SPELLBOUND

A WITCHES OF
CLEOPATRA HILL NOVEL

CHRISTINE POPE

Dark Valentine Press

This is a work of fiction. Names, characters, places, and incidents are either the product of the author's imagination or are used fictitiously. Any resemblance to actual events, places, organizations, or persons, whether living or dead, is entirely coincidental.

SPELLBOUND

Please contact the author through the form on her website at www.christinepope.com if you experience any formatting or readability issues with this book.

SPELLBOUND

CHAPTER ONE

"ARE YOU CRAZY?" CAITLIN MCALLISTER SAID, EYES WIDENING. Then she winced. "Sorry…wrong word."

"It's all right," Danica Wilcox replied with a shrug. Everyone had been tiptoeing around her for the past five months, but that didn't mean she hadn't heard the whispers anyway. All right, maybe no one had used the C-word out loud. They'd probably thought it, though, even if that thought was couched in euphemisms such as "Danica doesn't seem like herself."

No kidding. She didn't feel like herself, either. Ever since the rogue warlock Matías Escobar invaded her mind, Danica had been haunted by the sense that he'd stolen some vital part of her heart or soul, something she hadn't even realized she needed until it was gone.

She and Caitlin were sitting in the family room of the house that Caitlin now shared with her fiancé,

Alex Trujillo. Stacks of bridal magazines and catalogues were piled on the coffee table in front of them. Caitlin and Alex had set the date for early November—anything sooner would have probably been too hot down in Tucson—and Danica had come here to get the final fitting for her dress, even though the wedding was still almost two months off.

Well, that was the public reason Danica had given for coming to Tucson. She supposed she should be glad that her parents hadn't vetoed the trip altogether, since it meant driving several hundred miles all by herself. However, they'd probably decided that Caitlin's house was a safe enough destination. Besides, Matías was now securely locked up in a maximum-security facility, as were his two partners in crime. They certainly didn't present any threat, to Danica or anyone else.

"I have to go see him," she told Caitlin. "I need... closure."

"I'd think his being behind bars would be all the closure you need," Caitlin replied. Then she shook her head and retrieved her iced tea, which was sweating slightly despite the air conditioning going full blast, from where the tall glass sat on the coffee table. "Anyway, you know your parents would freak if they found out you'd gone within fifty miles of that place...and they'd kill me for letting you do it in the first place."

Her friend had that right, on both counts. But Danica had no intention of allowing her parents to discover her real reason for coming down here to Tucson. "Yeah, they probably would. But how would they know in the first place?"

At that reply, Caitlin frowned. "I don't want to lie to anyone—"

"Who says you'd have to lie? You just have to not say anything."

"That's totally splitting hairs, Danica."

She didn't say anything, just waited for Caitlin to cave. Which Danica knew she would. Caitlin hated confrontations. And maybe, just maybe, she'd realized that Danica's wish for closure wasn't quite as crazy as it sounded.

After a tense few seconds, Caitlin huffed out a breath. "Okay, fine. I'll cover for you. How long do you think it's going to take?"

"A little over three hours, I guess. It's about an hour and a half one way." Danica couldn't let herself feel relief. Not exactly. In one way, the very thought of facing her former tormentor made her stomach clench. But she also knew this was something she had to do, that she couldn't move forward if she didn't ask him the questions she'd been holding in for months. "If I leave in the next twenty minutes, then I can be there for the one-thirty visitation block."

Caitlin's eyebrows lifted. "Sounds like you already had this planned out. So why ask for my permission?"

It wasn't that Danica was asking for permission...more that she wanted her friend to understand why she had to do this. She'd learned quickly enough that visiting someone in a maximum-security prison wasn't exactly the same as stopping by a hospital to bring some flowers. First she'd had to submit to a background check, and then she'd had to call to schedule an appointment. Through all this, she'd had to use her real name, but that wasn't a big problem. Because of her fragile mental state, she'd never been called to testify against Matías after the ordeal. In fact, her name hadn't been included in the case at all, because there had been plenty of evidence to convict him of Roslyn McAllister's murder without dragging Danica's kidnapping into it.

"I just—I just wanted you to know. And I could have canceled the appointment if I had to. That's not such a big deal."

For a long moment, Caitlin didn't say anything. At last she nodded. "Okay. I'm not going to say I get it, not really, but...do what you have to do."

She still sounded dubious, so Danica asked, "Is Alex going to wonder where I've gone? I mean, I don't want to drag him into this, too."

Caitlin shook her head. "I haven't said anything to him because I figured it was your business. Luckily, you should be back here before Alex gets home from work."

He'd started a new job a month earlier, working in the marketing department of a local TV station. His dream job, according to Caitlin. Everything seemed to be going their way. Danica couldn't begrudge her friend her current happiness, but at the same time, she wished she could look forward to a future that was even half as idyllic.

In the meantime, she had an appointment to keep.

From the outside, the Florence prison facility didn't look nearly as intimidating as Danica had thought it would. All right, it was surrounded by tall fences topped by curls of barbed wire, and it seemed to be baking under the glare of the early September sun, but the buildings themselves looked new and sleek, some sections even covered in cheery bright red paint.

She sort of doubted the inmates thought of the place as cheery, however, no matter what color it had been painted.

The heat struck her as soon as she opened the door to her Land Rover and got out. Blinking behind her sunglasses, she followed the sign to the visitors' intake area. Clearly, she wasn't the only one coming to see an inmate this brutally hot afternoon; she found herself surrounded by a crowd of people, the majority of them women, and many of them with children in tow. That had to be rough, to only see your father a few times a year during visiting hours.

Thank God Matías had no real family of his own, only a sister he barely spoke to.

Despite the stifling heat, Danica had made sure to dress conservatively, so she was covered up, in jeans and a short-sleeved peasant top and ballet flats. The last thing she needed, after steeling herself to come here at all, was to be turned back because the officer in charge of the visiting room decided she was showing too much skin. Not that she really wanted to give Matías a show. He'd already seen enough of her body.

She had her driver's license out so she could show it to the officer on duty. His dark eyes flicked over it in a bored way, and then he checked a box on the sheet attached to the clipboard he held. "That way," he said, jerking a thumb over one shoulder. "Follow the signs."

Well, she was in it now. If she turned tail and fled, she might attract attention, even when surrounded by so many people consumed by their own worries. Swallowing, she followed the stream of visitors to a big room where the far wall was configured as a row of cubicles with small windows looking into them. In front of each window stood a small wooden-topped stool attached to the wall by a metal arm.

Danica had seen these sorts of setups in movies and television, but in person they appeared far more intimidating. More guards stood near the doors, and she walked up to the closest deputy and murmured, "Matías Escobar."

The guard pointed to the cubicle up against the farthest wall. "Over there."

She couldn't really feel relieved, not considering her surroundings, but she was slightly heartened that Matías had been assigned the cubicle over by the wall. At least that way she'd only have another visitor on one side of her, instead of both. The sorts of questions she intended to ask weren't exactly things she wanted overheard.

As she looked over at the cubicle, she saw a man approach and take the seat there. At once her heart begin slamming away in her chest. Never mind that she knew Matías couldn't hurt her ever again, that Angela and Connor Wilcox had burned the magic right out of him as their own form of punishment for his transgressions. It still took every ounce of willpower she possessed to force her feet to move in that direction, to propel her over to the stool that sat in front of the cubicle where Matías waited for her.

Somehow she made it, then sank down onto the hard surface of the provided seat. Not looking directly at Matías, she reached out and picked up the phone receiver attached to the wall. He did the same thing at almost the same time.

That hated voice, the one which still echoed in her dreams, came through the handset. "Hey, *chica*. Didn't expect to ever see you again."

She bristled. "Don't call me that."

"Okay, sure…Danica."

As much as she didn't want to, she made herself lift her eyes to his. A dark, mocking gaze met hers, but she didn't blink. She wanted to see him, to commit every feature to memory when her mind wasn't in a fog of his making.

In a way, she'd hoped all her memories of him would be false, that he'd made himself far more attractive in the magical brain haze he'd cast on her than he actually was in real life. But as she stared at him, she realized he truly was very good-looking, with those strong brows and straight nose and long-lashed black eyes. His hair was much shorter now, shaved down to almost stubble, and fresh tattoos marked his hands and arms. Still, she would have recognized him.

For months she'd imagined what she would say to Matías if she ever saw him again, but now, confronted by the reality of his presence, she found her mouth dry, the words she'd intended to utter choking in her throat. This was insane. She'd driven out to the back end of nowhere, and now she was just sitting here like an idiot, and—

"You look good," Matías said. "Of course, you always looked good." He smiled then, a slow, lascivious smile that told her he was remembering the nights they'd spent together.

Her blood seemed to freeze in her veins. Hands tightening on the knees of her jeans, she replied, "I can't say the same for you."

His smile only broadened. "That's kind of harsh, Dani." He ran one hand over the dark stubble on his head. "You don't like my prison 'do? But then, I do kind of remember you hanging onto my hair while I—"

"Stop it." Pausing, she risked a quick glance at the woman who occupied the stool next to hers, but she was hanging on to the phone receiver like it was a lifeline and speaking rapidly in Spanish, tears coursing down her cheeks. Unnerved by the display of emotion, Danica returned her attention to Matías. "You were *making* me do all that shit. I certainly didn't enjoy any of it."

"Could have fooled me."

Son of a bitch. She pulled the phone away from her ear and began to reach toward the cubicle wall so she could hang up. At once Matías' voice came from the speaker.

"Sorry. *Sorry.* Don't—don't hang up."

Eyes narrowing, she brought the phone back to her ear. "Then stop talking about that crap."

"I will."

He didn't exactly sound contrite, but at least it was a start. She drew in a breath before asking, "Have you seen your sister?"

His eyebrows lifted at Danica's words. Clearly, he hadn't expected her to ask that question. "Right after I was put in here. Not since."

Well, it was a long way from California to the prison here in Florence, Arizona, and Matías' sister Olivia had an infant to take care of. Danica kind of doubted that the young woman's civilian husband would much appreciate having his wife leave the baby with him so she could visit her jailbird warlock brother in prison.

She hesitated, not sure what she should say next. Matías shifted in his chair and sent her a piercing look.

"Why are you here, *chica*? I mean, really…*why*?"

Her stomach was so knotted with tension that she didn't even bother to re*prima*nd him for using that hated endearment. Now she understood why the woman in the cubicle next to hers was hanging on to that phone as if it were the only thing keeping her from drowning. Because sometimes when your world felt like it was falling apart, you needed something solid to hold on to. Danica could feel the hard plastic begin to slip under her sweat-dampened fingers. "I—I had to ask you something."

Another lift of his eyebrows. "Sorry, Danica...the good state of Arizona doesn't allow conjugal visits."

She scowled at the implication. "Fuck you, Matías."

"I wish."

God, this was the dumbest idea in the history of dumb ideas. Blood boiling, she once again moved to hang up the phone, and once again his voice stopped her.

"Wait. Don't. I'm sorry."

The note of contrition in his voice was almost genuine. She shot him a wary glance and waited, ready to end the call the second he said something out of line again.

"I want to hear what you wanted to ask me."

She hesitated. He sat there quietly, gaze fixed on her face, but he did look almost...well, not exactly sorry, but the mocking glint had gone from his eyes.

"Please."

Had Matías ever said "please" to anyone in his entire life? Maybe when he was trying to get into the pants of the Santiago clan's first daughter, back in

California before he'd come to Arizona, but Danica wasn't even sure about that.

This is why you came here, she told herself. *So just do it.*

Gathering a breath, she said quietly, "I need to know why."

"'Why'?" he repeated, looking confused. "Why what? Why'd I do it? You know that. I wanted a chance to be in charge. To be somebody."

No, she knew that. His methods were unthinkable, but at least she almost understood his motivations. He'd felt on the edge of things his whole life, allowed to be part of the Santiago clan on sufferance because of his refugee mother's healing gifts, but never really belonging to it. He'd seen the chance to seize the de la Paz family's *prima*-in-waiting as a way of getting the control he'd always wanted. It was horrible, but it was understandable.

"Not that," Danica replied, knowing she sounded desperate. In that moment, though, she didn't much care. "Why…*me*?"

Why did you spare me, when you bled Roslyn dry to power your hideous spells?

That was the question which lurked, unspoken, in her mind, but Matías seemed to understand. He shifted on his stool, eyes moving away from hers. For the first time, he appeared almost nervous. Nervous? That was a laugh. Matías was too full of himself, even stripped of his powers as he was now, to ever be truly ill at ease.

Then he said, "I liked you."

"Oh, please."

"No, I did." This time he did look at her, dark eyes narrowed. "You think I'm lying?"

She gave a helpless little shrug. Right then she didn't know what to think.

"That was my plan at first," he went on. "You know, to use both of you, alternating, so you'd last longer."

She shuddered. Maybe he didn't notice, because he went on,

"But then I decided that I didn't want to do that."

"Because you liked me." Why he would have preferred her over a golden girl like Roslyn....

"Yeah. I thought...." The words died away, and he shook his head before beginning again. "I don't know what the fuck I thought. That sure, I'd get Zoe because I needed the access to her *prima* powers, but that would just be for show. I'd still have you."

"What, as your little piece on the side?"

"I guess."

What the hell was she supposed to say to that? Was she supposed to feel grateful that this sociopath had thought she was hot, and so he'd keep her around as his bed buddy, even while he used the *prima*-in-waiting of the de la Paz clan as his personal steppingstone to power?

"That's messed up, Matías."

"It's the truth."

A long pause. He seemed to be watching her, waiting for her reaction, but all she could feel was an odd sort of numbness. It somehow seemed even more awful to know that Roslyn had died because Matías had decided he didn't want to use Danica in the way he'd originally intended.

"Okay," she said at last. "Thanks for being honest, I guess."

This time she did hang up the phone.

He made no move to stop her.

On the drive back to Caitlin's house, Danica kept wishing she'd had the guts to throw her belongings in the back of the Land Rover so she could have driven straight home to Flagstaff from the Florence prison facility. But she'd told everyone she'd be spending the weekend down in Tucson, going over wedding stuff with Caitlin, and if she'd bolted like that after being in Tucson for barely a day, her behavior would have raised even more eyebrows.

Actually, this whole wedding thing was making her a little crazy. Danica knew that Caitlin had tried to take as much of the burden off her as possible, had asked Roslyn's older sister Jenny to be her maid of honor, even though Caitlin had once hoped that Danica would fill that role. But no way could she do all the wrangling that being maid of honor involved. Jenny was still grieving over her sister's death, but she was also Caitlin's cousin. She'd already been maid of honor at several other McAllister weddings and knew the drill. And it seemed as if Jenny was glad to have something to take her mind off Roslyn's death.

Whereas Danica couldn't seem to focus on much of anything at all. She'd dropped out of school for now. Her parents told everyone that she'd be back, that this was just a temporary sabbatical, but was it?

She didn't know. She'd been intent on coming down here to confront Matías, to ask him the question that had been preying on her mind ever since she'd woken up enough to understand what had really happened during those days when she'd been the dark warlock's captive. And now that she had her answer, what the hell was she supposed to do?

Nothing, probably. She'd been doing a whole lot of that lately. Her parents had wanted her to see a shrink, but that experiment had been a dismal failure. No one in the Wilcox clan was a psychologist or even a counselor, and so she'd had to try talking to a civilian. And what was the point of that? She couldn't discuss any of the real details of her situation. No, she'd had to basically lie her ass off and say that she'd been drugged by Matías, when she'd actually been controlled by his unique—and extremely dangerous—magical powers of coercion.

After three visits to the psychologist, she'd put her foot down and said no way, that now she felt guilty about lying to her shrink on top of everything else, and that was the end of that. Ever since, she'd been loitering around her parents' house—she couldn't have stayed in the apartment she once shared with Caitlin, since Caitlin had moved in with Alex and Danica's parents wouldn't hear of their daughter living alone after what had happened to her—and not doing much of anything. Watching TV. Eavesdropping on other people's lives on Facebook. She'd probably be as big as a house, except the one thing that seemed to help was walking around the neighborhood. Her family's home was located in the Country Club Estates section of Flagstaff, and so there were plenty of artificial lakes to roam around, lots of tree-lined streets where she could walk and breathe in the clean air and not think about much of anything at all.

When Danica got back to the house Caitlin shared with Alex, there didn't seem to be any sign of him, even though it was almost six thirty. She parked the Land Rover on the street, and went up and rang the doorbell.

Caitlin let her in, eyes full of questions, but she appeared to realize that Danica wasn't much in the mood for conversation.

"Alex?" Danica asked briefly.

"He called about a half-hour ago. Something came up, so he won't be home for dinner."

"That sucks."

"I know. This is his dream job, so I'm trying not to say anything, but this is the fourth time in the last two weeks that he's gotten stuck there late." She sighed and pushed a lock of bright copper hair away from her face. "I'm doing my best to be understanding, but it's just tough sometimes. I want to be with him, you know?"

"I'm sure it'll be okay," Danica said, glad that she could focus on her friend's problems rather than her own. "He's new, so he's probably just trying to prove himself."

A nod, although Caitlin didn't look all that convinced. "Maybe. Anyway, since we're free agents, we might as well go out. I'll take you downtown."

And that was where they headed, to a restaurant Danica had wanted to try for a while, since it was owned by the same company that ran a couple of eating establishments up in Flagstaff. They ordered some truffle fries to nosh on, and each got a glass of wine. That was about all Danica thought she could manage; she'd never been much of a drinker.

Then again, after the day she'd had....

"You want to talk about it?" Caitlin asked, sipping at her glass of pinot grigio.

"Not really." How in the world could Danica tell Caitlin that her cousin had ended up dead because Matías had gotten a hard-on for her instead?

Luckily, Caitlin only nodded. Unlike a lot of people, she knew when not to push. "So…what now?"

"I don't know. Go try on those shoes you picked out. Get stuck full of pins at the bridal shop one last time. Go home."

"That's not what I meant."

Danica felt like telling her friend that she was the one who could see the future, so she should be advising Danica on what was supposed to happen next, not vice versa. But it didn't always work that way.

The malbec she'd ordered suddenly tasted sour, but she took another swallow anyway. "I'm just…I don't know. It's like I know that that asshole did a number on me, but I can't figure out a way to fix it."

"Maybe you don't have to fix it," Caitlin said gently. "Maybe you just have to learn how to live with it."

That option didn't sound very appealing. It wasn't as if Matías had given her an incurable disease. He'd messed with her head, messed with her body, but she was still alive, wasn't she? There had to be some way to get past what he'd done.

Her expression must have been dubious, because Caitlin shook her head. "I'm not saying it's something that's going to happen instantly. It hasn't even been six months yet."

"Six months is a long time. Look at how much your life has changed in the past few months."

Somewhat to Danica's surprise, Caitlin didn't smile at that comment. Her expression remained serious as she regarded her friend. "Yes, it's changed. And yours can, too. You just have to give yourself permission to change. Don't give Matías the power to permanently mess up your life."

When Caitlin made that suggestion, she made it sound so easy.

"Well, I'm trying not to," Danica replied, "but it's not going so great right now."

Caitlin opened her mouth to answer, but then she paused, her blue-green eyes going glassy. A casual observer might have thought that she'd simply had too much to drink, but Danica knew her friend better than that. She wasn't drunk.

She was having a vision.

"What are you seeing, Cate?"

A blink, and then Caitlin swiveled her head toward Danica. Her gaze was still a little unfocused, but she sounded normal enough as she said, "You need to go back to Flagstaff."

"Well, yeah, I was heading back on Sunday."

"No. You need to go back tomorrow."

"What about the shoes?"

"Okay, we'll go to the bridal store first thing in the morning. Then you need to go home."

"Do you want to tell me why?"

Another blink. "I can't say exactly for sure. I just get this feeling that you need to be there. I saw pine trees...quiet. It wasn't a neighborhood like where your parents' house is, though. Someplace near town, but not really *in* it. I did see part of one build-ing...it looked like it might have been a log cabin."

"'A log cabin'?" Danica repeated. What the.... Then, as understanding seemed to roll over her, "*Our* log cabin?"

"You have a log cabin?"

"Well, *I* don't," Danica replied. "It belongs to the clan. I guess it was the cabin that my great-great-whatever grand-uncle Jeremiah built when he brought all the Wilcoxes out to the Arizona Territory in the late 1870s."

"That cabin," Caitlin said firmly. "So it's seriously a for-real log cabin?"

"Kind of. I mean, we've updated it, because we all sort of share it for weekend getaways in the summer or whatever. But it still looks like a log cabin on the outside."

The dreamy look returned to Caitlin's eyes. "Getaways. That's exactly it, Danica. You need to get away."

"To the cabin?"

Caitlin nodded.

"By myself?"

Another emphatic nod.

Great, Danica thought. *My parents are just going to love this....*

CHAPTER TWO

"You want to do what?" Olivia Wilcox demanded, staring at her daughter as if she truly had lost her mind this time.

"I want to go stay at the cabin for a while. No one's using it, right? I mean, everyone's kids should be back in school, and—"

"No, it's not being used at the moment," Olivia said. "That's not the point."

Danica bit back a huff of annoyance. This was no time to sigh or roll her eyes or impatiently shift her weight from one foot to another the way she might have back in high school when her mother decided to be difficult about something. If Caitlin believed it was important for Danica to go to the cabin, then, damn it, Danica was going to that cabin. Even if Olivia Wilcox thought it was a crazy idea.

"Look, Mom," Danica said. "I just think a change of scenery might be a good thing. I can be quiet and still there, sort through some things."

"You can be quiet and still here. Mason's moved out, and your father's at work all day. And I'm gone half the time volunteering at the hospital."

Yes, her mother definitely liked to be the lady of good works. And it was nice of her to volunteer when she could be spending all day at the golf course or at Pilates or whatever it was the other über-fit housewives in their upscale neighborhood did to fill their days. But even though Danica had the house to herself a good deal of the time, it still wasn't the same as being truly, truly alone.

"I can...and I can't. Sometimes you need a change of scenery. It's just the other side of town. It's not like I'm planning to go rent a flat in Paris or something."

Now, there would be a change of scenery. Unfortunately, because of the territorial nature of the witch clans' world, such trips rarely happened, if ever. The Wilcoxes were now on more or less friendly terms with the de la Pazes, who held sway over the southern half of Arizona, and so it was no big deal for Danica to go and spend a weekend with Caitlin in Tucson. But Paris? Not going to happen.

Olivia's expression was a study in uncertainty. On the one hand, she probably thought it a good sign that her daughter was trying to strike out on her own instead of spending another day brooding in the house. On the other, that same daughter hadn't exactly exhibited all the signs of mental stability lately....

But because Olivia hadn't yet given a definitive no, Danica decided to push on. "I can be home in twenty minutes if something comes up. I know when you're there, that cabin feels like it's in the middle of nowhere, but we all know it really isn't. There's a phone and electricity and everything."

A long pause. "Have you talked to your father about this?"

"Well, no. I figured I'd ask you first."

Danica's mother didn't look exactly thrilled to have the burden of the decision placed on her, but then she shrugged. "If he's okay with it, then I guess it's all right. But how long are we talking about here?"

Good question. Danica really had no idea, but she knew if she left her plans completely open-ended, her mother would probably freak out. Olivia Wilcox was all about nice straight lines and not a whole heck of a lot of thinking outside the box, which was part of the reason she'd had such a difficult time dealing with her daughter after the whole Matías incident. Suddenly, Danica wasn't acting like Danica anymore, the go-getter daughter Olivia had raised gone, maybe forever, and she didn't know what to do about it.

"A few days to start," Danica said, hoping that would be enough. To tell the truth, she really had no idea how much time she'd need to spend at the cabin. Caitlin hadn't been very specific. "I'll see how it goes from there."

That answer didn't appear to reassure her mother, but neither did she raise any additional objections. And that, Danica figured, was probably as good as it was going to get.

Joseph Wilcox also didn't put up any roadblocks, except to say that Danica should call him if she found anything at the cabin that needed fixing. "It should be fine, but your cousin Cody was out there with some of his college buddies last, so God only knows what shape they left it in."

A warning Danica appreciated. Cody definitely knew how to party.

Her cousin Lucas was the keeper of the key to the cabin, so after she'd loaded up the Land Rover with enough changes of clothes and supplies to last her for a few days, she swung by his house first. She felt weird about calling, and figured someone should be around. It turned out Lucas wasn't home, but his wife Margot answered the door. At her side was their little girl Mia, who was probably the most beautiful child Danica had ever seen. And well-behaved, too, unlike Angela and Connor's hellions. Okay, Ian and

Emily weren't exactly hellions, but they did tend to keep their parents on their toes.

"I'll get the key," Margot said, stepping aside so Danica could come inside the entryway. Her gaze was curious but friendly. "So you're going up to the cabin?"

"Just for a few days," Danica hedged, since she really didn't feel like going into any detail.

"It should be pretty right now," Margot replied, somewhat diplomatically, since it was a little early to be going out there to see the fall foliage. Even at this elevation, the trees didn't really start to turn until the end of September.

"I think so."

Margot seemed content to leave the matter there for the moment, because she excused herself to get the key from Lucas' study. As Danica waited, she tried not to be too put off by the way little Mia just stood there and stared up at her with big brown eyes. The girl was only around two, but she seemed awfully serene for a two-year-old.

"Um, hi, Mia," Danica said.

Mia blinked, then extended the stuffed rabbit she held in one hand. "Bunny?"

"Yes, that's a bunny."

The little girl shook her head. "No, *bunny*."

Even spending time with her cousins' myriad offspring hadn't made Danica entirely comfortable around very small children. She was okay once they were old enough to more or less talk to, but toddlers were an entirely different matter altogether.

"It's a very nice bunny," Danica offered. Well, in actual truth, it was looking a little shopworn, but she supposed that tended to be the fate of most stuffed animals.

Mia shook her head, then marched over to Danica and pushed the toy up against her nearest hand. *"Bunny."*

Oh, lord. Danica took the stuffed animal, mostly because she didn't know what else to do. But what if Mia started to cry once she realized she wasn't holding on to her beloved toy?

Luckily, Margot reappeared at that moment. Obviously fighting back a smile, she said, "I see that Mia's given you her bunny."

"Yeah, she seemed kind of insistent about it."

"Well, it's no ordinary rabbit. It's magical."

Of course it is, Danica thought wryly. From the twinkle in Margot's dark eyes, she guessed that the other woman was playing along with some fantasy of her daughter's. "That's great, but, um…why did she give it to me?"

"Obviously, she thinks you need it."

Maybe I do need a magical bunny. That wouldn't the weirdest thing that's happened to me lately.

But Danica knew she couldn't drag Mia's stuffed animal along with her to the cabin. The kid would probably start crying the moment she realized the bunny wouldn't be coming back anytime soon.

Crouching down, she held the toy out to Mia, saying, "Thank you for the bunny, Mia, but I'm going to be staying up at the cabin for a few days. There are bears out in those woods, so I think the bunny might be safer here with you."

Mia's big brown eyes widened, and she reached out and snatched the bunny back with surprising force. "Bunny."

"That's right. You keep the bunny safe." Danica straightened, and Margot handed her a brass key on a woven lanyard.

"Just bring it back when you're ready. Lucas had a clean-up crew in there after Cody was done with the place, so everything should be in order."

"I hope he sent Aunt Diane and Uncle Chris the bill," Danica said darkly. Not that Lucas couldn't afford to absorb the cost, but come on.

"Oh, he did," Margot replied, her mouth curving in amusement. "They weren't exactly thrilled."

Served them right for letting Cody get away with murder. But Danica wasn't going to worry about that. Cody was his parents' problem, not hers.

Now she merely itched to get away and up to the cabin. What Caitlin had seen for her there, Danica didn't know for sure. But there was only one way to find out.

She thanked Margot and left, giving Mia one last wave before she headed down the walkway to where she'd left her SUV. Starting a family had been the last thing on her mind even before the Matías incident, but Danica thought she wouldn't mind too much, if it meant she could have a daughter as cute as Mia one day.

The route to the cabin actually took her through the heart of town, so Danica stopped at the grocery store to get a few things on her way out there. Usually the pantry at the cabin was kept decently stocked with canned food, but the frozen stuff was a lot tastier. She also got a sandwich from the store's deli section for that night, and a couple bottles of wine. True, she generally drank a glass at a time, but she'd just put the corks back in the bottles when she was done and make them last that much longer.

After that stop, she headed out on Fort Valley Road. By then it was a little past three in the afternoon, but Danica wasn't too worried about the time of day. There'd still be plenty of daylight for her to get settled, even with bumping the couple of miles over dirt roads to get to the border of the property. All around it was Forest Service land, and she wondered how her family had managed to hang on to its little piece of the woods for all these years.

Well, that wasn't too much of a mystery, she supposed. The Wilcox clan did have a long history of getting its own way.

The Land Rover soldiered along over the rutted road, and then she was turning onto the narrow lane that led to the cabin itself. All around her was the stillness of the pine forest, which was broken occasionally by stands of oak and sycamore, along with groups of aspen trees, their leaves shimmering in the afternoon breeze. Already she could feel herself relaxing. She might have been the only person for a hundred miles, even though she knew the main road wasn't that far off, and that there were plenty of houses nearby with people in them, should she need any assistance.

But why would she? Despite what she'd told Mia, these woods were perfectly safe. Maybe a black bear would amble by every once in a while, but in all the years she'd been coming up here, she had yet to see one. Deer and elk and squirrels and rabbits, sure. One time when Danica was around ten, she'd spotted a fox and nearly burst from excitement. But that had been it for anything remotely resembling a predator, unless you counted the hawks and the occasional eagle.

She came to a stop next to the cabin in a sputter of gravel. The property didn't have a true garage, only a storage shed, and so she'd have to leave the

SUV outside the whole time she was here. No biggie; it was already in need of a wash after that trip down to Tucson.

Moving her belongings and the items she'd picked up at the grocery store from the Land Rover to the cabin took less time than she'd thought. And it was just as Margot had assured her—the place seemed to be in more or less perfect condition, except for a little dust.

As she made her inspection, Danica reflected that none of her Wilcox ancestors probably would have recognized the place. It had become sort of a family tradition to update the property once every decade or so, and Lucas had been in charge of the last round of renovations. Not much could be done about the awkward shape of the cabin itself—it had begun life as a simple square and then had rooms added on as needed, before the Wilcox clan abandoned it altogether for a series of impressive houses closer to downtown—but now the interior walls had been covered in thick plaster and painted a warm parchment yellow, and the floors were gleaming new cherry wood.

Not exactly roughing it, but Danica was okay with that. She dropped her two weekender bags near the entrance to the kitchen and proceeded to put the food she'd bought in the shining stainless-steel refrigerator. That didn't take much time, either, so after that she took her bags to the master bedroom. She'd never slept there before, since in the past she'd always come to the cabin with her family. It would be a luxury to have that big king-size bed to herself. And the days had been mild, but maybe it would get cold enough to justify having a fire in the bedroom's stone hearth. The shed always had a good supply of wood, because even during summer visits people liked to sit out on the expansive patio to the rear of the cabin and gather around the outdoor fireplace there.

Once everything was settled, Danica went out to the porch and stood there for a long moment, letting the cool breeze wash over her face and tug at her long, loose hair. So very quiet here, except for the ever-present soughing of the pines, and the long, falling cry of a hawk high overhead.

Something within her seemed to relax, a tension she'd been carrying for so long she hadn't even realized it was there leaving her shoulders and neck. Up here, she wouldn't have to worry about her parents giving her the side-eye, or the awkwardness of running into friends at the store or at the mall and having them ask why she'd left school so abruptly. She'd more or less gone dark on Facebook, except to lurk, and she left texts and emails and phone calls mostly unanswered, but there wasn't much you could do about randomly running into people on the street.

She wouldn't have to worry about any of that here, though. The food she'd brought would last about four or five days, and then she could decide if she wanted to stay or whether solitude was something to be enjoyed in smaller doses.

Not that she would really lack for entertainment. Of course the cabin had electricity—she'd always wondered how much it had cost to run a line all the way out to the property—and satellite TV, along with some painfully slow Internet. And she knew the trails around here by heart, since she'd come out to the cabin with her family ever since she was old enough to walk. About a half-mile up the hill, you would come to a narrow ravine with a creek running through it, a creek that flowed year-round. She couldn't paint like Connor or write like Caitlin, but she could still go there with a book and sit and read while the water rustled away in the background.

Yes, this could work.

Lying down to sleep that night did feel strange, despite the promise of that king-size bed. She slept on a queen at home, so it wasn't as if she wasn't used to having room to move around in her sleeping arrangements. No, it was more that the bed faced the wrong direction, and it was so very dark out here. And quiet. She'd thought her parents' house quiet enough, since their neighborhood was fairly secluded and not that much traffic passed by, but this was so still she thought she could hear the whisper of owls' wings as they flew through the sleeping forest that surrounded the cabin.

She rolled over onto her side and squished the pillow a little to get it into the proper shape. That felt better. Problem was, when she shut her eyes, she seemed to see Matías staring back at her, that knowing half-smile on his lips, as if even now he was laughing at her, at her feeble attempts to put her life back together.

"Laugh's on you, asshole," she murmured into the darkness. "You're the one in prison."

And yet…hadn't he put her in her own kind of prison? Considering how circumscribed her life had been over the past few months, was she any freer than he?

No. She wouldn't allow herself to believe that. Sooner or later, she'd be released from the last remnants of his influence. Besides, didn't she owe it to Roslyn to make the best of her life that she could? Maybe Danica would never be as strong a witch as her sister Mason, who had an uncanny level of control over fire, and to a lesser extent over the weather as well, but there had to be something Danica could do with her own peculiar talent.

Yeah, great talent, she thought. *The ability to never be late. Well, not really late, anyway.*

Because Danica had discovered around the time she was eleven that she could always produce an extra five minutes whenever she needed them. Running late for school? No problem. Need a little more time to go over your notes before a big test? Not to worry. Spent longer than you'd expected getting ready for a date? The guy you were going out with would never know the difference, because time seemed to stop for the rest of the world while she went about her business.

She had to admit that it had come in handy, but there was nothing particularly interesting or showy about her gift. The clan could always use a seer or a healer or a weather-worker, but this? It didn't really seem to help anyone except herself.

A shadow passed by outside the window, and Danica startled, heart beginning to pound in her chest. She lay very still, ears straining into the silence, but she heard nothing.

Only an owl, she told herself, *passing over the moon.* There was supposed to be a full moon tonight, after all.

Except...that shadow had looked a lot bigger than an owl.

She'd locked the doors and most of the windows, but she'd left a few cracked open to let in some fresh air. Maybe someone had seen her coming out this way, thought that a young woman all on her own might be easy prey....

Stop it. Just stop it.

But she couldn't quite push the fear away, because she knew from personal experience that not all people were good, that some men did enjoy making victims of women. And she might be a Wilcox witch, but she wasn't that strong. Not really. Although she supposed that extra five minutes could come in handy if she had to flee an assailant.

Even that realization didn't seem to help, though. To make matters worse, she didn't have any weapons with her. Well, unless you counted the walking stick that was always propped up in a corner of the main room near the front door.

Better than nothing, she supposed.

She pushed back the covers and got out of bed, glad that she'd gone to sleep wearing a tank top and some yoga pants. At least that way she felt somewhat clothed. After slipping into the flip-flops she'd left by the side of the bed, she padded out into the darkened cabin. It wasn't completely black because of the moonlight streaming through the unlined curtains at the windows. Because of that faint illumination, she was able to go straight to the walking stick and wrap her hand around it. The smooth wood felt reassuring against her skin, although she had to admit she didn't know much about using the stick as a weapon. Knock it against the guy's head and hope for the best, she supposed.

If there was even anyone outside. For all she knew, she'd dozed off briefly and only dreamed that she'd seen someone moving past her window.

That didn't feel right, though. She hadn't been asleep, and she *had* seen something.

Tiptoeing in her flip-flops, she went from window to window, carefully lifting a corner of each curtain so she could peer outside. Each time she saw nothing, only moon-bleached grass and the dark, watching stands of pine trees.

By the time she'd made a complete circuit of the cabin, Danica was feeling like a complete idiot. No one had come by. Even if she hadn't been sleeping, her brain must have manufactured that shadow. God knows she was already enough on edge after her confrontation with Matías. She should have left that sleeping dog severely alone.

She couldn't do anything about that now, though, except go back to bed and tell herself to stop jumping at nothing. This experiment in solitude was going to be a big fat failure if she couldn't settle down.

Still, she'd take the walking stick back with her. No one was around to laugh at her paranoia, and she'd probably sleep better if she knew she only had to reach out and grab the stick if she heard or saw anything else.

A step toward her bedroom, and another. Then she saw it again—a tall shadow, this time moving past one of the front windows. The moonlight seemed to etch its outlines onto the fabric of the curtains.

It was definitely shaped like a man.

Heart pounding, she tightened her grip on the walking stick. Her cell reception was for shit out here, but the cabin had a landline. Unfortunately, the phone was all the way in the kitchen.

She hardly breathed as she inched her way into the kitchen, wincing when one of her flip-flops slapped a little too loudly against the wooden floor. The phone hung on the wall near the back door, and she abandoned caution and made a beeline for it, transferring the walking stick to her left hand so she could stick the handset under her ear and use her right hand to push the buttons.

Only...there was no dial tone. Nothing. Terror mounting, she jiggled the receiver several times, but the line remained dead. Had the person roaming around outside cut it, or had the phone line been gnawed by animals, or the pole itself been knocked over?

No way of knowing for sure right now, and she supposed it didn't really matter. Dead was dead.

Then she spied her purse, still sitting on the kitchen counter where she'd dropped it earlier. Thank God. It wasn't that far from the back door to where she'd parked the Land Rover. She'd grab her purse, get out her keys, and make a break for it. With any luck, the intruder would have wandered over to the far side of the house, and she'd have enough time to climb into the SUV and lock the doors before he could get back to her.

So much for solitude.

She reached in her purse and grabbed her key-chain, then slung the bag over her shoulder, keeping the walking stick in her left hand the whole time. Okay, so she was right-handed, but she still might be able to land a lucky blow. No way in hell would she go outside without something to protect her.

After fumbling a little with the back door's lock, she was able to get outside. A chill wind blew over her, tugging at the ends of her loose hair. She gave a quick glance around but saw nothing. Okay, she could do this.

Gravel crunched under her flip-flops as she hurried over to the Land Rover. Wincing at the noise, she looked around again, but the property appeared completely deserted, the only sign of life a few dead oak leaves moving as the wind picked them up and scudded them a few inches down the driveway.

She'd already punched the button on the key fob, so the SUV was unlocked. As she reached for the door handle, something seemed to flicker in her peripheral vision.

At once she whipped around...then almost dropped the walking stick she held.

He stood at the end of the drive, watching her. His dark hair blew around his face, seemingly driven by a wilder wind than the capricious nighttime breeze that had played with the oak leaves a moment earlier. The tails of the long black coat he wore also flapped in the breeze, showing a pale band-collared shirt underneath.

And...he was gorgeous, at least from what Danica could tell in the uncertain moonlight. Regular features, strong chin, the kind of mouth you'd look at and wonder what it was like to kiss. Which was crazy. She sure as hell shouldn't be thinking such a thing about an oddly dressed stranger roaming uninvited on her family's property.

But she was a Wilcox, and since he'd obviously spotted her, she was going to stand her ground. Anyway, she was only a few steps away from the Land Rover's driver-side door.

"Who are you?" she said clearly, her voice carrying on the night air. "What do you want?"

He didn't reply, but only stood there and continued to stare at her. Something in that gaze awoke a chill in her body...or maybe it was just the cold wind blowing down from the San Francisco Peaks.

"You're trespassing," she went on. She wouldn't let his silence unnerve her. Okay, she was extremely unnerved, but that didn't mean she intended to show it. "I know it's Forest Service land all around here, but this is private property."

His head tilted, and he glanced away from her to the cabin and then back again. Then he seemed to frown, and turned back toward the forest and began to walk.

There. That was better. He didn't seem inclined to argue with her, or prolong the confrontation. No, he was only walking calmly into the pine trees, his back to her, and…

…and then he was gone. It wasn't that he'd gone out of eyeshot. She'd been watching him the whole time, and it was as if he became blurry, then transparent, then…gone.

If she hadn't been holding the walking stick, she might have had her knees give way then and there. As it was, she clung to the stick, letting it hold her up, while she stared into the darkness where a man had just stood seconds ago.

Had she finally gone completely insane?

CHAPTER THREE

DANICA'S COUSIN MARIE LIFTED ONE ELEGANT BLACK EYE-
brow. "You think the cabin is haunted?"

"I—" Danica waved a hand, knowing she must
sound even crazier than usual. But really, when you
got right down to it, ghosts shouldn't be that crazy a
notion to anyone in their clan. After all, Angela saw
them all the time, or at least she used to. There probably weren't as many opportunities for hauntings in the
newish subdivision where she lived now, rather than
back in the former mining town where she'd grown
up. Forging ahead, Danica went on, "I don't know if it
was a ghost I saw, or if the cabin's actually haunted. I
just know I saw...something."

For a moment, Marie remained silent. They were
sitting in her living room; from upstairs, Danica heard
the faint whine of a Dremel tool grinding away and

guessed that Marie's husband Andre was working on one of his jewelry projects. When she did speak, the older woman sounded skeptical. "Our family has been using that cabin in one form or another for the past hundred and thirty years or so. As far as I know, no one has ever reported seeing any kind of spirit anywhere in or around the cabin, or experienced any kind of supernatural phenomena there at all."

"So you're saying I'm imagining things?"

"No, I am not saying that. I'm only saying that this is the first time I've ever heard of anything like this."

Of course it's the first time something like this has happened, Danica thought. *Because God forbid there should be any corroborating evidence to prove that I haven't finally lost my mind.*

Seemingly unperturbed by Danica's lack of response, Marie went on, "Are you sure it couldn't have been a trespasser? I remember when I was a girl and went up there often, every once in a while we'd get people stumbling onto the property, not realizing it wasn't part of the Forest Service lands."

"That's what I thought at first. But the man I saw disappeared by just sort of melting away…and there was also what he was wearing."

"Which was?"

Danica had thought about the stranger's clothes a good bit, attempting to brand every detail into her memory so she wouldn't forget. "Like something out of *Tombstone*. It's one of my dad's favorite movies, so I've seen it a lot. One of those long black frock coats, and the kind of shirts they used to wear in the 1800s. You know, with the band collar."

"I'm familiar with that, yes." Marie's mouth pursed slightly, and she added, "But I also know that we have a lot of historical re-enactors in this part of the world. Maybe he was off doing an encampment or something and got lost."

"An encampment on a Thursday night?" Danica scoffed. "I mean, I guess it's not outside the realm of possibility, but don't they usually have those things over the weekend?"

"I would assume so, but I'd say it's a more logical explanation than having a ghost suddenly turn up on the property." A lift of her slender shoulders, and Marie leaned toward the coffee table so she could pick up her neglected glass of iced tea. "But if you really want an expert opinion, you should call Angela. She's the one who knows all about ghosts. If there actually is some kind of spirit at the cabin, she should be able to call it forth and communicate with it."

The thought had crossed Danica's mind as well, but she'd decided that she should get some background from Marie before approaching Angela. After all, Marie was her cousin, and Danica had known her all her life. It was Danica's older sister Mason who was friendly with Angela, since they were closer in age. If Danica had exchanged even a hundred words with Angela in the three years since the two clans had been reconciled, she would be surprised.

But it seemed as if there wasn't much else Danica could do except talk to the McAllister *prima*. As Marie had said, Angela was the expert when it came to ghosts.

"Okay," Danica said after a brief hesitation, hoping the reluctance in her tone wasn't too obvious. "I'll see what she has to say."

And pray that she doesn't drag the twins along if we end up having to take a field trip back to the cabin....

That eventuality was avoided, however, because Angela had sounded positively cheerful about being able to leave Ian and Emily with her husband Connor so she could meet Danica at the cabin.

"If that's okay," Angela had added hastily. "I mean, if you don't want to go back there by yourself—"

"No, it's fine," Danica cut in. She hadn't felt any sort of ill will coming from the handsome stranger… ghost…whatever he was. It was only that his mere presence had been enough to give her the heebie-jee-bies. But going back in daylight didn't seem too scary. "When can you get out there?"

"I'll shoot for three, but if anything changes, I'll let you know."

That reply hadn't sounded too good to Danica, for multiple reasons. "Well, you won't be able to get me on my cell because I don't get any reception out there, and the landline in the cabin isn't working."

"Oh." For a second, Angela hesitated, and then she went on, "It's fine. I'll be there at three, come hell or high water. Or the twins."

Danica thought they were probably the most likely disaster scenario, but she held her tongue, and only said that sounded great and she'd see Angela later that afternoon.

And the McAllister *prima* had been there right on time. Well, only five minutes late, which, considering how far she had to drive, really wasn't too bad.

Angela parked her Jeep Cherokee next to Danica's Land Rover and got out, surveying the property with interest as she did so.

"Hi, Angela. You've never been to the cabin before?" Danica asked as she approached the other woman.

"No. Connor's talked about it, but I wanted the twins to be a little older before we came out here and roughed it."

Danica chuckled. "Well, I don't know if you can really call it 'roughing it,' after all the upgrades Lucas did a few years ago, but come on inside."

They both walked up the porch and went in through the front door. The weather had cooled down a little that day, and so Danica only had one window open. The curtains moved lazily in the breeze, but otherwise the main room was quiet and still.

"Wow, this is nice," Angela said, looking around approvingly. "But then, I guess I shouldn't be surprised, if Lucas was the one in charge of the renovations." Her expression turned businesslike, and she added, "Where did you first see him?"

They both knew she wasn't talking about Lucas.

"Outside the master bedroom window. Here."

Danica led Angela into that bedroom and pointed at the window in question. "I was lying in here, trying to fall asleep, when I saw a shadow go past. At first I tried to tell myself it was nothing, but I somehow knew it was more than just an owl, or whatever. So I got up and went out to the front room, and I saw the shadow again. That time I could definitely tell it was shaped like a man."

"And then when you went outside, you saw him clearly."

"As clearly as I'm seeing you." Well, that wasn't quite right. She and Angela were facing each other in a well-lit room in broad daylight, and he'd been standing outside in the dark. Even with a full moon, you couldn't see everything. She amended, "Okay, clearly enough. He just—he looked like a person. It wasn't until he disappeared that I realized he couldn't be real. I mean, not *real*, real."

A little frown was pulling at Angela's dark, perfectly arched brows. Almost with surprise, Danica noticed how pretty the *prima* actually was. They hadn't spent a lot of time around one another, and Danica supposed that in her mind she'd sort of built Connor's consort into a mythical, almost fearsome creature, the one person who'd managed to break the Wilcox curse after it had wreaked havoc on the clan for more than a century. Now, though, Danica realized that Angela was just another young woman like herself, a couple of years older, but still having to manage the problems of being a witch in a civilian world.

Still looking distracted, Angela said, "Show me where you saw him outside. I'm not getting anything at all here."

Disappointment flared in Danica, but she told herself she needed to be patient. The ghost or man or whatever he was had only gone past her bedroom window, whereas he'd been standing in one place at the end of the driveway for some time.

"This way."

She led Angela out of the cabin and down the gravel drive, almost to the place where it met with the dirt road that wound its way to the property.

Pausing there, Danica pointed at a spot a few feet away.

"I saw him right there."

Without speaking, Angela moved to the location Danica had indicated and then stood there for a moment, hands upturned and arms slightly outstretched, as if she was trying to feel the currents of the wind…or anything which might be riding on that wind. Her head cocked to one side, and her eyelids drooped slightly.

Danica wanted to ask if she was feeling anything, but she knew better than to interrupt a medium while she was working. Well, no, that wasn't quite right. Marie had said once that Angela wasn't actually a medium, but rather someone with the ability to see ghosts and speak with them like they were living people.

That man had looked real enough, at least until he had dissolved into the darkness and disappeared. So what did it mean that Danica had seen him? Twenty-two was a little late to be developing a newfound witch talent.

At last Angela opened her eyes and shook her head. "I'm not feeling a damn thing."

Of course she wasn't. So that meant Danica could add "having hallucinations" to the long list of things about her life that were completely screwed up.

Her expression must have fallen, because Angela said quickly, "Which doesn't necessarily mean anything. I know everyone likes to talk about my talent as if it gives me the ability to call ghosts to me and have them do whatever I want, but that's not true at all. I mean, I can reach out to a spirit and hope that he or she will respond, but making that connection is up to the spirit, not me. Maybe this man, whoever he was...maybe he only wants to communicate with you."

"I don't see how that's going to work," Danica replied. She knew she sounded gloomy, but she'd had so many setbacks lately that it was hard to feel too enthusiastic about anything. "I don't talk to ghosts."

"Ghosts in general," Angela corrected her. "If I've learned anything from talking with the spirits, it's that they generally have a mind of their own. You can't really force them to do anything. But it sounds as if this one was reaching out to you."

"So why didn't he say anything?"

"Maybe he couldn't right then. Or maybe he just hasn't decided what he wants to say. Time doesn't work the same way for ghosts as it does for us mortals. They don't think anything of disappearing for months at a time and then coming back and picking up a conversation as if they just broke it off a few seconds ago." She went quiet for a moment, appearing to ponder what she should say next. "What did he look like?"

Well, at least that part was easy enough. "He was handsome. Late twenties, I think. Dark hair, Wild West–looking clothes. He didn't have a hat or anything, though. Clean-shaven."

Angela appeared to absorb that information, then asked, "Did you get any kind of a feeling from him?"

"'Feeling'?" Danica repeated. "You mean other than, 'what the hell is this strange guy doing on my property in the middle of the night'?"

Angela grinned. "Yeah, anything other than that."

What had Danica felt, other than the need to get the hell away from the intruder? That moment when he'd been standing there, looking at her. He hadn't made any threatening movements. His face had been calm…maybe a little sad, if anything.

"Nothing, really," she said. "It wasn't as if he seemed evil or angry or anything like that. I guess it wasn't the man himself that scared me, just more the idea that someone was wandering around the property when I was all alone out here."

"I can understand that." Angela's tone was neutral, almost too neutral. As the consort of the Wilcox clan's *primus*, of course she would know all about the way Danica had fallen apart after the Matías incident. Angela would never be so crass as to mention the near-breakdown to Danica, but she probably was telling herself to step lightly, to not say something that would reference Danica's admittedly fragile mental state. "But if he truly doesn't feel like a negative spirit, then maybe you should try reaching out to him. Or have you decided not to stay here?"

"I don't know yet." True, her first instinct had been to pack her bags and get the hell out of there. But last night, after it became obvious that the stranger or ghost or whatever he was didn't intend to return, she'd actually managed to go to sleep, and slept better than she had in many months. The next morning had dawned bright and sunny, with no sign of anyone having been on the property, except some deer tracks off in the back forty. Besides, Caitlin had told her to come here, so this man—ghost or shade or whatever he was—had to be connected to what she had seen. Should she mention that to Angela? Maybe not right now. Just because Caitlin had had some kind of vision that told her Danica was meant to come here didn't necessarily mean that the ghost was connected to her friend's vision.

Anyway, Danica hadn't said anything to her parents, had talked to Marie in confidence. True, Marie might still go blabbing to her mother, but Danica didn't think so. The Wilcox seer had her faults, but breaking confidences didn't tend to be one of them.

Angela lifted her head into the wind, as if attempting to sense something of the mysterious stranger on its currents. Right then she did look something like a priestess of old, despite her T-shirt and jeans. Weren't the McAllisters descended from druids or something?

Danica couldn't remember, and maybe it really didn't matter. She shoved her hands into the pockets of her jeans and stared into the forest, toward the spot where the stranger had disappeared. Maybe it was her imagination, but it did seem as if she could see a faint trail there, a narrow pathway winding through the trees.

"It feels all right," Angela said at last. "Although I totally get it if you don't want to stay out here."

"I think I will stay," Danica said, surprising herself. Where had that come from? Had Angela's reassurance that no evil was lurking around the cabin convinced her, or was it something else? But the conviction began to grow in here that she needed to stay. It would be one thing if the stranger had done anything to approach her, or made an attempt to enter the cabin. He hadn't, though, had merely passed by outside. Besides, Caitlin had said that Danica was supposed to come here to the cabin. Maybe it was specifically to see the stranger, although she thought if that were the case, it might have been helpful if he'd actually said something to her.

"I probably would stay, too, if I were in your shoes. I love a good mystery. But here." Angela gestured for Danica to follow her over to her Jeep, which Danica did, feeling somewhat mystified. After opening the passenger-side door, Angela picked up something from the front seat and handed it over.

Danica took the device from her, eyebrows lifting. "A satellite phone?"

"Well, I'll feel better knowing we have some way of reaching you, and knowing that you can get a call out if you need to. Connor bought the phone when he used to go out hiking in the middle of nowhere, but he hasn't been doing much of that lately. So you might as well have it."

For some reason, the simple gesture made Danica's chest tighten. Yes, she'd had her parents hovering over her for the last six months, but she hadn't had much interaction with the rest of her family members, preferring to hole up with her misery. To see Angela, who probably had plenty of other things on her mind, show that she did care, that she wanted to make sure Danica was all right, meant more than she wanted to admit to herself.

Words seemed to fail her. She clutched the phone, and Angela reached out and put a gentle hand on one arm.

"Hey," she said. "Are you okay?"

Danica nodded. "I—I'm fine. Really. Thanks for this. That does make me feel better, knowing I can call if I need to."

Angela's green eyes were very sharp. "Just make sure you do, if it comes to that."

The *prima* didn't stay too long after that exchange. She seemed to listen to the wind one more time, then shook her head, as if exasperated with herself that she couldn't sense anything of the previous night's visitor. Afterward, she got in her Cherokee and drove off, waving to Danica as she headed back to the dirt road in a cloud of dust.

Still holding the satellite phone, Danica went inside the cabin, then set it down carefully on the dining room table. By then it was a little after four, so she still had a few hours before night fell. Plenty of time to go explore that little track she'd seen.

But because she'd wandered through these woods before and knew how time seemed to pass differently there, how you could wander for hours and have it feel as if only a few minutes had passed, she made sure to put the phone, some bottled water, a granola bar, and a compass scrounged from the kitchen junk drawer in the backpack she'd brought along with her, then shoved a sweater on top of everything, just in case. She threw the backpack over her shoulder, locked the front door of the cabin, and shoved the key into her jeans pocket.

When she'd gotten up that morning, she'd put on jeans and a T-shirt and her trail shoes, just because the ground around the cabin wasn't really suited for flip-flops, even if you weren't planning to go on a hike. She was glad of her forethought now, glad that she didn't have to delay to change into something more practical.

She crunched her way down the driveway and then cut off across open ground, heading to the trail she thought she'd spied earlier. And there it was, not much more than a thin line moving through the dry grass. But it was something, a sign that someone had come this way before.

Or something, anyway, she reminded herself. Elk could have cut through here, or deer. It didn't necessarily have to have been human feet that had crushed the vegetation.

This wasn't the way to the valley with the stream. Danica couldn't remember for sure if she'd ever come to this part of the woods or not, because, face it, one stand of ponderosa pines pretty much looked like any other. But it was still lovely, the air clean and fresh-smelling, the sunflowers and mulleins still blooming. Flagstaff hadn't yet had its first frost of the season, but she knew it was coming.

As she walked, she looked from side to side to see if she could spy any evidence that the stranger had come through here. Footprints, broken underbrush, even a discarded gum wrapper. But she didn't see anything at all, only dry pine needles that crunched underfoot and the warm gold of autumn wildflowers. It seemed clear enough to her that no one had come this way in a long while. Definitely not her cousin Cody and his band of rowdy frat boys. They probably hadn't gone any farther than the shed to get firewood for the outdoor hearth.

Danica came to a small clearing and stood there, gazing around her. Again, the place looked as if no one had visited it in a hundred years.

"Are you here?" she called out softly, but only the sound of the wind in the pines came back to her.

Then she heard the crunch of dead pine needles and turned quickly, heart pounding.

Two almond-shaped dark eyes surveyed her solemnly. The doe blinked once at Danica, then turned and moved quite calmly back into the forest, clearly not too startled by the stranger she'd just encountered.

So it was deer that had made the tracks through the trees. Danica's heart sank at that realization, even while she wanted to scold herself for thinking there could be any other explanation. She still could have completely imagined the stranger, after all. Angela sure hadn't been able to detect even the slightest trace of his presence.

Just go back to the cabin, she thought. *Read, or watch TV. Fix something to eat. He didn't even show up last night until after you went to bed.*

So she did just that. Television seemed too intrusive, so she got out her phone and the portable Bluetooth speaker she'd brought along, and turned on some music. Not the retro metal that always made Caitlin wince, but a playlist she'd put together specifically for her time in the woods—old-style country, Johnny Cash and Patsy Cline, and acoustic guitar, and some newer stuff that she'd thought would blend, like the Civil Wars and Zac Brown. It hadn't taken that much time to throw the playlist together, once Danica had told her mother of her intention to come here.

Out of respect for her surroundings, she kept the volume down, but the music was still enough to drown out the echoing silence of the woods, the sense that she was very alone out here.

Her gaze strayed to the satellite phone where it sat on the dining room table, and she relaxed a little. That phone was her lifeline, should she need it.

She ate frozen linguini and salad, and even popped open one of the bottles of wine. Just for a single glass, and then she stuck the cork back in it and returned the bottle to the kitchen. It helped, though. Took the edge off, which was exactly what she needed.

After she was done with dinner, though, and had washed her plate and wine glass and put them away, she realized she didn't feel like reading, or watching TV. She wanted...what?

To solve the mystery.

Two wooden benches sat on the front porch. The weather was getting a little chilly for lingering out there after nightfall, but she'd brought a jacket, and she could wrap one of the spare blankets from the linen closet around herself.

Besides, she couldn't think of anything better to do.

She retrieved her jacket from where she'd hung it up in the coat closet, then got the first blanket that came to hand, a heavy wine-colored cotton thing. After draping it over one arm, she headed out to the porch, although this time she didn't bother to lock the door to the cabin.

For all she knew, she'd need to beat a hasty retreat.

By then, full night had fallen. The moon hadn't come up yet, and so all was utter darkness, except for the broad star-spangled expanse of the heavens above her, the glittering belt of the Milky Way stretching from one end of the sky to the other. With the coming of night, the temperatures had dropped precipitously from their mild low seventies of the daylight hours, and Danica was glad of the blanket she'd brought with her. She wrapped it around herself now, thinking it was a good thing her parents had no idea of what she was up to at the moment. They'd probably start shopping for another shrink, stat.

Maybe it was crazy to be sitting out here, waiting for him to come back. Still, there was something to be said for waiting openly, looking straight into the darkness. She'd show him that she wasn't afraid.

And if it turned out he really was a lost re-enactor, and had decided to return tonight to apologize for trespassing, well...he *was* awfully good-looking.

She thought she saw movement in the darkness, and she stiffened, reaching out for the walking stick she'd brought with her. Telling her pounding heart that it was probably just the deer coming back didn't seem to do much good.

Whatever was moving out there was coming straight for her.

As it approached, drawing nearer to the little pool of yellow light cast by the fixture next to the front door, she saw that it was him.

Mouth dry, she stood, blanket falling to the bench behind her. He paused at the bottom step and stared up at her.

God, he really was gorgeous. The light was better here, so she could see that his eyes under the straight, dark brows were deep blue, his lashes long. A faint trace of dark stubble couldn't hide the strong lines of his jaw, or the curve of his lips.

"Who—who are you?" Danica asked, managing to find her voice. That wasn't so bad. She hardly sounded nervous at all.

He didn't answer, but only continued to look up at her. Now she could see more details of his clothing—the suspenders under the long frock coat, the shirt thinly striped in black and blue, the high black boots that seemed to mold themselves to his muscled calves. The toes of those boots were dusty, as was the hem of his coat. A gold chain disappeared into one of his pants pockets. A watch, she supposed.

Everything item of his clothing seemed perfect in every detail, but she knew re-enactors tended to be fanatical about their costumes. He probably should have been wearing a hat, and a waistcoat and a cravat or something. She didn't mind that he didn't have a hat; this way, she could see how his wavy dark hair flowed back from his fine brow.

"Are you lost?" she asked. Surely that had to be the logical explanation. But who would get lost in the exact same place two nights in a row?

At that question, his eyes widened. Then his gaze seemed to shift, as if he was looking at something over his right shoulder, toward the door of the cabin. Unnerved, Danica glanced in that direction as well, but she saw nothing except a few moths fluttering around the porch light.

Even as she looked back toward him, he staggered backward, one hand going to his chest. Dark blood began to flow down the front of his striped shirt.

Danica let out a gasp and began to run down the steps toward him. His despairing eyes caught hers, and he shook his head. As he lifted his hand from his shirt, she could see the hole there.

A bullet wound.

And then he was gone.

CHAPTER FOUR

So he was a ghost. There couldn't be any other explanation.

Danica sat at the dining room table, shaking, a glass of water next to her. When she'd run back into the house, she'd thought about pouring herself some more wine. But that was a stupid idea. She needed her wits about her—what was left of them, anyway.

Someone had shot him. One of her long-ago Wilcox ancestors? From what she'd heard through the family grapevine, they did sound as if they were hard men, used to getting their own way and not worrying too much about any civilian laws they might break to get ahead. Danica figured she could be objective about those family members when examining the problem, since that was all so very long ago. It was entirely possible that one of the Wilcox relatives wouldn't scruple at shooting someone in the chest, if the killing was something that turned out to be in their best interests. But why shoot the man at all? Couldn't they have used a more witchy way to get rid of him?

Maybe, she thought. *Or maybe they decided that shooting him was easier, and a lot less conspicuous.* Back in the day, Flagstaff had been a pretty wild frontier town. Would anyone have noticed an extra grave out in Boot Hill?

If Flagstaff had had a Boot Hill. She didn't know.

There was a whole hell of a lot she didn't know.

Now wasn't the time to focus on her shortcomings, though. She needed to think about this logically. According to everything she'd read, ghosts tended to haunt the places where they'd met their end, which meant the stranger must have been killed here at the cabin, or at least somewhere on its grounds. No wonder he was hanging around.

As to why…she couldn't begin to guess. Shooting someone that gorgeous seemed like an awful waste to her, but of course she doubted her Wilcox ancestors—Jeremiah and his brothers—were too concerned with such niceties.

If it had even been them at all. She supposed someone else could have been lurking around the Wilcox homestead and shooting trespassers or whatever, but that didn't seem very likely. Then again… when did they abandon this cabin and move to their fancier houses in town? She thought it was sometime in the 1880s. Family history had never interested her that much, except maybe the all-important tracking of how closely everyone in the clan was related to one another, and who was okay to marry and who wasn't. That whole cousins thing could get a little weird, which was why a lot of Wilcoxes married civilians. Such arrangements came with their own set of problems, but at least you didn't have to worry about inbreeding.

Not that even any of her distant, and therefore "safe," cousins had seemed that interesting to her. She'd hoped maybe she could meet someone at school. And then, when the world seemed to open up after the curse was broken, she'd thought she might meet someone in the McAllister clan the way her sister had. Problem was, she hadn't found any of the available McAllisters all that interesting, either.

Anyway, Danica realized that her knowledge of what the Wilcoxes had been up to back in the day was definitely sketchy. She could fix that, though. Tomorrow she could go into town, go to the historical society, dig through a few records.

And...what? If some random guy had really been gunned down on the Wilcoxes' old homestead, she kind of doubted there'd be an official account of the crime. She didn't know a lot, but she did know that no Wilcox had ever spent any time in jail. Which meant this murder—if it really turned out to be a murder—had been covered up.

Still, she might as well try.

What else did she have to do with herself?

The trip to the historical society did yield a few tidbits, including the information that the Wilcoxes had established their homestead in 1877, long before Arizona was a state and before the railroad even got to Flagstaff, but then moved into a series of five houses built on adjoining lots on Leroux Street in 1883. They'd begun as sheep ranchers, but later expanded into cattle ranching and lumber. And, unlike a lot of people in the boom and bust Wild West of the late 1800s, they'd always prospered, had always seemed to know when to invest and when to divest.

Danica thought that sounded as if they'd had someone like her cousin Lucas around, someone whose magical talent was luck, or at least a shrewd understanding of the financial markets. But interesting as that one piece of information might be, it didn't get her any closer to discovering the identity of the man she'd seen.

He didn't look like a Wilcox. True, he was tall and dark-haired, but his eyes were blue. She'd seen the old portrait of the original settlers, because almost every Wilcox household had a reproduction of it. The four Wilcox brothers, three of them with their wives—obviously, Jeremiah had been forced to perpetual widower state by the curse at that point—and their sister Emma with her husband. All of the Wilcoxes had black hair and piercing dark eyes. Not one set of baby blues among them. And the dead man wasn't Emma's husband, either, because he'd also had dark hair and dark eyes, if not quite as jet-black as those of the Wilcox siblings.

If only she could travel back in time, could see exactly what had happened. Now, *that* would be a useful talent.

She'd been walking back to her SUV when that notion struck her, and she stopped dead in the parking lot of the historical society, one hand clutching the strap of her purse.

What if...?

No, that was ridiculous. Sure, she could give herself an extra five minutes here and there, but that was only a few minutes, not more than a hundred years. Time travel in that sense didn't exist.

Although didn't she travel in time a little bit whenever she used her talent to buy herself those five minutes?

Since she realized she must look like an idiot, standing there in the parking lot with a gobsmacked expression on her face, Danica hurried over to the Land Rover and got in. She wished she could talk to

someone about this, but she had the feeling that anyone she broached the subject to would probably give
her some serious side-eye.

Except…Angela had seemed sympathetic. And
she'd done a bit of time travel herself, or at least astral
travel, when she met with Nizhoni and Jeremiah
Wilcox, two people who had been dead for more
than a century, and broke the curse. Surely Angela
would have better insights than anyone else.

Heart beginning to race, Danica picked up her
phone and pushed the button to make the call. Yes,
she and Angela weren't exactly close, but every clan
member had their *prima*'s and *primus*'s number pro-
grammed into their phones.

Just in case.

Angela had sounded a little puzzled on the phone, but
when Danica got to her house in Forest Highlands,
she just smiled and let her in.

"Connor's out back, playing with the twins, so
we shouldn't be interrupted. I hope," she added,
casting a dubious glance over one shoulder toward
the rear of the house. "It's the twins, so anything
could happen. But let's hope for the best."

She led Danica into the living room, saying, "I
don't let them play in here, so we can walk without
worrying about stepping on any Legos or stuffed
animals. Or the dog's chew toys." Her tone sounded

resigned, but from the light dancing in her green eyes, Danica guessed the *prima* really wasn't too concerned with the state of her house.

"It's fine," Danica said. "I know I'm kind of barging in without much notice. But I really needed to pick your brain."

"Pick away," Angela replied. "Although these days it's kind of fried, so I'm not sure how much help I'll be."

Now that the time had come, Danica wasn't quite sure of the best way to explain herself, at least in a manner that wouldn't sound completely off the wall. Then again, they were both witches. Off the wall kind of came with the territory.

"Well, first off, the man I saw is definitely a ghost. Last night, he came back to the cabin, and I—I saw him get shot."

"He was *shot*?" Angela asked, eyes widening.

"Here," Danica elaborated, pointing to the approximate spot on her own chest. "I saw it happen, and then he disappeared again."

For a second the *prima* didn't say anything. She seemed to hesitate, as if considering her words, and then remarked, "That's unusual. Most ghosts don't want to reenact their deaths. They don't like to talk about it. Not that I can really blame them."

"So what do you think it means?"

"I'm not sure, but it's obvious that he's trying to communicate with you. Maybe it's just that you're the first person he's resonated with, and he's trying to get you to understand what happened to him so he can finally move on." During this speech, however, she was frowning, as if annoyed at herself for not being able to sense the stranger's violent death.

Even if Angela was feeling frustrated, her comments sounded logical enough on the surface. But…. "I've been to the cabin before," Danica pointed out, "and I've never seen him. So why now?"

Again Angela paused. Her gaze flicked toward Danica and away, toward the tall windows across the room with their view of the surrounding ponderosa pines. Then she said, "Yes, but you hadn't been through a truly traumatic experience before. What happened to you this past spring…." The words trailed off, and she shook her head. "These things can leave psychic echoes, emotional residue. You're not the same person you were before. So maybe now, for whatever reason, you can resonate with this man, this spirit. He sensed that, and came to you for help."

The thought that what Matías had done to her had materially changed her in some way made Danica cold all over. She didn't want to be changed. Hadn't she spent the last six months desperately trying to get back to the person she used to be?

But if she had been changed, and there was nothing she could do about it, then she might as well make that change matter.

"Okay, maybe that's true," she said. "So what should I do next?"

"I'm not sure," Angela said frankly. "All the ghosts I've encountered were pretty chatty. They wanted to talk to me. But this man hasn't said anything, right?" Without waiting for an answer, she went on, "Do you even know for sure if he's really interacting with you, or just replaying a traumatic experience from his past?"

Danica shook her head, hating the feeling of helplessness she was experiencing. She *thought* he'd been trying to communicate somehow, but she just didn't know for sure.

"So that makes it a lot harder. Sometimes they only want to talk, to have an interaction that makes them feel as if they're alive again. I've gotten a few to cross over, but a lot of the spirits I've dealt with don't seem to care about that. They're clinging to this plane of existence, for whatever reason."

"What if—" They'd come to it now, and Danica knew she had to say the words. She just wished they didn't sound so ridiculous. "What if this ghost doesn't want to talk, or cross over? What if he wants me to stop his murder before it even happens?"

Dead silence. For the first time, Danica heard the ticking of the clock that hung over the huge stone fireplace, then, from farther away, a series of unearthly shrieks. A second or two passed before she realized the noise must have come from the twins playing with Connor in the backyard. Well, good. At least they sounded distracted.

Then Angela spoke, her tone almost too gentle. "How do you propose to do that?"

"I—" Danica hesitated, then said, all in a rush, "My gift. I mean, I always thought it was kind of a stupid gift, because what are you supposed to do with an extra five minutes? But that's a kind of time travel, isn't it?"

"Wait a second. So your talent is giving yourself an extra five minutes whenever you need it?"

"Basically, yes."

"Interesting. I've never heard of anything like that before."

Neither had Danica, but she didn't think that was anything to be proud of. She'd always wished she had a more well-known—and useful—magical talent. "Anyway, I was thinking about how you broke the curse, how you sort of had to expand your own gift to do it, and I was wondering if maybe I could do something similar. You know, figure out a way to work with my talent so I can go back a lot farther than just five minutes."

"That's...." From the befuddled expression on Angela's face, Danica guessed that the *prima* wasn't quite sure how to react to that proposal. "I don't know. Maybe there could be some way." She fell silent, clearly pondering the problem. Her mouth twisted, and she remarked, "I never thought I'd say this, but I almost wish your cousin Damon was still alive. He knew better how to manipulate our witch powers and spells than anyone I've ever heard of. He probably would have some insight on all this. As it is...." Her shoulders lifted. "But maybe you should talk to Lawrence, my father's great-uncle. He's the one who helped teach me how to do the spirit walk, to go outside the bounds of my body so I could talk to Nizhoni."

Although she knew it was far too early for any kind of real hope, Danica felt a surge of excitement nevertheless. "Do you think he can help me?"

"I don't know for sure. I mean, it was one thing for me to go into the spirit world. I still stayed here—my body, anyway. But you're talking about moving yourself back in time, interacting with people who were alive back then. That's something entirely different."

Yes, it was. And when Angela stated the matter so baldly, Danica realized how crazy the entire proposition sounded. However, the *prima* hadn't said no. "Can you talk to Lawrence?"

"Not really. That is, he doesn't have a phone, and cell reception is for crap out on the reservation. My father keeps trying to give him a satellite phone, but Lawrence says he's survived ninety-five years without one and doesn't see any reason to start now."

Ninety-five. That seemed immeasurably ancient to Danica, whose grandparents were only in their late sixties. "Are you sure he'd be up for something like this? I don't want to bother him—"

"Are you kidding? He'd love a chance to try to solve this puzzle. And I'd love to see him help you, but I don't think I can manage to disappear for a whole day. I could get one of the cousins to babysit, but then I'd have to explain why."

"It's fine," Danica said quickly. "All I'd need is directions."

At once Angela shook her head. "No, I wouldn't send you out there—for the first time, at least—without someone guiding you in. His house can be a little tricky to find. Would you mind going with my father? He drives out there about once a week anyway to check on things. I know he'd be happy to take you."

For a second or two, Danica hesitated. She didn't know Andre Begonie all that well, and it did feel sort of awkward to be driving off with him into Navajo country. But then, if this insane plan of hers actually worked, she'd be going a lot farther—metaphorically speaking, anyway—than the reservation. This was no time to be timid.

"Sure," she replied, making sure she sounded firm and upbeat, and not worried at all. "If you really think he won't mind."

"I know he won't. Let me go give him a quick call and see when he might be available."

"Thanks."

Angela got up from the couch and went into the kitchen, presumably in search of her cell phone. As she waited, Danica glanced around the room. It really was very tidy, with no sign that a couple of almost-three-year-olds lived here. Pictures of the children were scattered around—on the hearth, on a side table, on top of the low bookshelves under the picture window. They really were adorable, with their big green eyes and dark hair. One of the pictures was clearly a professional shot of the entire family, taken in the yard, it looked like, since Danica recognized the outlines of the house behind them. Everyone was smiling. Connor had his arm looped around Angela's waist and was leaning in toward her. The adoring light in his eyes made it obvious that he was just crazy about her, and Danica felt a little pang as she looked at the portrait. Would she ever find someone who looked at her the same way?

She quickly glanced away from the picture as Angela reentered the living room, phone held to her ear.

"Just a sec," she was saying. She paused and glanced over at Danica. "Is tomorrow okay?"

That sounded awfully soon, but, on the other hand, what the heck else did she have to fill her days? She might as well go and talk to this Lawrence person, and find out sooner rather than later whether her plan had any hope of succeeding. "Tomorrow's great."

Angela returned her attention to the phone. "That works. At ten?" Her gaze flicked to Danica, who nodded. "Okay, she'll meet you at your place at ten. Thanks, Andre." She ended the call and stuck the phone in her jeans pocket. "You're all set."

It seemed strange to Danica that Angela would call her father by his first name, but then, the *prima* hadn't met him until she was an adult. He certainly hadn't been around when she was a child, so maybe it felt more natural for her to call him by his given name rather than attempt to make up for lost time by saying "Dad" or whatever.

"Thanks so much," Danica said. "I really hope I'm not imposing or anything."

"You're not. As I said, Lawrence eats this stuff up. If he can't help you, I don't think anyone can."

That remark didn't exactly sound encouraging, but Angela was probably right. The Wilcoxes had some talented witches and warlocks among them, but Danica didn't know of anyone with the talent to bend time and space. And she doubted the McAllisters had anyone like that, either.

Danica got up from the couch, since she figured she'd taken up enough of the *prima*'s time already. "Thanks," she told the other woman, even though she'd said practically the same thing already.

"It's fine. Let me know how it goes. I'm really interested."

Most likely, nothing would happen at all, but Danica told herself to be positive. Lawrence had certainly helped Angela when she—and the whole clan—needed it most. After all, up here in the high country, lightning did sometimes strike the same place twice.

As much as Danica had enjoyed not having her parents hovering over every little thing she did, she knew she should call her mother while she was in town where she actually could get some cell reception. Luckily, though, Danica got the voicemail at the house, which meant she was able to leave a message saying that she was fine, and the cabin was fine, but something had gone funky with the land line. Not to worry, though, because she had a satellite phone, so she could still call out if necessary.

Danica didn't bother to explain where she'd gotten the satphone, and she didn't leave the number. Well, that was mainly because she didn't know it. She'd left the phone back at the cabin, since she hadn't thought she'd need it in town, where she could use her cell phone. She could always call again with the number…or not. The important thing was that she could make calls. That didn't mean she wanted to get pestered by people calling her, especially overly anxious parents.

The sun had begun to dip behind the trees to the west of the property by the time she got back to the cabin. She still had an hour or so until sundown, which was good, because she'd decided she wanted to go back into the woods. After more than a hundred years, there probably wasn't any trace of where the stranger's body had been buried, but Danica thought she should at least try to find his resting place, uneasy as it was. Maybe if she did that, he would understand that she was attempting to help him.

Dry grass crackled under her feet as she headed toward the clearing. Once there, she looked around, inspecting the ground and the trees with narrowed eyes, hoping she would see something out of the ordinary. But everything looked just as it should—a few fallen branches littering the ground, pinecones scattered here and there, mullein plants driving up yellow-tipped spikes.

There, though, on the other side of the clearing. Danica's eyes narrowed as she realized that another path wound away through the woods. It could go nowhere, but she had her compass with her. And she had some time before the sun really began to set.

This other path—if you could even call it that, overgrown as it was—snaked away to the north and west, moving over ground that gradually rose and became rockier. Danica had to slow her pace but kept on doggedly, although she knew there was a very good chance the trail would only lead her to another dead end.

She came to a small clearing, barely more than a wide space in the path. To her left, boulders protruded from the hillside, a few pine trees clinging tenaciously to the spaces between the rocks. On the other side, sycamores fought for space with the ponderosa pines. The trees' leaves hadn't begun to turn yet, but Danica thought she saw a patch of foliage high up on one that was just starting to turn gold.

As her gaze traveled back down from the treetops, she thought she saw an odd, pale scar on the lower trunk of the middle sycamore. She approached, thinking it must be a scratch left by a wild animal. Didn't bears sharpen their claws on tree trunks or something?

Her hiking boot hit a rock, and she glanced down. There wasn't just one rock, but a whole pile of them. And they didn't look like the reddish sandstone of the boulders above her, but instead were smooth and pale, clearly tumbled in a creek or riverbed. What the heck?

She looked back up at the tree. The scar she had noticed was only a few feet off the ground and consisted of two simple lines.

A cross.

Ice seemed to travel down her spine, and she stepped back quickly. Those rocks covering the ground...the cross on the tree....

It seemed she might have found the stranger's resting place after all.

Some might have thought the use of the cross odd, but, unlike the McAllister clan, who practiced their own form of Wicca, the Wilcoxes had always been nominally Christian, or at least paid lip service to Christian traditions so they wouldn't attract any unwanted attention. As to why her ancestors had gone to the trouble of burying the stranger, and then putting a cross above his unmarked grave out here in the woods, she couldn't begin to guess. Delayed-reaction guilt?

A shadow moved behind her, and she turned slowly, hoping it was a deer and knowing it probably wasn't.

He stood there, in silence as always. The sorrow in those piercing blue eyes made her want to go to him and put her arms around him. But, considering the way he tended to evaporate into nothing, she realized embracing him would probably be like trying to hug mist.

"I'm sorry," she said.

His gaze flickered to the meager little pile of stones, and his shoulders lifted. He tilted his head at her as if to say, *It's not your fault.*

No, it wasn't. But it could have been the fault of her great-great-etc.-grandfather, or great-great-uncle. In fact, she very much feared that was exactly the case.

Anyway, this one-sided conversation seemed to answer one of Angela's questions. Clearly, the ghost was interacting with Danica in some fashion, even if he couldn't seem to talk.

"I want to help you," she continued. "I don't know if I can. But I'm going to try. That is…if you want me to."

Then she waited, breath held, as the stranger regarded her with those sad blue eyes of his. For the longest moment, he didn't do anything, but only stood where he was. Maybe he couldn't really hear her. Was there some sort of disconnect between the land of the living and of the dead, so he could see her but not communicate in any meaningful way?

At last he took a step toward her, followed by another. The silence of his movements unnerved her; she should have been able to hear the crunch of dry grass under his high boots, the crackle of a twig as his heel descended on it. But she heard none of those things, only the heightened pounding of her heart.

He stopped at last, so close that she could have reached out and touched his face…if she'd dared. Everything about him seemed so solid, and yet…his chest didn't rise and fall, and she knew if she'd laid a hand where his heart was supposed to be, she would have felt nothing.

Since she didn't know what else to do, she stood there, holding herself as still as she could. She didn't want to frighten him away.

A hand reached up, as if to touch her hair. She fancied she could feel something, the tiniest brush of fingers against the loose strands, but that must have been the wind.

And then the echo of one word in her mind, nothing more than a whisper before he was gone again, fading away like mist in sunlight.

Yes.

CHAPTER FIVE

DANICA WAS GLAD OF ANDRE BEGONIE'S RELAXED, EASY-going manner, because after that encounter with her ghost the afternoon before, she still felt a little rattled.

Her ghost. Of course he really wasn't hers, but she couldn't help thinking of him that way. Of everyone who'd visited the cabin, she was the only one he'd reached out to, made contact with. That had to mean something.

They rattled along in Andre's ancient Jeep, all the windows rolled down. Danica wondered why on earth he hadn't bought a new car. Now that he was back amongst the Wilcoxes and not in hiding on the reservation, he certainly had the funds to do so. Maybe he simply didn't care about that sort of thing.

She would have liked to say she didn't care, either, but as they made their way out of Flagstaff and down into the desert lands where the Navajo tribal territory began, she found herself missing her Land Rover and its awesome air conditioning in a major way. Rolling down the windows only helped so much.

One good thing about that, though—the noise from the wind blasting through the Jeep kept conversation to a minimum, which worked just fine for Danica. She really wasn't in the mood for small talk. Not that Andre Begonie seemed like the chatty type. He guided them down the highway, gaze fixed on the road ahead of them, and didn't seem inclined to say much. Not in a taciturn or grumpy sort of way, but more like he was fine with being quiet if that was what you wanted. And right then Danica wanted it very much.

She was still trying to figure out how much she should say to this Lawrence person when she saw him. It was one thing to say you were being altruistic about wanting to go back in time and right an ancient wrong. Now, though, after the way the stranger— the spirit—had approached her, had reached out to touch her, she knew deep down that her feelings weren't terribly altruistic at all.

She wanted to save him because…she was pretty sure she wanted him.

Oh, God, that sounded terrible once she'd admitted her need to herself, especially in reference to a man who'd been dead for more than a hundred years before she was even born. Why did he have to be so damn handsome?

It was more than his looks, though. There was something…a pull…that Danica had never experienced with anyone else.

She wouldn't count what she'd felt with Matías, because that had all been a lie, an attraction based solely on the unholy magical power of coercion he possessed. He'd made her think that she wanted him, maybe was even in love with him, but it had nothing to do with what she actually wanted and everything to do with Matías' own sick desires.

But this man, whose name she didn't even know…she thought she wanted him. Which, again, was crazy.

Of course you couldn't be practical like your sister and fall for a nice McAllister boy, she thought wearily as she watched the dusty landscape flash by. *No, you had to find yourself attracted to a ghost.*

She must have made some sort of sound, possibly let out a sigh, because Andre looked over at her then.

"Sorry about all the wind," he said. "The A/C worked once upon a time, but I've just never gotten around to fixing it."

"It's okay," Danica replied automatically, even though she knew she was going to be a complete windblown mess by the time they got to Lawrence's house. "I don't mind it."

He seemed content with her answer, and returned his attention to the road. At least it looked as if they were getting close to their destination; he slowed down for some road construction, and then turned left a little bit before the trading post, which seemed to be where a lot of the other cars were heading.

No trading post for the two of them, however. Andre turned off onto a dirt road and seemed to be headed up toward a canyon. Danica could just make out some sort of compound through the swirling dust—a couple of one-story houses and a few out-buildings she didn't immediately recognize. A white pickup truck even more ancient than the Jeep they were riding in was parked under a huge old oak tree.

Andre pulled up next to the pickup and put the Jeep in park. "Well, here we are."

Danica nodded, then reached up to smooth her wind-tangled hair as best she could. Good thing she couldn't really see what she looked like. But then, she kind of doubted this Lawrence person would care one way or another if she looked like a walking disaster area.

She followed Andre to one of the two houses on the property. They looked nearly identical, and she wondered if he'd lived in one of them while he was out here in hiding, waiting for Angela to grow up so she could break the curse.

Although they'd left a mild day behind them in Flagstaff, the heat here was blistering enough for July. Andre knocked once on the door, said, "Lawrence, we're here," and then opened it to let them in.

Cool, somewhat damp air, obviously from a swamp cooler, swirled out around Danica. She stepped into it, glad of the relief from the merciless dry heat outside, then blinked as her eyes adjusted themselves to the darkness. The room was shabbily furnished, with a cracked leather couch, a battered coffee table...and a leather chair in one corner. In that chair sat an ancient-looking Navajo man, his bone-white hair pulled back into a ponytail.

"Forgive me for not getting up," he said. In contrast to his frail appearance, his voice was still deep and resonant. "These old bones of mine don't always want to cooperate some days."

"Oh, it's fine," Danica said at once. "Thank you for seeing me."

"Well, after my great-grandniece told me what you wanted to talk about, I knew I must speak with you." The old man's gaze flicked up at Andre. "We'll probably need some water."

Andre smiled and disappeared through a door in the far wall, presumably on his way to the kitchen.

Lawrence gestured toward the sofa. "Go ahead—sit down."

Danica did as instructed, setting her purse on the floor beside her. Although she'd wanted to talk to Lawrence, now that she was here, she couldn't quite think of how to phrase her request. Too often, subjects that sounded reasonable enough in her own mind turned into outright lunacy when she had to utter them out loud.

Luckily, Andre returned then with a couple of glasses of water. He set one down on the coffee table in front of Danica, then put the other on the TV tray next to the chair where Lawrence sat.

"Thank you," Lawrence said. "But I think Danica here would like to speak in confidence now. Andre, maybe you could go next door for a little while."

Andre didn't appear at all annoyed to be dismissed so summarily after playing chauffeur. "Not a problem. I wanted to go through my supplies and get some more stone rough for cutting anyway. I'll knock when I'm done and see if you're ready."

He offered Danica an encouraging smile, then let himself out.

She wished she felt encouraged. She glanced over at Lawrence, who was sitting quietly, dark gaze fixed on her. It seemed pretty obvious that he intended to wait until she spoke.

"Well, um…." she began, then paused, not sure where she should begin.

Come on, she chided herself. *You made Andre drive you all the way out here, so get on with it already.*

"I suppose Angela told you about the ghost?"

"She did."

"And she told you about my talent?"

"Something of it. She was somewhat startled, because she'd never heard of such a thing before." He'd been leaning forward slightly, but he settled back into his chair, letting out the slightest grunt as if the shift in position pained him. "Truthfully, Danica, I've never heard of a gift like that, either, although the magic of my people is different from the magic of your witch clans. But this must mean something."

Yeah, she thought. *It means I'm a freak, even in a clan of witches.*

But she didn't say anything, only nodded and hoped that she looked appropriately expectant and hopeful.

"For you to have seen this spirit when no one else has…this means something as well. Especially when speaking with ghosts is not your particular talent." Lawrence nodded to himself, and his black eyes, almost buried in wrinkles, glinted as a notion appeared to occur to him. "But when we speak of time, these things become more complicated. Time is a construct we place on the universe, so we can understand it. But the universe does not need time."

"It doesn't?" Danica responded, hoping she didn't look too puzzled. She'd taken enough physics courses to figure out her brain didn't really work that way. Even if getting an advanced degree in physics might have impressed her parents, following in her cousin Damon's footsteps when it came to a career choice probably wasn't going to happen. Instead, she'd switched her major to biology. She still wasn't sure what she would do with the degree…not that it mattered, since it didn't look as if she'd be finishing up that bachelor's anytime soon.

Anyway, it sounded as if Lawrence was about to launch into the sort of quantum discussion that tended to make her feel as if her brain was about to cave in. But if that was what it took to make her talent do something new and unexpected….

"Time is a human construct," Lawrence said. "Which is fine. We need that order in our lives. But the universe doesn't necessarily see time as something linear. And you'll need to see it as something more than that, if you truly wish to go to this man's time and right this wrong." He stopped then and seemed to study her face, as if attempting to determine whether she actually believed a wrong had been committed.

"I do," she said quietly. "That is, I know something terrible happened to him. I went up into the woods yesterday, and I—I found his grave. No one would have buried a man out in the forest like that if they weren't trying to cover it up."

"Ah." For a few seconds, Lawrence was silent, expression abstracted. "This is a terrible thing, and it is good of you to attempt to make it right. But do you understand—truly understand—what it will take to accomplish this task?"

Danica shook her head. Of course she didn't. Time travel, and ghosts, and ancient murders—she had no idea what she was getting herself into. But then in her mind's eye, she saw the stranger's face, the sorrow there, and she realized she didn't care that she was stepping off the deep end. She had to save him, no matter what.

"How could I?" she asked, but not in a confrontational way. She just wanted Lawrence to know that she was way out of her depth here.

He smiled. His teeth were very white, but oversized. Danica wondered if they were false.

"Of course you can't. This is good. If you had said you did understand, I would worry, because then you would be overconfident, and that can be dangerous. So," he went on, and again she caught that glint in his black eyes, "show me this talent of yours."

"Excuse me?"

"How does it work?"

"Well...." Really, there wasn't anything that spectacular about it. She'd look up at the clock in her room, or the time display on her phone, think, *I really need that five minutes now,* and then she'd just sort of have it. She could finish blow-drying her hair or putting on her makeup or whatever, and when she was done, the clock wouldn't have moved, and the display wouldn't have changed.

She explained all that to Lawrence as best she could, and he nodded. "Good. Do it now. Take your five minutes to go next door to talk to Andre."

That felt strange, since usually she took her five minutes in private, someplace where people weren't around to see that something odd had just occurred in their universe. Technically, though, time should seem to be passing normally for Andre, as long as she was with him.

Or would it?

Only one way to find out.

I need my five minutes.

The clock on the wall behind Lawrence stopped ticking. The swamp cooler continued to hum away, though, so it wasn't as if everything around her had been halted completely. Danica got up from the couch and went out the door, blinking against the glaring sunlight and wishing she'd thought to grab her sunglasses before she headed outside. She squinted as best she could and went over to the other house, which apparently had been Andre's, and where some of his belongings still remained.

He answered the door only a few seconds after she knocked. Looking down at her in some surprise, he asked, "Is everything all right?"

"I don't know yet," she said. "I guess we'll find out in a few minutes."

Her reply only seemed to puzzle him that much more, but he did step aside so she could enter the house. This place seemed much better furnished, and Danica wondered why Lawrence hadn't moved in here, if Andre wasn't using the place anymore. But maybe he liked his shabby old stuff.

"It's my talent," she explained after Andre had closed the door. "I'm using my five minutes. It looks as if you're experiencing them with me, because I'm with you, but Lawrence shouldn't even be able to tell that any time has passed."

Surprisingly, Andre didn't appear too confused by her remark. He nodded, saying, "Angela had mentioned you had some sort of gift of time, but she didn't go into any details."

"There's not much to tell. I get five minutes whenever I need them."

"And only five minutes? Nothing more?"

"Not as far as I can tell."

He seemed to consider that response, then asked, "What if you, I don't know, stacked them up against each other so you could make up even more time?"

She'd honestly never tried that, because having just five minutes had saved her ass on multiple occasions. Besides, she'd always been taught that a talent was a talent. If your talent was changing the direction of the wind, then you couldn't alter it to summon tornadoes, and if your skill lay in conjuring illusions, you couldn't suddenly make those illusions become real.

Then again, Angela had managed to shift her talent into something more, partly because of Lawrence's guidance. It could also have something to do with her growing *prima* power, or the way that power had joined with Connor's *primus* energy. No one had been able to say definitively for sure, and no one had done any real investigation. That had been Damon's area of expertise…exploring witch powers, analyzing them, using them to create spells no one else had ever heard of.

But Damon was gone, and she would have to figure this one out on her own. Well, not completely on her own. She had Lawrence to help her, and even if Angela couldn't offer any real assistance in terms of figuring out how to stretch that five minutes to a hundred years or more, she did seem willing to keep her mouth shut about Danica's activities. The only way her parents would ever find out was if Danica herself told them.

And that's not going to happen, she thought. *At least not until all this is over.*

Andre was watching her with some curiosity, and so she shrugged. "No, I haven't ever tried stretching out those five minutes. Maybe I will, to do…what I'm planning to do. But right now I'm just showing Lawrence how the basics work."

"Got it." He glanced over his shoulder, toward a short hallway that connected the front room with the rest of the house. "I'm still sorting through my samples, but if you want to come along, you're welcome."

Danica pulled her phone out of her jeans pocket. Best guess, she had about three more minutes to kill. "Okay."

So she followed him into what had once been a bedroom but now appeared to be a kind of workshop. Or at least it looked as if it once was a workshop; long tables lined the walls, but they were mostly bare, except for what looked like scars left from slips of a drill, and the odd burn mark here and there. But a few plastic bins still sat on the one table under the window, and some pieces of rough stone had been carefully laid out on the table's surface in front of them. Danica guessed that was the rough Andre had mentioned before he went out.

"So," she said, as he went over and began sifting through the contents of one of the bins. "You cut and polish all your own stuff?"

"Most of it," he replied, lifting a greenish stone so he could hold it up near the window, in the light. "I always get a better feel for what a piece wants to be when I start from rough. Every once in a while I'll trade one of the stones I've polished for one from a friend, but that doesn't happen too often."

"That's cool." Then she wanted to wince. Did she have to sound so…banal? Problem was, she really didn't know that much about jewelry-making, although she'd gotten the impression that Andre made a good bit of money from his work, that it had made its way into some of the higher-end shops in Flagstaff and Sedona.

He didn't seem to note the inanity of her reply, though, but only continued to work, setting pieces aside, occasionally stopping to put them in a leather bag he'd placed off to one side of the worktable.

Wanting to redeem herself, Danica asked, "Where do you get the rough? Do you mine that, too?"

A quick grin. In the flash of that smile, she caught something of the resemblance between father and daughter, although otherwise she wouldn't have said that Angela and Andre looked all that much alike. "No, I trade for it, or go to local gem shows. Although this past year I was able to go to the Tucson gem show for the first time. That was a little mind-blowing. I had no idea it was so huge."

Danica had only vaguely heard of the gem show, but she guessed it had to be an eye-opener, if only because it probably was the first time Andre had ventured so far afield from Wilcox territory. No, wait… that wasn't right. He'd gone to California to meet Angela's mother. But it still was most likely his first time going that far since his self-imposed exile out here in Navajo territory.

"It's great you were able to go," Danica said. "So much has changed…."

And she trailed off then, because she realized how much really had changed since Angela broke the curse. Big things, like the Wilcoxes never having to suffer through the loss of another *primus*'s wife, with all its resulting tragedy, and small ones, like being able to travel to a gem show in another clan's territory. And everything in between, like her own sister being married to a McAllister. If someone had told Danica a few years ago that her future brother-in-law was going to be a member of the Jerome witch clan, she would have told them to put down the crack pipe.

"It has," Andre agreed. "And all for the better."

Danica couldn't argue with that. True, her own life had pretty much gone into the toilet after the

Matías incident, but that had nothing to do with the Wilcoxes and the McAllisters. If she wanted to blame anyone, she supposed she could blame herself, since it had been her idea to go to Tucson in the first place. But no, her shrink had said it wasn't her fault, that she hadn't done anything wrong for wanting to enjoy spring break. All right, then maybe she should blame Simón Santiago, the nominal head of the witch clan in Southern California, for not warning Maya de la Paz that such a dangerous warlock had crossed over into her territory.

But what good would blaming Simón do? Done was done. Now Danica only wanted to get past all of that, and focusing on saving her ghost sounded like a pretty good distraction.

She pulled her phone out of her pocket again and checked the time. A hair past five minutes, which meant time should have started back up again for Lawrence and the rest of the world that wasn't in this small bubble with her and Andre.

"Looks like it's time to head back over," she said.

"And what does that mean for me?" he asked. "That is, am I always going to be five minutes ahead of the rest of the world?"

"No." It was something that had puzzled her at first as well, although by now she was used to the odd little step out of time she took whenever she used her power. "It's like…we get this five minutes, and

I can see it passing on my phone, but then when it's up, it's sort of…up. Like now." She held up the phone so he could see the display. "A few seconds ago, it said it was 11:42, but now it's showing as 11:37. We had that five minutes to have our conversation, but now we've used it up."

"Fascinating."

He really did look fascinated, too; his eyebrows were drawn together in thought as he gazed at the time display on her iPhone, and his head was cocked to one side. It felt a little strange to be standing there with him studying her phone like that, so Danica shrugged and said, a little too quickly,

"Well, I'd better get back to Lawrence."

"Sure," Andre replied. "I'm almost finished with sorting these stones, but if you need more time, just let me know."

Time. There was the conundrum. She supposed she could go back over to Lawrence's cramped little house and ask for another five minutes, then another, and another. Or maybe he wouldn't want her to do that.

Only one way to find out. She sent Andre a quick smile and headed back outside, then hurried over to Lawrence's house. A knock at the door, and he was telling her to come inside. When she entered, she saw that he was gazing up at the dusty clock on the wall, dark eyes speculative.

"So you had your five minutes, I suppose."

"I did." She hesitated, then asked, "What did it feel like to you?"

"Nothing. That is, it seems as if you went out that door only a minute ago, but of course it was more than that."

"It was." Danica advanced farther into the room and sat down on the little rush-bottomed chair, since it was closer to the leather one where Lawrence sat than the couch. "But…what am I supposed to do now?"

"What do you want to do?"

It felt as if they were speaking in circles…sort of like talking to her former shrink but without all the lying. Swallowing her frustration, Danica said, as evenly as she could, "I want to go back and save him. Whoever he is."

Silence for a long moment. The ticking of the clock seemed unnaturally loud, even against the background hum of the swamp cooler. It was dim enough in the room that she couldn't quite decipher the old man's expression. Empathy?

"And are you so certain he is one who should be saved?"

Well, there was a question. Danica didn't have a ready answer for it, because she honestly didn't know for sure. The stranger—the ghost—hadn't seemed threatening in any way. She hadn't sensed anything wrong or evil about him, and neither had Angela detected any sign of a negative presence on the property. But how much did that truly mean?

"I—I think he is."

"But you don't know. You say he was killed on your family's property. What if your ancestors were merely defending their own against him? You have no way of knowing what happened."

No, I don't, she thought miserably. *Not unless I can figure out how to get there and see for myself.*

But even as that thought passed through her mind, she somehow felt the wrongness of Lawrence's suggestion. This man was good. And, by all accounts, her Wilcox forebears weren't exactly angels. True, it turned out that Jeremiah had never kidnapped his Navajo wife, had actually loved her, but caring for one person didn't mean you weren't still capable of doing some pretty underhanded stuff if it suited your purposes.

"He was innocent," she said, her tone firm. "I just know it."

Lawrence smiled. "Well, then, let us find out for certain."

CHAPTER SIX

DANICA ENDED UP SPENDING THE ENTIRE AFTERNOON AT Lawrence's house. At one point Andre headed out, saying he was going to get lunch for everyone. Which he did, reappearing awhile later with takeout boxes with Navajo tacos—fry bread, beef, cheese, lettuce and tomatoes—for all three of them.

The food was delicious. Good thing, too, because she'd never realized how physically taxing mental exercise could be. Lawrence wanted her to meditate, to think of time like the air around her—eternally flowing, something to be breathed in. It was not a straight line, like the road that led back to the highway, but something ever-present, in all places at once and always.

Easier said than done. Because she'd taken yoga, Danica had learned how to be calm and still, how to keep her thoughts from darting this way and that, how to use her breathing to steady herself. Many times over the past six months, it seemed as if the practice was the only thing keeping her sane. Even so, she thought it was a pretty big leap to go from the quiet serenity of deep meditation to letting her consciousness flow through time like a trout swimming in a forest stream.

Anyway, a lot more than her consciousness would have to be involved if she wanted to succeed. This wouldn't be a spirit walk like the one Angela had taken on the astral plane to find Nizhoni and break the curse. Danica would have to find some way to take her odd facility with time and allow it to jump over the hundred-plus years that separated her from the ghost...or rather, the man the ghost had once been.

And thinking of those hundred years wasn't the right way to go about it. Centuries and decades only chopped up time into artificial units. They weren't *really* time.

Not that she could precisely say what time was. She only knew it didn't seem to be on her side at the moment.

She breathed in, trying not to be conscious of Lawrence sitting in his chair on the other side of the room. For this exercise, she'd moved to the couch, since it was far more comfortable, despite its shabby appearance. She thought of her gift, of how it could give her all the time in the world…if she would only let it.

That's right. Five minutes was a construct. Five minutes meant nothing to the universe. There was only time, moving around her and in her, pulling her along in its strong current. But a good swimmer didn't necessarily have to move with the current.

A wave of warm air washed over her. For an instant, Danica thought something had gone wrong with the swamp cooler. Her eyes opened, and she sucked in a breath.

The house was gone. She sat on a rock in the midst of a huge expanse of rolling grassland. A line of dark trees seemed to follow a river to the north and east, judging by the angle of the sun. Dark against the bright green of the grass, huge herds of cattle grazed.

So she finally had gone crazy.

She shifted on the rock where she sat, and realized the unfamiliar landscape wasn't completely unfamiliar. The box canyon behind her looked like the same one that backed up to Lawrence's property. At least, its contours were the same. The area seemed far lusher than the dry, dusty desert she'd left behind her.

Left behind in her own time….

A sensation of the air being pushed out of her lungs, as if she'd fallen flat on her face. She gasped, and blinked, and was back in the dim, damp confines of the living room where she'd first been sitting.

"You went," Lawrence said quietly.

"I—" Danica blinked and tried to pull in a breath. "I went…where?"

"That's for you to tell me, I suppose." His sharp black eyes were focused on hers. "This was not like Angela's spirit walk. I saw you sitting there on the couch, and then you were gone."

Back to whenever that had been, with these hills rolling green instead of dusty yellow, and cattle as far as the eye could see. "How long?"

"Less than a minute. And then you were back."

He seemed remarkably calm about the whole thing. Danica wasn't sure how she would have reacted if she'd seen him wink in and out of existence right in front of her eyes.

"I saw green hills," she said. "And a line of trees along the river—I guess they're still there today, but they looked thicker. And herds of cattle."

A nod. For some reason, he appeared almost sad. "That was this land, many years ago. The settlers overgrazed their cattle and moved on. It was greener then." He let out a sigh, hardly more than a soft breath, then went on, his tone far brisker, "So you did go back."

"But I was still…here."

"Yes. Your gift has always only given you the ability to move in time, not in space. When you do go back, you will need to make sure you are standing someplace that would have been safe back then."

Well, the family cabin had existed back in the 1880s, but she had a feeling her Wilcox forebears might not appreciate a strange young woman appearing out of nowhere in their living room… or whatever they called it back then. The parlor, maybe?

And then Danica realized she was thinking about traveling to that time as if it wasn't of much more consequence than getting in her SUV to go to the mall. She swallowed, glad that she was sitting down. Her knees felt a little shaky.

Okay, *really* shaky.

Lawrence was still watching her carefully. "What brought you back?"

"I don't—" She broke off there. She'd been about to say she didn't know, but she thought she probably did. It was when she'd consciously thought about what she'd just done, *when* she might have gone, that she'd sent herself right back where she'd started from. "Realizing I might have just gone back in time."

He chuckled. "Well, that means you know what you have to work on."

Andre drove her back to town not long after that. The sun was just beginning to set, glaring into her eyes even though she had her sunglasses planted firmly on her nose. As on the drive out to Lawrence's house, neither Danica nor Andre said much to one another. Her thoughts were churning.

I went back in time. I went back in time.

All right, only for a few seconds, but still. She knew she hadn't imagined what she saw. How could she have? She hadn't even known that those lands weren't always dried-up desert. Local history wasn't something covered in her school's curriculum, except the standard story about how a group of travelers had come to the area in July of 1876 and cut down a ponderosa pine so they could fly the American flag for the holiday, thus giving birth to Flagstaff's name.

If that story was even true.

Once they reached the house Andre shared with Marie, he pulled into the driveway. They both got out of the Jeep, and Danica absently thanked him for driving her. He seemed to understand that she didn't want to talk, so he only told her it was no problem, and that he'd be happy to take her again if she needed him to.

Maybe she would. She didn't know yet. Clearly, she'd managed a tiny jump back in time, but she knew a few seconds or a minute certainly wasn't enough for her to do anything about saving the man who had died on her family's land so many decades ago.

And maybe she should stop thinking about years and minutes and seconds, but that was just how her mind worked. At least she was able to turn that part of it off when it really counted.

Danica drove back up to the cabin in the gathering darkness. All was quite black when she got there, and she wished she'd had the forethought to at least leave the porch light on or something. Then again, she'd had no idea she would be spending that much time at Lawrence's house.

Time again. Always time.

Luckily, she kept a flashlight in the glove compartment of her Land Rover, so she dug it out and exited the vehicle, keeping the narrow beam fixed on the ground in front of her. The weather was getting to be too cold for snakes, but that didn't mean she couldn't put her foot wrong in a gopher hole or something.

The light passed over something solid and black, definitely not a rock. Boots, dusty. Danica gasped, flicking the beam upward.

He was standing in the driveway again.

Was it strange that the flashlight's beam didn't even pass through him? If she hadn't known better, she would have said he was just as solid as she was.

His eyes met hers. Again she felt that odd pull, that ache somewhere deep within her. She didn't know who he was or why he had died, although right then his shirt looked untouched, the bullet hole gone. Had he gotten rid of it, realizing that the sight of it disturbed her?

She didn't know. What she did know was that she wanted him.

After moistening her suddenly dry lips, she said, "I'm trying. I think—I think I can help you. But there are still a few things I need to figure out. You're from back then…but *when* back then?"

He continued to watch her for a few seconds, expression faintly puzzled. Then he nodded, as if something had occurred to him. Moving past her, still in that unnatural silence with no crunch of gravel beneath his feet, he went to the rear window of the Land Rover. It was coated with dust she'd kicked up on her drive back here; there hadn't been any rain for more than a week.

Danica stared at him, mystified, and wondered what the heck he was up to. She sort of doubted he was going to scribble "wash me" on the SUV's window.

Not exactly that, but he did reach out with one finger to touch the glass. A downward stroke, and then a couple of swirling motions, followed by a quick angled brush of his finger and a final stroke that mirrored the first one he'd made.

Heartbeat speeding up, Danica trained the flashlight's beam on the Land Rover's rear window. She halfway expected to see nothing at all—could ghosts even affect the physical world?—but what the flashlight revealed made her mouth go dry.

1884.

"That's when you were here?" she asked, even though she knew the stranger wouldn't—or couldn't—reply.

But he did. Not verbally, but he inclined his head.

That did narrow things down a good bit. Still....

"When in 1884?"

He paused then, glancing around him, although Danica wasn't sure what he might be looking at. Then he pointed at the trees, and at the sky.

Well, that was clear as mud.

"I don't understand."

A frown creased his brow. During their previous encounters, his features had been still for the most part, although Danica had noted the sadness in his eyes. Now, though, he looked almost frustrated.

No wonder, she thought, *if he's been waiting more than a hundred years to communicate with someone and then can't even speak when he finally finds a person who can see him.*

Then it seemed as if a sudden thought struck him. He stepped away from the Land Rover, moving purposefully toward the cabin. Danica hurried along after him, although she couldn't begin to guess what he might be up to.

The stranger stopped by the aspen tree that stood a few yards away from the eastern side of the house, then reached up and plucked one of its leaves, and let it fall to the ground. Watching this performance, Danica could only feel her own sense of puzzlement grow. She lifted her shoulders.

"I still don't—" But then she broke off as realization struck. "It happened when the leaves were falling?"

He nodded, relief clear in his face.

That would be mid- to late October in Flagstaff, depending on when the first frost had struck that year. There would probably be a record somewhere, in someone's almanac or a farmer's diary...something. She'd find out, one way or another.

"October 1884?"

Another nod. Then he smiled, eyes meeting hers, and the shock of that blue, blue gaze made her knees go a little wobbly. If he could have this effect on her now, when he was nothing more than a spirit, how the hell was she going to react when she met him in person?

If she could meet him in person. There were still so many variables involved here that she couldn't allow herself to be overly hopeful.

But she wouldn't express those doubts now. She wanted to comfort him as best she could.

"All right," Danica said. "October 1884. It's a date."

Another of those heart-melting smiles, and then he was gone.

God*damn*. She stood there for a moment, flashlight still trained on the spot where he had stood, but he didn't reappear. Then she took in a breath and headed for the front door of the cabin.

She had a lot of work to do.

Back to the historical society, where she explained that she was working on a paper for school. None of the older ladies staffing the place—clearly volunteers—seemed too surprised by her explanation. It probably was something that happened fairly often in this college town.

Danica did find an almanac that stated the first frost in 1884 fell on September twenty-second, which was very close to the average. Funny how she'd never really paid that much attention before, although her mother dutifully pulled in her potted ficus from the patio every year around that time. So the autumn leaves would have been at their height a few weeks later, and beginning to fall toward the end of the month.

That gave her the timeframe she needed, but what now? Everything she'd read seemed to indicate that Flagstaff during that era was beginning to bustle, but the population was small enough that the arrival of an unaccompanied young woman would raise more than a few eyebrows...unless the young woman in question was going to work in one of the young logging town's thriving saloons or whorehouses.

Neither of those options sounded very appealing to Danica. If she could come up with some way to get back there—and stay back there as long as her "mission" required—then she'd also have to think of a plausible cover story.

But poring through the microfiche—thank God the historical society had transferred all the old newspapers to that format back in the 1980s—she thought she might have found the answer to her problem. The first school in Flagstaff had been built in 1883, but the population was growing so quickly that the following year they hired a second teacher to come help out the town's one overworked schoolmistress. The young lady they hired, one Eliza Prewitt, never arrived, however. The mystery was never really explained, although Danica wondered if Miss Prewitt got cold feet about heading out to the wild, wild west all by herself and had instead decided to stay in her native Missouri.

Unfortunately, the accounts didn't include any old photographs or even descriptions of Miss Prewitt, so Danica had no idea whether she and that long-ago young woman shared any similarities in appearance. But pretending to be Miss Prewitt did seem to be the best course of action. It wasn't as if anyone back in 1884 Flagstaff would be able to look up her photo or her credentials in a central database.

Danica was feeling fairly pleased with herself after that discovery...until she was halfway back to the cabin and realized that simply taking on Miss Prewitt's identity wasn't going to be of much help when it came to disguising her own witch nature. All it would take was for Danica to get within ten feet of Jeremiah Wilcox or any of his family members, and they'd know she had witch-blood, the same as all the rest of them.

"Well, shit," she muttered as she turned off the Forest Service road and onto the gravel drive that led up to the cabin. Supposedly her cousin Damon had devised a spell to hide someone's witch nature—which was how Connor had been able to sneak into McAllister territory to meet Angela without her discovering who he was—but the secret of that spell had died with Damon. So she'd have to come up with some sort of a plausible explanation for being a single witch far from her own clan's territory.

Running away from a crappy engagement or marriage seemed the best idea. Back in the Victorian era and earlier, the witch clans hadn't been quite as freewheeling about letting their members choose their prospective spouses as they were today. Again, that sort of thing would be very difficult to check. Even so, she would still have to find out who the witch clans in Missouri actually were. The Wilcoxes hadn't had much contact with other clans, for obvious reasons, but Danica figured Marie would know.

Which of course she did. She raised an eyebrow at Danica's request, when she came down into town the next day to visit her cousin, but Marie said calmly enough, "Missouri? That would be the Landons, for the most part. Up near the Iowa border, there's some spillover from the Rollins clan." Her gaze sharpened. "Why do you need to know about the Missouri clans, Danica?"

Her question seemed to make it clear that neither Lawrence nor Andre had said anything to her about Danica's time-traveling plans. "Um…just curious," Danica replied, knowing how stupid that answer probably sounded. She'd certainly never shown any particular interest in the witch clans in other parts of the country before then.

Luckily, though, Marie wasn't the sort to pry. She shrugged, asked how Danica was faring at the cabin, and seemed willing to let the matter go. And after a few more minutes of conversation that really didn't go anywhere, Danica was able to make her escape.

So, she could be Eliza Prewitt, of the Landon clan. No one should think it particularly strange that her last name wasn't Landon, since of course other family names tended to get mixed in as a clan grew and intermarried with civilians and whatnot. The only reason the Wilcox clan had so many actual damn Wilcoxes was that Jeremiah had been one of four brothers. And hadn't one of those brothers had just sons and no daughters? She couldn't remember for sure; her own great-great-great-whatever-grandfather was Wyatt Wilcox, the only son of Jeremiah's younger brother Edmund.

Danica had another reason for coming to town today besides seeing Marie. After poring over old maps of the town and and a number of architectural sketches, she thought she had a pretty good idea of which streets existed back in 1884 and which ones weren't even yet a twinkle in a city planner's eye. At the corner of San Francisco Street and Phoenix Avenue, just below the train depot, there had been a row of businesses, including the general store. That seemed a safe enough place to try her second trip back in time…but her first in a populated area.

She parked at the depot and walked down to the spot she'd chosen, which was under a huge oak probably as old as the city itself. It was now just a little past two in the afternoon, and so the street wasn't too busy. Even so, she made sure to stand in a place where she wouldn't be directly visible to passersby. The last thing she wanted was for anyone to see her wink in and out of existence in broad daylight.

In preparing for this moment, Danica had understood that she couldn't just pick a date and use that as her target. Dates were meaningless, arbitrary numbers assigned by people who needed to create some order from the chaos that was the universe. No, she had to keep the images she'd seen in the old photographs she'd studied fixed in her mind—what the streets had looked like, what the people were wearing. The fall color on the trees. All of those details would help to pull her toward that one place where she could go to help the stranger.

So…the leaves of the tree above her head would be golden, and there would be no true sidewalks, just packed earth. The men would have frock coats like the one her ghostly visitor wore, or possibly sheepskin jackets, if the day was cold enough. They'd all be wearing hats. The women would be wearing bustle dresses, or possibly plainer skirts and what they called shirtwaists, or blouses, depending on their social status. In the background there might be the mournful whistle of a train as it pulled into the station, and the clopping of horses' hooves. And....

She had to stop visualizing at that point, because what she'd imagined in her mind's eye was suddenly there on the street before her. Only now it didn't have the sepia tones she'd somehow imagined must tinge everything in that long-ago era, but instead blazed before her in full color. The bright bay coats of a team of horses pulling a buggy. The almost eye-searing purple and green plaid of the bustle dress one woman wore as she climbed the steps into the general store only a few yards from where Danica stood in the shelter of the oak tree. A little girl's golden hair, worn in a neat braid halfway down her back.

All that, and above a sky with the deep, serene blue of autumn, and billowing white clouds gathered up near the top of Humphreys Peak. The air felt colder than Danica had expected, but she realized this must be mid-October, not the mild day in early September she'd left behind her. All of the men she saw wore coats, and the women had shawls wrapped around their shoulders as they went about their business.

Holy shit, she thought. *I'm really there.*

But she couldn't let her thoughts dwell on the miracle of her standing here in Flagstaff in 1884. No, she had to let herself drink in the scene without thinking too much about how she was able to do so.

At the same time, she realized she couldn't stay here too long; she was wearing jeans and a long-sleeved T-shirt, not exactly the sort of attire considered proper for a young woman of the day. So far, it didn't seem as if anyone had noticed her standing there in the shadow of the oak tree, but she couldn't count on it to conceal her forever.

Pulling herself away was harder than she'd thought, however. She wanted to keep standing there and absorbing everything, from the clean tang of fresh-sawn pine on the air to the undeniable scent of horse manure—not as bad as she'd feared, though. A group of men not too much older than herself, all of them in rough coats in brown or black, emerged from one of the buildings across the street, laughing. From the unsteady way they walked, it seemed clear enough to Danica that they'd just had a few too many beers or whiskeys or whatever the pour of choice might have been back in 1880s Flagstaff. One of them straightened slightly, though, and looked across the street at her, shock seeming to register on his face as he took in her attire.

Oh, crap. Time to go.

Danica immediately thought of the present day she'd left behind, with cars lining the streets and people moving along the sidewalks, absorbed in texting or checking their email or surfing the Web. The college students who used to be her classmates—the guys with their faux lumberjack beards and the girls who didn't think anything of going to school or to the store while still wearing their plaid flannel pajama bottoms.

And, just like that, she was back then. Back now. Whenever. Traffic whirred past, and off in the distance somewhere, Danica could hear a girl talking loudly on her phone, saying quite without embarrassment that she'd seen him sticking his tongue down the throat of that skank at the party, and—

Good old twenty-first century, Danica thought, cringing inwardly. In that moment, she wasn't sure she wouldn't take the scent of horse manure over having to listen to one more unguarded cell phone conversation.

Even so, she couldn't help experiencing a flood of triumph. She'd gone back then, had seen what this very street looked like more than a hundred years before. In addition, she'd been able to control her coming and going.

She might really be able to go back and stay there long enough to make a difference.

In the meantime, though, she still had a lot of work to do.

CHAPTER SEVEN

"You want to do *what?*" Olivia Wilcox said, staring at her daughter as if certain she hadn't heard her correctly.

Danica was already beginning to regret coming home, but she didn't have that much choice. What she had to do next required access to the Internet and her bank account. And she could only think of one even halfway reasonable-sounding excuse for suddenly wanting to acquire a wardrobe of Victorian dresses and accessories.

"I think I'm going to try cowboy action shooting," she said.

"You've never shot a gun in your life," Olivia pointed out.

True enough. "They just *call* it that. You don't actually have to shoot anything if you don't want to.

A lot of people just like to get dressed up and watch the shooting matches."

Olivia crossed her arms, frowning. "And where did all this come from?"

Well, Mom, I met a ghost, and he's really hot, so I need to see if I can go back in time and save him so he doesn't become a ghost. But for that, I need some bustle dresses.

Yeah, right.

Danica shrugged. "I met some guys who were doing practice shooting out in the woods. It sounded like fun."

"'Some guys'?" Actually, her mother didn't sound all that disapproving as she asked the question. There might have been a hopeful note in her voice, as if she thought Danica meeting "some guys" might be healthy step in the right direction, even if the guys in question liked to dress up in Wild West clothes and shoot guns on the weekend.

"Yes," Danica replied, lying furiously. "One of them actually goes to Northern Pines, but we'd never met because he's getting his degree in mechanical engineering and none of our classes ever overlapped. He was out shooting with his older brother."

There, that sounded safe and family-oriented. And a nice young man who wanted to be mechanical engineer? Catnip to someone like Olivia Wilcox. She still wasn't entirely thrilled that Mason had gotten married to someone who worked as a carpenter, who didn't even have a college degree. Never mind that, up until a few years ago, the McAllister clan didn't really have access to a four-year college, not unless they wanted to get a dispensation from the de la Paz family to study down in the Phoenix area. Danica had never heard of any of them doing that, though; they hadn't seemed too inclined to wander very far from the territory they called their own.

"Oh, well, if you're not actually going to be doing any shooting...." Olivia let her words trail off and then shrugged. "It sounds as if it could be fun. Is it very expensive?"

"It can be," Danica admitted. "But I just need to get a wardrobe together. At least I won't be buying any firearms."

Her mother seemed to think that over before giving another slight lift of her shoulders. It looked as if she'd realized that there were worse things a daughter could be spending her money on. At least this all promised to be vaguely educational.

"Well, I suppose there isn't any harm in it. Just don't go too crazy with the dresses and all that, at least until you've really decided whether you're going to keep at it or not."

"Thanks, Mom," Danica said, and went to give her mother a quick hug. Olivia appeared vaguely startled—her daughter hadn't been all that

demonstrative lately, ever since the Matías incident—
but she smiled as Danica hurried out of the kitchen
and back to her room.

Time to start spending some *serious* money.
Thank God for the stipend all Wilcox clan members
received, because she sure needed it now.

She bought herself a membership so she'd have
access to the shooting society's bulletin boards and
chat rooms. That seemed to be the easiest way to
get a line on a local dressmaker who specialized in
costuming re-enactors. A quick perusal of the ready-
made dresses that were available had told Danica
they wouldn't do her much good—she might not be
an expert on Victorian costume, but she could tell at
a glance that the gowns she was looking at weren't
anything like the ones she'd seen during her brief
flashback into 1884.

Luckily, she found the person she was looking
for in Prescott. Once upon a time, going there for
fittings would have been out of the question, since
Prescott was in McAllister territory, but none of that
meant much these days. Danica was able to get herself moved to the head of the woman's line, so to
speak, by offering to pay a thirty-percent rush fee.

The dressmaker, whose name was Jackie, arched
an eyebrow when Danica explained what she wanted.
After giving her new client a once-over, she asked,

"A schoolmistress? Are you sure? Most of my clients who're your age want to be saloon girls, or maybe Annie Oakley or Calamity Jane."

Danica assured her that she wanted to look like a respectable young lady, and ordered a week's worth of underthings, along with a corset, plus four gowns, two of them cotton, one in lightweight wool, and the last a dinner gown in silk. Maybe that was being extravagant, but surely it couldn't hurt to have at least one really nice dress.

Right, for when your ghost takes you out to dinner, she mocked herself. But she just couldn't resist that dark teal silk brocade Jackie showed her as part of her swatch collection. It was too gorgeous to pass up.

"And they'll be accurate?" Danica asked anxiously.

"Totally accurate," Jackie assured her. "I've been studying Victorian clothing for almost twenty years now. You'll look just like you stepped out of a fashion plate. And go here for all your accessories," she added, giving Danica a business card that was lying in a silver dish on her coffee table. "Louise makes awesome hats, and she can get your gloves and reticules and shawls, everything else you need. You'll be the best-dressed young lady in northern Arizona."

Danica hoped so. Or at least, she hoped that nothing she ended up with would make her look out of the ordinary. She had to blend in as best she could.

After writing Jackie a scarily large check—and that was just for the deposit—she headed home, hoping that the dressmaker really knew what she was promising when she said the whole wardrobe would be ready in two weeks. Yes, it wasn't as if she had to make everything by hand, but still, that seemed like an awful lot of sewing.

Then it was back home to place her accessories order online, choosing two hats, a couple of shawls, shoes that were supposed to be exact reproductions of ladies' boots from the 1880s, stockings…so much that Danica wondered where she was going to store it all.

Right, in the carpetbag she ordered as well.

And money. She found someone in Flagstaff who sold antique coins and bought several thousand dollars' worth of silver dollars that would be usable in the Arizona Territory of the 1880s. Well, several thousand dollars to her; the actual face value of the coins was a couple of hundred bucks, which she hoped would be enough. But it had to be, in a time when you could buy a new pair of shoes for only two or three dollars. Plus, if she was really journeying back in time to pose as the new schoolmistress, it meant she would presumably be getting paid something for her efforts.

Even though the thought did scare her a little, Danica wouldn't allow herself to worry about the whole teaching thing too much. All right, she hadn't finished college, but she remembered reading about Laura Ingalls Wilder, who'd taught school when she was younger than Danica was now, and definitely hadn't had the benefit of a college education. And hadn't Anne in the Anne of Green Gables books done basically the same thing before she was actually able to go to a real four-year college? Anyway, Danica thought she should be able to fake it. The hardest part would be making sure she didn't let anything slip that people wouldn't have known back in 1884. And the kids…well, she'd spent enough time around all her Wilcox cousins that she was used enough to children of all stages of development. It wasn't as if she'd be teaching nursery school; it sounded like most kids back then started school around six. Besides, little Victorian children had to be better behaved than some of the terrors she'd had to deal with at family gatherings.

While she was waiting for her new wardrobe to be finished, Danica read as much as she could about Flagstaff in the 1880s, about the Arizona Territory in general, and about anything else she could think of—Victorian manners and deportment, politics of the day, popular music, dining, and more. She knew some of her newfound knowledge wouldn't be all that applicable, since she kind of doubted a rough frontier town like Flagstaff was the place for afternoon teas or grand balls, but it never hurt to sock the information away in case she needed it. Also, she read as many novels of the period as she could, trying to absorb how people spoke and thought, and also watched movies set in that era, even if she wasn't sure how accurate any of them might be.

When she wasn't reading, she was staying studiously out of the sun so the last of her late-summer tan could completely fade away—sun-browned women were definitely not in vogue in the 1880s—and spending hours in front of the mirror, fighting with her long stubborn hair until she could force it into a more or less reasonable facsimile of the styles she'd seen in old portraits and books of fashion plates. No way would she cut bangs, which seemed to be very "in" in the mid-1880s, but after leaving her hair braided at night so it would have soft waves in it, she was able to pull it up into a heavy looped plait at the back of her head. A few ornamental hair combs she'd found in a local antique shop, and she figured it would pass.

One time she did drive up to the cabin, just so her ghost wouldn't think she'd abandoned him. But although she waited until nightfall, and sat on the porch as the air grew steadily colder, he never materialized. Maybe it was enough that he now knew she was planning to help him, and so he saw no more reason to drop hints for her.

Feeling strangely disappointed, she'd returned home. Her parents had gone out that night—it was a Friday—and so she wandered the house by herself, thinking of how big and empty it felt, and wondering what her ghost would have thought of the place. The granite and stainless-steel kitchen probably would have mystified him, as would the large TVs in the family room and her father's study. But the couches and the tables and all that...they weren't exactly Victorian in style, but they were still recognizable. Things hadn't changed all that much.

She realized then she was just trying to reassure herself, that if she stopped to think about all the thousands of ways 1884 was different from the twenty-first century, her head would probably explode. Anyway, she'd already committed to this, and she would just have to roll with whatever happened.

Jackie emailed her the next morning and said the dresses were ready. A mixture of excitement and fear sent Danica's stomach roiling, but she made herself email back, saying that was great and she'd be by around two to get her new wardrobe.

That appointment took longer than she'd thought, because Jackie made her try everything on, including the corset. It had been laced in such a way that the strings came out in a pair of loops at the center back, and Danica looked at it in some mystification.

"It's so you can tighten it yourself," Jackie explained. "I know a lot of the time, you re-enactor girls don't have someone to help you get dressed."

Danica tried it out, and, sure enough, the corset tightened up beautifully. Not too tight, though—she was already slender, and she wasn't trying to be Scarlett O'Hara. She just wanted to look accurate.

All the dresses fit perfectly, and they all buttoned up the front, which meant Danica could get in and out of them easily, even though she was sure she was going to knock something over with that big wire-framed bustle petticoat. Oh, well, it was still probably better than trying to manage a hoop skirt. And Jackie did show her how to sit down in it, how to surreptitiously gather up the draperies at the back of the skirt and the cage bustle with them, so it sort of collapsed when she sank down into a chair. The whole process wasn't as difficult as she'd feared.

The last gown Danica tried on was the teal silk dinner dress, and it was hard not to stare at herself in the mirror as she inspected that one. Jackie had really outdone herself—the gown had black braided trimming with dangling glass beads, and the skirt was wonderfully draped and pleated. Danica had to hope it would survive being stuffed in a carpetbag.

"It's stunning," Jackie said, looking over the entire ensemble with a critical eye, as if making sure for herself that everything was draping and falling where it was supposed to. "Where are you planning to wear this one? The big convention in Vegas?"

"Um…yes," Danica replied. She had absolutely no idea what the dressmaker was talking about, but face it, the gown wasn't the sort of thing you'd wear tromping around in the dirt at an outdoor shooting range.

"Well, I hope you don't mind attracting attention!" Jackie chuckled, clearly not realizing that the very *last* thing Danica wanted to do was attract attention.

Well, except for a certain handsome ghost….

She paid the balance due on the commission, then gathered up everything and took it back out to her SUV. It did all seem like far more than could fit in the carpetbag she'd ordered. Maybe she should've bought two.

You'll be wearing one dress, she told herself, *along with all the underpinnings. It'll be fine.*

She supposed it would have to be.

That night Danica didn't sleep well. Just nerves, of course. But she also knew she didn't want to make her debut in 1884 looking wan and tired, and eventually she drifted off to sleep.

Since she'd already told her mother that she would be going to an event the next day, Danica figured it was safe enough to get dressed at home.

Since she now knew that the bustle sort of collapsed when she sat on it, she thought she'd be able to drive while fully garbed, even if it might feel a bit awkward. Careful deliberation had led her to decide that the best place to "materialize"—for lack of a better word—was on the train platform itself, since Miss Eliza Prewitt was expected to arrive by train. Danica just hoped no one would notice that she'd never actually gotten off the train car itself.

The blue and green plaid gown seemed like the best traveling dress, so that was what she put on, shaking fingers working the row of velvet-covered buttons up the front. Garnet and gold earrings she'd bought at a local antique store, and a matching ring. Hair in the heavy looped crown of braids at the back of her head, and the black velvet hat with its jaunty plumes perched just so.

"Holy moly," her father said as she descended the stairs. He was just coming out of the kitchen, a glass of iced tea in his hand. "You're looking right purty, little lady."

"Oh, God, Dad," Danica replied with a roll of her eyes. "That's a terrible John Wayne impression."

"Yes, it is," he agreed amiably. "But that is a great getup. You look like you walked right off the set of *Tombstone*."

Which, considering what a fan he was of the movie, was pretty high praise. "Thanks. Now I just

have to see if I can maneuver into my car in all this."
She didn't bother to mention that she'd packed everything she wouldn't be wearing the night before, then smuggled it down to the Land Rover while both her parents were still asleep. Going to a Wild West reenactment was one thing, but taking along a bunch of changes of clothes was sure to raise questions she didn't want to answer.

"Well, I'll open the door to your carriage for you."

Danica just smiled and shook her head. "Where's Mom?"

"Oh, she had to run to the store for a couple of things. I'm sure she'll be sad she missed your debut, but I suppose you can show yourself off to her when you get back."

If I get back, she thought then. No, that was just silly. She'd already proved that she could return to the present very easily. The hard part was going to be keeping herself back in 1884.

"Okay. Well, the event starts at eleven, so I'd better get moving."

They both went out to the garage. When Mason still lived here, Danica was the odd one out who had to park in the driveway, but now Danica's Land Rover occupied the garage's third bay. She actually did need her father's help to hand her up into the driver's seat, mostly because the corset prevented her from bending the way she was used to when sliding in behind the steering wheel. But eventually she was more or less in place, although the feathers on her hat kept getting jammed up against the SUV's headliner.

"Have fun!" her father called out as she hit the remote to open the garage door.

Somehow she summoned a smile. She wasn't sure how fun it would be...but she had a feeling her trip to the past was going to be something of an adventure.

Danica was able to park in the Amtrak station's parking lot. Leaving the SUV worried her a little, but then she reassured herself that this was time travel, after all. She'd come back within five minutes of leaving, no harm, no foul. And if the worst happened....

Well, the Land Rover would get towed, and her parents would be notified, since their name was on the title along with hers. And they'd spend the rest of their lives wondering what had happened to their daughter.

Stop it, she thought. *Just stop it. Why defeat yourself before you even get started?*

Her inner voice more or less shut up after that. She clambered out of the SUV and went around back to retrieve the carpetbag. Several people in the parking lot immediately gave her the side-eye, and she couldn't really blame them. Most travelers taking the train didn't do so while wearing a voluminous plaid bustle gown. Then again, the gown had its uses, because she was able to block part of the vehicle with her skirt as she slipped the car key into one of those little magnetic holders and secreted the little box in one of the rear wheelwells. She'd decided that was the safest thing to do, because the key would have been a hideous anachronism back in 1884...and what if she managed to lose it?

Ignoring the stares, Danica headed up to the platform. One woman did call out, "Are you in a play?"

Luckily, she'd prepared herself for these sorts of questions. "No," she replied. "I'm here to do a photo shoot for the Chamber of Commerce. It looks like the photographer's late, though."

"Oh, that's fun," the woman replied, but she didn't say anything else as Danica breezed on by. Photo shoots weren't exactly the most exciting thing in the world, unless supermodels were involved or something.

After making her way to the spot she'd decided on, Danica paused on the platform and drew in a breath. No one was out here with her, since the next train wasn't due for several hours. That was partly why she'd chosen to come at this time of day—the chances of anyone seeing her suddenly disappear were fairly low.

All right, then. She shut her eyes, imagining the nip in the air from the last time she'd gone back to that earlier Flagstaff. The golden leaves on the oak trees. And then the shiny black locomotive, stopping next to a platform of pine hewn from the forests above town. The swirl of coal smoke from its engine, and the waiting people in their hats and frock coats and bustle dresses.

The smell of pitch, and the mournful cry of a train's horn. Danica opened her eyes, and all around her were people in Victorian garb alighting from the train, families mostly, but here and there a man or woman alone, someone who was invariably greeted by a waiting family member or friend.

And then a woman's voice, calling out, "Miss Prewitt? Miss Eliza Prewitt?"

Oh, Danica thought, *that's me.*

She turned and saw a sturdy-looking woman in her forties approaching, black gown swishing over the wooden planks of the platform, a quizzical expression on her face. "You *are* Miss Prewitt, aren't you?"

"Yes, ma'am," Danica replied.

The other woman didn't exactly sigh with relief, but she did appear to relax slightly. "Oh, excellent. I am Mrs. Marshall, the other teacher at the school here. Everyone thought it would be best if I came to meet you."

No wonder Mrs. Marshall was relieved. Eliza Prewitt was supposed to have arrived at the beginning of the school year, but now it had to be mid-October, and she was only just showing up. Well, the truth of the matter was that she never actually appeared, but Danica saw no reason to comment on that, not when she was coopting the young woman's identity for her own use.

"Oh, thank you, Mrs. Marshall," she replied, hoping nothing in her accent or choice of words would give her away as someone from a lot farther off than just St. Louis, Missouri. "I do appreciate that. And I do wish to apologize for my late arrival, but there was a family emergency that delayed me. I did send a telegram—"

"Which never arrived," Mrs. Marshall said, looking annoyed. "I keep saying that we need a new man in the telegraph office, but no one ever listens to me." She leaned closer to Danica and added in conspiratorial tones, "He drinks, you know."

Danica's eyes widened. Apparently Mrs. Marshall took that as the correct response, for she nodded vigorously, the plumes on her hat dancing.

"I know. Scandalous! But I fear, Miss Prewitt, that you will find Flagstaff a rough town, especially for someone from a civilized place like St. Louis."

"I'm sure it will be fine, Mrs. Marshall."

"Well, I hope it will be, for I do need the help at the school. And there is quite a good boarding house here in town, which is where I will take you now."

With that, she turned and began to stride purposefully toward the edge of the platform. Still clutching her carpetbag, Danica followed. She wanted to look everywhere, take in everything she saw, but she worried Mrs. Marshall might view any kind of gawking as an example of very unladylike curiosity. But surely it wouldn't be too awful to study things just a little bit as she passed. After all, "Miss Prewitt" was a newcomer here; some interest was only to be expected.

As they crossed the street, the two women had to dodge heavy wagons, some filled with unhewn logs, others with smooth-planed boards clearly fresh from the lumbermill. Men on horseback went by, several of them sending stares in Danica's direction that weren't exactly what she'd consider polite. She kept her chin up and didn't return those stares. After all, it wasn't so strange that they'd be looking at a young woman newly come to town, especially since it was probably obvious that she was on her own.

Luckily, their destination was only a few blocks away. Mrs. Marshall led Danica up the steps of a two-story clapboard house, painted white with green shutters. She knocked, explaining, "This is Mrs. Wilson's boarding house. She has four rooms to let for genteel young ladies like yourself. She'll take very good care of you."

And watch me like a hawk, I'm sure, Danica thought. Getting some private time with her "ghost" might turn out to be something of a challenge. At the same time, though, it was probably just as well that she had some protection from the types of men she'd spotted on the walk to the boarding house.

The door opened, and a thin, tall woman with iron-gray hair looked out at the two of them. She wore a gray gown, and so she seemed almost all gray. Except her eyes—they were bright blue, and gave Danica a shrewd up-and-down glance.

"You must be Miss Prewitt," she said. "I'm Mrs. Wilson. Your room is ready—although I'll have to change the sheets again, as I made up the room more than a month ago, when we thought you'd be arriving."

"I am so sorry—" Danica began, but Mrs. Wilson only held up a hand.

"You're here now. Why don't you and Mrs. Marshall wait down in the parlor here while I freshen up your room?"

There was no way to decline that offer, so Danica nodded and then followed her companion inside. The front room, or "parlor," was jammed full with two sofas, a low marble-topped table, a pair of carved chairs, and a matched set of curio cabinets stuffed with hand-painted china, butterflies under glass, and what looked like an odd assortment of Indian arrowheads.

"I've just put the tea on," Mrs. Wilson said. "I'll bring that out first, and then go tend to your room."

"Thank you," Danica said, somewhat weakly. It was one thing to pop back in time, look around for a minute or so, and then go back where you belonged. It was quite another to be standing here in this shining example of overwrought Victorian interior decorating and talking about having tea. But she knew she couldn't let herself dwell on that, had to act as if all this was perfectly natural.

Flow with it, she told herself. *Don't think about it. Just be it.*

Mrs. Marshall offered her thanks as well, then made her way over to one of the velvet-upholstered couches and settled herself on it, disposing her own voluminous bustle with the ease of long practice. Danica wasn't sure she was quite that graceful about the procedure, but she did manage to sit down on the other sofa without incident.

"It was a good thing you came in on a Saturday," the other woman said. "For if it had been a weekday, I would have been in school, and someone else might have had to fetch you. Perhaps Mr. Wilcox."

Somehow Danica managed to keep herself from stiffening. "Mr. Wilcox?" she asked, hoping she had injected the correct amount of innocent curiosity into her tone.

"Oh, yes. He's one of our more prominent citizens here. And his family has a good number of children attending the school."

"So he has a lot of children?"

Something in Mrs. Marshall's brisk manner seemed to falter. "Well, not Mr. Wilcox himself. He has only the one son. Mr. Wilcox's wife passed away some years ago."

So people here seemed to think of Nizhoni as Jeremiah's wife, even though Danica knew they'd never been formally married.

"Oh, I am sorry to hear that."

"Well, it can be a tragedy, but life does go on. However, I was speaking of his extended family. Mr. Wilcox came here with his brothers and sister, and their spouses and children. There are seventeen children among them."

"My goodness!" Danica exclaimed. Her study of the period had instructed her that a well-bred young lady didn't dare utter anything stronger than that. Even so, she thought she sounded like an idiot.

Mrs. Marshall didn't seem to notice, however. Nodding, she said, "Now you see why we had so much need of a second teacher. Why, we have forty-three children to instruct this school year, which of course is far too many for any one person to manage."

Danica couldn't imagine trying to ride herd on forty-three children at once, let alone kids of all different ages and learning levels. "That is a good number."

"Indeed," Mrs. Marshall replied.

However, Danica couldn't help noticing how the other woman's eyes narrowed during that exchange. Damn, had she goofed somehow? Maybe when the "real" Miss Prewitt had applied for the position, she'd been told how many students were attending the Flagstaff school. Well, there wasn't anything Danica could do about the slip-up now, so she tried to look as innocent as possible.

Luckily, Mrs. Wilson returned then, carrying a silver tray with a hand-painted tea set floridly decorated with roses. She set the tray down on the marble-topped table, then said, "I'll just see to your room now, Miss Prewitt."

"Thank you so much."

The mistress of the boarding house departed, and Mrs. Marshall took it on herself to serve, pouring some of the fragrant steaming liquid into the teacups. There was cream and sugar, and although Danica generally took her tea black, she picked up one sugar cube with a pair of silver tongs and carefully dropped it into her cup, then stirred in a small measure of cream. Her companion did the same, although she didn't seem too concerned about being sparing with the cream.

"And tomorrow there is church, of course," she remarked, apropos of nothing. Fixing Danica with a steely gray stare, she went on, "I assume you will be coming to the Methodist services?"

Her tone seemed to indicate that Danica would burn in eternal hellfire if she indicated another preference. Since she hadn't even been inside a church since her cousin Anna got married almost a year ago, Danica really didn't have an opinion one way or another, and in fact hadn't even considered the question of church when she was making her preparations for her trip into the past. A stupid oversight; a lot of social activities back in the day tended to center around a person's church.

"Of course," Danica said quickly.

Mrs. Marshall smiled. She actually had quite good teeth, a detail that made Danica wonder if the article she'd come across in her studies had been accurate after all, the one that said people in the Victorian era had better teeth than one might expect, since they consumed less sugar, and processed foods hadn't yet made their appearance. She hoped it was true. Yes, she'd seen the ghost's teeth when he smiled at her, and they had seemed fine, but you never knew.

"Very good," Mrs. Marshall said. "You can come with me and my boys. It'll be an excellent opportunity for everyone to meet you before you start in at the school on Monday."

"Boys?"

"Yes, William and Matthew. They're nine and thirteen. Their father has been gone these three years"—she pulled a blindingly white handkerchief from her reticule and dabbed at her eyes—"but I can manage, thanks to the school."

And how hard that must have been, to be left widowed in this rough frontier town with two young boys to raise. Danica couldn't even begin to imagine it. "I'm very glad I could come to assist you. And I look forward to meeting your boys." She wouldn't let herself worry too much about that ominous reference to meeting "everyone." Would that group include the Wilcoxes?

A little shiver went over her at the thought.

What would they be like?

CHAPTER EIGHT

DANICA FOUND OUT SOON ENOUGH, SINCE MRS. MARSHALL appeared at the boarding house promptly at five minutes before ten on Sunday morning, both her boys in tow. They grinned at Danica, apparently not self-conscious at all, and she smiled back. They both had their mother's wavy brown hair and gray eyes, although they looked as if they'd end up being blessed with a good deal more height than she possessed. Maybe their father had been tall.

That morning, Danica had put on her wine-colored wool gown, since it seemed a little dressier than the two cotton outfits she had. She was still trying to come to grips with the realization that she'd spent an entire night here, had slept in the narrow white iron bedstead in her room and hadn't blinked back to the twenty-first century as soon as her eyes closed.

And she'd survived the bathroom as well. At least Mrs. Wilson's boarding house, which she proudly proclaimed to be completely modern and up to date, had an actual bathroom, with a primitive flush toilet and a bathtub. Saturday nights were bath nights, although Danica was informed that she could purchase another bath on Tuesday evenings for an extra dollar per week. That seemed a fair enough trade-off, although she was having a hard time coming to terms with the notion of only bathing twice a week.

Despite that privation, no one around her seemed to be particularly stinky. She wasn't sure why, exactly, but she'd take it. In the back of her mind, she'd worried that she'd meet her handsome ghost and find out he reeked of sweat. However, that didn't seem to be as big an issue as she'd thought it would.

Half the town seemed to be heading toward the simple rectangular building with the tall steeple on top. Danica trailed along dutifully as Mrs. Marshall pointed out the people she thought she should know—"Mr. Brannen, who has the general store down on San Francisco Street, and Mr. Reilly, who owns the livery stable, and Mr. Ives, the banker"—but as far as she could tell, she couldn't see any sign of the Wilcoxes.

Or her ghost. It was hard to scan the faces around her without seeming too obvious, but Danica just had to look. Unfortunately, she didn't see anyone she recognized.

Her spirits sank, even though she told herself it was entirely possible that the stranger didn't attend this church. He could be Catholic—Mrs. Wilson had mentioned there was also a Catholic church in Flagstaff—or he could be the type who didn't feel compelled to get up and go to services every Sunday.

For all she knew, he wasn't even in town yet. She had no idea whether he was a resident or someone who'd only been visiting. Her cramped little room had a calendar from a baking powder company hanging in it, with the days past already carefully crossed out by her landlady, and so Danica knew it was now October twelfth. The leaves all around were golden and orange and brown, but they hadn't begun to really fall yet, so her ghost shouldn't yet meet his fate at the hands of the Wilcoxes for a few more weeks.

If one of them was truly the person who had killed him.

Mrs. Marshall directed Danica to a pew located in the approximate center of the rows of benches on the right-hand side of the church. She took the seat nearest the aisle, while Matthew, the older of Mrs. Marshall's two boys, sat next to her, with his brother on his right and their mother providing a bookend for the little group. Matthew didn't look at all discommoded by having to sit next to the new teacher;

in fact, his eyes twinkled, and he scooched a little closer to her than was strictly necessary.

Hot for teacher? she thought with a grin. Well, their hormones did start to rage around that age. At least the older boy would be in his mother's class, and not Danica's.

All around, people were filing dutifully into their pews, taking their positions as if they'd been assigned in advance. Maybe they were. Didn't there used to be fairly rigid customs about who sat where in church?

Danica noticed that several pews up near the front on the left-hand side remained empty, although the rest of the church was nearly full by that point. All around, people spoke in quiet voices, waiting for the services to begin.

Then it seemed as if a shadow fell on the space, although she realized in the next second or two that it was simply because a large group had entered the foyer, blocking a good deal of the bright morning light streaming in through the open front doors of the church. She blinked, while at the same time experiencing the inevitable tingle she always felt when in the presence of witch-kind.

The latecomers had to be the Wilcoxes.

This time, it was almost impossible not to stare. How couldn't she, when she was seeing her ancestors in the flesh, instead of in a faded sepia-toned photograph?

That must be Jeremiah Wilcox in the lead, a black-haired boy of about six walking next to him. Danica could tell that the Wilcox patriarch noted her immediately—he didn't exactly pause, but there was the slightest hitch in his step before he continued toward the pews that must have been held aside for his family. Black eyes under heavy black brows surveyed her quickly, and something about that shrewd regard made Danica hold her breath.

Of course he would be able to tell she was a witch. All she could do was pray that he wouldn't also be able to tell she was a Wilcox.

He said nothing, though, and went on to take a seat, the rest of his family members trailing after him. All of the adults also seemed to notice she was not like the other churchgoers, but they appeared to take their cue from Jeremiah and didn't react, except for possibly the briefest of hesitations. None of the children—and damn, there *were* a lot of them—seemed to notice anything out of the ordinary, but again, they wouldn't. The ability to sense other witches awoke at the same time a witch's or warlock's talent began to show itself, and the oldest of those children appeared to be around nine, too young for their powers to have started to develop.

Then they were all sitting down, and Danica let out a sigh of relief. From here, she could study them more or less surreptitiously—except for one of the wives, who was quite blonde, the family seemed to be uniformly dark, and better dressed than most of the citizens of Flagstaff she'd seen so far. Well, that made sense; the Wilcoxes had always been prosperous, even as long ago as this.

The minister, a tall man in late middle age, with thinning hair and a bushy beard to make up for it, approached the pulpit. Danica took that as her cue to more or less tune out. She wasn't here to be preached to, but to attempt to fit in as best she could. Of course she stood at the appropriate times, and fumbled along with singing hymns the real Eliza Prewitt probably knew by heart, but otherwise, she was far more interested in trying to soak in as many details about the Wilcoxes as she could, from the heavy gold drops hanging from one of the wives' ears to the gleaming raven-black hair of Jeremiah's little boy. He seemed darker than all his cousins, who were uniformly dark-haired, but then, Jacob Wilcox was half Navajo.

At last the service ended, and Danica rose from her pew in relief. Even with all those petticoats and that cage bustle protecting her rear end, she'd begun to feel the bite of the hard edge of the pine bench against the backs of her thighs. She headed toward the exit, the two Marshall boys behind her, and Mrs. Marshall—lord, Danica didn't even know her first name yet—bringing up the rear.

As she made her escape outside, though, she could practically feel Jeremiah Wilcox's black eyes boring into the back of her neck. Crap, he wasn't going to make a scene here in front of everybody, was he?

Although of course she'd never heard him speak before, she somehow knew the strong, authoritative voice cutting through the chatter of the crowd must be his.

"Mrs. Marshall. Is this the new teacher?"

"Why, yes, Mr. Wilcox. Miss Prewitt?"

Reluctantly, Danica came to a halt and then turned back toward the schoolmistress. Although the rest of the Wilcox contingent kept going, probably because the children seemed intent on climbing the hay bales that separated the churchyard from the street, Jeremiah had stopped to one side, Mrs. Marshall standing next to him.

"Yes, Mrs. Marshall?"

"Miss Prewitt, may I present Mr. Wilcox? He was one of the guiding forces in getting the new school-house built."

Since she knew she couldn't do anything else, Danica extended a hand, saying, "Very pleased to make your acquaintance, Mr. Wilcox."

Those black eyes had looked piercing in the portraits she'd seen of him, but they were nothing compared to the reality of them, fixing on her face as if he could somehow drill down into the very essence of her being. Somehow she managed to repress a shiver, while at the same time being very glad of the thin kid covering her fingers so she wouldn't have to touch him flesh to flesh.

When he spoke, however, his words were commonplace enough. "And very pleased to meet you, Miss Prewitt. I hope your journey here was not too taxing?"

"Oh, no. The train was quite comfortable." Of course she was lying, since she actually hadn't been on the train at all, but she'd seen movies with Victorian railcars, and they always looked like fun, with the dark wood and the plush upholstery and the dangling fringe on the curtains that framed the windows.

"I'm glad to hear it." He let go of her hand, but didn't look away. "I hope you don't think it's an imposition, Miss Prewitt, but I was wondering if you would have a spare few minutes this afternoon? So I might discuss some school matters with you, that is."

Oh, hell. Danica knew he didn't really want to talk about the school—he wanted to find out why a young unaccompanied witch was in his territory, so far from where her clan must actually reside. "Well, I was having supper at Mrs. Marshall's—"

"But not until five," she broke in. "You would have plenty of time for a talk. And you know, Miss Prewitt, Mr. Wilcox is a very busy man. You should be glad that he is willing to take the time to talk to you about the school."

Which ostensibly was the reason why she'd been invited to Mrs. Marshall's home for supper. However, Danica knew she didn't dare protest. Surely meeting with him in the parlor at her boarding house couldn't be too dangerous. Mrs. Wilson had said she might have "gentleman callers," as long as they didn't presume to leave the parlor, and were gone by five o'clock.

Anyway, there didn't seem to be much point in further protests. Danica had known this confrontation would come; she'd just hoped it wouldn't arrive quite so soon.

"Oh, I am glad," she said. "I'm much obliged to you, Mr. Wilcox. Perhaps this afternoon around two o'clock?" There. That sounded polite enough. She hoped.

"I'll see you then, Miss Prewitt," Jeremiah replied.

And though his tone was pleasant enough, Danica couldn't help thinking of those words as a threat.

Meals were included with her room at the boarding house, but on Sundays Mrs. Wilson expected her guests to fend for themselves after breakfast, and to make their own meals using the contents of the pantry. Although there were four rooms to let, only two were currently occupied—Danica's own, and another by a young woman named Clara DeWitt, who had come out west with her ailing mother in the hopes that the drier air would aid her mother's tuberculosis. Mrs. DeWitt had succumbed after only a few months, unfortunately, but Clara remained, mostly because she didn't have the funds to return to Ohio.

"Not that I'd really want to," she'd told Danica the night before in a conspiratorial whisper as Mrs. Wilson left the dining room to bring in dessert. "Arizona Territory is so much more exciting. Besides, there are so many more young men here than young women. I just have to decide which one I want."

Since Clara was currently working as a clerk in Mr. Brannen's general store, Danica guessed she had many opportunities to inspect those young men. She was pretty enough, with big blue eyes and thick sandy-blonde hair, and so she probably could pick and choose.

After church, Danica had gone back to the boarding house while attempting to ignore the growing knot in her stomach. All right, Angela's experiences on her "spirit walk" had revealed that Jeremiah really wasn't such a bad guy after all, but in person he was kind of intimidating. Danica knew she'd have to keep on her toes around him.

Apparently Clara had gone to church with Mrs. Wilson, although Danica hadn't seen them there. But Clara had certainly seen her, because almost as soon as Danica came in the front door, Clara pounced.

"What did Mr. Wilcox have to say to you, Eliza?"

Wonderful. Danica had been contemplating raiding the kitchen to see if any of those amazing buttermilk biscuits from breakfast were left over, but she realized her midday snack was going to be delayed.

"Nothing, really," Danica replied. "He only wants to discuss some school matters with me. He is one of the trustees, isn't he?"

"I suppose so," Clara said, looking somewhat let down. Then she perked up a bit. "But isn't that why you're having dinner at Mrs. Marshall's? To discuss the school?"

Right then, Danica really wished it was possible for well-bred Victorian young ladies to tell someone to mind their own fucking business. Since it wasn't, she allowed herself a small lift of the shoulders and said, "Yes, but I suppose Mr. Wilcox will want to talk about more of the business aspects, while Mrs. Marshall is going to discuss the curriculum with me."

There, she thought in some triumph. *That sounded dry and boring enough that hopefully Miss Thang here will move on to something else.*

Danica's hopes appeared to be borne out, because Clara let out a small sigh. "Oh. Yes, that's probably it." But then her mouth pursed, and a certain glint entered her eyes. "He is so very handsome, though, don't you think?"

Jesus, that's my great-great-great-granduncle you're talking about. Then Danica realized she'd probably left out a "great" or two. Not that it really mattered. "I suppose I hadn't thought about it." And maybe she should have been asking the other girl for more information, but something about her fellow boarder set Danica's teeth on edge. She figured she'd find out most of what she needed to on her own.

Clara shot her a disbelieving look, but appeared to decide the matter wasn't worth pursuing. "By the way, Mrs. Wilson always says she won't cook for us on Sundays, but there's vegetable soup to go with those leftover biscuits."

Perfect. A light meal, just enough to fortify her for her meeting with Jeremiah Wilcox. Danica had been a little worried about having to scrounge for herself; it wasn't as if she could wander off down the street to Chipotle for a burrito.

She smiled and thanked Clara for the information, and headed toward the kitchen. The Wilcox *primus* would be here in an hour, and Danica knew she had to be on her game when she saw him, or this whole enterprise might be over before it had even gotten started.

When he arrived, Jeremiah Wilcox knocked politely on the door, just like any normal caller might. No lightning bolts, no puff of smoke. Not that Danica had really expected him to do anything that would call attention to himself. The Wilcox clan had survived all those years precisely because they knew how to blend in.

"Mr. Wilcox," she said politely as she held open the door for him to enter. Mrs. Wilson had told her that she should treat the boarding house as her own home, and that meant greeting her own callers, as the older woman didn't employ any servants, except a boy who came around once a week to clean up the yard and take out the garbage.

"Miss Prewitt," Jeremiah Wilcox replied. He stood just inside the entryway, dark eyes taking in every detail of the interior of the house. "It's such a fine day. I was wondering if perhaps you would like to walk with me?"

Damn. Danica had been counting on the protection Mrs. Wilson's presence would provide. She was in the little sitting room off her own bedroom, knitting away at what looked like a scarf or muffler. Not that the landlady would be of much use if Jeremiah

Wilcox really tried anything, but to go strolling off with him, alone?

His gaze flickered upward, and Danica heard the distinct creak of the topmost stair. Clara lurking up there, probably, trying to listen in, just in case the conversation between the two of them ranged to topics a little more interesting than her teacher's contract.

Time to acknowledge defeat. No, she really didn't want to go off somewhere with Jeremiah Wilcox, but neither did she want Clara to overhear anything they might have to say to one another. Trying to explain away a discussion about witch clans would be a nightmare.

"Of course, Mr. Wilcox," Danica said. "Just let me go fetch my shawl and hat." That was right, wasn't it? A lady wasn't supposed to go outside without her head covered.

She managed a smile before heading up to her room to retrieve the items in question. As she did so, she saw Clara's door shutting quietly.

Yeah, about what I thought.

After settling the shawl around her shoulders and securing her hat with a pin, Danica descended the staircase. "All ready, Mr. Wilcox."

For a second, it looked as if he was going to offer her his arm, but instead he reached out and opened the door. "After you, Miss Prewitt."

Relieved, Danica stepped out onto the porch and waited for him to shut the door firmly behind them. "There's rather a fine park two streets over," he said. "I thought we could walk there."

That sounded safe enough. A park in the afternoon on a nice October day—there had to be families there with their children, or at least other people walking around and getting some fresh air. Taking a constitutional, as the Victorians might have put it. Not exactly the sort of place for a dark warlock to try something nefarious.

All right, Jeremiah Wilcox wasn't *really* a dark warlock. Even so, he was someone who didn't care much about the rules...which meant he was still dangerous.

Danica fell in beside him as he led her down the porch steps to the dusty street. No wonder women of the day had detachable dust ruffles that buttoned onto the inside of their skirts and petticoats; otherwise, their gowns would quickly become too filthy to wear.

It was good to distract herself by thinking about such trivialities, because then she couldn't focus as much on the insane realization that she was walking down the street in old-time Flagstaff with the family's patriarch by her side. Danica didn't think of herself as short, even by modern standards, but the man walking next to her seemed to tower over her. But maybe that was partly because of the long black coat and wide-brimmed black hat he wore.

They reached the park, which was a little oasis in the center of town, with a pond off to one side and a nice stand of aspen trees, now flaming yellow, on the other. The grass was yellow as well, but probably fresh and green in the summer months. She found herself wondering if they skated on that pond in the winter, with those funny skates people used to strap on over their shoes.

More distractions….

Jeremiah stopped near the stand of aspens, in a spot well away from the children playing near the pond, or the young couple that had spread a blanket on the frost-yellowed grass and were sharing some kind of picnic meal. Yes, he stood a decorous distance away from her, and they were clearly in plain sight of anyone who might pass by. Even so, Danica had to struggle to keep herself from shaking.

Voice quiet, he said, "What are you doing in my territory, Miss Prewitt…if that truly is your name?"

She swallowed. "Just as you were told, Mr. Wilcox. I've come here to teach school."

An eyebrow lifted. "One young witch, all alone? You're clearly not one of the de la Paz clan, and I don't think you're one of the McAllisters, either. You don't have that look about you."

No, the McAllisters in general were much fairer. Danica had let her tan fade, and her eyes were hazel instead of the black and brown that tended to dominate the Wilcox clan, but her hair was still as sooty as Jeremiah's own. "That's true enough, Mr. Wilcox," she said. "I'm one of the Landons. I truly am from St. Louis, and Eliza Prewitt is my real name."

He didn't say anything, but only stood there, seeming to consider her. It was so hard not to flinch under that steady black gaze. She was acutely conscious of so many details about him—the long, elegant nose and high cheekbones, the muted dark green brocade of his waistcoat, even the stickpin of carved jet in the cravat at his throat. As Clara had said, he was very handsome.

And scary.

"I don't know of any clan that would allow an unmarried young woman to venture alone so far from her family's territory, particularly without asking for permission first. Perhaps you would like to explain yourself?"

No, she wouldn't, not really. But she'd cooked up a story precisely for this eventuality, so she knew she'd have to trot it out. "The advertisement for the teacher ran in the St. Louis papers. I suppose Mrs. Marshall and the other trustees were casting their net wide to make sure they would—would have a good pool of candidates. I saw the advertisement and applied without my family knowing anything about it."

He didn't blink. "Now, why would you do that, Miss Prewitt?"

"My—my father wants me to marry a cousin I don't much care for, and he refuses to listen to my concerns on the matter. So I decided the best thing to do was to run away."

"All the way to Arizona Territory? That seems rather drastic, don't you think?"

"You wouldn't think it drastic if you'd met my cousin."

Jeremiah smiled then, the laugh lines crinkling around his eyes. It was sort of amazing what that smile did to his face, because he instantly transformed from good-looking but scary to downright drop-dead gorgeous.

And if that isn't the creepiest thing ever to be thinking about your great-whatever-granduncle....

He said, "Still, quite a bold step. If you'll forgive me for asking, why the delay in your arrival in Flagstaff? If you truly were attempting to get away, I would have thought you'd be on the first train out of St. Louis once you received the acceptance letter from the trustees here."

Damn. That wasn't an angle she'd considered before he asked about it. Thinking furiously, she said, "Well, that was because my father found out what I was planning. He had clan members, elders, watching me day and night."

"So how did you make your escape?"

"I—well, after a week or so, he began to have some of my cousins keeping guard on the house, since the elders were needed elsewhere. My cousin Mary and her brother Edward were sympathetic to my plight, so one night they smuggled me out of my room and down to the train station. That is how I got away."

"How very enterprising of them. I hope neither of them faced any repercussions because of their role in aiding your escape?"

"I—I don't know," Danica said, hoping she looked appropriately concerned about these nonexistent "cousins" of hers. "I suppose the elders might have given them a talking-to. But once I was gone, what could they do about it?"

"Besides follow you out here to bring you home?"

"Oh, I don't think they would do that."

"And why not?" His eyes narrowed; the smile was quite gone by now. Clearly, Jeremiah Wilcox did not look too thrilled at the prospect of a possible horde of angry warlocks descending on Flagstaff to bring their wayward clan member home.

"Well, because—" She floundered for a few seconds, because she really couldn't think of a good reason. Yes, the witch clans tended to stay in their own territories, but that didn't mean they couldn't venture forth when extenuating circumstances arose. And she supposed going after a runaway daughter might be one of those extenuating circumstances. Widening her eyes and attempting to look as guileless as possible, she said, "Because my cousin would think me ruined, just for coming all this way without a chaperone, and so there wouldn't be much reason to pursue me, would there?"

"I should think there would be a good many reasons," Jeremiah replied, and something about the way his gaze lingered on her face made Danica go cold inside. He couldn't really be looking at her like that...could he?

Well, why not? It wasn't as if he had any idea who she was, except a young unattached witch who'd suddenly popped up in his territory.

Lovely.

"My cousin Alfred is quite taken with notions of propriety," she said, in as prim a tone as she could manage.

Jeremiah flashed her another one of those brilliant smiles. "Well, Miss Prewitt, I think you'll discover that out on the frontier, we're not quite as rigid about such things. But I thank you for telling me the truth. You may consider yourself safe here. Mrs. Wilson will take excellent care of you at her boarding house, and I'd like to formally extend to you the protection of the Wilcox clan."

That was quite a proposal to make, and not one that the head of any clan would offer lightly. It meant they would be compelled to come to her aid, should she need it, and that she would be treated as a family member in any witch-related matters.

Of course, she actually *was* a Wilcox, and so was due that sort of consideration because of her birthright, but obviously Jeremiah didn't know about any of that...and couldn't.

This was getting complicated.

"Th-thank you, Mr. Wilcox," she managed. "I can't tell you how much I appreciate your kind offer, especially when I am trespassing here—"

"You're not trespassing," he broke in, but gently. "You've come here to teach our children." His gaze sharpened somewhat. "You *do* know how to teach school, I assume?"

"Oh, yes," she lied. All those children she'd seen in church looked well-behaved enough. And she'd always been an excellent student. How hard could it be?

If he detected that massive prevarication, he didn't give any sign of it. "Well, then, we should all get on famously. But let me take you back to your boarding house. I should think you'd want to be rested for your first day tomorrow."

This time, he did offer his arm, and Danica knew it would be horribly rude to refuse it after the kindness he had just shown her. She looped her own arm through his, and let him guide her back to Mrs. Wilson's house. The whole time, she was conscious of the curious stares of the town's inhabitants as they passed by. They had to be wondering who she was, and what she was doing in the company of Jeremiah Wilcox.

Then again, she was beginning to wonder the same thing.

CHAPTER NINE

THANK GOD MRS. MARSHALL WAS SO VERY ORGANIZED, OR Danica might have wanted to run back to the twenty-first century after that first day of school. To have to stand in front of twenty-one pairs of curious eyes and act like she knew what she was doing...it would have been torture if she'd been forced to truly wing it. But Mrs. Marshall had left behind detailed notes on what needed to be taught that week, and had lined up all the textbooks on Danica's desk so she wouldn't have to go hunting for them in the bookcase.

True, at dinner the night before, she had discussed the school somewhat, saying that they'd divided the classrooms by age, and so Danica would have the younger set, ranging from six to ten, and then Mrs. Marshall would teach the older students, the eldest of whom was seventeen. Danica was somewhat relieved to hear that. Having to ride herd on a bunch of six- and seven-year-olds sounded scary, but not as scary as pretending to be an authority figure to kids who were only five or six years younger than she was.

But Mrs. Marshall had seemed more interested in Danica's talk with Jeremiah Wilcox than going into any great detail about the curriculum. Of course Danica couldn't tell her the truth, so she fumbled her way through saying that Mr. Wilcox only wanted to welcome her to Flagstaff, and for her to let him know if there was anything she needed.

"That was very polite of him," Mrs. Marshall said, but her gaze was frankly curious, as if she guessed there was something Danica wasn't telling her.

You have no idea, Danica thought.

Luckily, though, Mrs. Marshall didn't seem inclined to presume on their short acquaintance by pursuing the matter further, and she shifted to the much less fraught topic of the weather, and how "Eliza" would find it quite different from St. Louis.

"Oh, the snow we get sometimes!" she exclaimed. "But luckily, it is only a few blocks from Mrs. Wilson's place to the schoolhouse, and the men do a good job of clearing the main streets so we can get around."

Danica hoped sincerely that she would be long gone from here before the first snows appeared, but the weather in Flagstaff could be kind of crazy. She remembered several times when they had been hit by snowstorms well before Halloween. Recalling those events, she thought of the one shawl she'd brought with her and made a mental note to stop in at the general store sometime this week to see what she could get to beef up her meager cold-weather wardrobe.

But at least the topic of Jeremiah Wilcox had been dropped, and that was the most important thing.

Now, after spending six hours teaching everything from arithmetic to geography to the planets in the solar system—*but not Pluto,* she fiercely reminded herself, *since it hasn't been discovered yet*—she felt like she wanted to fall over from exhaustion. Not because any of the children had acted out. They were actually far better behaved than she had expected. The only real incident had been the frog that escaped Clay Wilcox's pocket and jumped all over the room before Danica could shoo it out the door, a task accompanied by the shrieking laughter of the children.

Well, all the children except Jacob Wilcox. He'd sat quietly as his desk, watching the commotion through black eyes eerily like his father's. Thinking about it later, when she had a chance to catch her breath, Danica thought his behavior did seem rather strange, but he was a solemn little boy, answering correctly when called on, but certainly not volunteering anything. Maybe it was simply that he took his position as the next *primus* seriously, and so didn't want to join in with the antics of the other children.

Some people might have said he missed his mother, but Danica knew that couldn't be right. Nizhoni had died when Jacob was just a baby. But hadn't Jeremiah remarried twice before both those wives met violent ends, and he finally realized that Nizhoni's dying ravings weren't ravings at all, but a curse that would haunt the family for generations?

Reflecting on those tragedies, Danica thought that maybe Jacob had a pretty damn good reason for being such a sober little guy.

Even though she wanted to go straight back to the boarding house and collapse face first on her bed—standing all day in a corset, high-heeled boots, and a ten-pound dress was not for the faint of heart—she knew she needed to stop in at Mrs. Marshall's room first to give a report on her first day at the Flagstaff school. When she got there, though, she paused at the doorway, because she could see the other woman was occupied, talking earnestly to a tall sandy-haired boy who didn't look that much younger than Danica herself.

"Yes, I understand that the mill pays two dollars a day," Mrs. Marshall said. "But you could command a good deal more than that if you finished your education."

The boy shrugged. "Money's money now, Mrs. Marshall, and they're hiring. My ma's got another baby on the way, and my pa says it's time I helped out."

Mrs. Marshall's shoulders slumped. "Very well, Daniel. I understand that you need to contribute to the family. But if you could try to keep up with your reading—"

A smile that showed a set of very white, crooked teeth. "Yes'm. I'll do my best. Thanks for all you've done."

And that seemed to be the end of the conversation, because he headed for the door, forcing Danica to step out of his way. He shot her an admiring grin before sauntering off toward the street.

"Does that happen often?" she asked, coming inside as Mrs. Marshall was wearily stacking the books on her desk.

"More often than I'd like. If it's not the mills luring them away, it's the ranches. I suppose they don't see the value in book learning if they're going to be handling a saw all day, or sitting on a horse." She shrugged, then asked, "And how did everything go today?"

"Just fine," Danica replied. "Except for the frog Clay Wilcox had hidden in his pocket deciding it wanted to explore the schoolroom."

"Oh, was that commotion I heard over there earlier this afternoon? I almost came over to check, but it sounded as if you got them quieted down quickly enough."

Thank God Mrs. Marshall had held off. It would have been too embarrassing to be bailed out by her fellow teacher on her very first day of school.

"Yes, I was able to shoo it out the door before all he—well, before the children got too out of hand." Damn, that was close. Danica had a feeling the older woman wouldn't exactly be thrilled to hear her new teacher saying "hell" like it was no big deal.

If Mrs. Marshall had noticed the near-slip, she didn't mention it. "It sounds as if you did very well, Miss Prewitt. My advice now would be to go home and have some tea, and rest as best you can. You'll have to do that all over again tomorrow."

Well, hopefully without the frog. Although the next day it could be a snake. Not that Danica was afraid of snakes, but she could only imagine that trying to chase one down while wearing a bustle skirt would be even more difficult than catching a frog.

"Oh, I will," she said. "But I thought I'd go over to Brannen's general store first. There are a few things I'd like to get, now that I've settled in a bit."

Mrs. Marshall nodded. "Well, enjoy your shopping, then. I need to get home to make sure my boys are doing their chores. I sent them on ahead, because Daniel needed to talk to me, but William will get distracted, I'm afraid."

She sounded exasperated, and Danica couldn't really blame her. She couldn't imagine having to teach all day and then have to ride herd on two young boys, all without any assistance at home.

After murmuring something noncommittal, Danica said her goodbyes and headed over to San Francisco Street. The wind had picked up, blowing down from the San Francisco Peaks, and she thought her decision to buy some sturdier outerwear was beginning to sound like a pretty good idea, even though her feet ached and she would have killed for jeans, a T-shirt, and some tennis shoes right about then.

The streets weren't too crowded, mostly because the millworkers wouldn't get off shift until six, and a lot of the housewives were probably beginning to fix dinner and wait for their children to come home from school. Even so, there were several horses tied up to the hitching post outside Brannen's general store, both looking a little dusty, as if they'd just come into town from riding one of the cattle or sheep ranches on Flagstaff's borders.

Danica opened the door and went in. The interior of the store smelled of warm pinewood and coffee and something else she couldn't quite place, something sharp and aromatic. Two men in sheepskin coats stood off to one side, inspecting a set of knives that Mr. Brannen had laid out on the counter. A third man, his back to the door, was at the far end of the shop, his head bent over something, although Danica couldn't see what it was.

"Why, Miss Prewitt!" Clara called out from behind the counter. "What brings you in?"

Oh, damn. Danica had almost forgotten that her housemate worked here. She was really too tired for Clara's chattiness, but since she'd already been spotted, there wasn't much she could do about it now.

"I was hoping you might have a heavier winter cloak," she began, stepping farther into the store.

"Oh, we have several," Clara replied, looking eager. It was probably a lot more interesting for her to show clothes to Danica than farm implements or cooking utensils to the men and women who usually came into the shop. "Black, or brown, or we have a nice dark green."

"May I see the black one and the green one?" It couldn't hurt to look at both. Lord knows she'd brought enough money that she could afford a couple of cloaks, and more. The thought of having to cycle through the three daytime dresses she'd brought with her for possibly weeks didn't sound very appealing, and she added, "Do you have any ready-made clothing besides the cloaks?"

Appearing startled by the request, Clara said, "I'm afraid not. That is, we have some work shirts and trousers for men, but you'd need to go to Mrs. Adams, the dressmaker on Birch Avenue, for something for yourself. We do have a nice selection of fabrics."

Of course it couldn't be that easy. Danica noticed that Clara wore the same warm brown dress trimmed in black that she'd had on the day before, so clearly people here weren't too concerned about recycling their wardrobes. But if this Mrs. Adams was as fast as Jackie, her twenty-first-century counterpart, had been about making up some new gowns, then the wait shouldn't be too bad. Her research had already told her that the sewing machine had been in use for decades by this point; it wasn't as if Mrs. Adams would have to construct Danica's new gowns by hand.

"The fabrics are over there," Clara added helpfully, pointing to the far wall, near where the one man still stood at the counter.

"Thank you, Clara." Danica headed to the spot her housemate had indicated, at the same time hoping the man standing there wouldn't be too much in the way. These damn bustle dresses did take up a good deal of space, and she wasn't anywhere close to being an expert in managing hers.

As she approached the section where bolts of fabric had been set on the wooden shelves in neat stacks, the third man in the shop looked up suddenly.

Bright blue eyes met hers.

Oh, my God. Danica stopped suddenly, aware that she was staring, but also unable to tear her eyes away from him. He did not look that much different from the last time she'd seen him, since he now wore the same long black coat and high black boots. Today, though, he did have on a waistcoat in a deep steel blue, and a black puff tie fastened with a gold stickpin completed the ensemble.

Also, she knew that if she reached out to touch him now, he would be real, and not a ghost. Not that she would ever do something so crazy. She could only imagine what his reaction would be if she sidled up next to him and then poked him in the arm, just to make sure he wasn't another apparition.

After that one long heart-stopping second, he offered her a polite smile and returned his attention to the objects on the counter before him, which she realized now were several different pocket watches, most of them silver, but one gold. Danica remembered the gold chain he'd worn, the one that disappeared into his pants pocket. Had he bought that watch and chain here at Brannen's?

Far more important than that single detail, however, was the realization that he had looked at her and not shown one ounce of recognition. She wasn't quite sure why she'd expected him to know who she was. He'd made contact with her more than a hundred years from the present day. So why on earth would he have the foggiest idea who she was here and now?

Because they'd made some sort of connection, and she'd thought it would carry back to his former life. If time truly wasn't a river that flowed in only one direction, shouldn't some echo of their interactions have come to him now?

But it hadn't, and Danica's heart sank a little. She would have to find some way to make a whole new connection, and then guide him away from the Wilcoxes somehow.

Well, that's going to be fun.

"Do you see anything you like?" Clara asked, coming up behind Danica. Over one arm were draped both the green and the black cloaks.

Danica didn't quite startle. "Um…yes," she said quickly. It was so hard to pretend that everything was fine, and that the man standing only a few feet away meant nothing to her. "The black and brown plaid, and that dark green."

"I'll just get those out for you while you take a look at these." Clara laid the cloaks on the countertop, then glanced past Danica to the stranger. "Have you made a selection yet, Mr. Rowe?"

The stranger looked up. "Thank you, Miss DeWitt. I believe I'll take the gold one." He had a precise way of speaking, almost clipped, though his tone was rich and resonant enough.

Clara flashed him a brilliant smile. "Then would you like me to wrap that up for you?"

"Oh, it's not a gift. I somehow lost mine on the train ride out here, so this is a replacement. Just let me know how much."

"Twenty dollars," she replied, with the slightest flinch, as if worried he would decline once he heard how expensive the watch actually was.

But he didn't blink, and instead pulled a pair of coins from his pants pocket and laid them on the countertop. "Thank you for your assistance, Miss DeWitt." For the slightest fraction of a second, his gaze flickered toward Danica, but she saw only the mildest curiosity in his face. Then he picked up the watch and looped its chain around a button on the front of his waistcoat before dropping the timepiece itself into the pocket apparently designed for that purpose.

He left then, even as Clara retrieved the gold coins he'd left behind and placed them in her own apron pocket.

"Who was that?" Danica asked, hoping she sounded only idly curious.

Clara batted her eyelashes. It was obvious enough what she thought of the stranger. "A *very* welcome newcomer. His name is Robert Rowe. I believe he came in on the same train you did. Didn't you see him?"

"No," Danica replied. "I think I would have remembered him if I had. He must have been in a different car."

"I should say you should have remembered him! I don't know if I've ever seen a more handsome man."

Repressing a grin, Danica remarked, "And just the other night you were saying how handsome Mr. Jeremiah Wilcox is."

"Well, they both are, aren't they?" By that point, Clara had gone back around the counter and had begun to pull the bolts of fabric Danica had chosen down from the shelf. Clara set them down and lifted an eyebrow, clearly expecting Danica to reply.

"I suppose so, yes." Pretending to be interested in the cloth, she ran a hand over the top bolt so she could feel the smoothness of the fabric beneath her fingers. It felt very similar to the lightweight wool of her good "churchgoing" outfit. "Do you know why Mr. Rowe has come to Flagstaff?"

Clara darted a look at Mr. Brannen, but he still seemed to be occupied with helping the two men

Danica had noted as she entered the shop. Apparently satisfied that the shop's owner wouldn't notice her indulging in a little gossip, Clara said, "Well, it seems that he's quite wealthy, and is looking to purchase one of the land parcels to the west of here so he can start his own ranch." She let out a little sigh, then shook her head. "I'd set my sights there, but I think Mr. Robert Rowe is a little too fine for the likes of me. But you, Eliza…."

"I didn't come out here to 'set my sights,'" Danica said, a little more sharply than she'd intended. "I came here to teach school."

That reply earned her a skeptical look. "I don't doubt that you did, but surely you wouldn't turn your nose up at him, should he show an interest."

"Well, he certainly didn't show any interest just now." That realization sent a little pang through her. Maybe it shouldn't exactly have been love at first sight, but surely he should have exhibited a spark of curiosity, of attraction.

Lord knows Jeremiah Wilcox had.

Danica repressed a shiver, even as Clara said, "I should think he'd be too well-mannered to stare at a woman he'd just met. And there aren't that many eligible girls here in Flagstaff, when you get right down to it, so I think you would have an excellent chance with him."

"If he's here because he's starting a ranch, I should imagine he must be fairly busy. Besides," Danica added, going cold as a sudden thought came to her, "it could be that he's already married."

"No, he isn't. Did you see a ring on his finger?"

Back in the twenty-first century, going without a ring was no indication that a man was unmarried, but Danica decided it was probably better not to mention that particular fact. "No."

"Well, then. At any rate, I *did* ask around, and Beth, the chambermaid at the Hotel San Francisco, said he was quite unaccompanied, and gave no indication of having a wife."

Which didn't mean much. Mr. Rowe could have left his wife behind, wherever he came from. "That's quite a bit of sleuthing, considering he just came to town on Saturday."

Clara flushed. "I'm sure there was nothing improper in my asking. We're always curious about new arrivals around here."

Especially young, handsome, rich ones, Danica thought wryly. On the other hand, Clara's poking around did seem to have its uses. The fear that this Mr. Rowe might have a wife had mostly subsided. Coming here to start a ranch sounded innocuous enough, but Danica couldn't help wondering what he might have done to run afoul of the Wilcoxes.

Simple trespassing didn't seem to be a good enough reason for putting a bullet in someone's chest.

"I suppose you would be curious, in a town this size." Danica turned toward the cloaks, which she'd been neglecting all this time, and felt the heavy wool, the smooth silk of their linings. Yes, that would be much better than a thin challis shawl. "I believe I'll take both of these cloaks, and then however much of the fabric you think I'll need."

Clara appeared somewhat surprised by her request. "Well, are you going to use the same pattern as one of your own gowns? You should know from that how much it would require."

Which made logical sense, except that Danica hadn't been involved at all in the construction of her Victorian wardrobe, except to show up for a fitting and to pay Jackie her fees when everything was delivered. She certainly hadn't provided the fabric, and she'd only given a token glance at the line items on her final bill. It just hadn't mattered that much.

"Well," she said, "I'm not completely sure how I'll have them made up. I suppose Mrs. Adams could guide me in that."

Luckily, that reply seemed to put Clara off the scent. "True. If I get you ten yards of each, that should be enough. And if it turns out that Mrs. Adams needs more, you can come buy it as necessary."

Ten yards sounded like what you'd need to make a set of draperies, not a dress, but Danica had to admit there was a lot of fancy draping going on with these dresses. They probably did take up a lot of fabric.

She nodded, and Clara went to cut the lengths of cloth and then folded them and put them together with the cloaks. The total bill was quite a lot, far more than Mr. Rowe's twenty-dollar watch, but Danica handed over the coins to Clara without blinking. After this, she should be set, and anyway, she still had plenty of money left over for any other contingencies that might arise. She had to wonder what Clara would think of the five grand a month she got as her Wilcox "stipend." The poor girl would probably fall over in a heap, and then start asking what in the world such an heiress was doing, teaching school out here in the hinterlands.

After everything had been safely wrapped up in brown paper, Clara offered to have Danica's purchases sent directly over to the boarding house so she wouldn't have to carry them there herself. That sounded like a great idea, considering how much her feet were aching by that point. Since she'd had to mail-order her boots, Danica hadn't had the opportunity to really try them on. They'd felt all right for a few test runs around her carpeted bedroom, but now, after standing on bare boards in them for hours and hours, she just wanted to get back to Mrs. Wilson's house and tear them off her feet as soon as possible. Even seeing the mysterious Robert Rowe wasn't quite enough to erase her discomfort.

Well, unless he follows me back to Mrs. Wilson's and offers to rub my feet for me, she thought with a grin, one she quickly hid so Clara wouldn't ask what on earth she was smiling about.

Danica limped her way down the front steps of the store and then into the street. While she couldn't claim to know the town very well yet, she had noticed that it looked like she could take a shortcut through a little alley between the feed store and the livery stable, and come up on Phoenix Avenue that way, instead of going the long way around by walking decorously on the actual streets themselves.

That sounded like a great idea. She headed off in that direction, and had just entered the shadows between the two buildings when a tall figure interposed itself in front of her. A gasp escaped her lips before she realized that the man who stood before her was none other than Robert Rowe himself.

"Miss Prewitt?" he said. "I need to talk to you."

CHAPTER TEN

Danica was so confounded by this apparition—and by the fact that he knew her assumed name—that she could only blink up at him for a few seconds. Then she managed to pull herself together enough to ask, "I beg your pardon?"

He smiled, but the blue eyes regarding her were cold. "At first I thought you must be one of the Wilcoxes, but I was informed by my innkeeper that you've just lately come here from Missouri. Are you one of the Landons?"

He knew she was a witch. How could he know that? Was he a warlock himself? But no, Danica hadn't gotten any sort of ping from him, hadn't felt that weird resonance she always experienced when she first met another of her kind.

Somehow she managed to recover herself enough to say, "I'm not sure what you're asking, Mr. Rowe. Who are the Landons?"

His brows, straight and expressive, drew together, shadowing his eyes. "If you've truly come from Missouri, then you know very well who the Landons are. There's no use denying it, Miss Prewitt—you are a witch. Just as you know the Wilcoxes are witch-kind as well."

Crap. *Crap.* "Very well, yes, I am a member of the Landon clan. And clearly you were able to sense who I am. But why can't I sense that about you?"

"We all have our peculiar gifts, we witches and warlocks. One of mine is being able to block my nature when the situation calls for it. Since I'm now in Wilcox territory, I thought it only wise to make sure they could not tell I was not an ordinary mortal like everyone else in this town." He paused then, eyes flicking over her dispassionately. Under that cool gaze, Danica found herself hoping that she didn't look as tired as she felt. "Well, everyone else except you, it seems."

"Am I supposed to be happy that you don't think I'm an ordinary mortal?" she retorted. Yes, he was gorgeous, but she sure as hell wasn't seeing anything in this cold-voiced man of the sorrowful ghost she'd met up at the cabin. Right then she thought she liked the ghost a whole lot better.

As for his talent, well, she'd never heard of it before, but that didn't mean much. Talents disappeared, or seemed to die out, only to appear generations later. Damon had supposedly created a spell to hide a witch's "tell" from others of their kind. For all Danica knew, he'd been inspired because he'd read of other people, like Robert Rowe, who possessed that gift naturally.

"You're more than that, Miss Prewitt," he told her. "You're something of a mystery. You're not a member of the Wilcox clan, and yet I observed you in quite close conversation with Jeremiah Wilcox yesterday. So he must also know that you're a witch."

"You were *spying* on me?" This just kept getting better and better.

"As I said, I was observing you. Or rather, I was observing Mr. Wilcox, and noted that you were with him."

"Why would you be spying on Jeremiah Wilcox?"

Robert Rowe's mouth tightened at her use of the word "spy" once again. Right then Danica had to tell herself not to focus too closely on those lips, the ones that only a few short days ago she'd thought looked just about perfect for kissing. Well, she sure as hell didn't feel like kissing him now.

Mostly.

After sending a quick glance past her, as if to make sure no one was walking by on the street who might overhear their conversation, he said, "I would not call it *spying*, Miss Prewitt. I was sent here for a reason."

"What kind of reason?" she asked, feeling unaccountably annoyed. Misplaced familial loyalty? Maybe. Jeremiah Wilcox didn't know who the hell she was, but she knew he was connected to her, even across all those years and down all those generations. The thought that Robert Rowe had come here on some sort of mission which involved the Wilcox patriarch wasn't sitting particularly well with her at the moment.

"I'm not at liberty to say."

"Oh, of course you're not." Danica crossed her arms and glared up at him. "But now that you've determined I'm a witch, and have also determined that I am not a Wilcox, I don't believe we have anything further to say to one another." Maybe that wasn't the best reaction, but right then she felt as if she needed to get away from him, if only to sort out her muddled thoughts.

She shifted, as if to brush past him, but he moved as well, blocking her way. Although she doubted that he intended her any real harm, the irritation she felt was tinged with worry. Just what the hell *was* he doing here?

Not buying a ranch, that was for sure. Unless he was using the ranch purchase as a convenient cover.

Crossing her arms, she said, "Mr. Rowe, you do know that if I screamed right now, things wouldn't go very well for you."

He didn't appear particularly distressed by that threat. "Possibly. They might not go very well for you, either. You know how we all must do our best to avoid attracting attention."

Son of a—"What is it you want from me, Mr. Rowe? Clearly you have business here with the Wilcoxes, but that should have nothing to do with me."

"If I may ask, what precisely are *you* doing here, Miss Prewitt? If you're truly from St. Louis, then you're quite a long way from home."

I'm here to save your skin. Although at the moment, I'm beginning to wonder if you were worth the effort.

But no, that wasn't true. Even if he was doing his best right now to annoy her, that didn't mean she had any intention of standing by and letting him get shot down by one of the Wilcox clan.

She gave him the same answer she'd given Jeremiah Wilcox. "I'm here to teach school."

"There were no schools in St. Louis that needed teachers?"

"I needed to get much farther away than that."

Although she certainly wasn't a mind reader, Danica didn't need that ability to see he wasn't at all convinced by her reply. But he said nothing, only stood there and surveyed her with those frosty blue eyes of his. Funny how they had seemed so much warmer when he wasn't actually alive.

Right then, she would have welcomed someone coming down the little alley. The interruption would have been awkward, but at least it would have broken up this tense *tête-à-tête*. But while there were certainly people passing by on the streets to either side, no one seemed particularly interested in the narrow, shadowed space she and Robert Rowe currently occupied.

She planted her hands on her hips and said, "If you must know, I'm here because I'm avoiding a very unwelcome match my parents tried to force on me. It was better to come to the wilds of the Arizona Territory than to be married off to my awful cousin Alfred. So please, Mr. Rowe, feel free now to lecture me on my irresponsibility and lack of loyalty to my clan."

To her surprise, his expression softened, and his eyes lost their frosty glint. "My apologies, Miss Prewitt. I fear you have formed rather the wrong opinion of me. I would certainly never presume to lecture you about something like that. I assume you had a very good reason for not wishing to make the match."

"Oh, well—" Danica floundered for a second, trying to decide how she should reply. His words had mollified her, but they'd also knocked her off balance a bit. She'd assumed he was going to get all sanctimonious on her, but that didn't seem to be his intention. "That is quite all right, Mr. Rowe. But you see now why I've come all this way."

Much farther than you would probably ever believe....

"And Jeremiah Wilcox knows of this? I understand that he's one of the trustees of the school."

"Yes." She hesitated, then decided she might as well be as truthful as she could. After all, she would have to gain Robert Rowe's trust somehow. She did find herself somewhat heartened that he wasn't entirely unsympathetic to "Eliza's" plight. "I had to tell him the truth. He understood that I was in a difficult situation, and so he offered me his protection."

Once again Robert Rowe seemed to go ice cold. "Oh, he did, did he?"

"I thought it quite a gallant gesture," Danica replied, nettled. "He did not have to do that."

"Perhaps not, but Jeremiah Wilcox, I have heard, rarely does anything that does not serve his interests. I am quite sure his main intention was to make you feel indebted to him."

"I am indebted to him. For his consideration, and his kindness. It was certainly not what I had expected."

She all but flung these words at Robert Rowe, and his lips pressed together. "You should be careful,

Miss Prewitt," he said. "He is a powerful man, and I understand that he has given you reason to feel grateful. But you would do well to fear his intentions. I have heard that he does not have the best of luck in his wives."

Having delivered that shot, he nodded brusquely at her, then moved swiftly away before she had a chance to do anything but open her lips to retort that Jeremiah Wilcox's luck with wives had absolutely nothing to do with her. But since she'd been left standing there, alone, she closed her mouth in grim silence and stalked off toward Mrs. Wilson's boarding house.

Luckily, the lady of the house sat down with Clara and Danica for dinner that night, and so Clara was deprived of an opportunity to gossip any further about Robert Rowe. Instead, the conversation was confined to far more innocuous subjects, such as Danica's plans to commission Mrs. Adams to make a few more dresses for her, and how the teaching had gone on Danica's first day.

Clara appeared consummately bored by those topics, but she didn't try to interrupt, and only ate her chicken and dumplings in uncharacteristic silence. She brightened a good deal, however, when Mrs. Adams said, "It appears the trustees are going to hold a harvest dance at the school this Friday evening."

"Oh, I was hoping they would!" Clara exclaimed. "I heard Mrs. Finley talking about how they would have dances at the school, but they hadn't held any since Ma and I—well, since I've been here."

Danica couldn't help noticing how Clara stumbled at the mention of her mother, but since Mrs. Wilson seemed to be purposely ignoring that brief awkwardness, she decided she'd gloss over it as well. "A dance at the school?" she asked, setting down her knife and fork. "Where on earth do they hold it? Both classrooms are filled with desks."

"In Mrs. Marshall's room. The men will move the desks in that schoolroom over to the one where you're teaching, Miss Prewitt. Then there will be plenty of space for dancing."

That sounded like quite the undertaking, but she supposed all those desks probably could fit in her room, if the men got creative about where they put them. "Isn't this sort of short notice? That is, to go to all that work."

Mrs. Wilson made a pshawing noise. "Not at all. I think they'd been discussing the matter for a bit, but today they decided on the date. So now you girls will have something to look forward to."

Clara all but clapped her hands together in excitement, but Danica couldn't help experiencing a sudden sinking feeling. Sure, she'd studied the clothes and the manners and the local history as best she could. One thing she hadn't bothered with very much was music or dance, thinking she wouldn't need to know any of that.

It looked as if she was about to be proved wrong. Wonderful.

It turned out that Clara was willing to help, since it had been a while since she'd attended any kind of dance, either. Although Danica still felt bone-tired at the end of the day, she roused herself enough to go into the parlor after dinner, pull off her boots, and practice the waltz and the polka with her house-mate, along with more arcane dances such as qua-drilles and the Virginia reel.

"Of course, it's a lot easier when you have more people to dance with," Clara said, stopping to catch her breath after leading Danica through a figure of the reel. She put a hand against her waist, as if her stays felt too tight, then sent a curious glance in Danica's direction. "I'm surprised you aren't more familiar. Surely you must have danced back in St. Louis."

"Oh, we did," Danica replied, searching franti-cally for a reason as to why she would be so clue-less about something every young woman her age should be well acquainted with. "It's just—I was rather sickly for some years, and so I often had to sit out."

That reply earned her a dubious glance. True, Danica knew she was slender enough, but she didn't exactly look like someone who had been confined to her sickbed for long periods of time. But then Clara gave a small lift of her shoulders, as if the reason for Danica's general cluelessness about the popular dances of the day wasn't really her concern.

Despite her worries about her general lack of expertise, Danica couldn't help feeling a little thrill of curiosity about the upcoming dance. She and Robert Rowe hadn't exactly parted on the best of terms after their encounter on Monday afternoon, and maybe in the congenial setting of a dance, he'd be a little friendlier.

Or he could not show up at all, she told herself. *He's just come to town, so who knows if he was even invited?*

That thought sobered her. She had absolutely no idea what the protocol was for these sorts of things. Was everyone in town invited, or was it even an "invitation" sort of thing? Maybe everyone who wanted to come, did. That might be a little problematic. Some of the men she'd passed on the street were pretty rough-looking. She wasn't sure she wanted to do a St. Cecilia Circle—whatever the heck that was—with one of them, let alone be held close in a waltz.

Now, with Robert Rowe...maybe. Danica was still irritated with him for the way he had acted, although that irritation had mostly given way to curiosity by the time Friday rolled around and she was up in her room, changing out of her plaid day-time dress for the teal silk one. Would Robert even come to the dance? He didn't exactly seem like the social type. Then again, it would give him an excel-lent opportunity to spy on—sorry, *observe*—the Wilcoxes. Surely they would be there, if the trustees were sponsoring the dance.

A sudden suspicion came to her, and she frowned. Jeremiah Wilcox couldn't have pushed for this dance so he would have an opportunity to see her socially, could he? No, that was ridiculous. She hadn't seen hide nor hair of him since their conversation after church on Sunday, and besides, Mrs. Wilson had said that they'd held one of these harvest dances before, last fall after the school had newly opened. This just had to be a coincidence.

Danica adjusted the carved tortoiseshell comb in her hair, and then slipped a garnet necklace around her throat. She'd bought the necklace to match her antique garnet earrings and ring, but because her daytime dresses all had high necks, she hadn't had the opportunity to wear it yet. Now, though, it gleamed against the bare skin of her chest, which felt strange after being so buttoned up all week.

The gown wasn't too provocative, was it? When she'd tried it on, she'd loved the way it revealed just a hint of cleavage but wasn't too low-cut. Well, low-cut by her standards. It now seemed almost daring. Unfortunately, there wasn't much she could do about it at this late date.

A dab of lip stain, and a bit of powder to take the shine off her nose. She hadn't dared to bring any real makeup, but the lip stain was subtle enough, and powder was completely period-correct. The reflection looking back at her from the slightly warped mirror looked pretty glam compared to her workaday self of no makeup at all and high-necked gowns, and she hoped it wasn't too much. Again, she couldn't do much to change it all now.

She made her way down the stairs, the silk of her skirts rustling elegantly against the steps. Mrs. Wilson and Clara were already waiting in the parlor. Clara practically gasped when Danica entered, and even the imperturbable Mrs. Wilson's eyes widened.

"Goodness, Eliza!" Clara exclaimed. "You look like a princess!"

"Oh, I don't know about that—" Danica began, but Clara waved her hand.

"Things must be mighty fine in St. Louis, for you to have a gown like that." Her expression fell, and she looked down at the mid-blue dress of wool crepe she wore. Danica knew it was her Sunday gown, and the only thing Clara would have deemed suitable for an important event such as a dance. Still, it did rather pale in comparison with Danica's teal silk.

"Well, my mother had it made up for my last birthday party," she said, hoping the explanation would be enough to quell the light of jealousy she saw in Clara's eyes. "It's certainly the finest gown I've ever had." Which wasn't even a lie. This thing definitely put the strappy little beaded number she'd worn to prom to shame.

"Both you girls look lovely," Mrs. Wilson said briskly. "That gown is just the color of your eyes, Clara, and is very becoming. Now, we should be going. It never does to be the last to arrive."

Clara didn't seem inclined to argue, but pulled on her brown wool cape. Danica had brought her own black wool cloak with her, draped over one arm, and so she slipped it over her shoulders. It was now getting cold enough at night that a shawl would never have been sufficient.

The three women went out of the house and hurried up the street toward the schoolhouse. Light streamed from all its windows, and as they approached, Danica could already hear music coming from within. Maybe that was better; she could slip in while people were dancing and watch for a bit, get her bearings that way.

Admission was a quarter, with the proceeds going to the upkeep of the school and its grounds, as well as to books and whatever else might be needed. For all she knew, some of it might also be going to pay Mrs. Wilson for her room and board. Said room and board seemed to be the bulk of Danica's own compensation, although she would also receive the princely sum of twenty-five dollars at the end of every month. Lord knows what everyone would think if they discovered she had some ten times that stashed away in the drawer that held her stockings and assorted undergarments.

Danica's untrained eyes told her that those in attendance were dancing some sort of quadrille, although she couldn't begin to guess which one. Her studies of books and films set in the period had only told her so much, after all. The room truly had been cleared of all the desks, with Mrs. Marshall's large oak desk called into duty as the admission table. She wasn't the one who sat there, however, but Mrs. Adams the dressmaker, who took Danica's quarter and praised her gown.

"Why, if you don't look like something out of *Godey's Ladies Book*!" she said. "I'd love to be able to work on something that fine, although I must say the Wilcox ladies do get themselves up very well."

Her gaze moved toward the other end of the room, where Danica could just make out the Wilcox brothers and their wives, along with their sister Emma and her husband. They were all dressed very beautifully as well, in silken gowns in shades of deep blue and plum and dark wine red.

And there was Jeremiah, too, in his long black coat, a crimson waistcoat gleaming beneath. His eyes caught hers, and Danica quickly glanced away. The last thing she wanted him to think was that she'd been deliberately looking at him.

She pretended to be studying the room instead. It did look very transformed, with the swags of autumn leaves over the windows and all the desks gone, replaced by men and women in all their best finery. From what Danica could tell, there did seem to be some subtle segregation going on here. There were probably some forty people in attendance, but she could tell they all consisted of what Mrs. Wilson might have referred to as the "better people"—the shopkeepers and their wives, the property owners. No sign at all of the rougher sorts who worked at the mills, or the women who served drinks at the saloons. Not that Danica really knew any of them, either, but she'd passed enough people on the streets during her time here that she could recognize who'd been excluded tonight.

That number seemed to include Robert Rowe. At least, she didn't see him anywhere, even among the smiling, shifting dancers. The music was being provided by a woman seated at an upright piano in one corner, a fiddle player standing next to her. Getting the piano in here must have been quite a feat, and Danica had to salute the organizers for that accomplishment, as well as managing to make the room look like a welcoming place for a party, and not the plain rectangle of a chamber it actually was.

Off to one side was a refreshment table with a punchbowl. That seemed to be the safest place to go, especially since Clara had forgotten to pout about her gown as she spied a tall fair-haired man a few years older than either she or Danica, and hurried off to speak to him. Mrs. Wilson was more sedate about taking her place with a group of middle-aged women who chatted in a corner, but it seemed clear enough that neither of Danica's companions felt compelled to keep her company this evening.

Well, fine. She didn't need anyone to babysit her. All right, as the dance ended and people headed for the punch bowl, she could tell that a good number of eyes were on her, whether admiring, curious, or, as in the case of some of the women, more than a little jealous. How was she supposed to know that a dress like this would have been too flashy for Flagstaff? At least her cover story about being from St. Louis probably helped, as did the cash she'd flashed at Brannen's earlier in the week. It wouldn't take too much for people to figure out that she hadn't accepted the teaching position because she was in need of the cash.

The punch was tasty, although definitely not alcoholic. Just as well. She was going to have a hard enough time remembering half the dances Clara had taught her without being tipsy into the bargain.

After thanking the woman who was pouring the punch, Danica moved off to one side so she would be more or less out of the way. People were already pairing off for the next dance, but Danica noticed none of the men seemed inclined to ask her. Intimidated by the dress, or simply because she was still more or less a stranger here, an unknown quantity?

It was probably for the best. She could stand here and observe, and at least have the opportunity to wear the beautiful gown Jackie had made for her. Meanwhile, Clara could get some dancing and flirting out of her system. Yes, there she was, already standing up with the fair-haired man, the two of them facing another couple, as more and more people went out to the dance floor to form a large circle composed of sets of two couples, all in their little groups of four.

Oh, lord, which one was that dance, anyway? Not that it really mattered, since it seemed pretty obvious she'd be sitting this one out. Danica lifted the cut-glass cup of punch to her lips and took another sip, hoping that she looked as if she was having a great time. If Robert Rowe didn't show up, this whole evening was going to be pretty much a bust.

"Miss Prewitt?"

Jeremiah Wilcox's voice.

Danica started, but not badly enough that she spilled any of her punch—and, she hoped, not so badly that Jeremiah would notice.

She turned toward him. "Good evening, Mr. Wilcox," she said steadily, although it was impossible to ignore the admiration in his gaze as he regarded her. From anyone else, such a look would have been flattering. From the man who was her great-great-etc.-granduncle?

Not so much.

"I couldn't help noticing you didn't have a partner for the Spanish dance. My sister Emma and her husband Aaron could make up a new quartet—if, of course, you're amenable."

Could she turn him down? Maybe, but it wouldn't be very politic, and might even seem ungrateful, considering how he'd offered her the protection of the Wilcox clan.

"Certainly, Mr. Wilcox. It's very kind of you to ask." Even as she replied, however, Danica found herself praying that those impromptu practice sessions with Clara would be enough to keep her from completely embarrassing herself.

He smiled. "Let me take care of that for you," he said, then plucked the half-drunk cup of punch from her fingers so he could return it to the woman who was watching the refreshment table. She seemed to be keeping track of whose cup was whose, fortunately. And if not...well, Danica's immunizations were up to date, and she rarely got sick anyway.

Jeremiah took her by the hand and led her to the dance floor, where they were met by his sister Emma and her husband. One could have almost mistaken Aaron Garnett for another Wilcox brother, since he was also tall and dark. However, his hair wasn't quite as sooty, and his eyes were a warm brown instead of Jeremiah's piercing black.

"Emma, Aaron," Jeremiah said. "This is Eliza Prewitt, our new teacher."

"Very nice to meet you," Emma said. She was a lovely woman, probably right around thirty, with creamy pale skin that contrasted startlingly with her black hair and eyes.

"Pleased to make your acquaintance," Danica murmured, while Aaron Garnett echoed more or less the same sentiment.

The piano and the fiddle together sounded a single chord, while everyone bowed or curtseyed to their partners. From watching the previous dance, Danica remembered half a beat too late that she was supposed to do so as well, and she had no idea whether her curtsey to Jeremiah Wilcox looked completely awkward, but there wasn't much she could do about that.

He affected not to notice, and as the dance began, she experienced a wave of relief. This was one of the dances where you held your partner's hand and then the hand of the man opposite as you slowly went around in a circle. Not too hard, and nowhere near as intimate as a waltz. She could do this.

Except for the part where, once you'd done the little set of movements with the group of people in your starting quartet, you were supposed to waltz with your partner around the circle until you came face to face with the next couple, and it started all over again. Danica tensed as Jeremiah's arm went around her waist, but she could tell that he held her lightly, wasn't attempting to pull her so close that it would be improper.

Even so, she hardly dared to breathe as they went around and around. This was way too close to him—her hand on his shoulder, his on her waist, the warmth of his fingers seeming to burn through the silk of her dress and the metal bones of her corset, all the way down to the skin. Part of her wanted to run away right then and there, because this was all just worlds of wrong.

Worlds of wrong because you're making it that way, she scolded herself. *It's just a goddamn dance. He's not doing anything improper.*

Which was true enough. A surreptitious glance from under her lashes told her that all the men were holding their partners more or less the same way, although the man Clara danced with had her pressed up a little more closely than the rest of them. She didn't seem to mind, and seemed to be laughing at something her partner had just said.

"…enjoying yourself?"

Danica reluctantly returned her attention to her own dance partner. Jeremiah's expression was pleasantly neutral, a not-quite smile touching his mouth. Had he noticed her unease, or was he merely trying to keep from smiling at her clumsiness? So far she'd avoided stepping on his toes, but….

"Oh, yes," she lied. "They've done a lovely job of decorating the room. I'd hardly recognize it."

"Wait until you see it at Christmas. I think the ladies on the decorating committee make it a point of honor to outdo themselves."

God, if she was still here by Christmas…. But no, that wouldn't happen. Robert Rowe had been killed when the leaves were falling from the trees, long before Christmas rolled around. Whatever was going to happen would have to happen in the next several weeks.

She didn't know whether to be worried or relieved about that.

What she did know was that she needed to at least pretend she was having a good time. From somewhere she summoned a smile and put it on, rather the same way she'd put on her fancy dress to prepare for the evening. "That does sound wonderful. Do you usually have white Christmases here?"

"Every year since I've been here," he returned with a smile.

After that they reached the next couple, and had to move through the simple figures of the dance again. It was a relief when Jeremiah let go of her waist, and when it was time to waltz again, she found herself a little more prepared. They only had time for brief bursts of conversation on safe topics—the weather, the school—before they reached the next couple they had to dance with.

The music ended once they'd made a complete circuit of the dance floor, and afterward Jeremiah bowed courteously enough and led Danica over to where she could retrieve her half-drunk cup of punch. He murmured his thanks for the dance and headed back to the group of chairs in the far corner where his other family members had congregated.

Danica let out a sigh of relief, glad that he hadn't attempted to remain at her side. Maybe he thought doing so would have been too conspicuous.

But then she looked up, and her breath caught. Robert Rowe had just entered the room, blue eyes scanning the crowd as he moved past the table where he'd paid his admission. Those eyes caught hers, and his lips curved up in a smile.

Danica couldn't help smiling back at him, although the two of them certainly weren't on what one could call the best of terms. Appearing to ignore the admiring glances of the unattached young ladies present, and the murmurs of some of the older women, he cut through the crowd and came straight toward her.

"Mr. Rowe," she murmured as he paused by her side.

"Miss Prewitt." His gaze seemed to take in her gown, the darkly winking garnets at her throat. "I hope you won't think I'm being too forward in saying that you look very lovely this evening."

"Thank you, Mr. Rowe. I don't believe that's too forward." Not too forward at all. It was nice to know that he'd noticed she was female. Up until this moment, she hadn't been sure.

"Then I am relieved." He gave a quick glance around the hall. "I had no idea Flagstaff could be this…civilized."

Was that supposed to be an insult? The real Miss Prewitt couldn't have taken it as such, considering this was certainly not her hometown. "It can be a surprising place. So where are you from, Mr. Rowe, that you're so quick to take the measure of a town's civilization?"

He didn't appear to be offended. No, he grinned at her, blue eyes glinting, and Danica experienced a certain melting sensation in her midsection that had nothing to do with her tight-laced stays. "Massachusetts, Miss Prewitt. Boston, to be precise."

Well, no wonder he didn't have a very high opinion of Flagstaff. Then her eyes narrowed. She knew the Wilcoxes had traveled here from Connecticut, having been driven out of New England by a group of witches and warlocks there who weren't happy with Jeremiah's experiments with magic. You didn't have to look too hard to see where her cousin Damon had gotten that particular talent. But if Robert Rowe was from Massachusetts, did that mean he was one of those crusading New England warlocks?

No, that couldn't be right. There was no way he would dare to come anywhere near Jeremiah Wilcox, who might not be able to sense that Robert was of witch-kind, due to his own particular gift, but who would surely recognize his face if he'd seen it before.

She risked a quick glance over where Jeremiah sat with his family members. To her dismay, he seemed to be looking at her—or rather, looking at both her and Robert. The Wilcox *primus* didn't appear too thrilled, either; his mouth had thinned, and his heavy black brows were pulled together. But even for all that, she couldn't detect any awareness in his expression. He might not like that she was standing there and talking with Robert Rowe, but it didn't seem to be because of who the warlock from Massachusetts actually was.

In a way, that might be worse. Otherwise, he had to be wearing that expression because he didn't like seeing her talking with another man.

Somehow she managed to chuckle, then said, "Well, Mr. Rowe, I can see why you might not have a very high opinion of Flagstaff, if you've truly come from such a cosmopolitan place as Boston."

His gaze seemed to warm as he looked down at her. "Let us just say that I'm rapidly revising my opinion."

Was he flirting with her? What had brought that on? The last time they'd spoken, he'd been almost hostile. It was remotely possible that he'd decided he hadn't been very gentlemanly with her, but she doubted that was the case. In fact....

There it was. Just the quickest flicker of his eyes toward the corner where the Wilcoxes sat, so fast that if she hadn't been looking for it, she probably would have missed it altogether.

Robert Rowe wasn't flirting with her because he was attracted to her. He was flirting because he'd noticed Jeremiah's interest, and he was trying to get a rise out of the Wilcox *primus*. Why, she wasn't sure, but she guessed it must have something to do with Robert's reasons for being here in Flagstaff.

Anger flared, and she said tartly, "I'm not sure that's necessary, Mr. Rowe. After all, they do say that first impressions are the most lasting ones."

After flinging that retort at him, she turned on her heel and stalked away. Maybe it would be a horrendous breach of protocol to simply walk out of the dance, but no way did she intend to stay there and have to dodge Robert Rowe and Jeremiah Wilcox all evening. It was only a few blocks to Mrs. Wilson's boarding house, after all.

Luckily, her cloak was hanging on the coat tree near the door, so she pulled it off and settled it around her shoulders even as she hurried down the front steps of the school. A few people standing by the doorway shot her curious looks, but she didn't see either Clara or Mrs. Wilson, and so she was able to make her escape mostly unnoticed.

Well, except for Robert Rowe. He hastened after her, matching strides as she continued her way down the street, studiously not looking over at him.

"Miss Prewitt, did I say something to offend you?"

"Oh, stop with the act," she snapped. "Of course you did."

"'Act'?" he repeated, sounding puzzled.

"You're doing it now, too."

By then they'd reached the corner of Leroux Street and Birch, and she turned down toward the boarding house.

Robert protested, "I'm afraid I don't know what's upset you so much."

Danica ground to a halt and turned to face him. "Do you really think I didn't notice how you were only talking to me because you wanted to see how Jeremiah Wilcox would react?"

"Miss Prewitt, I do think you're getting the wrong impression—"

Oh, the hell with this. She let out an exasperated huff and kept walking. And of course he stayed right with her, sticking by her side like a goat-head thorn she'd picked up in her shoe while hiking.

Then there was the awkwardness of actually reaching the boarding house, and having him follow her right up the stairs. She stopped there and faced him, arms crossed. "Yes, Mr. Rowe, I am getting the wrong impression, because you have followed me all the way to the front door of my house, even though I thought I made it quite clear that I didn't want to talk to you. So please, go back to your hotel and leave me alone."

He only stood there, watching her closely. The kerosene lamp mounted on the wall next to the front door seemed to flicker into his face, providing enough light for Danica to see his features, although she couldn't read his expression. And she realized how alone they were, how everyone else was off at the dance, and he could do anything he liked.

Well, maybe not anything. After all, he didn't know which powers she possessed. He didn't know that hers was novel but all but useless to her at the moment, since it seemed to be entirely focused on keeping her locked here in 1884. If she attempted to give herself that extra five minutes so she could walk calmly away from him and then lock the door behind her, she'd only find herself back in the present. She couldn't risk not being able to get back here, even if she currently felt as though she wouldn't mind terribly if one of the Wilcoxes did manage to drill a hole in Robert Rowe.

Then he said, "You're right. I did want to see how Jeremiah Wilcox would react. But I have my reasons."

"Which are?"

Robert glanced out toward the street. It was utterly empty, dry leaves rustling in a chill wind that had begun to blow down from the north. "I'd prefer not to speak out here. Where could we talk in privacy?"

Privacy? There was a laugh. From the time she got up in the morning to the time she went to bed at night, Danica felt as if there was always someone watching what she did, whether it was Mrs. Wilson and Clara at the boarding house, or Mrs. Marshall and Danica's own pupils at the school. Really, she had to wonder how anyone ever got away with anything in a place like this. Flagstaff's denizens seemed so…omnipresent.

She said, "I have no idea, Mr. Rowe. I doubt that anything you wish to say to me is something you'd want overheard by Clara DeWitt. She does have a tendency to eavesdrop. And I'm afraid Mrs. Wilson is not much better." It had been on Danica's lips to invite him in to talk to her now, but that would give entirely the wrong impression. To have him inside the boarding house with her while they were all alone? If anyone ever learned of it, her reputation would be ruined, and she could say goodbye to the teaching position, the only thing that gave her an excuse for being here in Flagstaff.

"What about at the school on Monday, after you're done teaching classes for the day?"

He really wasn't going to let this go, was he? Danica wanted to say that wouldn't work, but actually, she could probably manufacture an excuse to stay after Mrs. Marshall had gone home. Something about the floors needing an extra sweeping, or whatever. Although Mrs. Marshall was very dedicated, she had her own boys to look after, and so she tended not to linger at the school, but took her grading with her. And although it felt strange to her that Robert Rowe was willing to wait until Monday to have their conversation, Danica knew that was really the only solution. There would certainly be no privacy at the boarding house over the weekend.

"Oh, very well," she said, knowing that she sounded ungracious in the extreme. "Come by a little after four. That should be safe enough."

"Thank you, Miss Prewitt." He hesitated before adding, "I appreciate the chance to clear the air between us."

Danica didn't know how much air would actually be cleared, but she only nodded. "Then I'll see you Monday at four."

He gave a small bow, not much more than a tilt of his head, and then he headed back down the porch steps.

She stood there in the light of the kerosene lamp, watching him go, and let out a breath. Somehow she had thought this would be so very easy, that she would go to him and tell him his life was in danger, and that she'd come here to help him. Now, however, she was discovering that he had an agenda and a mind of his own, and that things weren't working out at all the way she'd expected.

This was going to be a very long weekend.

CHAPTER ELEVEN

OF COURSE CLARA HAD TO CORNER DANICA THE NEXT morning. "Whyever did you leave so quickly? You only danced one dance!"

"I—I wasn't feeling very well. I believe the punch didn't agree with me."

Clara sent her a skeptical look at that weak reply and opened her mouth to argue further, but after Danica made it clear she wasn't going to answer any more questions—nor comment on her dance with Mr. Jeremiah Wilcox—the other girl more or less gave up. Anyway, she had to be at the store at nine thirty, and so was more or less out of Danica's hair.

The remainder of Saturday was taken up by grading papers and helping Mrs. Wilson around the house. If the landlady had questions of her own about

Danica's conduct the night before, she kept them to herself, for which Danica was eternally grateful.

Church on Sunday was only slightly less awkward, but at least Jeremiah made no move to approach her. Lord knows what conclusions he'd drawn from her precipitous flight on Friday evening. Had he even seen her storm out? Hard to say, as he'd been sitting at the far end of the room, with a crush of dancers between them. But word had probably gotten around, the way it always seemed to in this small town.

Robert Rowe was conspicuously absent from the Methodist congregation. Danica didn't know if that was because he attended a different church, or whether his clan was more like the McAllisters and worshipped in the old ways. If he did, he was probably keeping that particular fact well hidden. People around here tended to give you the side-eye if you even admitted you were Baptist. Wiccans would definitely be beyond the pale.

And school the following Monday…well, school was school. By that point, Danica had more or less broken in her uncomfortable boots, and broken in the students as well. Or maybe they had broken her in. At any rate, she was used to the routine, used to having to shift from subject to subject throughout the day. In a way, having to teach so many different things to children of so many different ages kept things interesting. It probably beat teaching five periods of algebra, day in and day out. Besides, there was the undeniable fascination of seeing and interacting with the children who were her aunts and uncles many generations past, as well as her own great-great-great-grandfather Wyatt, who was a well-behaved child and somewhat bookish, quite unlike his cousin Clay.

But then it was the end of the day, and the last of her students had trooped out. At lunch, Danica had informed Mrs. Marshall that she was going to stay behind and do some extra tidying up, as well as take care of that day's grading at a proper desk instead of Mrs. Wilson's dining room table. Apparently Mrs. Marshall saw nothing strange about this explanation, because she nodded and said she hoped Danica would have a nice, productive afternoon.

Productive? Probably not. But hopefully informative.

She did pick up the broom and sweep out the classroom. It seemed better to perform that chore first, since it would be pretty obvious if it was left undone. She'd just have to catch up on the grading later. Luckily, compositions written by seven-year-olds were fairly easy to blow through in an afternoon.

The back door creaked open, and Danica turned, broom still in her hand. Robert Rowe entered, then quickly shut the door behind him.

"Did anyone see you?" she asked.

"No," he replied. "At least, I'm fairly certain no one did. I made sure to wait until the street was empty until I came onto the school property, and of course I came in through the back door."

That would have to do, she supposed. Right then, it felt strange to be standing there with him looking at her, all alone in an empty classroom. Danica recalled the broom she had clutched in her hand and went to replace it in its spot in the corner behind her desk.

"All right," she said. "So we've somehow managed to be alone so we can talk. What did you need to tell me?"

"Perhaps we should sit down."

She gave the desks a dubious glance. Would her bustle even fit into one of those things?

"Go ahead and sit in your own chair, Miss Prewitt. I can manage."

There was an undercurrent of amusement in his tone, but she chose to ignore it and went ahead and pulled her chair out from behind the desk. As she sat, Robert somehow managed to wedge himself into one of the student desks, his long, boot-clad legs sticking out in front of him.

Danica found herself stifling a smile of her own. "So, Mr. Rowe. Perhaps now you can provide some illumination?"

Before she asked that question, his blue eyes had held a glint she was already beginning to recognize, but his expression sobered abruptly as soon as the words left her mouth. "You know I told you that I had come here from Massachusetts."

"Yes."

"Did you also know that the Wilcoxes are also originally from New England, from Connecticut?"

This was going to be tricky, because she would have to push aside all the things she knew about her own family history and feign a convincing ignorance. "Are they? I hadn't heard that. But everyone here in Flagstaff is from somewhere else, I suppose."

"True enough." Robert fell silent for a moment, clearly deciding what he should say next. Danica waited as patiently as she could, but she really wished he would just spit it out. Then he seemed to straighten in his cramped seat, clasping his hands on the desk in front of him. They were good, strong-looking hands, still lightly tanned. He wore a gold ring with a carved sapphire on the pinky of one hand, but there was no sign of a wedding band, not even a paler border of skin at the base of his ring finger. It was silly to be looking for it, but....

After a long pause, he continued, "In the case of the Wilcoxes, however, they did not leave Connecticut of their own volition. No, stories had been circulating for several years, ever since Jeremiah Wilcox and his brothers and sisters broke away from their parent clan, and Jeremiah began calling himself the *primus*, after an old tradition that all the other clans had long since abandoned. But in the beginning, Jeremiah didn't appear to be doing anything much out of the ordinary, and so the neighboring clans saw no reason to interfere."

"But you did interfere at some point?" Danica asked. Of course she already knew the answer to that question, since it was ancient family history, but she really wanted to know what sort of spin Robert would put on the story of the New England clans driving the Wilcoxes out of the area.

Even though she'd kept her tone neutral—or thought she had—Robert frowned, as if detecting a hidden rebuke. "We did have to intervene, but I assure you, it was only as a last resort, Miss Prewitt."

"Eliza," she said. All this formality was beginning to wear on her nerves. She knew she didn't dare give him her real name, but at least they could dispense with the "Miss" this and "Mister" that. "Please."

He looked startled, but then nodded. "If you wish…Eliza. Then of course you may call me Robert. I suppose it is just as well that we're on a first-name basis, since we are sharing confidences with one another."

Well, not exactly. He might be about to confide in her, but Danica knew she didn't dare tell him the truth about who she really was, or where—*when*— she'd really come from. But she smiled, and he seemed to take that as a signal to continue.

"Stories began to circulate, stories of strange spells and even stranger occurrences. I'm sure I don't have to tell you, Eliza, that the survival of all our kind depends on secrecy, on keeping our true natures hidden from the rest of the world. If one of us grows careless, drunk with power, then he puts all of us at risk, not merely the members of his own clan."

Danica nodded. She couldn't really argue with that statement. It was the one rule all the clans followed, no matter what else they might believe.

"As I told you, Jeremiah and his immediate family were part of a larger clan, the Winfields. After his father passed away, Jeremiah declared himself *primus*, and he and his family moved to a new town some distance away from Winfield territory. Everyone kept watch on them, but at first nothing seemed to be that untoward about their behavior."

"But then?" Danica asked. This was the first she had heard of anything about the Wilcoxes breaking off from another, larger witch clan. True, all the family stories seemed to be horribly vague about exactly what had happened before Jeremiah and his immediate kin were driven out of Connecticut. She'd always assumed that was because the records had been lost.

Now it sounded more as if Jeremiah had purposely made sure that information was buried.

"Then the stories began," Robert replied, looking grim. "Of disturbances like storms from nowhere, and the ground shaking, and strange lights in the woods outside the town where the Wilcoxes had settled. This aroused the concern of the Winfield elders, and they went to speak with Jeremiah. As you can imagine, that conversation did not go well."

"What happened?"

"He told them it was none of their business, that they were trespassing on his clan's territory, and to leave and never bother him again. The elders replied that it was their business, if whatever magic he and his clan were dabbling in awoke the suspicions of the non-magical folk in the area. And then Jeremiah and his brothers cast some sort of spell that was like a raging wind no one could withstand, blowing the Winfield elders right out of town and dumping them in an open field almost a mile away." Robert's mouth compressed. "The thing is, my mother is a Winfield, and it was her father who was injured in that assault. Only the skills of the Winfield clan's healer kept him from succumbing to those wounds."

So this was personal, at least on a certain level. That only made matters worse, but she could see why Robert would have reason to think ill of Jeremiah Wilcox.

As for the rest…well, the family stories had always spoken of how powerful Jeremiah was, but obviously Danica hadn't yet had the opportunity to see any of those powers firsthand. And after hearing what Robert had just told her, she didn't think she wanted to.

"And so your people came back in force," she said.

"Yes. It was clear that the New England witch clans couldn't allow someone so powerful, and with such a disregard for their laws, to remain in the area. The elders of the clans from Massachusetts, Connecticut, and New York all converged on Killingworth, which was where the Wilcoxes had settled. Even as strong as Jeremiah and his brothers were, they couldn't hope to prevail against the combined powers of more than twenty elders. They were defeated, and given enough time to pack what belongings they could, and take their wives—or, in Emma Garnett's case, her husband—with them. Of course the family had far fewer children at that time. Emma's and Samuel's eldest were only babies, and neither Jeremiah nor his other two brothers had any children yet."

A lot of fun that must have been—having to pack up your whole life and haul a couple of infants most of the way across the country in a covered wagon or whatever. No, that didn't sound exactly right. Danica had always gotten the impression that the Wilcoxes had taken a train as far west as they could, then bought provisions and whatever else they needed in New Mexico before heading into Arizona Territory. She had the vague impression that Emma Wilcox had offered help to the *prima* in Santa Fe, healing her ailing son, and that was why the Wilcoxes had a good relationship with the Castillo clan in New Mexico, when otherwise they had been isolated from the rest of the witch clans.

It was also on that trip that Jeremiah's first wife had passed away. The family had no real details on her death, except that it had happened on the road between Santa Fe and Flagstaff. Neither was there any real information as to why Emma Garnett hadn't been able to heal her, but witches with healing powers weren't infallible. Some diseases had no cure, magical or otherwise.

"But...." Danica began slowly, thinking over what Robert had just told her. "You got rid of them. They haven't bothered anyone in Flagstaff, as far as I can tell. Really, from what I've heard other people say about the Wilcoxes, it sounds as if they're model citizens. So why come all the way out here to 'observe' them?"

Apparently, Robert had had enough of his cramped seat, because he eased himself out of it and stood, then came over to lean against the side of her desk. She was still safely tucked behind it, but that didn't change the way he seemed to tower over her. If she got up and stood as well, she'd look far too obvious, so she remained where she was, hoping he couldn't detect the way her heart had begun to beat a little faster as soon as he got near.

"Because we had to make sure they hadn't gone back to their old ways. We listen, Eliza. Rumors come to us—slowly, when they have to travel all the way from Arizona Territory, but we do hear them. So we knew that the Wilcoxes eventually settled here... and we also know that the family seems to have suspiciously good luck in everything it does, whether ranching, or mining, or selling timber to the local sawmill."

Suspiciously good luck was the hallmark of the Wilcox clan. Danica didn't bother to deny Robert's claim on that subject, because she knew it was only the truth. Whether that famous luck had attracted too much attention...that was the real question. She hadn't really heard any conversation on the topic since she'd come here, but she'd be the first to admit that she hadn't been offered much opportunity to get out and mingle. At the time, posing as the town's new schoolteacher seemed like the best cover story she could come up with. However, she was learning the hard way that her assumed role took up a large chunk of her days.

Robert, on the other hand, had no real occupation to fill his time, and his guise as a prospective landowner gave him the chances he needed to speak to the locals, to range around the area and get the lay of the land, so to speak.

Maybe she should have posed as a saloon girl after all. She probably would have heard more gossip that way.

"Perhaps they really are that lucky," she ventured, earning herself a tilted eyebrow and a highly ironic look.

"It's much more likely that they're making their own luck," Robert said. "We heard rumors of such a power back in New England, but the Wilcoxes' darker experiments were of more immediate concern. Now, though, they once again run the risk of making themselves far too conspicuous."

"And if people begin to ask questions?"

"Then we'll have to consider what to do next. If the Wilcoxes were the only witch clan here in Arizona, it might be one thing, but the McAllisters are not all that far away, down in the mining town of Jerome. They are a small clan, and don't have the means to withstand any real scrutiny if people really start asking questions about newcomers who exhibit unusual behavior."

Danica hadn't even considered that aspect of the problem. The de la Pazes were far away in the south of the state, and big and established enough that any blowback from a witch-related scandal up in Flagstaff probably wouldn't affect them too much, but the McAllisters hadn't been in Jerome much longer than the Wilcoxes had been settled in Flagstaff. Or at least, that was what she recalled. McAllister history had never interested her all that much.

But because Robert was worried about the McAllisters, that meant their fate could be an issue here as well.

"What do you plan to do?" she asked, not sure whether he'd really tell her the truth or not. After all, he seemed worried by Jeremiah's interest in her, and where that might lead. She wasn't about to flatter herself that Robert Rowe disliked the connection because he himself was attracted to her. Throughout this entire conversation, he'd sounded cool and dispassionate, talking to her more like a business associate. In a way, that was gratifying; at least he had the decency to speak to her as an equal. But she also wouldn't have minded just a bit of heat in those baby blues of his.

"At the moment, as I said, I'm observing." He hesitated, then pushed himself away from the desk and went to the window. The warm afternoon light cast his fine profile into sharp relief, like a cameo of a Roman god Danica had seen at the antique store when she was shopping for period-appropriate jewelry. "My talent isn't merely hiding my own witch-born nature. I can also sense when another witch or warlock is using their gift."

"You can?" For some reason, his admission alarmed her. Could he tell that her own very strange temporal ability was currently working overtime to keep her anchored here in his own present?

"Yes. I've felt brief bursts from the Wilcox compound—that is, the five houses they built next to one another over on Park Street. But I know that Emma Garnett is a healer, and with all those children, it's very likely she uses her gift regularly to heal all their bumps and bruises and fevers, even if she can't share her healing abilities with the community at large." His shoulders lifted, and he turned back toward her. "The other bursts of power I'm sensing…I'm not sure. One of the brothers must have the gift for luck—I don't know which of them it is. Not Jeremiah. His talents are showier than that."

"Which means he must not have been using any of them," Danica pointed out. "That is, if he had done anything even half as spectacular as what you described was happening back in Connecticut, people would notice. Of course, I haven't been here very long, but in that week, I've certainly not seen anything out of the ordinary, except perhaps that tremendous rainstorm we had on Wednesday. I don't believe I ever saw it rain like that back in St. Louis."

She'd halfway hoped Robert would smile at her remark, but he only shook his head, his expression still far too serious. He said, "And then there's you, Eliza."

"Me?" she said, pulse beginning to speed up. In what she hoped was a suitably casual fashion, she added, "I hope you're not lumping me in with the Wilcoxes."

"No, it's not that." He frowned and took a step toward her, then stopped. "There's something different about you. As if you're using your power all the time at a very low level. I've never experienced anything like it before."

Crap. She supposed he would pick up on that, because even if she wasn't paying it any particular attention, her talent was always working in the background, making sure she stayed here rather than slingshotting back to the present where she belonged.

Since he still watched her with that frown pulling at his brows, she knew she needed to say something to explain the strange phenomenon he was sensing. Only...what?

After casting about wildly for anything that might work, she said, "Very well—I fear you have caught me. My talent is illusions. I actually have red hair, but I thought the dark brown more becoming."

"You don't have a redhead's complexion."

"That's because I'm hiding my freckles as well."

At that reply, he did smile. "Ah, well, I suppose that would take a good deal of ongoing effort." His expression turned sober again, though, as he added, "You don't have to tell me, Eliza. If you want to keep your secret, then do so."

Danica could hear the disappointment in his tone. While it was true that witches and warlocks generally did not discuss their particular talents openly, Robert had told her of his, and it seemed rude not to share hers with him as well. But she couldn't do that. For one thing, telling him why she was here would mean revealing that she was a Wilcox, and she didn't know how he would handle such a revelation. Clearly, he wasn't too keen on the Wilcox clan.

Since she didn't know how to reply, an awkward silence fell between them. She hated this. It would have been so much easier if he'd just fallen for her at first sight. Then she could have persuaded him to stay away from the Wilcoxes and….

And what? Put him on the next eastbound train, wave goodbye, and walk away?

She realized she hadn't actually followed this little scheme through to its most logical conclusion. Or maybe she'd hoped the attraction would be mutual, and then once they'd confessed their undying love for each other, she could have told him the truth. After that…lord only knows. She didn't fancy the idea of having to stay back here in 1884, but could she get him to return to the present with her? How would that even work?

When she'd been researching Flagstaff's past at the historical society, she hadn't known Robert's name. She'd pored over as many old photographs from that year as she could, but she'd never seen him in any of them. It made sense; people weren't snapping selfies all the livelong day back then the way they were now. But because she hadn't known who Robert was, she also wasn't able to track down any information about him. If he truly did end up killed by one of the Wilcox men and buried in the woods, his story would stop there.

His story would stop there.

Danica had never really experienced the sensation of her heart missing a beat, but it did right then. Because he had no future, she could give him hers.

"What is it?" he asked then, taking another step toward her. "Something just lit up your face like the Fourth of July."

"I—" Something told her now was not the time to confess all. "I wish I could tell you, Robert. And I think I will…only not today."

That rather muddled statement only made him shake his head. "I worry about you, Eliza. To be here alone, with no one to watch out for you—"

She wanted to snap that she could take care of herself, thank you very much, but she also realized in the next second that Robert wasn't being a sexist pig, only a man of his time. Back then, most men considered it their duty to look after the women around them.

Even so, she couldn't help saying, "Well, Jeremiah Wilcox did offer me the protection of his clan. So I wouldn't say I am completely alone."

At once Robert's blue eyes took on that shuttered expression she disliked so much. "And I believe I told you, Eliza, that you would do well to fear Mr. Wilcox's attentions."

"He hasn't paid me any particular 'attention,' as you put it." Maybe she was being disingenuous in making that particular denial. Or maybe she just really, really didn't want to acknowledge to herself what those looks and glances from Jeremiah Wilcox might actually mean.

"It didn't appear that way when he was dancing with you."

So Robert had seen. And, judging by the tight set of his jaw, hadn't liked it very much. Danica experienced a little start of satisfaction at that realization. Maybe he wasn't quite as uninterested as he pretended to be.

"I'm sure he danced with several of the ladies," she retorted. "I can't say for sure, of course, since your own behavior forced me to make my exit before I intended to."

"That's not what I heard," Robert replied, mouth still hard. "Mr. Jeremiah Wilcox is not one for dancing, by all accounts. That he would stand up with you, when he hadn't done so with anyone else, was quite the cause for some gossip."

Oh, hell. Danica wondered why Clara had never mentioned such a thing to her in all her chattering, then realized that, because of her tendency to shut the other young woman down whenever she even began to utter Jeremiah's name, Clara had probably decided it wasn't worth bringing up the subject. "Well, that may be, but I can't control what Mr. Wilcox does or doesn't do. Surely no one can fault my behavior."

"No, not at all," Robert said. This time his tone was almost dry, but there was a flicker in his eyes Danica couldn't quite read as he added, "More than one person has said you were very clever indeed, to get the richest man in Flagstaff paying such attention to you so soon after your arrival in town."

Oh, they had, had they? So this was what people did before Facebook and Twitter…spent their days gossiping, apparently. All right, that was mostly what people did on Facebook, too, only it didn't give Danica the same creepy feeling as realizing that everyone was talking about her behind her back.

Especially when she hadn't actually given them any-thing of substance to talk about.

"Oh, yes," she shot back, voice equally ironic, "that's precisely why I came here. I learned that one of the trustees was rich and handsome, and so I made sure to put myself deliberately in his way."

"So you think he's handsome?"

"I think most people would acknowledge that fact."

"That isn't what I asked."

"Well, clearly you think that I think he is, so I'm not sure why you bothered to ask in the first place."

"Because—" Robert bit down on the word, as if making sure he wouldn't allow himself to say any-thing else. Not looking at her, he flicked an entirely imaginary speck of dust off the lapel of his frock coat, then said, his tone hard, "Because Jeremiah Wilcox has put four wives in the ground. Now it has been almost two years since the last, and I fear he tires of his single state. I would hate to see you become his fifth victim."

Danica's irritation melted away as if it had never been. He must care about her a little bit, or he wouldn't be saying such things. Hoping that Robert could hear the truth in her voice, she said, "I have no desire to be Jeremiah Wilcox's wife." And lord, a truer statement had never been spoken. Even if they hadn't shared that familial connection, tenuous as it might be after so many generations, she knew what eventually happened to Jeremiah's wives…what had happened to *all* the Wilcox wives, until Angela had come along to break the curse.

It did seem as if Robert could tell she was being sincere, since he took another step toward her. Now they were only a foot or so apart. If he wanted to, he could reach out and touch her arm, take her hand. Anything to show that his wasn't the impersonal concern she feared it might be.

Another silence fell. Outside, the light had begun to slant toward sunset. It painted a rectangle of gold on the sleeve of Robert's coat as it poured through the window, and warmed his blue eyes almost to green. The air seemed to thrum between them, heavy with things neither one of them had the courage to say.

Before she could even react, he was moving to her, one arm going to her waist so he could pull her close, the other caressing her cheek. Danica wanted to close her eyes at the exquisite tenderness of his touch, so different from—

No, she would not think about *him* right now. Not with Robert holding her the way she'd dreamed he might.

"I told myself I would not do this," he said, his voice barely above a whisper. "This is not what I came here for."

It would be a lie if she told him the same thing. In the back of her mind, she had hoped he would feel the same attraction for her that she did for him. Their stormy interactions after her arrival here had dimmed that hope, but now she realized he'd only been fighting his feelings, knowing that he should be concentrating on the task he'd been given, and not falling for the very unexpected witch he'd met.

So she only stared at him, mute, and tried to tell him with her eyes that it was all right, that she wanted him as well, and they'd find some way to make all this work so their involvement wouldn't upset his plans.

She must have been successful in getting her message across, because in the next second he bent toward her, pressing his mouth against hers. His lips did feel just as good as she'd hoped, and he smelled good as well, of something just faintly spicy. Cologne, or hair tonic? She had no idea, and supposed it didn't matter, because in the next second she felt his tongue touching her lip, but gently, as if he wasn't sure how she would react.

Maybe properly brought up Victorian ladies didn't French-kiss, but Danica didn't care about that. She wanted to taste him…wanted all of him, although she knew better than to ask for anything more than this still rather chaste embrace at such an early stage in their relationship.

She opened her mouth to him, felt him pull her even closer as they explored one another, all the worry and the weariness of the past week gone as if it had never existed. It was enough to be here in his arms. Her stranger. Her ghost.

No, she shouldn't have thought that. Because then the terrible memory surfaced in her mind, the one where that long-ago bullet struck him once again, red blossoming against the white of his shirt.

She didn't recall making any sound, but she must have, for in the next instant he was pulling away, expression worried as he stared down at her. "Eliza—was that wrong of me? I apologize if—"

At once she held up a hand. She didn't want him thinking that she regretted the kiss. Her only regret was that it hadn't happened sooner. But oh, the agony of hearing him say her borrowed name! After a kiss like that, she should at least have been able to hear him call her by the name that was truly hers.

"No—no, Robert. Don't apologize. I—I wanted you to kiss me."

"Then what is it? There was such a look of sadness on your face."

"I—" Oh, God. She had no idea what she could say to him. "I suppose I was only startled. In a good way," she added hastily. "I was so worried that you disliked me."

"Disliked you?" he responded, clearly startled. Then he shook his head, as if at himself. "That is entirely my fault. For I felt an attraction to you from the very moment I saw you in Brannen's store, and yet I kept telling myself that I couldn't indulge such a weakness, that I had been sent here by my clan for a reason, and that reason was not to give my heart to a beautiful stranger."

Hot blood rose to Danica's cheeks. "You think I'm beautiful?"

His eyebrows lifted, and then he gave her a lopsided smile. "You must know that. After all, I assume you look in a mirror each morning to arrange your hair, and so you must be able to see how lovely you are."

"I—" She shook her head. "Robert, you must stop making me blush. Anyway, when a woman looks in a mirror, she only sees the hairs that are out of place. She's not studying her own looks."

"Well, you should, if you're so unfamiliar with them." He came close to her then, bending down so he could press his lips to her cheek. Every nerve ending thrilled at his touch, even at so chaste a kiss. "My dear Eliza, you are a very distracting young woman. But even with that, I can't allow myself to become too distracted."

"I understand," she said. "But really—I think you're looking for problems where there are none."

Something about him seemed to stiffen. "Are you trying to defend the Wilcoxes?"

No, she would *not* let herself become annoyed by his reaction. Not after that kiss. "Of course not. All I'm saying is that I've seen nothing that suggests you should be worried about them. Yes, I've only been here for a little more than a week, but during that time, nothing out of the ordinary has happened. And no one else seems to have anything bad to say about the Wilcox clan. Do you find it so difficult to believe that Jeremiah and his family might have learned something from their experiences in Connecticut, and so are trying to be as circumspect as possible?"

From the way he set his jaw, she thought he was having a very hard time believing it indeed. All right, he'd seen for himself—or at least heard firsthand accounts—how much havoc the Wilcox brothers could wreak. And she knew they weren't angels, not by a long shot. But neither were they devils.

When Robert spoke, his voice seemed weighted with uncertainty. "But the way their luck never runs out—"

"I know," she said. "They haven't been very cautious in that. Look at it this way, though—if no one here in Flagstaff knows anything about our witch clans, that we even exist, why would they even suspect such a thing as too much luck in the first place?

People can have strings of good luck without there being any kind of magic involved. So I don't see why you can't go back and report that to your elders."

As soon as she made the suggestion, though, Danica regretted it. Yes, he'd get on the train and go back to Connecticut. He'd be safe, but where would that leave her…the two of them?

He seemed to be thinking the same thing. "And would you come, if I left?"

She blinked at him, not sure how to reply. In all the scenarios she'd imagined, she'd never thought of leaving Flagstaff but staying in 1884. Could she do that?

Robert would be safe, but she would be trapped in a time that wasn't hers, a world where she'd be alone, except for Robert Rowe. Her family would never know what had happened to her. Could she do that to them, all for an attraction that was still very new and fragile?

Reaching out, he took her hands in his, grasped them tightly. She could feel the slight roughness of calluses on his fingers. So he wasn't entirely a city boy.

"I could not leave this place if you weren't with me," he said, voice taut with need. "I know it must sound mad to you, but after tasting your lips, I know why I felt drawn to you from the first moment I saw you, even though I tried to fight those feelings." He paused then, and his eyes caught hers, their blue so mesmerizing that she knew she couldn't look away even if she tried. "I never thought I would settle down. My family despaired of me, but I was doing the work of our clan, and that was enough. Or so I thought. Now I know why I waited all this time. But now that I've found you, I can't bear the thought of leaving you behind. Please, Eliza—tell me that you'll come away with me when all this is done. Tell me you'll come back with me to my home."

What could she say to such a plea? She'd never had anyone look at her this way, like he'd just gotten a glimpse of the promised land and didn't dare let it go.

Danica drew in a breath, then nodded. Maybe agreeing with him was crazy, but really, the whole situation was crazy. And she knew what he meant. She'd never felt this way before, either. It was supposed to happen that way for many witches and warlocks, this pull toward the person who was their other half, but she'd always thought the idea a fairytale, something that sounded good but couldn't possibly happen in real life, since she'd never experienced even an echo of that kind of attraction. Now, though....

There was really only one way to answer. "Yes, Robert. I will come away with you."

CHAPTER TWELVE

DANICA WOULD HAVE ASKED HERSELF JUST WHAT THE HELL had possessed her, but she already knew the answer to that question. Robert Rowe's mouth had possessed her, and the shape of his lips, and the sweet taste of his kiss.

Be careful what you wish for, the old saying went. She'd wished she could be with him, and now it seemed as if she might get that wish. A wish that included a world without her family—or at least a family she could acknowledge. Without her friends.

And without Internet, tampons, or toilet paper. They used newsprint here. She'd sort of gotten used to it, but some days she felt as if she'd cheerfully axe-murder someone for a couple of family-size packs of Northern toilet tissue. The tampons weren't as much of a concern, since she'd had her period right before

she time-jumped back to 1884. Anyway, she'd gotten a birth control implant last spring, only a few
weeks before the ill-fated trip to Tucson, so her
period wasn't much of a bother. If she stayed here,
the implant would have to remain in her arm, she
supposed, although the hormones it was supposed
to be dispensing would eventually run out.

But, setting aside all the triviality of those lost
conveniences, could she do this? Give up everything
to be with Robert Rowe?

Once again, she saw that bullet hitting his chest.
If she changed his past, then the future would
be unknown. And if she disappeared into nine-
teenth-century America, would that mean she'd
never be born? What would change? Would Matías
Escobar have found other victims to fuel his dark
spells?

She shivered. Maybe it wouldn't be Robert
Rowe's past they'd end up sharing, but her future.
Could she tell him the truth, convince him to come
back to future Flagstaff with her rather than remain
here?

Right then, she just couldn't say for certain.
True, by their very nature, witches were more open
to the strange and unusual than the rest of the population, but no one in her present seemed to know
of anyone else who possessed her time-bending abilities. So maybe that meant there hadn't been any

time-traveling witches back here in the past, and so Robert would have no other precedents to rely on. He'd only have her word that she had come from a time other than now.

Danica sat on the narrow bed in her room at the boarding house, papers scattered around her. After she and Robert had parted, and he'd hurried out the school's back door, she'd gathered up her work and brought it back to the boarding house. Since Mrs. Wilson thought she'd stayed late at the school to grade papers, Danica couldn't spread them out over the dining room table the way she usually did. No, she was trying to work through them as best she could using the lap desk she'd bought a few days earlier at Brannen's general store. "Trying" being the operative word. She couldn't seem to focus.

Of course she couldn't. Robert Rowe had kissed her. He wanted to take her away from here. But only after his work was done, whatever that meant. And she worried that the longer he stayed, and the more he snooped around, the more chance there was of him being driven toward whatever circumstances had caused the confrontation at the Wilcox homestead.

Someone knocked softly at the door, and Danica called out, "Come in."

Clara entered, looking quite mysterious. She cast a glance over her shoulder toward the hallway, then shut the door behind her.

Repressing a sigh at this furtive behavior, Danica asked, "What is it, Clara?"

The other girl came to the foot of Danica's bed and surveyed the mess of papers there. No doubt Danica herself was looking quite a mess as well—she'd taken off her boots and her bustle, and also removed the heavy pins from her hair. But she hadn't been planning to leave her room again, now that they'd all eaten dinner, and so she'd thought she might as well make herself as comfortable as possible.

However, considering the way Clara planted her hands on her hips and shot her a knowing smile, Danica was beginning to think she would've been wiser not to respond to that knock.

And she should have made sure her door was locked.

Since she couldn't do anything about it now, she waited for Clara to respond. Clearly, the other girl had something she wanted to get off her chest. And, judging by the smile playing around her lips, it wasn't anything Danica particularly wanted to hear.

At last—probably because she'd decided that she'd drawn out her significant silence long enough,

Clara said, "What was Mr. Rowe doing at the school this afternoon?"

Wonderful. And he'd sworn that he'd taken care to make sure no one had seen him enter the school's grounds. Restraining herself, she circled "wander" on Clay Wilcox's composition and changed it to "wonder," then said, "I'm afraid I don't know what you're talking about."

"Oh, is that a fact?" Clara crossed over to the small rickety chair at the dressing table, and pulled it out and sat down. Eyes avid with curiosity, she said, "Because I know what I saw, and that was Mr. Rowe walking toward the school and then cutting around to that vacant lot before he came up to the back door and went inside."

This just kept getting better and better. Danica set down her pencil. "He—he wanted to apologize for something he said to me at the dance on Friday evening. That's all."

"So that was why you stormed out the way you did?" Clara nodded, as if satisfied that one mystery had been solved at least. Without waiting for Danica to reply, she went on, "But why would he hold off until Monday to apologize?"

"Because that was the first time he had the opportunity to do so in private," Danica said, giving the other girl a pointed look.

That remark didn't seem to deter Clara, however. She leaned forward. "So what did he say that upset you so much?"

"I'm afraid that's between Mr. Rowe and myself." Seriously, Danica wanted to pat herself on the back for not losing her temper outright. As it was, her words were becoming more and more clipped, and if Clara had any sense, she'd shut up and go away.

Unfortunately, her curiosity seemed to override any judgment she might happen to possess. "I didn't know you were even acquainted enough for him to have said something rude to you."

"It wasn't rude. It was a misunderstanding. That's all." Danica retrieved her pencil, then picked up a few papers at random and shuffled them in what she hoped was a sufficiently significant way. "But I do need to finish with these papers before I go to sleep—"

That comment finally seemed to sink in. Clara got to her feet, a look of irritation passing over her features. "I was only trying to *help*, Eliza. Why, if anyone else had seen Mr. Rowe going into your classroom when you were all alone there...." She let the words trail off, and lifted one golden eyebrow in a suggestive manner.

Yeah, because of course what I really wanted was for him to bend me over my desk and take me then and there. Actually, come to think of it...

"If you're suggesting anything improper, Clara, then go ahead and say it. I was there, and nothing happened. Mr. Rowe and I spoke for some time, and cleared the air between us. That's all." *And he kissed me in a way no one ever has before….*

But she would never say such a thing to her housemate, obviously.

Clara crossed her arms. "Of course *I'm* not suggesting anything. I'm only saying that's what other people would have thought, if they'd seen it for themselves. So perhaps you and Mr. Rowe should be more careful with your…conversations."

"I'll bear that in mind," Danica said icily. "But since I do have these compositions to grade—"

"Of course," Clara broke in. "I wouldn't want to keep you from your important work."

She flounced out then and shut the door. At least she didn't slam it, probably because she didn't want to get scolded by Mrs. Wilson, or worse, have the landlady start making inquiries as to why the two girls had been quarreling in the first place.

To steady herself, Danica reached for the pitcher of water that had been sitting on the table next to her bed, then poured some into the ceramic cup that sat next to it and took a large swallow. Too bad it wasn't something stronger. She really had never been that into drinking, unlike a lot of her friends, but there were times when she could definitely use the calming effects of a beer or a nice glass of wine.

But not a margarita. She knew she'd never drink one of those again, not after suffering the effects of the drugged—or bespelled—cocktail Matías had given her.

And he was absolutely the last person she should be thinking of right now. Instead, Danica wrenched her thoughts back to Robert Rowe, to the way his mouth had felt against hers, of how strong his arms had been. That was what it felt like to be with a real man. She wondered how old he was. A little older than she, maybe in his late twenties.

Right, she thought, *so that makes him about a hundred and fifty years older than you are.*

Sighing, she shook her head at herself, then got back to work.

After their confrontation, the two girls maintained a frosty distance. Danica could tell Mrs. Wilson noticed right away that something was wrong, but she didn't comment on it. Most likely the landlady had enough experience housing young women under her roof that she knew these things had a tendency to blow over.

As she made her way to the school, however, Danica couldn't help fretting over what Clara had said. The other girl might have been trying to be deliberately spiteful, but at the same time, Danica knew that she would have to be more careful. If there was even the slightest hint of impropriety, she knew her job would be on the line. And she had to maintain that pretense for as long as necessary. If the trustees decided to dismiss her because they thought she was a "loose woman"—despite everything, the ridiculous phrase brought a smile to her lips—then she wouldn't have a lot of options.

Except saloon girl, she thought wryly. *Maybe Jackie was seeing into the future when she asked if I wouldn't rather have that kind of costume.*

Or seeing into the past, Danica supposed. Either way, she didn't think that was very likely. Jackie was a hell of a dressmaker, but she was still a civilian. She didn't have the ability to see into the future or the past.

As she climbed the steps to the school, Danica did her best to erase the worried pucker she knew must be creasing her brow. The last thing she wanted was for Mrs. Marshall to ask if anything was wrong.

Or one of her students. Several of the little girls had sort of latched on to her, eager to know more about her life back in Missouri, taking in every detail of her wardrobe and her hairstyles. Danica had stuck with the heavy braided crown at the back of her head because it was easier than some of the fussy curls she'd seen other women in town wearing, but she'd overheard one of her older girls—Annabeth Lindsay—saying she thought it looked terribly romantic. Danica didn't know about romantic, but she'd been around enough of her younger cousins to know that sometimes they tended to hero-worship people whose style they admired. If that was happening here, then she needed to mind herself and act as if everything was just fine.

Easier said than done. It was difficult to walk into the classroom and pass the exact spot where Robert had kissed her, and pretend nothing was wrong. But she did her best, going to her desk and setting the little satchel she carried on top of it so she could remove the papers she'd graded the night before. She put them off to one side, then opened the desk drawer where she kept the chunk of white quartz she used as a paperweight. She'd found it out in the schoolyard and thought it was pretty. Caitlin claimed quartz had calming qualities. Danica didn't know about that, but the white stone had proved useful.

Sitting near the front of the drawer was a folded piece of cream paper. Danica didn't recall putting it there. Frowning, she pulled it out and unfolded it, even as her students began to file into the classroom. She'd never seen the handwriting before—strong and slanted, and far more legible than anything she could manage, although she'd been laboriously keeping her own writing as clear as possible so no one could complain about her penmanship. However, she recognized the writing as Robert's at once, even before she read the words of the note.

Dearest, I'll be away for a few days, as I'm riding west of town to survey some land to purchase. I wish I could have let you know some other way, but Charles Royer approached me last night with the opportunity, and of course I could not come speak with you at the boarding house without causing all sorts of gossip. I should be back no later than Friday. Take care, and know that I will be thinking of you the entire time I'm gone.

The note was signed with a single "R." Danica traced the letter with one fingertip, thinking of his fine, strong hands holding the pen that had written the note. It would be all she had of him for the bulk of the week, it seemed.

She pushed back her disappointment. Robert had a façade to maintain, just as she did, and so getting upset at the lengths he must go to hide his true reasons for being in Flagstaff wouldn't do anything to improve the situation. Anyway, she tried to tell herself sensibly, with the way Clara was lurking around and spying on everything she did, even having the opportunity to be alone with him would have been difficult.

What had people done back in the day when they were "courting"? Sneaked around a good bit, she imagined. Or rather, if a young man made his intentions known, then he could come and visit a girl's house and spend time with her. But since it seemed obvious to her that Robert wanted to keep their developing relationship a secret, Danica doubted she'd see him sitting in the parlor of her boarding house and drinking tea anytime soon.

Her students began trooping in then, and she hastily shoved the note back in her desk drawer. As usual, the Wilcox children arrived together, all ten of them in her class, ranging from Susan, the eldest of the group at nine, down to little Victor, who had only turned six the month before school began. The two eldest children—the ones who had been infants when the New England elders ran their family out of Connecticut—were in Mrs. Marshall's classroom. Danica had the vague impression that there were several more at home who were too young to come to school yet. Clearly, that early generation of Wilcoxes had taken the suggestion about being fruitful and multiplying to heart.

But they were all good kids, even the mischievous Clay and the too-solemn Jacob. Thank God for that. Although this whole teaching thing got a little easier each day, Danica knew it would have been a complete nightmare if the Wilcox children had decided to form a cabal against her, for whatever reason.

She wondered about that, since they were such a tight-knit family. Maybe Jeremiah had put the fear of

God in them. Not that she much liked the sound of that, either. She didn't really want Jeremiah Wilcox championing her causes.

Well, whatever the reason for their continued good behavior, she'd take it. And then it was time to put all such thoughts out of her head, because the rest of her students were coming in and taking their seats. For the next few hours, all she'd need to think about was making sure she adequately covered the material Mrs. Marshall had laid out.

In a way, that was a relief. At least when she was explaining how to carry the one, or writing a list of spelling words on the chalkboard, she didn't have time to think about Robert Rowe, and how much she'd miss him while he was gone.

One interesting development did crop up during Robert's absence. The day after Danica had gotten his note, she stayed late to grade papers, working until the light began to fail. She knew she needed to finish up soon, since Mrs. Adams, the dressmaker, had sent word that the new gowns Danica had commissioned were ready, and the errand of going to pick them up needed to get handled before she was due back at the boarding house for dinner. Just as she was locking the schoolroom door, she saw movement across the street, then realized that movement was Clara, obviously headed home from her day at Brannen's general store.

There wasn't anything so noteworthy about that. What did make Danica sharpen her gaze was the realization that Clara wasn't alone, that at her side walked the tall blond man Danica had seen the other girl with at the harvest dance. And not only were they walking together, but also holding hands.

Well, then. The unknown young man must have made some declaration to her, or Clara would not have allowed him to be quite so intimate with her in public. While Danica was still irritated with Clara's nosiness, at the same time she couldn't help but be relieved. If Clara had a man to distract her, then maybe she wouldn't be quite so eager to know everything about Danica's personal life.

Not that she had much of a personal life right now, thanks to Robert's scouting trip. She understood the need for it, but she hadn't counted on missing him so much. It was as if the kiss they'd shared had awakened a hunger inside that only the sight of him, the sound of his voice, could satisfy. At least he'd be back on Friday. That wasn't so bad. Danica thought she could survive another day or so without him.

She hoped.

Mrs. Adams' shop was just a few doors down from Brannen's store. Danica passed by his shop without stopping to peek in the window, just because she didn't want to get distracted and be too late about picking up her new dresses. Even after being here for almost two weeks, she still found something very novel about a store that sold the sorts of things you couldn't even get outside an antique shop.

The new gowns both looked lovely. Danica made the appropriate appreciative noises over them before paying Mrs. Adams the balance due for the commissions, then waited for the dressmaker to wrap them up in brown paper so they could be easily transported back to the boarding house. It would definitely be a relief to have four dresses to work in, along with the good one for church and the dinner dress for whatever other special occasions cropped up. Danica didn't expect too many more of those, however; it wasn't as if the community got together and held a dance every week. Which, considering the blowout she and Robert had after the last one, was probably just as well.

She tucked the brown paper parcel under her arm and headed back out to the street. By that point, the sun had already disappeared behind the hill to the west. What the heck did they call it now? In her time it was Mars Hill, but in 1884 the astronomers had yet to take over the heavily wooded height. The wind picked up, chill, promising another night of frost.

As she was passing Brannen's store, a tall figure emerged from the doorway, the tails of his long black coat flapping in the breeze. Danica tensed, because she recognized him right away.

Jeremiah Wilcox.

She hadn't seen him since the day after the dance, and even then he'd only given her a small, polite nod. Just as well, because being around him was awkward, to say the least. But now there didn't seem any way avoid him without seeming far too obvious.

He lifted his hat to her. "Miss Prewitt."

"Mr. Wilcox." She paused in the street as he approached her. He, too, had a parcel tucked under one arm. It seemed a little late to be shopping, but she wouldn't dare to ask what had brought him to Brannen's. "I was just headed home."

"Then please, let me escort you."

If there had been a way to decline without sounding ungracious, she would have. As it was, she had to smile and thank him for his courtesy. The only real saving grace in the situation was that he didn't offer her his arm, possibly because of the package she carried.

"And how are things at the school?" he inquired.

"Very good, thank you. Why, Clay hasn't smuggled in anything more dangerous than a set of marbles all this week."

She'd meant the remark as a joke, but Jeremiah didn't smile. Instead, the faintest frown touched the corners of his mouth, and he said, "Has Clay been giving you any problems? I'll make sure that my brother Samuel speaks to him, if that's the case."

"Oh, no," she replied hastily. The last thing she wanted was to get Clay in trouble with his father… or his uncle. "There was only the frog that one time. He's a good boy. All of your family's children are very well-behaved. And your son Jacob is quite the scholar. I hope he doesn't find the lessons too dull. I would suggest that he study with Mrs. Marshall's group, but they are a good deal older than he."

Even this praise didn't seem to please Jeremiah all that much. He nodded at her words, but even in the dimming light he appeared abstracted, as if what she'd told him had confirmed a truth he didn't want to acknowledge. "He reads all the time. Indeed, we're always ordering books from back east for him."

"Well, that's a good thing, isn't it?"

"He should play more. A boy that age should want to roughhouse, but Jacob doesn't. I fear it's because he's seen more than his share of tragedy, and knows how fragile life can be." Jeremiah glanced over at her, but quickly, soon returning his attention to the rutted street ahead of him. "I don't know how much you've heard of that, Miss Prewitt."

Of course Danica knew the whole sordid story, of Nizhoni's curse and the two ill-fated marriages that followed—not to mention the wife who had died on the journey out to Arizona Territory—but she had to pretend that her knowledge only extended to what she might have heard in passing during her short time here in Flagstaff. "I know that his mother passed away when he was only a baby," she said, her tone cautious.

A brief gust of wind caught at Jeremiah's coat tails again. In the fading light, he seemed even taller and blacker than before, like some grim figure of impending doom. Maybe he was, but Danica knew the only doom he could call his was the curse that Nizhoni had brought down upon him.

"And my two wives after that," he said then. "It has been…difficult. My sister Emma takes special care with him, but even so, an aunt can't replace a mother. And of course he sees how it is with his cousins, how they all have one another, and he has only me."

"I'm so sorry," Danica managed. What else could she say, after all? Nizhoni had been raving with a deadly fever when she brought down her curse on the Wilcox men. She had to have been out of her mind, for otherwise she would have realized that the curse would doom her son to a motherless existence, would sentence all the men of that line to a world where they would be forced to raise their children alone.

More than anything, she wished she could tell Jeremiah that it would all be made right one day. A day far in the future, true, but at least the day would come when no Wilcox *primus* had to mourn the loss of a young wife, when the head of the Wilcox clan could have more than one child. The image flashed into her mind of the picture on Angela and Connor's mantel, the two of them happy and in love, their arms around their beautiful children. Connor was this man's great-great-great-great-grandson, and Danica had to believe that Jeremiah would be proud of him, proud of what he and Angela had done to bury the past and bring a better future to both the northern Arizona witch clans.

But she couldn't tell Jeremiah any of that, because such knowledge might cause him to make different decisions from the ones he'd already made, and any change in the past could alter Danica's future beyond all recognition. She didn't dare risk that, because she could be risking her very existence.

His shoulders lifted slightly. In that gesture, she could see the weariness of a man who'd come to the realization that he was doomed to live his life alone, and her heart ached for him, even though she knew she was powerless to do anything to change his fate.

Then he said, his tone altered, "It's fortuitous that we met today, though. My sister Emma was scolding me this morning, saying that I've been remiss in not inviting you to dinner with the family. As trustee, I should have shown you more hospitality."

Danica knew she couldn't refuse. But at least he had said "with the family." It didn't sound as if he was inviting her over to have dinner with him alone.

"That's very gracious of you, Mr. Wilcox," she replied. "I do appreciate the gesture."

"Then come to Emma's house tomorrow evening. Jacob and I generally take our meals there, so we don't feel quite so alone in our own home."

She could imagine them sitting at a long, polished table with only two place settings. Yes, that would be horribly lonely. Surrounding himself with the noise and chatter of his sister's family might do a good deal to decrease Jeremiah's feeling of isolation.

Until he and his son returned to their own empty house, at least.

But she couldn't let herself think about that, because otherwise the odd tightness in her throat would only get worse. "That sounds lovely, Mr. Wilcox. What time?"

"We sit down to dinner at six thirty, so a little before that. Ten Leroux Street."

"I look forward to it."

By then they were approaching the little white fence that surrounded Mrs. Wilson's boarding house. Jeremiah stopped at the gate, then tipped his hat to Danica again. "Have a very good evening, Miss Prewitt. I know my sister will be pleased to hear that you're coming to visit. And I will see you then."

He moved off, heading toward Leroux Street and the family that awaited him. Jacob must already be at Emma's, perhaps writing his composition on the Battle of Bunker Hill while his father was off finishing up his business at Brannen's general store. For some reason, that mental image made Danica even sadder. She could imagine the little boy sitting on a chair in a corner, writing away on a lap desk while his cousins laughed and joked and played around him.

Then she shook her head and told herself that she needed to get a grip. Yes, it was all very tragic, but she couldn't do anything to change the situation. At least Jacob had a loving extended family, an aunt who clearly was concerned about him and did her best to be there for him. It wasn't the same as having a mother, but it was definitely better than nothing.

Anyway, she needed to focus. Because tomorrow she'd be sitting down with the whole clan, or at least a big chunk of it, and she needed to mentally prepare herself for that. One verbal slip, and this could all be over.

And what she'd do then, she had no idea.

CHAPTER THIRTEEN

THE NEXT DAY, DANICA DIDN'T LINGER IN HER CLASSROOM after school. She gave the floors a desultory once-over with the broom, then gathered up her things and headed home so she could change for dinner. Not into the teal-blue silk gown—it was far too dressy for such an occasion, and would send the wrong message—but her wine-colored wool, the one she wore to church.

At least Mrs. Wilson hadn't seemed too surprised by the Wilcoxes' invitation. "Oh, yes, they had Mrs. Marshall and her boys over to dinner when she was first hired at the school, so it's only fitting that they would extend the same courtesy to you," she'd said. "I'll just make up something small and light tomorrow, since it'll only be Clara and me." The landlady smiled slightly. "Well, unless she tries to invite that young man of hers over. He came to sit with her in the parlor this evening, you know. You just missed him, as he left a few minutes before you came home."

"I wondered, when I saw them together at the dance—"

"Oh, yes," Mrs. Wilson said briskly. "Elias Hansen is a fine enough young man, and just got a promotion at the sawmill. Clara could do much worse. If they're not married by Christmas, I shall be very much surprised."

She'd bustled off then, claiming she needed to check on the potatoes. Danica reflected that Clara's good fortune could be good fortune for her as well; if Clara was occupied with this Elias person, then she probably wouldn't have much energy left over for snooping. She certainly hadn't batted an eye that night at supper when Mrs. Wilson informed her that Danica would be going to the Wilcoxes' for dinner the next evening. Or maybe Clara was still irritated with Danica, and so didn't wish to reveal her own curiosity about that unusual event.

When Danica descended the stairs at a little before six o'clock, she did hear the low rumble of a masculine voice coming from the parlor. Elias again, apparently. So much for Mrs. Wilson's strictures about no male visitors after five. Possibly she'd made an exception, considering that Clara didn't even get off from work at the store until five thirty.

It really didn't matter one way or another. Danica did catch a glimpse of the two lovebirds as she headed out the door, but she only smiled. Not that she thought they'd even noticed her; they weren't kissing, but they were sitting pretty close to each other on the sofa.

Go for it, you crazy kids, she thought as she shut the front door. Then her smile abruptly faded. She could do with a kiss of her own right about now. Three days had gone by since Robert last kissed her, and she ached to see him again. Well, he'd be back tomorrow, and maybe they could do something about making up for lost time. Exactly what, she wasn't sure. Would Mrs. Wilson buy the excuse of taking a walk in the autumn woods? Possibly. But that sounded like the best plan. Go for a walk, meet at a predetermined place, and melt into his embrace as the aspens shimmered like liquid gold around them.

The mental image sent a tremor through Danica. She still wasn't quite used to her physical reaction to Robert. After Matías, she'd worried deep down that she'd never want a man to touch her again, that she'd shy away from even an attempt at intimacy, but she certainly was eager enough to be in Robert's arms. Her mother had been right when she'd told Danica that all you needed was the right person. Those with witch-blood did have a tendency to get married young, since many of them could sense their compatibility with the person who was exactly right for them, even on the occasions when that person happened to be a civilian. Danica hadn't felt it yet, but she also hadn't been too worried about the situation; after all, she was only twenty-two. But this thing with Robert....

Now she knew exactly what that sort of connection felt like.

But she also knew she needed to push thoughts of him aside for the rest of the evening. None of the family lore had ever mentioned the original Wilcox brothers having any kind of mind-reading abilities, but better safe than sorry. Her personal life was her personal life, and it shouldn't be any of their business who she was seeing after she was done with her duties at the school. However, Robert's very business here meant he'd be in the Wilcoxes' cross hairs if even a hint of it got out to them, and so it was better to leave him aside for now, even if doing so gave her a mental pang.

The night was dark, with no moon. Even so, enough of the houses had kerosene lamps on their front porches that she could see her way. Danica wondered when the streetlights had been installed. Probably not for another decade or so. This part of town wasn't quite populated enough yet to justify the expense.

At least the Wilcox compound—for lack of a better word—was well lit. All five of the houses had lights shining from what seemed to be every window. And they were fine-looking buildings, too, newly constructed and neat, each two stories high. They were exactly the sorts of homes that people paid top dollar for these days, wanting to keep as much of the "old Flagstaff" alive as possible. However, her own family hadn't lived on this street for decades and decades. Danica knew that large parts of Flagstaff had burned down and been reconstructed. It was possible that the Wilcox houses had been casualties as well, and they'd gone on to build even bigger and better homes in other parts of town as their fortunes continued to rise.

Number 10, Emma's house, was the one in the middle. Had she chosen that spot, as the only woman in her generation, or was it her brothers' subtle way of making sure she was protected? No, that was probably a silly idea. Aaron Garnett, Emma's husband, looked fully capable of taking care of his wife and family.

And you'd have to be tough, just to marry someone with four brothers…especially when those brothers happened to be the Wilcox clan.

Repressing a smile, Danica let herself in the garden gate and then climbed the front steps. The front door had been painted dark red, and the reflection of the kerosene lamp mounted on the wall next to it seemed to dance in front of her eyes.

If she waited, she knew she'd only lose her nerve. So she reached up and tapped the brass knocker twice, but not too smartly. She didn't want to sound as if she was too eager.

A young woman Danica had never seen before opened the door. Since she had a neat white cap on her head and an apron over her calico dress, Danica assumed she must be the housemaid or something.

"Yes, miss?" the maid asked, her Irish accent clear even in those two syllables.

"I'm Miss Prewitt. Mrs. Garnett is expecting me for dinner."

"Oh, of course, miss. This way."

She stepped aside so Danica could enter. This was definitely a step up from the cabin the Wilcoxes had first shared when they came to Flagstaff. The floor underfoot was gleaming oak, overlaid with Persian carpets, and the walls were covered in fancy striped wallpaper in green and gold. A low table with a Boston fern in a Chinese pot sat up against the wall facing the door.

As the maid led Danica farther into the house, she saw that the decor was much the same. Dark and ornate, but tasteful, not like the explosion of chintz in Mrs. Wilson's beloved parlor.

Voice came down the hallway, both male and female, and a moment later Danica was ushered into the dining room, where the Wilcox family seemed to be assembled, except for Emma herself. Here was a long dining table, much like the one she'd imagined Jeremiah and his son sitting at, but this one had places set for ten.

The husbands and wives...and Jeremiah Wilcox and me.

That seemed a little too neat, but she didn't have time to think about the setup any longer, because the maid curtseyed and said, "Miss Prewitt," then headed back out to the hallway.

Jeremiah came forward at once and greeted her, then commenced with the introductions. Danica had seen all of them at church and at the dance, but had only been formally introduced to Aaron and Emma. Now she met Samuel and his wife Grace, Edmund and Lida, and Nathan and Jennie. That seemed like quite enough to keep track of, but even so, Danica couldn't help noting that none of the children seemed to be present.

"I don't see any of my students here," she said.

Grace and Lida exchanged a smile. Grace was the one Danica had noted before, the lone blonde in this family of dark, handsome people. She smiled now, saying, "Oh, Miss Prewitt, you see quite enough of them in the daytime, I should think. No, they are all at their respective homes with their nannies, so we can all converse like adults. Besides, there certainly wouldn't have been room at the dining room table for all of them!"

No, there wouldn't. It was a very long dining room table, but even so, Danica didn't think it could accommodate much more than a dozen people.

The idea that the Wilcoxes had servants did surprise her a little, though. It was hard enough to keep civilians from finding out that witches were real without having them live with you day in and day out.

There didn't seem to be a delicate way to ask how they managed it, so she decided to put her questions aside for now. "That's true," she replied instead. "That would have to be a very long dining room table!"

Several of the men chuckled, and Jeremiah said, "I believe we're just about ready to sit down, Miss Prewitt. If you would allow me?"

He guided her to a spot directly to the right of the place setting at the head of the table. Seeing it, Danica felt her heart sink a bit. So she would have to sit next to him all through dinner? For some reason, she'd thought she would be buried safely amongst the brothers and sisters, but it seemed they were all now sitting next to their spouses, carefully alternating the men with the women, although the place to Jeremiah's left remained empty.

Danica soon saw why. Almost as soon as everyone had sat down—the men politely pulling out the chairs for their wives, while Jeremiah did the same for her—Emma Garnett appeared, smoothing the overskirt of her dress.

"The first course is ready," she announced.

Course? Danica thought. *How many are there?* The food she'd been served at Mrs. Wilson's boarding house was surprisingly good, but fairly simple. Certainly her landlady didn't bother with any nonsense about "courses."

But it seemed the Wilcoxes took their reputation as one of the leading families in town seriously. As Aaron Garnett was holding out her chair so his wife could sit down, the little Irish maid who had let Danica into the house now entered the dining room, a large tureen of soup in her hands. She set it down in the center of the table, and then one by one, the assembled diners passed their bowls to Edmund, who was seated closest to it, so he could fill the bowls with what looked like some sort of creamy concoction.

All right, so it wasn't exactly a *Downton Abbey* sort of setup where everyone had a footman standing behind them, ready to take care of their every whim, but the formality of the arrangements was still more than Danica had bargained for. At least she didn't fumble too badly when passing her bowl, nor when having it returned to her.

To her surprise, everyone fell silent for a moment so Jeremiah could murmur a brief blessing.

"Dear Lord, thank you for your bounty, and for what we are about to receive. Amen."

All the Wilcoxes murmured "amen" in unison, and Danica hastily did the same. So were they actually religious, or was the habit of trying to fit in so deeply ingrained that they would follow the customs in their own homes, even when no one else was looking?

That was another question she didn't dare ask.

They all ate in silence for a moment or two. The soup was very good; some kind of potato recipe, although it couldn't be vichyssoise, since it was hot. Then Samuel said, a glint in his black eyes, "And how are you enjoying Flagstaff so far, Miss Prewitt?"

"Very much," Danica replied, not sure why he would be wearing that odd expression. "The scenery is very beautiful."

"Quite different from St. Louis, I would imagine," Edmund put in.

"Yes, quite different," she agreed. "But I find that change can be broadening to the mind. Don't you?"

"I think all of us Wilcoxes feel that way," Jeremiah said. The grim expression he'd worn the day before was quite gone now. In contrast, a small smile played around the corners of his mouth. "Or else we would have stayed back in New England."

"Oh, is that where you're from?" Might as well play the innocent.

"Yes, Connecticut."

"Then this must have been a very big change for you. Why the move out west, may I ask?"

She held her breath, wondering if she might have gone too far with that question. Still, she was curious to know how he would answer.

The clink of his spoon as he set it down in his soup bowl seemed unnaturally loud. He paused, then said, "It was made known to us that it might be better if we went in search of a change in scenery. And so we did."

"Oh," she said, not sure how to reply to that statement. What would the real Miss Prewitt have done? Probably not have been here in the first place, but that was a problem for another day.

"I fear my brother has made you uncomfortable," Emma remarked, sending Jeremiah a sideways look from under her long lashes. "He is not always the most diplomatic of men. But truly, it became... unpleasant...for us to remain in Connecticut. At the time, the papers were carrying stories of the expeditions that had come out here to Arizona Territory, and we thought we should see it for ourselves, although I'll confess that our original plan was to carry on and go all the way to California."

"What made you stay?"

Emma's dark eyes flicked upward, although Danica couldn't quite tell what she might be looking at. The other woman smiled, then said, "When we arrived here, we didn't think any other place could be more beautiful. So why bother to go any further?"

A warmth in her tone told Danica how much Emma truly did love this place. Who could argue with that? Danica had lived in Flagstaff her entire life, but even so, every time she was coming home—say, from visiting Caitlin in the southern part of the state—her heart would lift again when she caught sight of the San Francisco Peaks rising above the town, and saw the miles of pine forest that stretched away on every side.

Danica smiled back at her, as Samuel said, "Besides, the land is good. Ranching, lumber—we knew we could make our own fortune out here."

It was on the tip of her tongue to say that much was obvious, judging by the fine houses they'd recently built, but she decided such a remark would probably be too personal, or at the very least considered crass. She might not have absorbed every nuance of Victorian society—far from it—but talking about money was never in good taste.

"Yes, Flagstaff has been very good to us," Nathan added. He seemed to be the quietest of the brothers, and Danica thought probably the youngest, too. He didn't appear to be that much older than she was, even if he did already have a wife and several children.

"And I hope our brood isn't plaguing you too much," Aaron Garnett said. "I know they can be a little overwhelming."

"Oh, not at all," Danica replied immediately. "They're all very good children. Besides," she added, "it's not as if I have to teach all of them. Mrs. Marshall has her share as well."

That comment elicited a chuckle from the group, as she'd hoped it would. Even Jeremiah smiled as he picked up his spoon and finished off the last bit of soup in his bowl.

"Still," Samuel said, "I'm curious as to what brought you to Flagstaff, Miss Prewitt. Surely there were opportunities for you closer to home. After all, our kind rarely travels too far afield unless compelled to do so."

"Samuel," his wife said, sounding exasperated, "I am sure that is Miss Prewitt's business, and none of ours."

Danica had been thinking more or less the same thing. Clearly, Jeremiah had not passed along any of her confidences, which made her much more inclined to think kindly of him. At the same time, she didn't see any real reason not to let the whole family know of her reason for being here.

Well, her manufactured reason, anyway. She couldn't tell them the actual truth.

"No, that's quite all right, Mrs. Wilcox. I'm sure there's been a good deal of conjecture on the subject. My family wished me to make a marriage I didn't at all want, and so when I saw the position here advertised in the papers, I applied. Truthfully, I did not think they would accept me, as I did not have any true experience, although I did get my teaching certificate back in Missouri. But the position was offered me, and I made my escape."

She fell silent then, trying to gauge their response to her revelation. The women all looked more or less sympathetic, Emma especially so. Her husband Aaron only nodded, while Edmund and Nathan appeared vaguely embarrassed, as if they were wishing that their brother had not pressed the issue. As for Samuel, his eyebrows went up, and for the briefest instant his gaze flicked from her to Jeremiah, then away.

Danica really didn't want to think what that was all about, although she was beginning to have her suspicions. She reached for her glass of wine, which she hadn't touched up until that point. As she sipped the claret, she tried to get a quick read on the other people seated around the table. Aaron Garnett looked neutral enough, his wife troubled, but again, there it was—just that quick flicker from Jeremiah to Danica and back again from the other two brothers, Edmund and Nathan.

The exchange only confirmed her fears. Yes, this was a social call, a dinner that Emma had thought overdue, but to the other Wilcox brothers, it was more than that. They'd wanted Danica—Eliza, that is—to come here so they could take her measure for themselves. Nizhoni had died raving, and Jeremiah's two wives after her hadn't fared much better, but they weren't ready to give up yet. They wanted their brother and *primus* to have a wife, and who better than a young unattached witch who had more or less been dropped into their laps?

Danica wanted to believe she was imagining things, that her mind was manufacturing undercurrents here that simply didn't exist. Unfortunately, her instincts were telling her differently.

At that moment, the maid reappeared to remove the soup tureen, then came back a minute later to set down a platter heaped with roast chicken, already carved for easy serving.

"Thank you, Bridget," Emma said, and the girl bobbed her head before heading back into the kitchen. She returned with a bowl of string beans and another of mashed potatoes, setting them down next to the platter of chicken.

After seeing the glances the brothers had exchanged, Danica thought she'd completely lost her appetite, but she knew she had to see this evening through to the end and then make her escape as best she could. She accepted a portion of chicken breast and potatoes and vegetables, then smiled her thanks to Bridget, who gave her a hesitant smile in return before going on to dish up everyone else's meal.

Apparently realizing that no one had actually commented on Danica's confession, Lida said, "I think that was very brave of you, Miss Prewitt, to come to a place you knew nothing of. But didn't anyone from your family attempt to fetch you back?"

"Not that I know of," Danica replied. "Although I suppose I made it rather difficult for them, as I did not say precisely where I was going."

"And your clan has no tracker?" Samuel asked.

Again there seemed to be an unwelcome undercurrent to his question, and Danica forced herself not to bristle. "Not as such, no. We have several people who are quite good at finding lost objects, and my cousin Thomas has something of a reputation as a dowser, but no one who can locate missing people."

This reply elicited some nodding, but no one contradicted her. How could they, really? The Wilcoxes might have passed through St. Louis on their way here to Arizona—her knowledge of which railways went where was foggy at best—but even if they had, they wouldn't have lingered. Witch clans were never all that happy about members of other clans passing through their territory, but as long as they minded their own business and didn't stay longer than strictly necessary, no one tended to make too much of a fuss about it.

Well, except when it came to the Wilcoxes. Lord knows the other two Arizona clans had been a lot stricter about the whole thing until very recently, even if Maya de la Paz had allowed Connor Wilcox to get his master's degree down in the Phoenix area. However, Danica doubted the Landons back in 1877 Missouri could have known much about the family of witches that passed through their territory before continuing west, if that was even the route her ancestors had taken.

Anyway, the Wilcoxes couldn't have known anything about the talents of the Landon clan, and that was why Danica didn't feel too bad about telling lies left and right. Anything to keep them from guessing the truth.

And thank God none of the Wilcoxes are like that cousin of Alex's, the private detective who can tell if someone's lying or not. Then I'd really be up a creek.

"Well," Emma said briskly. "It's unfortunate that you found yourself in such a situation, but lucky for the Flagstaff school. I know my nieces are quite taken with you."

"Oh," Danica replied, feeling blood rush to her cheeks, and wondering if the others would notice in the flickering gaslight, "I'm sure I make my mistakes. But it's always good when children look forward to going to school."

With some surprise, she realized that they mostly did. Oh, they had their squirmy moments, but she couldn't really blame them for that. At least it was considered normal to let them out for a short recess several times a day so they could run around the schoolyard and chase each other and scream. Danica feared that some of these screaming games might involve playing at Indians, but since no one had actually been scalped, she'd decided it was probably better to not even try lecturing a bunch of seven- and eight-year-olds on political correctness.

"No mistakes that we've heard of," Samuel said with a false heartiness that Danica didn't believe one bit. "And since my Addie is known for telling tales out of school, believe me—we would have heard."

That was probably true. Addie—short for Adeline—Wilcox was something of a tattler. Right then, Danica found herself very grateful that Jeremiah's youngest brother Edmund was her great-great-etc.-grandfather, and not the slimy Samuel. There was something about him that made the back of her neck crawl, although his other children besides Addie didn't seem to exhibit any of his less-than-attractive qualities.

Somehow Danica managed to essay a smile in response, and, seeming to notice that she appeared uncomfortable, Emma steered the conversation onto safer topics, such as the news that a man named Conroy had bought the parcel at the corner of Aspen and Humphreys Street and planned to build a hotel there. This led into a lively discussion on how much the brothers thought the price of lumber might rise, what with everyone building, building, building, and before Danica knew it, Bridget was bringing them all apple pie, and the meal was winding toward its conclusion.

What was supposed to happen next, Danica didn't know for sure. In most of the movies she'd seen, this would be the time when the "menfolk" retired to some other room to drink brandy and smoke cigars, but this wasn't exactly London, or even New York or Boston.

As Bridget came in to clear away the empty dessert plates, Jeremiah said quietly to Danica, "Let me walk you home."

She wanted to demur. But there was no way he'd let her go home in the dark by herself. Flagstaff had calmed down a good bit from the crazy days before the rail came through, but she'd been startled more than once by hearing shots fired in the night, mostly coming from the saloons over on Humphreys Street. As far as she knew, no one had been killed outright, and the gunshots were merely the result of scuffles between men who'd had too much whiskey. Even so, Danica figured the chances of her being allowed to leave alone were roughly the same as her announcing to everyone present that she was their future great-great-etc.-grandniece.

So she rose from the table and thanked Emma for the wonderful meal, and told everyone how it had been lovely to meet them. With the notable exception of Samuel, it actually had. She certainly couldn't see anything in the Wilcox clan of the devils the New England witches seemed to think they were.

She went out to the foyer, where her cloak waited for her on the coat tree in the hallway. Of course Jeremiah already wore his long frock coat, but he retrieved a heavy overcoat as well and drew that on as Danica was fastening her cloak's clasp at her throat. She couldn't really blame him for dressing warmly; the temperature outside was probably already in the low forties.

Jeremiah opened the front door for her, and she stepped out onto the porch, then waited while he closed the door behind him. This time, he did offer her his arm, and because she knew she couldn't refuse it, she looped her own arm around his and allowed him to guide her down the porch steps.

Although she still couldn't help feeling awkward, Danica had to admit that it was probably a good thing he was guiding her along. The night had remained stubbornly black as pitch, with no moon. And now it seemed that some clouds must have moved in, because the stars weren't visible, either. The night felt as if it was crowding close, pushing in on the two of them as they made their way along the dark street.

"It was very kind of your sister Emma to invite me for dinner," Danica ventured then, since the quiet between the two of them practically begged to be filled. "Please thank her again for me."

"I will. I hope you didn't find all of us together too overwhelming."

"Not at all." She chuckled, adding, "If all the children had been present as well, then yes, that might have been a bit overpowering."

"Oh, no, we would never subject you to that, not when you must put up with them every day at school."

His tone was warm...a little too warm. Danica risked a quick glance up at Jeremiah, but it seemed his own gaze was fixed on the street ahead of them, eyes intent on any obstacles or ruts that might cause her to stumble. Besides, it was far too dark to really see anything of his expression.

"I wouldn't call it 'putting up,'" she said lightly. "But I will agree that it was a nice respite." She hesitated then, wondering if she could ask the question that had come to her during dinner. After all, they were entirely alone. Off in the distance, she could hear faint ghostly laughter and the rumble of men's voices coming from the saloons on Humphreys Street. Here, though, they had no one to overhear what they were saying. "Is it difficult, to have"—she broke off then, because she'd almost said "civilians," and as far as she could tell, that wasn't a term used by the witches of the nineteenth century to describe their non-magical counterparts—"to have people who aren't witches working in your household?"

"Not as difficult as you might think." This time he did look down at her, expression speculative. "Didn't you have servants back in St. Louis? Forgive me, but your dress and your manners seem to indicate that yours must be a fairly prosperous clan."

Oops. She'd really put her foot in it there. At the same time, she couldn't help but be perversely pleased that he'd praised her manners. She'd been unable to let go of the worry that she might do or say something so out of line that someone would surely call her on it. But if Jeremiah Wilcox hadn't noticed anything….

"Um—we did, but it did get to be so tiring trying to keep our natures a secret that sometimes I wondered if it might not be better to take on those tasks ourselves."

He laughed, but quietly, not much more than a chuckle. "I suppose I can see how you might think that. But we do not have so many—a maid and a nanny and a cook for each household, and no one else, and only the nannies live in. And of course the nannies will not be with us forever, but only until the youngest of the children reach ten or eleven."

Some of them would be there all too soon. In the next year or so, the oldest Wilcox children would start to come into their own powers, and Danica imagined that would be quite the party, having to conceal those powers from the young women who cooked and swept and kept an eye on the nursery. But maybe their duties were more focused on the younger children, and so wouldn't be around the older kids, the ones just beginning to test their talents.

"At any rate," Jeremiah continued, "we're all used to concealing our abilities from the rest of the world, aren't we? It's best the children learn that discipline early on, so that it's second nature to them when they're out of the classroom."

His remark made a good deal of sense. Danica had never really thought about it that way. And it would have been difficult for the Wilcox wives to manage all those children and keep their households running smoothly. It wasn't as if they had the modern world's labor-saving devices like vacuum cleaners and washing machines. Even with all those conveniences, Danica's mother had a cleaning service come in every week to do the heavy lifting, and Danica had never really thought about whether or not Janine or Marcy, their two regular house cleaners, ever noticed anything out of the ordinary. That wasn't the same as having someone live with you day in and day out, however.

"I can see that, although I never had a nanny. It was just my sister and me."

"Does she know where you've gone?"

No, Danica thought then. *She has absolutely no idea that her sister is off someplace a hundred and thirty years ago....*

"I wanted to tell her, but I decided not to," she said. "I hope—that is, I do plan to write to her when I can, so she knows that I'm well. But I thought it safer to wait a bit."

By that point they had reached the white picket fence that surrounded Mrs. Wilson's property. Jeremiah paused there, looking down at Danica as he quietly slipped his arm from hers.

"Do you really have anything to fear from this cousin of yours? From the way you spoke of him earlier, I gathered the impression that he would not come after you."

For some reason, she found herself flushing. However, the light from the oil lamp near the front door was probably dim enough that Jeremiah wouldn't be able to tell that she had blushed.

"Not my cousin Alfred," she said hastily. "But I fear my father would still attempt to fetch me back, if he knew where I was, and that wouldn't do. Even if Alfred would not want such an independent-minded wife, there are others in the clan who might not be quite so choosy."

"I see." Another hesitation, one so long that she wondered if Jeremiah intended to say anything else at all. Then he went on, "Perhaps it is not my place to say this, Miss Prewitt, but if you should ever find yourself in need of additional protection, you have only to say the word."

He took her gloved hand then, raising it so swiftly to his lips that she didn't even have time to react. Then he turned and hurried back the way he came, as if he didn't want to wait and see what her reaction to that unexpected gesture might be.

All Danica could do was stare after him, heart racing. She'd hoped he would ignore the odd attraction he felt for her, would tell himself that he didn't dare risk having another young woman fall prey to Nizhoni's curse.

Unfortunately, that didn't seem to be the case. And Danica had absolutely no idea what to do about it.

CHAPTER FOURTEEN

ON FRIDAY MORNING, DANICA HAD TWO THINGS TO BE grateful for. First, that she had school to occupy her, so she couldn't spend too much time brooding about the kiss Jeremiah had bestowed on the back of her hand and what the hell she was supposed to do about it; and second, that Robert would be coming back today. He hadn't been very specific about when, but she supposed that made sense. It was sort of hard to file a flight plan when you were out riding the range.

Still, there had been the way he'd left her the note in her desk drawer. She wasn't quite sure how he'd managed that particular feat, except that door locks didn't generally mean much to witches and warlocks. But maybe he planned to contact her again that way, and so she might as well leave him a note, just in case.

While the children were out shrieking around the schoolyard during the lunchtime recess, Danica took a piece of paper and her fountain pen, and quickly scratched out a note.

Tomorrow I will tell Mrs. Wilson that I plan to take a walk in the aspen groves up on Thorpe Hill. Meet me there at one o'clock if you're able. Eliza.

She decided it was better to leave his name off the note. Robert would know it was meant for him if he found it, and if anyone else should come across it, better that no one would be able to tell for whom it had actually been intended.

The rest of the afternoon, she found herself jumpy, gaze jerking toward the window every time she heard horses pass by on the street. That led her to make a colossal mistake in the long division problem she'd been demonstrating on the board, and she had to hastily erase it and start over while her students shared a laugh at her expense.

Stop acting like a complete idiot, she scolded herself. *Even if Robert does happen to come riding by, he certainly won't stop and interrupt you while you're teaching. You need to be patient.*

The problem was, after that unexpected and unwelcome display from Jeremiah the night before, it wasn't all that easy to quell her anxieties. Not that she planned to tell Robert anything about Jeremiah's advance, small as it had been. She sort of doubted he would take it very well, and the last thing she wanted was to provoke him into the kind of impetuous action they might all end up regretting.

No, right then she'd settle for merely having him hold her so she could breathe him in after missing him for most of this week. Funny how she could crave his presence so badly when she'd only spent a few hours around him. None of that seemed to matter, though. She only knew that she wanted him, and soon.

Somehow she managed to survive the rest of the day, then wished all the children a good weekend. As he passed, Jacob Wilcox looked up at her with dark eyes far too wise for such a young face, and Danica had to keep herself from glancing away. Of course his father wouldn't have said anything to him about what had happened after he walked the schoolteacher home the night before, but still, it was unnerving, as if Jacob somehow had the ability to see deep into her soul.

That was ridiculous, though; Jacob was far too young to have started developing any of his witch talents, even if he did tend to be precocious in other ways. All the same, Danica couldn't help experiencing a feeling of relief after the boy went on through the doorway and joined the rest of his cousins for the walk home from school.

She picked up the broom and dutifully swept the classroom, then lowered all the blinds and made sure the wood-burning stove had been well tamped down. The weather was growing increasingly chilly, and she'd started the stove going earlier that week.

Mrs. Marshall walked her part of the way home, her boys running ahead. "How was your week?"

"Just fine," Danica replied. She really didn't feel like talking, but she knew she had to at least be polite. "I think Oliver Wilcox has finally mastered his five times tables. But then, I suppose I'll have to see how much he remembers come Monday morning."

The other woman smiled and shook her head, although her expression grew sober soon enough. "I heard you had dinner at Emma Garnett's house last night."

Funny how everyone spoke of Emma, not Aaron. Danica couldn't exactly say that the one Wilcox sister's husband was a nonentity—he seemed like a nice enough man—but as usual, the Wilcoxes took first place in most people's conversation. "Yes," Danica said, her tone casual. "Didn't you dine with them when you first arrived?"

"Yes," Mrs. Marshall replied, "and several times after that. They've always been very gracious about it, invited my boys to come as well. But I don't think it's quite the same situation."

Danica could only hope that her expression was one of innocence, and incomprehension. "Why not?"

"Well, Miss Prewitt—" Mrs. Marshall broke off there and shook her head. The pheasant feathers that topped her brown velvet hat danced with the movement, although her expression was serious enough. "I don't wish to presume, but since you are here quite alone, without family…." Her words died away, and she glanced around, but her boys were clearly far enough ahead of the two women that there wouldn't be any chance of them overhearing what was said. "I can't say anything against Mr. Wilcox, because he's always done well by the community here, and he takes such a great interest in the school."

Of course he does, Danica thought. *His nieces and nephews make up more than half the student population.* But she only nodded, hoping that would be enough to spur Mrs. Marshall on.

Then again, she had a good idea as to what the schoolmistress intended to say.

"But he's also suffered tragedies, and after burying four wives…." Again she paused. "All I am saying is that you should be careful."

"I didn't come out here to get a husband, Mrs. Marshall," Danica said baldly.

"No, of course not! I did not mean to imply such a thing. But I am sure that is what Miss Baker thought, and Miss Terrell."

"Were those his other wives?" Maybe asking the question was bordering on gossip, but right then, Danica didn't much care. She knew that Jeremiah had married twice more after he buried Nizhoni, which was sometime after he'd lost his first wife on the journey out here, but she knew nothing of the women's names, or how they had come to be Jeremiah's wives.

"Yes," Mrs. Marshall replied. "Miss Baker was from Brigham City—what they're calling Winslow now. I don't know how she met Mr. Wilcox, precisely, for that was before I came here to Flagstaff. I had the story from Mrs. Adams. She has no reason to love Jeremiah Wilcox."

Danica lifted an eyebrow at that statement. The dressmaker was certainly too old to have had any kind of fling with the *primus*.

"Oh, not like that, no," Mrs. Marshall said hastily. "Miss Terrell was her niece, who came out here from Kansas City to assist in her shop. Pretty thing, with the loveliest curly blonde hair. You can imagine she caught the eye of Mr. Wilcox soon enough, and they were married only a few months after she arrived in town. Millie—that is, Mrs. Adams—tried to warn her niece that Mr. Wilcox had already buried three wives, but she would have none of it. She laughed off her aunt's warnings and said she wasn't superstitious, and that she wanted to live in a fine house with servants and have a fine man at her side. And then she was gone within six months."

After delivering this sad little history, the schoolmistress plucked a handkerchief from her reticule and dabbed her nose with it before saying, "So you see why it might not be the wisest thing in the world to be encouraging Jeremiah Wilcox's attentions."

"I'm not encouraging his attentions, I assure you," Danica told her as she tried to tamp down her irritation at being the subject of such unwanted gossip. At the same time, she didn't want Mrs. Marshall to think she was annoyed with her. After all, the schoolmistress was, in her way, trying to protect someone newly come to town and not possessing all the facts of the matter. "I would hate for that to be the impression everyone is getting, because nothing could be further from the truth."

"Well, that is a relief."

By then they had reached the corner where they needed to part, as Danica's path lay one way and Mrs. Marshall's another. The boys were waiting there, looking impatient, so Danica said quickly, "Thank you for your concern, Mrs. Marshall. But it's really nothing you need to worry yourself about."

The schoolmistress nodded, her expression a study in relief. "Then you have a lovely weekend, Miss Prewitt. I expect we shall see you in church on Sunday."

She sailed off then, her sons following in her wake. Danica hesitated on the corner for a few seconds, watching them go. The boys' footsteps brought up little puffs of dust, since it hadn't rained for almost a week. A cart filled with freshly cut logs from somewhere on the mountainside passed them by, and farther up the street two ladies in shawls and hats crossed ahead of several men—ranchers by their clothing—who were riding along toward Humphreys Street and its saloons.

All in all, it was an ordinary enough scene, the kind that Danica had gotten used to during her tenure here in the past. But a shiver passed over her, one she didn't think she could entirely blame on the cold breeze blowing down from the San Francisco Peaks.

Had those other two wives of Jeremiah's seen their doom coming, or had it hit them from nowhere, like an icy hand rising from the grave?

The rest of the evening was prosaic enough, and quiet, since Elias had come to fetch Clara and take her out to dinner in the Hotel San Francisco's dining room.

"Just like being in New York!" Clara had exclaimed, eyes dancing. Apparently, she'd forgotten all about her quarrel with Danica, or at least had put it aside now that she had something far more interesting—namely, Elias Hansen—to occupy her thoughts.

Danica somehow doubted that the local hotel's dining room could compete with the Waldorf, but she didn't argue. It was good that Clara was going out on an actual date, even if it did make dinner at the boarding house that night a somewhat subdued affair.

"I thought I'd go walking up on Thorpe Hill tomorrow afternoon," Danica announced as Mrs. Wilson set down the plate of fried chicken she'd made for dinner.

The landlady gave her a curious look. "Whatever for?"

"Well, the aspens look like they're in full color right now. I thought I'd collect some leaves so we could mount them and study them in class on Monday."

"Study leaves?" Mrs. Wilson shook her head. "I'm not sure what the point is in studying something that we're all going to be raking out of our yards in the next week or so, but then, I don't pretend to know much about teaching."

I don't know much about it, either, Danica thought then. *But I'm still trying to pretend.*

She only shrugged, though, saying, "It never hurts to know a little more about the world around you," and Mrs. Wilson lifted her shoulders as well.

"That may be. Do be careful walking alone, though. I'm not saying you wouldn't be safe, but there are some rough types here, even though the town has gotten much better over the past year or so. Just keep an eye out, and don't stray too far."

Danica promised she would do all those things, and the conversation languished after that. She was glad to make her escape up to her room, where she tried to read the copy of *Ivanhoe* that Mrs. Marshall had lent her, but her thoughts kept wandering.

What in the world was Jeremiah thinking, anyway? No, he had no idea that he and Danica were related, but he had to know by this point that Nizhoni's curse seemed to be sticking. From what Mrs. Marshall had said, it sounded as if both Wife #3 and Wife #4 were civilians. Had he tried to circumvent the curse that way? Maybe now he was thinking he should try a witch again, since the experiments with the civilians hadn't worked out so well.

Well, it really didn't matter what his reasoning might be, since Danica sure as hell wasn't going to indulge him in it. She did pity him, since he really hadn't done anything to deserve Nizhoni's curse, but she couldn't help him. His salvation still lay far in the future.

With an almost physical effort, she turned her thoughts toward Robert. Would he even think to go back and look in her desk drawer? She'd put the note there in the hope that he would try to leave another message for her, then find the one she'd left for him. At least, that was her plan.

Maybe she should have left a letter for him at his hotel. No, that was a terrible idea. Doing so would have sent a clear signal that a connection did exist between them, and it was better for everyone involved if she and Robert kept this whole thing on the down-low, so to speak, for as long as possible.

Danica sighed then, placing her neglected book on the bedside table. Since she'd known she wouldn't be venturing out of her room after dinner, she was already in her nightgown, face washed and teeth brushed. She turned down the wick in the kerosene lamp next to her bed, then sent a brief prayer out into the universe.

She would see Robert tomorrow. She *would*.

Because this was supposed to be only a simple walk in the woods, Danica tried not to make too much of a fuss with her appearance. She did put on her new green wool gown, since Robert had never seen it, but it was a simple enough dress, with a plainly draped

bustle and a high-necked bodice whose only embel-
lishment was the velvet collar and row of velvet buttons down the front. Even so, she still dabbed on the
tiniest bit of the lip stain she'd brought with her, and
rewound the braid she wore on the back of her head
at least four times before she was satisfied with it.

If Mrs. Wilson noticed that Danica had taken
particular care with her appearance, she didn't show
any sign of it after her tenant descended the staircase to have her lunch of cold chicken and bread,
accompanied by some apple preserves. Afterward,
Danica said she was setting out and wouldn't be back
for a few hours. That should give her the rest of the
afternoon.

And if Robert didn't show up?

Well, this walk would be cut very short. But he
would appear. He had gotten the note. She just knew
it.

That was more wishful thinking than any kind
of clairvoyance; Danica knew she didn't possess
those sorts of skills, unlike her friend Caitlin. But as
she pinned on her hat and took one more look at her
reflection in the hallway mirror, she couldn't help
feeling a stir of excitement.

She did go out the back door, just because the
last thing she wanted in that moment was to have
the misfortune to bump into Jeremiah Wilcox. Not
that he'd taken to haunting her street—yet—but she

did seem to have picked up the habit of running into him when she really didn't want to.

The rear of Mrs. Wilson's property backed up to open land, with a trail that led away from the settlement and up toward Thorpe Hill. Danica set out in that direction, glad that her boots were more or less broken in by now, and that the heels weren't too high. She should be able to manage the path well enough, even if a pair of hiking boots would have been a hell of a lot more practical.

The clouds of the night before had mostly cleared away, although a few still ringed Humphreys Peak, making it look like the mountaintop had grown a gray beard sometime during the evening hours. Snow glimmered on those peaks now, although none had fallen in town, and a brisk wind blew from the northeast. Danica wondered if she'd made a mistake in only draping her shawl over her shoulders rather than bringing her cloak. But no, the climb would keep her warm enough. She'd be fine.

From up here on higher ground she could see more of the town, the way it was beginning to spread to the east, following the railroad tracks. Although it would burn down and be rebuilt before taking on its present-day shape, Danica was still able to make out the basic contours of the city she knew. Strange to think that the descendants of the people she'd met here could still be living there, more than a hundred years hence.

Then she had to turn her attention to the path, which was becoming increasingly rocky. At least there was only one stand of aspens on Thorpe Hill, making her destination easy enough to spot. Yes, there were also oaks and sycamores showing their autumn colors, but the aspens blazed brighter than any of them.

Danica didn't want to look at the sycamores. They only made her think of that rocky grave high above the old Wilcox cabin, the one where Robert had been buried.

But he hasn't been buried there yet, she thought fiercely. *And he won't be. I'll find some way to stop it, even if I have to hop a train tomorrow for Boston and never see my home again.*

That sounded very brave. She wondered if she would have the strength to follow through with that plan if matters were forced to such a pass.

Pushing the thought aside, she climbed the rest of the way to the aspen grove. Up here, all was quiet, the only sound the wind whispering through shimmering golden leaves. If the train came through, she'd probably be able to hear its whistle, and likewise for the one that sounded at the lumbermill at close of day, but she'd be long gone from here by then, one way or another.

At the center of the grove was an old ponderosa pine stump. Danica contemplated sitting down on it, since she really had no idea how long she'd have to wait. But that might stain her new dress, and it wasn't like she could take the thing to the dry cleaner's to repair the damage.

A crunch of leaves made her turn. A man was approaching along a different path than the one she'd taken, coming in from the north. His dark coat flapped in the breeze, and for one hideous second Danica thought that Jeremiah Wilcox had followed her up here, tracking her with one of his own incomprehensible talents. But then she caught sight of his blue eyes, smiling at her, and she realized it was only Robert. He'd probably taken a circuitous route so no one could guess at where he was headed.

But enough of logic. She ran toward him, forgetting propriety, forgetting that she was probably supposed to act like a good little Victorian woman and wait patiently for him to approach her. His blue eyes lit up as their gazes locked, and he quickened his pace, holding out his arms. She fell into them like someone coming home, rejoicing in the strength of his embrace, the way he held her against him, his mouth seeking hers at once.

So much for Victorian propriety.

The kiss seemed to last forever, the golden leaves shimmering around them like an echo of the warmth she felt rippling through her entire body. At last, though, Robert raised his mouth from hers, a smile lighting up his face.

"Am I to guess from this greeting that you missed me?"

"No, I was hoping you'd stay away a day or two longer," she replied with a grin.

"Ah, I couldn't do that. Not when I kept thinking of the sweetness of your kiss."

"So why didn't you come back sooner?"

His smile faded. "Sometimes business compels us to do things we'd rather not. But I did find a good piece of land—and was able to buy it out from under the Wilcox clan's noses."

That sounded like a terrible idea. "Why on earth would you do something like that? Are you *trying* to provoke them?"

"More or less."

Her expression must have registered her alarm, because he took her gloved hands in his, holding them tightly. When he spoke, his tone was gentle but urgent at the same time.

"My dear, it's necessary to provoke them. If they continually have everything going their own way, then they'll have no need to use their magic. And if they don't use it, then I don't have any way of gathering evidence against them."

"That sounds like entrapment." As the words left her mouth, Danica wondered if the Victorian concept of the idea was the same as it was in her own time. But she couldn't take back what she'd said. Not that she particularly wanted to. It was one thing to catch the Wilcoxes doing something underhanded of their own volition. However, setting up a situation so they'd be forced to react was an entirely different matter.

Robert's brows drew together, and his voice was considerably colder as he replied, "You might call it such. I was tasked with gathering as much knowledge as I could, and that might mean engaging in practices you find questionable."

Goddamn it. She really didn't want to argue, not after spending days apart. And if she got too vigorous in her defense of the Wilcox clan, Robert might start asking why she seemed so sympathetic to their cause.

"I'm sorry," she said then…although she wasn't. Not really. "I suppose I didn't quite understand. But what are you going to do with this land you bought? Surely you don't intend to stay here and become a rancher, do you?"

The smile returned, even as he shook his head. "No. That land was bought with my clan's money, and they'll decide in the end if they want to keep it—for it should be a good investment—or sell it off after a reasonable period of time has passed."

Meaning it might end up in Wilcox hands anyway at some point. "I suppose that makes sense. But really, Robert, what you're doing is dangerous. Yes, the Wilcoxes aren't able to sense that you're also a warlock, but that doesn't mean they won't retaliate if you get in their way."

Again she saw the image of that faint cross scratched on the sycamore tree, only a few miles from here, and she had to swallow past the sudden lump in her throat.

A frown touched his features. Out here, in the bright autumn sunlight, Danica noticed the beginnings of a thin line between his level brows.

Voice even, he said, "I know how to protect myself."

"Against all of them?" She still had no clear idea exactly what Jeremiah's talent was, but she knew he was powerful, probably one of the most powerful warlocks of his generation. And that didn't even take into account his brothers' various abilities, whatever they might be. Obviously, they'd been enough to create some spectacular shows back in Connecticut, and that was enough to frighten her now.

Robert didn't respond right away, confirming her suspicions that he would be hopelessly outmatched if he tried to engage all of them at once.

There was no real shame in that; she didn't know of anyone with those kinds of skills, although maybe her cousin Damon could have managed it when he was still alive. Or maybe not. After all, Damon was Jeremiah's direct descendant, and she didn't know for sure whether the powers he'd passed on had grown stronger down the generations or not.

Distress must have been clear in her face, because Robert bent and kissed her, but gently, as if trying to reassure her. "My dear, it will be all right. Some feathers will be ruffled. That's all."

She was far from convinced, but she nodded and even managed a smile. "You are quite the crusader, aren't you, Robert?"

To her disappointment, he didn't smile in return. "When the circumstances warrant it, yes." He hesitated for a moment, fingers tightening on hers. Then he said, "We know what it's like to be the objects of persecution. The Winfields—for that is the clan I'm associated with, as my father does not have witch-blood—have been in New England since the early seventeenth century. The Landons came later, and then to Maryland before finally moving on to Missouri, correct?"

Danica could only nod mutely. Her cousin Marie hadn't told her anything of her borrowed clan's history, only that they were the dominant witch family in Missouri. Of course Robert had no reason to deliberately attempt to mislead her, but Danica found herself praying that her silent agreement wouldn't send up a red flag.

Interesting that his father was a civilian, though. She wondered if the practice of marrying civilians was as common here in the 1880s as it was in her own present-day clan. Somehow she doubted it. And if Robert's mother was a Winfield, then that meant he had to be related to the Wilcoxes somehow, if only remotely. It seemed she couldn't get away from being involved with a distant relative.

"Well, then, your people wouldn't know what it was like to have ancestors of theirs burned at the stake," he went on, tone grim. "We know the price of discovery. The stakes—if you'll pardon the word—are simply too high."

"You really don't think anyone would burn witches at the stake in this day and age, do you?" Danica asked sharply, shocked into speech. All right, the need for secrecy had been hammered into her ever since she was a small child, but that was mainly so the witch clans wouldn't have reporters and reality TV personalities crawling up their butts with cameras and recorders.

"No," Robert said, although he had paused before answering, as if he had stop and think the matter over carefully first. "To be honest, I'm not sure what would happen. What I fear—what we *all* should fear—is how our lives would be changed for-ever if we were discovered. Perhaps not anything as immediately terrible as being put to death, but ostra-cized…kept separate…forever viewed with suspi-cion and fear. This is what we're all trying to avoid, Eliza, and why I have to know precisely which pow-ers the Wilcoxes do wield, and how much of a threat they might pose."

When he described the situation that way, Danica found it difficult to argue with him. She could say that the Wilcoxes were far more circumspect than that, and that they knew what was at risk here just as well as anyone else. But clearly they didn't, or they wouldn't have created such a stir back in Connecticut. That had been some time ago, though, and maybe Jeremiah had learned some restraint during the intervening years. He hadn't done any-thing since her arrival in town that would raise any eyebrows.

Well, except for possibly appearing a little too interested in Flagstaff's new teacher.

She swallowed. "I understand that, Robert—I do. But…." Should she tell him of her suspicions about Samuel? Something about Jeremiah's next-youngest brother just rubbed her the wrong way. That could have been a personal thing, though. Every once in a while she'd encounter someone she disliked from the beginning, and for whatever reason, Samuel

Wilcox seemed to have gotten himself admitted to that small but select group. Nathan and Edmund seemed unobjectionable enough, although Danica had the distinct feeling they'd fall in line with pretty much anything Jeremiah asked them to do.

And Jeremiah...it was probably better not to analyze her feelings about Jeremiah too closely.

"But you're worried," Robert said softly as she fought her own inner battles. "I understand that. Truthfully, I'm somewhat worried myself. My talents help to warn me when another warlock intends to use his powers against me, but that can only go so far. And, as you said, it is four against one. Five, if you count Aaron Garnett, and I suppose we must, since he acts with his brothers-in-law in everything."

"Then why on earth would your clan send you out here alone?" Danica asked, knowing desperation had begun to seep into her voice, even though she was doing her best to prevent it from doing so.

"Who else could they have sent? The Wilcoxes would have immediately sensed who and what any of my clan members are. As they did with you, Eliza, except that you are one woman on your own, and no one they could possibly see as a threat."

No, she thought then, *they see me as something very different. Although I have a feeling you wouldn't much like how they're seeing me at the moment.*

But that was a problem for another day. She'd have to hope that the men staying at the Hotel San Francisco weren't quite the gossips that the town's women had proved to be. With any luck, Robert wouldn't learn anything of Jeremiah's interest in her until they were safely away from here.

Wherever that might be. Or whenever.

"I suppose you're right," she said at length. Gently, she let go of one of his hands so she could reach up to touch his cheek, feel the slight roughness of the dark stubble along his jaw against the palm of her hand. In that moment, she wanted him so badly she was sure he must be able to sense the desire that seemed to flame its way along every vein.

Perhaps he did, because he pulled her to him with the hand he still held and lowered his mouth to hers, lips meeting, tongues touching. The need in Danica's body only intensified, almost cramping in its intensity.

The worst part was that she didn't know how she'd even be able to satisfy that need. She couldn't go to his hotel, and he certainly couldn't come to the boarding house. Unlike a couple of her friends, she'd never been the type to get a thrill out of having sex outdoors, but right then she thought maybe it wouldn't be so bad, if that was the only way she and Robert could get any kind of privacy. Of course, they'd have to do it soon, or it would be too cold even during the daytime for that sort of activity.

If he would even be amenable. Oh, he wanted her, that was easy enough to tell, but he was a man from a different era than hers, a gentleman. If they were intimate, he would think he had "ruined" her. Nothing could be further from the truth—especially since her implant would keep her from getting pregnant—but there was no way Danica could try to explain any of that without telling him who she was and where she'd come from.

All things considered, she should probably tell her raging hormones to be patient for a little while longer.

She didn't know how long the kiss lasted. There were no clocks out here, only the sun moving imperceptibly overhead, and the sound of the wind rustling in the aspens' yellow leaves. Finally, though, Robert lifted his mouth from hers, his breathing sounding ragged.

"You—" He stopped then, blue eyes seeking hers and holding them, as if he wanted to drown within her gaze. "I've never met anyone like you, Eliza."

Somehow Danica knew she needed to break the moment, or she'd be saying things she knew she shouldn't. It hurt somewhere deep within to keep the truth from him, but the time to reveal those particular truths wasn't now. Some instinct told her the moment wasn't right for that.

"You mean there was no one else?" she asked. "Not ever?" She had a hard time believing that of someone as strong and passionate and handsome as he was.

He shook his head, expression grim. "I told you that my clan despaired of me. Courtship, marriage—I knew it was expected, but there was never a woman who came into my life who made my heart lift the way it does when I look at you. Now I know why. I had to wait for you, Eliza, wait for the match of my soul."

Speaking of hearts, hers was melting right about then. She didn't kiss him, but put her arms around him, felt him tighten his around her as well. Oh, how she wished she didn't have that damn corset on. It felt like an impenetrable barrier composed of steel and cloth, and she wanted it gone.

All right, if she was going to be perfectly honest, she wanted all her clothes gone. And his.

That wasn't going to happen, though, so she had to settle for the feel of his embrace, the deep, steady breaths that made his chest rise and fall beneath her cheek, the strong, slow beating of his heart.

She had to make sure that heart kept on beating.

CHAPTER FIFTEEN

SAYING GOODBYE TO ROBERT HURT FAR MORE THAN DANICA expected—hadn't he just gotten back in town?—but after lingering in the aspen grove some time longer, holding one another, sharing more kisses, talking quietly about what they might do after he was done with his fact-finding mission, she knew she must get back to the boarding house. There was really only so much time a person could spend gathering autumn leaves.

Speaking of which....

She hastily picked up as many as she could from the clearing, Robert smiling and pitching in to help as he went a little farther afield and also collected some from the oaks and sycamores.

Those damn sycamores again.

Of course, in her haste to get up here, she'd neglected to bring along anything like a basket to actually hold the leaves.

"Your skirt?" Robert suggested.

That could work. Danica set down on the tree stump the little pile of leaves she'd collected, then took up the edges of her apron-style overskirt so it formed a little bowl. Then he took his own set of leaves and placed them carefully in her skirt, followed by the ones that waited on the ponderosa pine stump. A few threatened to flutter down over the edges of her overskirt, but otherwise she thought she should be able to get the collection back to the boarding house more or less intact.

Robert looked as if he was fighting back a smile. "Are you sure you'll be able to climb down from here while holding your skirt like that?"

"I suppose I'll have to. I don't know what I was thinking, running out of the house like that without a proper basket. Actually," she added with a grin, "I know exactly what I was thinking. I was thinking about you, Robert Rowe, so I suppose I can say that all this is your fault."

Shaking his head, he bent down and kissed her on the cheek. "Of course it is. Well, do be careful, Eliza. Do you think we can meet like this again tomorrow?"

Her smile faded. "I doubt it. There's church, and I'm not sure how many times I can use this particular excuse. I do hate the way we have to sneak around!"

"Not for much longer," he promised. "And I will come to church tomorrow, just so I can see you, even if we can't even speak."

That was something. Maybe it would be torturing herself, but better to see him and not be able to talk than have to go another day without being around him at all.

She nodded, then began to make her careful way back down the path that led to Mrs. Wilson's boarding house. After a long pause, she heard Robert's feet crunch on the leaves, and knew that he'd stood there for a moment, watching her walk away, before turning to go as well.

For some reason, that image made her heart ache even more.

Danica's landlady raised an eyebrow at the pile of leaves perched precariously in her tenant's overskirt, but she didn't say anything as Danica mumbled something about forgetting her basket, then hurried up the stairs so she could relieve herself of her burden. The leaves ended up in a messy heap on top of her dresser, since there wasn't anyplace else for them to go. Then she more or less collapsed on the room's single chair so she could press her fingers to her lips, recalling the touch of Robert's mouth against hers.

God, she wanted him here, wanted him to push her down into the feather mattress, wanted to feel his body on top of hers, in *hers*. And that sure as hell wasn't going to happen anytime soon.

At least Saturday night was bath night, so she was allowed the luxury of having the bathroom to herself for a good half-hour, letting the warm water lap at her skin. She cupped her hands around her breasts, wishing more than anything those were Robert's hands, not her own. Just the mere thought brought on a throbbing heat between her legs. Maybe she should reach down, give herself the relief her body obviously needed.

Something about that felt wrong, though. Not the act itself—she'd certainly done so enough times when she was between boyfriends—but the thought of pleasuring herself when she knew it would only be a counterfeit of the contact she really wanted. Letting out a sigh, she reached for the Castile soap that sat in a little tray on the table next to the bathtub, then ran it over her arms. She'd already washed her hair separately, using the basin in the stand up against the wall. The bar soap designed specifically for washing hair that she'd bought at the general store did a better job than she'd expected, although once a week she did use a lemon rinse to get the residue completely off. Even so, she found herself wishing on more than one occasion that she could get her hands on a bottle of real modern-day shampoo.

All of which was just a distraction to keep her from thinking about Robert. Not that she was having much luck; as she got out of the bathtub and began to towel herself off, she couldn't stop herself from wondering what it would be like to take a bath with him—or, better yet, a real shower. That fancy rain-shower setup her cousin Lucas had installed in the master bedroom's bath during the last redo of the cabin would be just about perfect.

Right. Like that was going to happen. She didn't even have the guts to tell Robert where she'd come from, so it was quite a jump to go from the current status quo to imagining him in the shower with her, letting the water sluice down over both of them while she ran her hands over his naked body.

Still, it made for a nice mental image.

Danica reflected if someone had told her a few weeks ago that she'd actually look forward to going to church, she would have laughed in their face. That particular Sunday morning, however, she found herself continually glancing at the clock, willing ten o'clock to roll around. Which it did eventually. Or rather, five minutes before the hour, which was when she and Mrs. Wilson and Clara set out.

It was a blustery sort of day, the sky gray and lowering. Once or twice Danica felt a stray drop of cold rain sting against her cheek, and she prayed the skies wouldn't open up until they were all safely inside. Clara kept peering this way and that, clearly looking for her Elias. She'd already announced at breakfast that she intended to sit with him that morning in church. Mrs. Wilson had only smiled indulgently, which seemed to indicate to Danica that her landlady more or less figured the engagement was a foregone conclusion.

At least Mrs. Marshall had sent a gracious little note over the day before, saying that she hoped Miss Prewitt would join her family in their pew again, so Danica didn't have to worry about where she would end up. As to where Robert would decide to seat himself…well, that was the real question. He hadn't been in church at all last week, but probably no one had thought much of it, since he was new in town and didn't have any family or connections here.

They ducked inside the church just as the rain began to fall in earnest, and Danica let out a sigh of relief at the fortuitous timing. Her velvet hat would have been a wreck if she'd gotten caught in the storm. Fall in Flagstaff could be tricky; sometimes it was dry but chilly, sometimes stormy and wet. Either way, she made a mental note to stop in at Brannen's general store after school on Monday to pick up an umbrella. A girl couldn't be too careful after all.

After she murmured to Mrs. Wilson that she was going on to Mrs. Marshall's pew, Danica stepped forward, barely paying attention as Clara moved quickly to the pew immediately to their left and settled herself next to Elias Hansen. Without being too obvious, Danica scanned the assembled crowd, but she didn't see Robert anywhere. The Wilcoxes were already seated in their pews near the front, thank God.

She smiled a good morning at Mrs. Marshall as she sat down, although she was feeling anything but cheery. What if Robert had decided not to come after all?

No, she wouldn't let herself think that. He probably planned to slip quietly into the back so he wouldn't attract too much attention. She'd just have to try to catch a glimpse of him after church got out.

The low buzz of murmured conversation slowly died down as Reverend Pierce made his way to the podium. A few seconds later, however, the murmurs rose again. Even though Danica knew she shouldn't, she shifted slightly on the hard wooden bench so she could risk a quick glance backward.

Yes, there was Robert sliding into the very last pew on the left-hand side. His eyes caught hers, but only for a second before he looked away. But that was enough—for now, anyway. She'd seen him, and he'd acknowledged her as much as he could without revealing too much.

Heart beating a little faster, Danica turned toward the front of the church again. There were a few curious glances sent toward the pew where Robert sat, but no one said anything about why he had turned up in church today when he hadn't attended before, and, thankfully, the Wilcoxes didn't seem to have moved at all.

Probably too busy keeping all those kids in line to pay attention to what's going on way in the back pew, Danica thought with some gratitude. From what she could see, Clay did seem a little squirmy this morning, although actually, the rest of the Wilcox children were sitting obediently enough next to their parents, eyes fixed forward.

Since this was her second go-round at the church, she was a little more prepared for the next hour, dutifully standing and singing the hymns at the appropriate intervals, then pretending to listen intently as Reverend Pierce delivered his sermon. In reality, she was thinking of how handsome Robert looked in his blue brocade waistcoat—why did that style have to go out of fashion, anyway? It was so much more attractive than anything the guys she knew wore—and what other stratagems she could cook up to get the two of them alone together. Too bad neither of them possessed a talent for teleportation. Then she could have easily popped herself into Robert's hotel room, or him into her room at the boarding house, although she had to admit that scenario wouldn't be ideal. Clara's ears were much too sharp.

Throughout the service, which seemed interminable, rain drummed away on the roof of the church, and Danica had to keep herself from sighing. She'd get soaked on the way home, and there wouldn't be any lingering in the churchyard and exchanging meaningful glances with Robert if this kept up. Damn the rain, anyway, although she knew they needed it.

But, just as they stood up to sing "Nearer My God to Thee," the dull background roar died away, although she could still hear water dripping from the eaves. She couldn't quite let out a sigh of relief, but something inside her seemed to relax slightly. Yes, it would be muddy as hell, and she'd probably have to borrow Mrs. Wilson's wire brush to get the mud off the hem of her dress after it had dried thoroughly, but at least she wouldn't have to worry about looking like a drowned rat.

After the final hymn, everyone sat back down to hear the minister make that week's announcements—the Ladies Aid Society would be giving a supper the following Tuesday, and volunteers were needed to come rake the churchyard in the next day or so. Finally, though, it was all over, and Danica was able to squeeze her way out into the aisle and head toward the back of the church. Mrs. Marshall and her two boys followed, but Danica wasn't paying any attention to them. Instead, her eyes sought out Robert Rowe in the crowd, taller than almost everyone around him, except Clara's Elias, the Nordic transplant from Minnesota.

Robert didn't look back at her, though. No, she realized that would be too obvious. He'd probably linger in the churchyard under some pretext and would find a way at that point to glance in her direction, as if merely performing a casual survey of the crowd to see who was in attendance.

"Miss Prewitt?"

Damn, a Wilcox. But not Jeremiah. It had been his sister Emma addressing her.

As much as she really didn't want to, Danica slowed her steps so the other woman could catch up to her. The other members of the clan kept moving forward, including Jeremiah. However, he did tilt his head at her and smile slightly, so Danica knew she could do nothing else but smile in return, even though her heart was not in the expression at all. Her response seemed to satisfy him, though, because he appeared to nod, as if to himself, before following his brothers outside.

But Emma lingered off to one side in the entry-way, clearly wishing to speak. Danica waited with her as the rest of the churchgoers filed out of the building, although she wanted to scream in frustration. What if Emma took too long, and Robert decided not to wait? That tiny glimpse Danica had caught of him was definitely not enough to last her for any amount of time.

If Emma noticed her frustration, she didn't show any sign of it. Serene and pleasant as always, she said, "I just wanted to let you know what a lovely time we had when you came over the other night."

"I had a lovely evening as well," Danica responded, knowing she had to be polite. Anyway, she liked Emma and didn't want to seem rude, even if Danica's every nerve ending was tingling with the need to get out of the church and into the yard, where she could see Robert.

"Oh, good. We were thinking we would like to have you back. Perhaps Wednesday?" A faint hint of a dimple appeared in her cheek as she added, "You see, I must confess that we all do get rather tired of looking at one another. Having a new face at the dinner table is always a pleasure."

Was there a way to decline? Probably not. The sad thing was, if she could have simply gone to dinner with Emma and her husband, or even with Edmund and Nathan and their respective wives in the mix,

Danica wouldn't have minded so much. They were all pleasant enough people, and she had to admit there was something fascinating about seeing these ancestors of hers in the flesh, and trying to discover the small mannerisms and inflections that reminded her of people she knew in the present day. There was definitely something in Nathan's easygoing manner that reminded Danica of her cousin Lucas.

Being around Jeremiah, however, was an entirely different matter.

"Oh, that's very kind of you," she began, hedging. Danica had no idea whether Emma was colluding with her brothers to get her to hook up with Jeremiah, but she did know that the more time she spent in his company, the more awkward things were going to get. Of course, this wasn't the Middle Ages; it wasn't as if anyone could force her to do anything she didn't want to do. The Wilcox brothers must have their own particular powers, but coercing people the way Matías had been able to didn't seem to be one of them. Thank God.

She was still searching for a polite way to decline when she heard raised voices from outside. Men's voices, angry, although she couldn't make out the words.

"Oh, no," Emma said. "That sounds like Samuel. I'm sorry, Miss Prewitt, but we'll have to discuss this later."

She gathered up her silken skirts and hurried for the door, Danica right on her heels, or at least as closely as she could follow without stepping on the other woman's modest train. What on earth could have provoked Samuel to create a scene in the yard outside the church, of all places?

The answer came to her almost immediately. Robert was out there—and he hadn't exactly been working to endear himself to the Wilcox clan.

As she feared, Robert stood near the gate, the Wilcox men gathered around him while their wives held the children at a safe distance. The rest of the congregation also seemed to be standing a few feet off, although Reverend Pierce hovered near Edmund Wilcox's elbow, as if he knew he should probably intervene but wasn't too eager to do so.

"…no-good swindling sonofabitch!" Samuel was growling. "We should've run off your sorry fancy-pants ass the second you got off the goddamned train!"

The crowd gasped collectively at that threat. Bad enough to have a confrontation in the churchyard at all, but to take the Lord's name in vain on Sunday?

Jeremiah's voice was low, but commanding. "Samuel, that's enough."

"That's not enough! He stole that land right out from under us!"

Danica wanted to groan. She'd known that "deal" Robert was so proud of would most likely cause trouble. True, she hadn't thought that trouble would erupt so soon, or quite so spectacularly, but….

And the awful thing was, she couldn't do a damn thing about it. For a second or two, she'd had the wild notion of running right smack in the middle of things and interposing herself between the two men. Creating a scene like that, however, would only make matters worse. For the moment, Jeremiah appeared as if he was attempting to defuse the situation. If she went down there and gave the impression that she was trying to defend Robert, she didn't want to think of what might happen next.

It looked as if Reverend Pierce had finally gotten up his nerve, because he took a step forward and said, "Gentlemen, if you have a real estate dispute of some kind, this is not the place to settle it. There are women and children present."

Samuel only sneered, but Jeremiah nodded. "Of course, Reverend. We didn't mean to make a scene." His gaze flicked toward Robert for a second, as if to say, *This isn't over.* His next words, however, were addressed toward his brother. "Samuel, I think it's best that we go home. What's done is done."

Again Samuel's lip curled. The pretty blonde Wilcox wife—Grace, if Danica was remembering correctly—stepped forward and laid his hand on his arm, murmuring something too low to be overheard. He shook, rather like a horse when a fly landed on it, but he didn't remove her hand. After a long pause, he nodded, jaw tense, then stalked off through the churchyard gate.

The rest of the Wilcoxes followed him, the children looking puzzled but seeming to understand that it was better for them not to say anything. Emma brought up the rear, and sent a quick apologetic glance back at Danica. Their conversation would clearly have to be picked up at a later date—a much later date, which was fine by her. Maybe Emma would decide everything was a bit too unsettled right now and abandon the idea of having Danica back over for dinner.

And Robert...well, he hadn't moved, stood silently as the churchgoers murmured amongst themselves and cast furtive glances in his direction. Most of them appeared more puzzled than anything, although there were a few who seemed almost angry. Wilcox supporters, probably; they didn't own the sawmill, but they did have large timber and ranching interests, and a number of people on their payroll. Anyone who depended on them for their bread and butter probably wouldn't be too big a fan of someone cutting them off from an opportunity to expand their empire.

It could have been the presence of Reverend Pierce, who hadn't moved from where he stood, either, and watched his flock with narrowed eyes, as if willing them to try anything. Apparently no one wanted the wrath of God to descend on them, because everyone began obediently filing out the gate as well. Mrs. Wilson and Clara had been lingering near the edge of the crowd, but the landlady caught Danica's eye at that point and tilted her head, clearly expecting her to come over and join the two of them.

Since there certainly wouldn't be any opportunity to talk to Robert, not after this whole debacle, Danica did as Mrs. Wilson clearly wanted and went to meet them, then headed out to the street. At the last minute, she risked a glance at Robert, who was buttoning his coat against the cold, face impassive. But his eyes did meet hers for a second before he glanced up at the sky, as if trying to gauge whether the rain intended to start again soon.

In that brief second as they looked at each other, Danica could have sworn she'd seen a pleased glint in those sapphire-blue depths, as if this was exactly the outcome he'd hoped for.

And she couldn't begin to figure out why.

CHAPTER SIXTEEN

OF COURSE, CLARA COULD TALK OF NOTHING ELSE AT SUP-PER except the nasty little confrontation in the churchyard. She'd gone off with Elias afterward for a walk, despite the muddy streets, and came back full of information provided by her beau.

"Elias says that Mr. Rowe went out and bought this piece of land that the Wilcox brothers had been bargaining over for weeks," she explained, although Danica already knew all about that particular tidbit. "Offered full price, which *no one* does. The news of it came down late Saturday afternoon, when Mr. Royer—the man who sold the land to Mr. Rowe—came into town to put up at the hotel and buy a train ticket back east. He said he couldn't wait to get out of this damned town."

"Clara, a proper young lady does not say things such as 'damned,'" Mrs. Wilson scolded her, even as she passed along a bowl of whipped sweet potatoes.

All innocence, Clara widened her big blue eyes at the landlady. "Why, I was just repeating what Elias told me that Mr. Royer said. It's a *quote*."

Despite her worries about Robert, Danica had a hard time to keep from grinning at the look of consternation on Mrs. Wilson's face, as if she knew there was something fundamentally wrong with Clara's argument but couldn't quite put her finger on it.

"Anyway," the girl continued, undaunted, "that's why Mr. Samuel Wilcox was so upset, because apparently he'd been doing most of the negotiating, and then to have all his hard work just stolen out from under him!"

Although she knew she probably should have kept silent, Danica found herself compelled to come to Robert's defense. "I'm not sure you can call it stealing when he bought that land fair and square. If the Wilcox brothers wanted it so badly, maybe they shouldn't have tried so hard to get Mr. Royer to lower his price."

That argument made Clara twist her brow in thought, while Mrs. Wilson said mildly, "I suppose one could say that, Eliza, but the truth of it is, no one much likes it when a slick stranger comes into town, thinking he can do anything because he has enough money in his pockets."

"I'm fairly certain that Mr. Rowe made it quite clear that he intended to purchase land in the area," Danica replied. "So I'm not sure why everyone's acting like he swooped in under cover of darkness and outright stole it."

"Oh, you're just saying that because you're sweet on him," Clara shot back, and Danica felt her blood run cold.

As calmly as she could, she said, "Don't be ridiculous. I have no idea where you would have gotten that impression."

Flushing, Clara retorted, "I saw the way you looked at him in the churchyard! Not that I can blame you, because he is such a very fine-looking man, but—"

"Clara, that is quite enough," Mrs. Wilson said in quelling tones. "Eliza has not shown any evidence of partiality toward Mr. Rowe. Sometimes I think you make these things up in your head so life can be as exciting as those novels you read. I'm quite sure your late mother would not approve of your choice in reading materials."

That cutting remark made Clara pout and retreat into silence as she dished herself another slice of pork roast. Quiet reigned at the table for the next few minutes as the three women ate what remained on their plates and studiously avoided looking at one another.

Clara finished first, and got up and went into the kitchen, where she set down her plate and silverware with a quite unnecessary clatter before flouncing out of the room and heading up the stairs. For a long moment, neither Danica nor Mrs. Wilson said anything. Then, because the silence was beginning to become too heavy, Danica ventured, "What do you think the Wilcoxes will do about the situation?"

"'Do'?" the landlady repeated. Under her gown of gray wool, her shoulders lifted. "I'm not sure how much they *can* do. Oh, Mr. Samuel Wilcox will make a rumpus, because that's what he does. But I'm sure his brother will get him calmed down eventually. Mr. Jeremiah Wilcox is very good at that sort of thing. His brothers do seem to follow his lead in most things."

Yes, that tone of authority in Jeremiah's voice was not something most people would want to contradict, even a hothead like Samuel. Ironic that Jeremiah Wilcox of all people should be the voice of reason in the family.

"Well, that's good to hear," Danica said. "I'm sure no one wants a long-running dispute over such a minor thing."

Mrs. Wilson's thin mouth quirked, as if she had to repress an ironic smile. "Oh, my dear, that's not what I said. Mr. Jeremiah Wilcox may keep the peace in this instance. But he never forgets."

That night Danica lay awake in her bed, staring up at the ceiling. Since it was very dark, she couldn't see much of anything. However, even though she knew she had to get up and teach school the following morning, she couldn't seem to keep her thoughts from running this way and that, stubbornly refusing her inner exhortations to her brain for it to shut up so she could get some sleep already.

More than anything, she wished she could get to Robert somehow so they could talk—*really* talk. The cold glitter in Samuel Wilcox's dark eyes had frightened her more than she wanted to admit to herself at the time. That was the look of a man ready to commit murder. Yes, Jeremiah had talked him down, but how long was the resulting peace going to last?

Not for very long, probably. The nights were getting colder and colder, and more and more leaves had begun to fall from the trees. Danica had the sense of time running out, slipping away from her.

But no, she couldn't think about time too much, or it might end up betraying her. She'd managed to stay rooted here in 1884 for more than two weeks now, true, but if she started obsessing over the unknown day when Robert met his demise and wondering if it was today, she'd probably throw a wrench into the whole thing. She couldn't take that risk. What if she slipped back to the present and couldn't make herself return to this chilly October so many years before she was born?

She rolled over, hugging the feather pillow to her. If only it could be Robert she held like this. She would protect him, even if it meant throwing herself in front of that bullet. Surely even Samuel Wilcox wouldn't shoot an unarmed woman—especially the woman his own brother wanted.

That was a truth she'd been trying to avoid for as long as she could, but Jeremiah's interest was something she could no longer ignore. Thank God he wasn't actually anything like the man family legend had turned him into, a man they'd said had forcibly taken a Navajo woman as his wife because he wanted her powers for his own. As it turned out, Nizhoni had gone to Jeremiah willingly enough. He would never force himself on Danica. Even so....

The pillow wasn't offering much solace, so Danica turned once again on her back and let out a deep sigh. This wouldn't be her first nearly sleepless night—she'd had plenty of those after being released from Matías' spell, her mind forcing her awake so she wouldn't have to suffer another nightmare of him touching her, that strangely insidious voice of his seeming to penetrate every pathway of her brain.

Losing all that sleep hadn't been fun, but it was still better than the alternative.

Now, though, she realized she was going to have to tell Robert the truth about herself, and about why she was here. He might think she was crazy, but making that long-overdue confession was the only thing she could think of to dissuade him from his pursuit of the Wilcox brothers. He might have a finely honed and special talent, but it wasn't like the gift Caitlin's fiancé Alex Trujillo possessed, the unique ability to create a barrier that no spell, no weapon, no *anything* could get through.

No, she knew all too well how vulnerable the man she loved really was. She'd seen the bullet strike the ghost-Robert's chest, seen the blood well up to stain his shirt front.

All right, she would talk to him. When and where, she had no idea, because she had the sick feeling that the Wilcoxes were going to be watching his comings and goings like a hawk. But she'd figure something out.

She had to.

All during school the next day, Danica had to fight to keep her eyelids from drooping. Yes, she'd finally fallen asleep sometime during the darkest watches of the night, but the little sleep she'd gotten wasn't nearly enough to keep her from feeling as if she was going to pitch right over if she didn't pay attention. And of course in 1884 there wasn't much chance of nipping out to the nearest Starbucks for a shot of espresso. She'd had a second cup of coffee that morning with breakfast, but the caffeine had worn off much too quickly.

It also didn't help that Susan Garnett, Emma's eldest daughter, solemnly handed a note over to Danica before she went to take her seat. "Mamma told me to give this to you, Miss Prewitt," she said with some pride. Clearly, she felt honored to be burdened with a task as momentous as acting as a courier for her mother.

"Thank you, Susan," Danica replied, then went to her desk and put the note in her drawer, to be read while the children were at lunch recess. Unfortunately, it was the only note in there; she'd checked when she first came in this morning, just to make sure Robert hadn't attempted to contact her that way, but the drawer was empty of anything except the usual assortment of pen nibs, blotting papers, and unsharpened pencils.

The morning passed more or less without incident, although Danica did have an instant of utter brain fade during the geography lesson when she couldn't remember the capital of New York. However, since little Annabelle Wilcox gleefully supplied it, beaming that she'd remembered such an important fact, all was not lost. Even so, Danica was very relieved by the time lunch rolled around and she could get a few minutes to herself. Although she didn't find herself that eager to read Emma Garnett's note, she knew she had to out of courtesy, if nothing else.

Danica poured some water into her cup from the dipper and pail that sat in one corner of the room, then unfolded the note. Emma's handwriting was clean and precise, if not as spikily perfect as the copperplate handwriting Danica had seen in the books on Victorian life and customs she'd studied to prepare herself for this journey into the past.

Dear Miss Prewitt,

I must apologize for my brother's behavior. I fear he suffered a setback in the family business the day before, one he found particularly provoking. However, that does not excuse his outburst.

I do hope that one scene wasn't enough to dissuade you from coming for dinner on Wednesday evening. If you're amenable, please tell Susan that your answer is yes. She does enjoy being our little messenger. We would expect you a little after six o'clock once again.

Very truly yours,

Emma Garnett

So much for the hope that Emma had forgotten all about her invitation to have Danica return for dinner. She allowed herself a sigh as she folded the note and put it back in her desk drawer. Maybe she could find some way to lie and say that she had too many papers to grade, but since she hadn't assigned any compositions that would be due in the specified time frame, the lie would be easy enough to discover. And then Emma would start to wonder why the schoolteacher had felt the need to lie about such a thing....

No, better to go and be as circumspect as possible. Jeremiah would probably offer to walk her home again, but since Danica really hadn't given him any encouragement, maybe he would hold off on making any gestures like that awkward kiss on her hand. Well, she could hope, anyway.

She had just enough time to eat her own lunch of cold chicken and an apple before it was time to go out and call the children back into the classroom. They all trooped dutifully in. As Susan Garnett passed Danica's desk, she gestured for the little girl to come toward her. Looking slightly puzzled, Susan did as requested, then looked up at Danica with big dark eyes.

"Please tell your mother that I would be delighted to come over on Wednesday evening," Danica said, and Susan smiled at once.

"Oh, thank you, Miss Prewitt! She'll be so pleased." Then the little girl's face fell as she sighed. "I just wish the party wasn't only for grownups."

"I can understand that, Susan, but there isn't quite room enough at your mother's table for everyone, is there?"

The little girl appeared to consider Danica's reply, then nodded reluctantly. "I suppose so. But Mamma makes all the best things for when company comes over, and there's never anything left for me or my brothers to try."

Susan sounded so plaintive that Danica had to quickly smother a smile. Some things clearly hadn't changed too much in the last hundred years or so; she remembered all too well the bacon-wrapped dates her mother used to make for cocktail parties, and how she and Mason used to plot to swoop down and steal a few before anyone noticed.

"I'll try not to eat too much, so maybe there will be something left over," she promised the little girl, and Susan smiled and headed back to her seat.

After all, Danica thought as she went to get her list of that week's spelling words so she could write them on the board, *trying to avoid your uncle's attention all night will probably kill my appetite anyway.*

If the town was still buzzing with gossip over Samuel Wilcox's confrontation with Robert Rowe, Danica

didn't hear anything of it. Although she lingered at
the school longer than was strictly necessary in the
hope that Robert would make a return visit to see
her, he didn't appear, and she didn't have any plausible errands at Brannen's store so she could hear
what people were saying for herself. Likewise, Clara
and Mrs. Wilson were uncharacteristically subdued
at dinner that evening, possibly because of their spat
the night before.

All Danica could do was tell herself that if something truly terrible had happened, they would have
heard of it, even at Mrs. Wilson's boarding house.
Flagstaff was too small for word not to get around
quickly.

Despite that, Danica resolved to do something to
reach out to Robert that day, even if it meant being
so forward as to send a note to him at his hotel. As
it turned out, there was no need for that, because
when she opened her desk drawer that morning
at school, she found a folded piece of cream paper
there, one she didn't remember tucking under the
spare pen nibs.

Robert's bold handwriting leaped out at her
immediately.

*Dearest, I know you must be fretting. I wanted to
leave you a note yesterday, but I saw one of the Wilcox
brothers—Edmund, I think it was—walking a little too*

close to the schoolyard, and so I thought discretion was the better plan. Believe me when I tell you that everything is going well, although I'm certain they're plotting something. Once again I had that twinge which told me they were using their powers, although I can't say for certain precisely how.

Today promises to be fine, so come and meet me in the aspen grove after school if you can.

I'll count the hours until I can hold you again.

—R

Closing her eyes, Danica held the note to her chest and remembered once again the way his mouth had felt against hers. Three days since they'd last spoken, kissed, been lost in one another's embrace. It felt more like three weeks.

The clamor of the children outside in the schoolyard made her hastily fold the note and put it in her desk. They knew better than to snoop into anything she had out on her desk—or at least Danica was fairly certain they did—but better to be safe.

She would go up to see him in the aspen grove, no matter what happened. His comment about one of the Wilcoxes passing by the property worried her somewhat, but perhaps the brother in question had only been on his way to the store or the barber or something completely innocuous like that. True, the school was somewhat out of the way if you were headed to either of those destinations. On the other hand, after the rainstorm on Sunday, the weather had turned beautiful, cool but bright, and it was entirely possible that whoever Robert had spotted was taking a roundabout route in order to enjoy the weather.

However, she was glad of his warning. It wouldn't deter her from going to see him—the proverbial herd of wild elephants couldn't keep her away—but she would be careful.

And then she had to put those thoughts aside, because the children were crowding into the classroom. The day would feel longer than ever, but she would get through it. She'd have to, so she could see Robert again.

Once her students had been gone for a good forty minutes, time measured out in the slow ticking of the clock on the schoolroom's back wall, Danica decided it was safe to leave. She went over the classroom floor with the broom, taking her time, and then made sure to give her surroundings a good visual sweep as she went out to empty the dustpan before determining that no one seemed to be around. Mrs. Marshall and her two boys had left at least a quarter-hour earlier.

The coast was clear.

Danica wrapped her shawl around her shoulders, then slipped out the back door and locked it.

After glancing around one last time, just to be safe, she hurried along the path that joined the one which led up to Thorpe Hill. A minute or so later, she was safely among the pine trees, and far less likely to be spotted by anyone passing by on Park Street.

As Robert had promised, the day was holding fine, the sky a bright, clear sapphire shade without a single cloud to mar its vast blue expanse. Despite that, the temperature was chilly enough, a brisk wind seeming to cut right through her layers of clothing. Maybe she should have worn her new green wool gown, even though she'd been saving that for dinner with the Wilcoxes the following evening.

Never mind, she thought. *You'll soon have Robert to warm you up.*

Not that she'd really needed a reason to spur her on, but her strides lengthened after that thought occurred to her, although she could only walk so quickly because of her dragging skirts. After two weeks of wearing these getups, she was more or less used to them, but hiking-friendly they were not. At least the path really wasn't that steep, and now that the frost had begun in earnest, the brush had begun to die back enough that it wasn't quite so in the way.

Aspen leaves fell in a flurry of gold on the autumn wind. Standing in the center of them was Robert, his head lifted to the sky. Seeing him like that made Danica's heart beat a little faster—but not in the way she'd expected. Something about the image of him surrounded by all those falling leaves once again brought home to her how little time they probably had left.

Be brave, she told herself. *You can do this.*

There was really no way to sneak up on somebody while wearing a bustle dress. Dry leaves rustled under her trailing skirts, and Robert turned around immediately. His teeth flashed in the bright sunlight as he saw her, and then he was hurrying forward, arms outstretched.

Whatever words she'd planned to say abandoned her as he pulled her against him and devoured her mouth with his, kissing her as though they'd been separated for months. Danica surrendered to him willingly, because kissing him was so much easier than talking. She welcomed the rush of heat through her body, the all-consuming need that seemed to take over whenever they were together like this. Maybe it was partly that she was denied his presence so often, that they had to steal these moments together rather than be out in the open the way she so desperately wanted to be. Whatever the reason, she knew she'd never reacted this way to anyone else.

In that moment, she was almost jealous of Clara and her Elias, just because no one gave them the side-eye when they walked down the street together. In fact, everyone seemed to view their engagement as practically settled already. But because of Jeremiah Wilcox's interest in her, Danica knew she couldn't be open about her relationship with Robert. Tempers were already strained enough; she wouldn't be the match to set that particular heap of dry kindling alight.

Besides, once she told Robert the truth, he'd understand why she'd become increasingly anxious about his interactions with the Wilcox brothers. And he'd understand why his "mission" would need to be abandoned—they might be experimenting with their powers, but the Wilcoxes weren't about to risk being banished from their new home here in Flagstaff. Danica and Robert could slip quietly away, and soon enough wouldn't even be a footnote to history.

Slip away to where, she still didn't know. He wanted her to go back to New England with him when this was all done, but could she? More importantly, was her gift strong enough to keep her permanently anchored here in the past? For all she knew, she'd already been straining her strange temporal talent to its utter limits.

Maybe the real question was, to *when* would they slip away?

Robert lifted his mouth from hers, then took a step backward. "Eliza, is everything well with you?"

Immediately, she summoned a smile. "Of course. That is, I feel much better now that I'm with you. But this situation with the Wilcoxes—"

"My dear, there's nothing to worry about. I set them back a bit, that's all. The important thing is to see how they'll react. I'll wager that Jeremiah is none too pleased with his brother's outburst, for it only brought attention on them that he didn't want. So I can't imagine that any of them will do anything conspicuous, at least for a little while."

"You sound very sure of yourself."

He reached out to push a stray strand of hair, loosened by the wind, away from her face. His fingers felt so warm, so strong, that she wanted to rub up against them like a cat. Smiling, he said, "I wouldn't presume to say that I'm sure of myself. Rather that I know Jeremiah Wilcox doesn't want to do anything to upset the position he's gained for himself and his family in this town."

"If that's the case, then you might as well stop there," Danica told him. "For your whole point in being in Flagstaff was to make sure there was no chance of anything happening here like what you described in Connecticut. As far as I can tell, the Wilcoxes are acting like model citizens. So why not leave it be, and just go back and report that there's no chance of them exposing the rest of us?"

For a few seconds he was silent, watching her carefully. His eyes might have been captured from the sky itself, their clear blue shades almost identical. When he spoke, his tone was gentle, as if he knew how much the situation distressed her, even though she hadn't said anything so far to make him change his mind. "Because they *are* using their magic somehow. To what purpose, I haven't yet been able to ascertain. Perhaps they're only weaving spells of good fortune so that the setback they suffered because of losing out on that land deal will be reversed quickly. I can't tell for sure."

"If that's all they're doing," Danica said, "then again, I don't see why you need to stay. They already have a history of being lucky, so no one is going to think it that out of the ordinary if they snatch victory from the jaws of defeat, so to speak." Even as she made the argument, though, she experienced the sinking feeling that whatever protests she put forward might not be enough. Robert had been given his mission, and he would see it through, no matter what.

Once upon a time she might have been more admiring of such dedication to the needs of his clan, but she knew what was at stake.

"Robert," she began, wondering how on earth she could even begin this conversation. *Just so you know, I'm actually a Wilcox. And by the way, I'm also from the future* didn't sound quite right. But she had a feeling that no matter how she phrased her revelation, she stood a very good chance of Robert thinking she'd completely lost her mind. Since he hadn't interrupted her, was clearly waiting to see what she was about to say, she took a breath and went on, "There's something I need to tell you—the reason why it's so important that you don't stay here. That *we* don't stay here," she added quickly as he began to frown.

"What is it, Eliza? I can tell it's upsetting you, whatever it is."

Start at the beginning. "Well, the first thing is, I'm not—"

A crunch of dead leaves stopped her. She looked over her shoulder, startled, even as she told herself that the sound must have been a deer, or maybe a rabbit or squirrel. Cold flooded over her as she realized this little sanctuary she and Robert had created for themselves was no sanctuary at all.

Because standing at the edge of the little grove was Edmund Wilcox.

CHAPTER SEVENTEEN

HE STARED AT HER AND ROBERT, EYES NARROWED. BELATEDLY, she realized that Edmund must have been out hunting; a shotgun was propped up against one shoulder, and he had several quail strung over the other.

For the longest moment, no one said anything. Danica's brain babbled at her, *Well, it could have been worse—at least it's Edmund, and not Jeremiah or Samuel.* Even so, she knew this was bad. Very bad.

Robert was the first to speak. Tone casual, he said, "Afternoon, Mr. Wilcox."

"Mr. Rowe." Edmund's dark gaze moved from the other warlock to Danica, appraising her.

In that moment she was unutterably relieved that the younger Wilcox brother had come across her and Robert while they were only talking. Or had he seen that kiss they'd shared? No, he couldn't have. There were too many dead leaves underfoot to really sneak up on anyone around here, unless you were a ninja or something. As far as she knew, Edmund Wilcox was certainly not a ninja.

Then he said, "Emma thought we should have quail for supper tomorrow evening. Do you like quail, Miss Prewitt?"

Danica had never eaten quail in her life, but she managed to stammer, "Well, um, yes, I do."

He nodded, eyes still wearing that squint. Normally, she would have said he seemed to be fairly easygoing and quiet, but right then the narrow-eyed look he wore would have been worthy of Clint Eastwood. Ignoring Robert, he continued, "It can be dangerous, walking up here alone. Best that I escort you back to Mrs. Wilson's place."

Great. What the hell was she supposed to do now? She risked the smallest of glances at Robert, and his mouth tightened. Then, inconceivably, he gave a tiny nod. He wanted her to go with Edmund.

Well, no, he didn't *really* want that. But he also didn't want to risk a confrontation. Right now, Edmund was playing it cool, for whatever reason, but if Danica was to decline his offer, he would probably press the issue…and things could get pretty ugly from there.

Inwardly, she flared with anger, wishing she could tell Edmund that where she went and who she was with was certainly none of his business. However, she had a pretty good idea that the real Eliza Prewitt would never have done such a thing, so Danica swallowed her rage as best she could and said evenly, "Why, thank you, Mr. Wilcox. That's very obliging of you." Then she did look over at Robert as guilelessly as she could. Nothing about any of this was normal, but she had to act as if the two of them had merely been having a casual chat in the woods. She certainly couldn't appear upset about leaving him before she even had a chance to tell him the secret she'd been concealing for too long.

Of course Edmund couldn't offer her his arm, because of the shotgun he carried and the group of quail strung over his shoulder, but he gave her an unsmiling nod and stepped back slightly so she could move past him on the path. She went, skirts dragging on the fallen leaves, the sound a scratchy counterpart to the sigh of the wind in the trees. He fell in just slightly behind her, but more off to the side so he didn't run the risk of treading on the trailing hem of her skirt.

For a long, awkward moment, neither of them said anything. Then, because she had to break the silence somehow, and because she felt she'd better at least try to deflect some of Edmund's suspicions,

Danica said, "That must be quite the popular path. I walked it once before, to gather some leaves for one of my lessons, but I thought I'd go back today to see if that one oak had dropped any of its leaves. I thought I might make a garland for Mrs. Wilson's mantel."

She paused then, flicking a quick glance back at Edmund. His face was impassive; because Danica had only spent an hour or so in his company, she couldn't call herself at all familiar with his expressions or his moods. However, since he hadn't called her out on her flimsy lie, she decided she might as well forge ahead.

"I was quite surprised to see Mr. Rowe, but he explained that he liked to walk that particular path because one can see the town so well from up on the hill. He was pointing out to me all the buildings that were being planned."

"Any of them his?" Edmund asked, tone dry in the extreme. No doubt he was wondering if Robert Rowe intended to buy up parcels within the town limits as well.

"I don't believe so," Danica replied, trying to keep the edge from her voice. "That is, he didn't mention anything along those lines."

A murmur of "good," and that seemed to be the end of Edmund's contributions to the conversation. He strode along in her wake, seeming content to remain silent. Actually, "content" wasn't quite the right word. Danica could practically feel the speculation in his gaze, the way he kept turning over her meeting with Robert in his mind, picking it apart for anything that could be construed as suspicious.

Well, it probably all looked suspicious to Edmund, but as long as he hadn't actually seen anything more incriminating than the two of them talking, she thought she might be able to escape this unfortunate discovery more or less unscathed. What Edmund intended to say to his brother Jeremiah, Danica had no idea. Maybe Edmund would keep his mouth shut altogether.

No, that was probably wishful thinking. But maybe if Jeremiah got the news and was angered by it, he'd cancel her invitation to dinner at Emma's house tomorrow evening. Danica was just fine with that, although she didn't like the idea of making Emma go to all that work, only to have her dinner guest be a no-show.

Either way, this was all just speculation. For now, Danica could only walk along calmly and pretend as if nothing was wrong. And when Edmund guided her straight to Mrs. Wilson's front door, Danica thanked him for escorting her home, even managing to smile, although she wasn't sure how convincing the expression actually was.

He only nodded and tipped his hat to her, then headed off toward Park Street. Taking a breath, Danica slipped inside the house and shut the door behind her, relieved beyond measure that Clara was still at work and Mrs. Wilson was clattering away in the kitchen, obviously prepping for dinner. Right then, Danica didn't want to talk to anyone. She tip-toed up the stairs and went straight to her room, where she locked herself in before sinking down onto the chair. Suddenly, even though she never laced her corset all that tightly, it felt as if she couldn't breathe.

It's okay, she told herself. *It's all going to be fine.* After all, Edmund had been pretty mellow, all things considered. Since she'd acted as if leaving Robert behind was no big deal, Edmund might just brush the whole incident aside.

Unfortunately, she had the feeling things wouldn't be at all fine.

When she went into the schoolhouse the next day, she held her breath as she opened her desk drawer, praying that Robert had left a note for her. But the only note there was the one from Emma Garnett, still sitting more or less where Danica had folded it and stuck it off to one side.

Disappointment stabbed through her, although she knew that, logically, Robert would need to keep his distance from the school for a while. He'd already spotted Edmund in the neighborhood the day before their ill-fated meeting in the woods, and so he'd have to wait until he thought it safe to approach her.

And no reprieve from dinner at the Garnett household, either. Little Susan Wilcox came up to Danica and said that her mamma was looking forward to seeing Miss Prewitt for supper that night, and to remember to come a little after six.

Managing the best smile she could, Danica told Susan she was very much looking forward to it as well, and that seemed to be the end of the matter. No hope of escape there, obviously.

That afternoon Danica didn't linger at the school, but took the few papers which needed grading back with her. She knew she'd need the extra time to get ready, because she wanted to change out of her plaid day dress and into the nicer wool gown, now that it had been carefully brushed to remove any sign of her rendezvous with Robert in the woods the day before.

And quite possibly it was foolish to care what she looked like for this dinner she didn't even want to attend, but she had to act as if everything was quite normal, and that meant showing Emma Garnett and her extended family the proper respect. It might be the longest dinner of her life, but Danica was determined to do all the right things. Tomorrow...well, she'd find some way to talk to Robert tomorrow, no matter what, but she'd worry about that then.

For now, she had to put on her game face.

The night promised to be windy and cold, so she slipped her cloak around her shoulders and headed down the stairs, pulling on her gloves as she did so. Mrs. Wilson was busy in the kitchen, but Clara sat in the parlor, reading a book. Where Elias might be, Danica didn't know, but she supposed he couldn't come over to visit every night.

"Dinner with the Wilcoxes again?" Clara inquired, closing her book on one finger so she wouldn't lose her place.

Technically, it was dinner with the Garnetts, but Danica didn't bother to contradict the other girl. "Yes," she replied. "Mrs. Garnett was kind enough to invite me for dinner again."

"You're spending a lot of time with the Wilcoxes, it seems. Folks are beginning to talk."

Danica refused to let herself be irritated by that remark. "Oh, are they? Well, I suppose people must have something or other to keep themselves occupied. I don't let myself worry about it too much."

Arching an eyebrow, Clara said, "Butter doesn't melt in your mouth, does it? But then, I suppose I might be the same way if I'd managed to attract the attention of someone like Mr. Jeremiah Wilcox."

You couldn't be further from the truth, Danica thought, but she only said, "I'm afraid you've misunderstood the situation, Clara. Mrs. Garnett invited me to dinner, and so of course I accepted. Mr. Wilcox had absolutely nothing to do with it."

"If you say so."

From the way Clara delivered this statement, Danica could tell she was both unconvinced and more than a little annoyed. But it was already past six, and she didn't want to be late. "I do say so, Clara. But you have a lovely evening."

Having put a period to the conversation, Danica sailed out of the room, then on through the front door and down the steps. The wind caught her immediately, struggling to yank her hat right off her head. Because it was anchored with several hatpins, it certainly wasn't going anywhere, but Danica gritted her teeth anyway and hoped she wouldn't be a complete disaster by the time she got to Emma's house. With the wind came the scent of pine, familiar enough even in her own time, but overlaid here with the sharp scents of freshly hewn lumber from the mill. At least the air was fresh enough that she could barely smell the horse manure.

Would it rain? Danica squinted up at the sky, but although more and more clouds seemed to be gathering, they didn't look heavy enough yet to be truly threatening. Thank God. This dinner was going to be difficult enough without getting trapped in the Garnett house by an inconvenient rainstorm.

She went up the neat front walk and knocked on the door. This time, little Susan opened it, and Danica gave her a surprised look.

"Are you the doorman tonight?"

"Door *girl*," Susan replied. "I have to go upstairs soon, but Mama said I could answer the door, since I was the one who took you the note inviting you to dinner."

"Well, that was very considerate," Danica said, trying not to smile. It was clear that Susan took her duties seriously, and it wouldn't be right to seem as if she was making fun of her.

Susan nodded. "And she said I could bring you to the dining room, after you've hung up your hat. You can put it there." She pointed to the hall tree, and Danica reached up and pulled out her hatpin, then removed the little velvet hat and did her best to smooth away the damage the wind had done to her hair. Afterward, she hung the hat on one of the hooks, and took off her cloak as well.

Through all this, Susan had been waiting patiently. Once she saw that Danica was done, she said, "It's this way to the dining room, Miss Prewitt."

Of course Danica remembered how to get there—the house was big, but not that big—but she let Susan dance ahead, dark sausage curls swinging down her back, as she led her teacher to meet the rest of the family. As she followed, Danica took in a calming breath, telling herself that this was all going to be fine. Certainly there was nothing in the little girl's manner to indicate that tonight's dinner was anything more than another gesture of hospitality from one of the town's leading families to the school's new teacher.

When Danica entered the dining room, however, she could almost feel the eyes of the Wilcox brothers boring into her. Of them all, Jeremiah was the only one who looked even somewhat relaxed, but maybe he was just a better actor than the rest of them. Oh, sure, they all still rose and greeted her politely, even as Emma thanked her daughter and sent her upstairs to be with her brothers and their most likely besieged nanny. That minor courtesy, however, was certainly not enough to calm Danica's nerves. Edmund had obviously been telling tales out of school, and she had no idea what the hell she was going to do about it.

But then Emma came up to her and said, "Good evening, Miss Prewitt. I'm so glad you could join us tonight. Edmund shot some lovely quail yesterday, so I was able to make this dinner a little more special."

"That sounds wonderful," Danica managed. So…had Edmund talked to his brothers, but not to his sister? Maybe. She still had the impression that

Emma and the other wives didn't know anything about what their husbands were plotting.

If they even were plotting at all. Maybe Danica was just being paranoid. Somehow, though, she doubted it. She could sense undercurrents here that had absolutely nothing to do with her imagination.

Emma led her to the same seat she'd occupied at dinner last week, the one to Jeremiah's right. At least Danica had been expecting it this time, so her place at the table didn't come as a complete surprise. After she'd settled herself, Jeremiah picked up a cut-crystal decanter of dark wine and poured a measure into the glass before her. Again, nothing obviously different from last time, when wine had also been served, but she couldn't help experiencing a stir of apprehension. What if one of the brothers had tampered with it somehow? After all, she still didn't have a clear idea of what all their various talents might be; maybe one of them had a facility with potions.

No, that really was being paranoid. They wouldn't do anything so blatant as attempt to drug their children's schoolteacher. Besides, Jeremiah had passed the decanter on to Nathan, who poured for his wife Jennie before the decanter again was handed off to the next waiting brother, this time Samuel.

Danica couldn't ignore the dark, flickering glare he sent her. She'd been halfway expecting that, however. None of the Wilcox brothers were particularly fond of Robert Rowe, but with Samuel the antipathy had morphed into downright hatred, as far as she could tell. Right then she was glad all the Wilcoxes were present and accounted for, because that meant they couldn't be going after Robert. He, she guessed, must be safely tucked away in his hotel. Was he sitting down to dinner there, just as she was here?

The ache of need that washed over her then was both unexpected and unwelcome, and she pushed it away as best she could. She couldn't allow herself to moon over Robert while surrounded by all these Wilcoxes. This was one place where she needed to keep on her toes.

Bridget, the maid, brought in the soup course, and after a brief prayer—probably more for Bridget's benefit than because the Wilcoxes were truly religious—everyone settled down to eat.

"I heard you were gathering leaves for autumn garlands, Miss Prewitt," Edmund's wife Lida said, and Danica paused, soup spoon halfway to her mouth. Crap, how the hell was she supposed to reply to that? Recovering herself, she responded,

"Oh, yes—I thought it might be nice to be a little festive." She added, hoping to turn the conversation to a more neutral topic, "Halloween is coming up so soon. Do you do anything much to celebrate here in Flagstaff?"

"Reverend Pierce is not overly fond of the notion of Halloween," Lida said with a smile. "But we don't want to deny the children their fun, so we do carve pumpkins, and we have a small gathering where the boys and girls bob for apples and play other games."

"I remember you playing a few of those games as well, not so long ago," Grace put in, looking sly. "Didn't you gaze into the mirror on All Hallows' Eve to see who would be your one true love?"

"Yes, and I saw Edmund's face, so I think that worked out very well."

Everyone chuckled, while Danica put on her best polite smile. She hadn't even thought to research Victorian Halloween customs, but clearly the day wasn't celebrated quite the same way here as it was back in modern-day Flagstaff.

Just as well, she thought. *If I'd had to see one more "sexy" version of something as a Halloween costume, I'd probably throw up.*

"You're always welcome here, Miss Prewitt," Jeremiah said then. His dark eyes held hers for a moment, and she swallowed. "Some of the young men here in town do take the holiday as an opportunity to…run wild, shall we say?…and so it might be better for you to be here with us rather than at Mrs. Wilson's boarding house."

That sounded ominous. How much trouble could the young men in the town really get into? But then she remembered how many of them seemed to wear pistols at their side, and how she often heard at least one or two gunshots emanating from Humphreys Street on Friday and Saturday nights, after everyone at the mill had gotten that week's pay.

"Thank you for the invitation, Mr. Wilcox," Danica replied. "That does sound like a much better way to spend the holiday." *And please God that Robert and I are long gone by then. Wherever or whenever that might be.*

After that Bridget brought in a large tray with the quail, and then bowls of rice and dressing and some kind of fruit sauce that smelled positively decadent. The conversation shifted to whether the Presbyterians were really going to buy that lot on the corner of Sitgreaves and Aspen Street, or if it would instead be the site of yet another hotel.

Danica was content to remain silent during most of that discussion; she knew the Presbyterians would win out, since the church they'd built back in the late 1880s still stood. In fact, she'd walked by it plenty of times when going to the art shows the city held in the park behind Flagstaff's city hall. She never could seem to get a decent parking place at those things and always had to hoof it for a few blocks.

If anyone noticed her silence, they didn't comment on it...although she couldn't help the way Jeremiah's gaze seemed to inevitably stray in her direction when he thought she wasn't looking. Not good. Whatever Edmund had or hadn't told him about seeing her with Robert, it didn't seem to have dissuaded the leader of the Wilcox clan from wooing her.

Dessert was bread pudding with a whiskey sauce so alcoholic that Danica was surprised they didn't light it on fire, just for show. It was also insanely good, and she had to force herself to turn down a second helping.

On top of the wine, it would knock you on your ass, she thought. Not that she had much room for any more food; one good thing about corsets was the way they tended to restrict your food intake.

And here they were at the end of the meal, and there hadn't been any scenes, nor any real awkwardness, except for those disquieting glances from Jeremiah. Danica was about to let out a small sigh of relief when he said, "Miss Prewitt, may I speak with you privately?"

The words were phrased as a request, but she knew she had no real choice. "On what subject, Mr. Wilcox?"

"As I said, I would like our discussion to be private. If you would come with me back to my house?"

Danica hesitated, trying to ignore the way all the others were watching them—the brothers' expressions somehow greedy, their wives appearing somewhat puzzled. What Jeremiah was asking of her was highly improper by the standards of the day, after all. Even so, she knew she had been backed into a corner.

Apparently noting her discomfort, he said, "My son and his nanny—and the housemaid—will all be there. You need not worry about being alone with me."

That was being a bit too bald-faced about the situation, even though only family members were listening. Danica let out a nervous laugh, saying, "No, of course not. I'm sure it will be fine." She turned toward Emma. "Thank you for another lovely meal."

She got to her feet then, the rest of the men rising courteously. Their wives stood as well, although they stayed where they were as Danica exited the dining room and went toward the entry hall. With shaking fingers, she retrieved her cloak from the hall tree and draped it over her shoulders, then picked up her hat, although she didn't bother to put it on.

Jeremiah came in behind her and draped his overcoat on his left arm, apparently deciding he wouldn't need it. "We're just going next door," he explained. Then he offered her his free arm, and she felt compelled to take it. Well, that wasn't so bad; at least she'd walked with him this way before. And, as he'd said, they were only going one house over.

Even so, the air was chilly enough against her face, promising another hard frost that night. Without speaking, Jeremiah took her down the front path and over to the cleared dirt that passed for a sidewalk, and back up the walkway that led to his own front porch.

Like Emma's house, his was a big wood-framed structure, not quite big enough to be called a mansion, but certainly imposing enough, with its multiple chimneys and overhanging gables. A lot of room for a man and his son, plus a couple of servants, but Danica knew practicality probably didn't have a lot to do with the choices made in building the house. It had been designed to show off its owner's wealth.

When they went inside, she saw that the décor wasn't all that different from what she'd seen in Emma's place. Maybe more burgundy and dark green than green and gold, but still, it had the same feel. Had she helped Jeremiah to decorate it? Danica wasn't exactly sure of the timeline when it came to his two civilian wives. Obviously, Nizhoni was long gone before this house had been built, but maybe Mrs. Adams' niece or the wife before her had a hand in its decoration.

"Let us go into the study," Jeremiah said quietly. He led her from the foyer into a large room off to one side, where a fire crackled in the stone hearth. The stone looked local, but the carved mahogany mantel must have been shipped in from someplace back east.

And while the room appeared pleasant and welcoming enough, with the cheery fire and the shelves of books and the mess of papers on the desktop, Danica couldn't help experiencing a chill as Jeremiah shut the double doors behind them.

"I fear that Jacob is overly inquisitive," he said by way of explanation, no doubt noticing the nervous flicker of her eyes toward those closed doors. "He should be in bed by now, but his nanny has a tendency to doze off, and then he slips out of his room more often than not."

This revelation didn't particularly surprise her. Yes, Jacob was a very good student, but he also seemed to be ruled by his own whims, whims that didn't always coincide with what was considered proper.

"Of course," she murmured.

"Please, sit down," Jeremiah said, gesturing toward a mahogany chair with a seat and back of striped silk. Its mate sat only a few feet away, a marble-topped table between them. On that table was a decanter of some dark liquid. Port, possibly.

Danica hoped he wouldn't offer her any. Between the two glasses of wine she'd had with dinner and the whiskey sauce on the bread pudding, she already felt a little off.

But not so off that she didn't really, really wish she could be just about anyplace other than here.

Then he did say, "A small glass of port?"

She shook her head at once. "No, thank you. I fear your sister's whiskey sauce was stronger than I'd anticipated, and I haven't much experience with drinking port." After making that reply, she did settle herself in the chair he'd indicated, since remaining standing would have seemed rude.

Smiling, he took a seat as well. Danica noticed that he didn't reach for the port himself, as if deciding to abstain since she wouldn't be having any. What would be the demure thing to do here? Fold her hands in her lap and wait for him to speak, since he was the one who'd requested this meeting in the first place?

That sounded like the best plan.

So she folded her hands and look over at him with an expression of what she hoped was mildly interested anticipation.

He seemed to take that as his cue, because he said, "I do realize, Miss Prewitt, that my invitation must have seemed somewhat irregular to you."

Danica lifted her shoulders. Yes, it was irregular, or at least by the mores of the current time period, but she wasn't about to admit that. Hoping she sounded calm, she replied, "I can understand that some topics might be too sensitive to be discussed in front of the rest of your family."

Her words seemed to relax Jeremiah. He leaned against the back of his seat, even as he nodded. "Thank you for understanding, Miss Prewitt."

"Eliza," Danica said then, although she wasn't quite sure what had prompted her to make that particular offering. Noting his look of surprise, she added, "After all, if we are to have private discourse, then we might as well do so on a first-name basis, don't you think?"

A nod, and the beginnings of a smile around the corners of his mouth. Damn. If he wasn't her great-great-etc.-granduncle...and if she'd never met Robert Rowe...Danica realized she might have harbored some impure thoughts about this man. Jeremiah said, "Well, thank you, Eliza. I do appreciate the gesture." He paused for a few seconds, then went on, "Do you realize the risks you're taking, associating with Mr. Rowe?"

So there it was. Clearly, Edmund had gone straight to his brother with that particular piece of intelligence, even though he couldn't have seen her doing anything except having a private conversation in the aspen grove. Fighting the sudden dryness in her mouth, Danica said, "I wasn't aware I was taking any risks at all. Our meeting was a chance one. I'd gone up there to gather leaves—"

"For your garlands, yes," Jeremiah broke in. "A useful excuse, I would imagine, for those times when you desired some privacy. But when I see a witch new to my territory associating with a warlock who has no affiliation with my clan, I have to wonder."

It took a second or two for Jeremiah's words to sink in. But then Danica blinked. "Warlock"? But Robert's talent was to hide his witch nature from others of his kind. How could Jeremiah Wilcox have possibly detected his origins?

"You appear surprised," Jeremiah said. "That is understandable. But you should know that I realized who Robert Rowe was as soon as he entered Flagstaff's town limits."

That revelation was so positively flummoxing that Danica could only stare at the Wilcox *primus*, unable to formulate a cogent reply. So if Jeremiah had known who Robert was all along....

Somehow managing to find her voice, she said, "I'm not quite sure what you mean."

"Oh, yes, you do, even if you don't wish to acknowledge the fact. Mr. Rowe came here from New England, and it did not take that much effort to put those pieces of the puzzle together."

"But...." Danica let her words trail off. Could she challenge Jeremiah by revealing that she knew the particulars of Robert's gift, that his gift should have camouflaged his true nature from Jeremiah Wilcox and anyone of witch-blood in his immediate vicinity? Letting slip that particular fact would probably make matters worse.

Another one of those half-smiles. "Eliza, as *primus*, I have many gifts, chief of which is the ability to detect interlopers in my territory, even if otherwise their natures should have been hidden to me. Mr. Rowe has the unmistakable scent about him of those holier-than-thou witches back in New England. Granted, he is too young to have been one of the gang who actually drove my family from our home territory, but I knew upon first meeting him that he was connected to them somehow."

"So…why didn't you do anything about it?"

"To what end? You know as well as I do, Eliza, that to initiate any kind of open conflict with others of witch-blood is to attract the scrutiny of outsiders. We clans may have our differences, but we all adhere to one code, a code which dictates that our survival is contingent on remaining hidden, on making sure that those who don't possess magical powers are never able to discover our true selves."

Recalling what Robert had told her about the Wilcoxes on that particular subject, Danica said, "So why the displays in Connecticut? If you knew doing so would attract the scrutiny of outsiders—"

Jeremiah lifted a hand, and she subsided. Tone heavy, he said, "I see that Robert has told you something of the reasons for our being here. Yes, there was some…experimentation…occurring. But I will also assert that it would not have attracted the attention of those without magical powers, since we took care to hold our 'experiments' in the remote woods where no one could observe us. The reactions of the Winfield elders, and those in the greater New England area, were certainly not proportionate to our crime, if you could even call it that."

For a few seconds, Danica said nothing. What Jeremiah had just told her didn't seem to jibe with Robert's explanations of the events that had driven the Wilcox clan from Connecticut. Which was the truth—Robert's story, or Jeremiah's?

As with most conundrums like this, she guessed the truth lay somewhere in the middle. Also, Robert had taken the Wilcox attack on the Winfield elders more personally than he otherwise might, since his grandfather had been among those injured. Not to excuse what Jeremiah had done, but Robert couldn't exactly be called impartial here, either.

"Perhaps not," she said, knowing she'd paused too long to answer. "I wasn't there, so I find it difficult to comment one way or another. But Mr. Wilcox—"

"Jeremiah."

She took in a breath. "Very well…*Jeremiah*. I understand that you are a trustee for the school here, but I was not informed that such a position gave you the right to make inquiries about my private life, even if that might involve interactions with a war-lock from a clan you have no reason to think kindly of."

A long silence followed that remark. Jeremiah watched her carefully, the firelight reflecting in the depths of those dark, dark eyes. At last he said, voice quiet, "Do you truly believe it's because I'm a trustee that I have these concerns?"

Damn. *Damn.* There it was, the issue she'd been trying to dance around almost the entire time she'd been here. "I'm afraid I don't understand," she began, but he shook his head.

"I think you do, Eliza. And to see you sharing company with a man like Robert Rowe—"

"Oh, because you're the far superior option?" she retorted, feeling wounded on Robert's behalf. Realizing how awful her rejoinder had sounded, she hurried on, "I'm sorry. That was uncalled for. But surely I've done nothing to give you the impression that I was interested, have I?"

"No," he said, that one word sounding as heavy as lead. Right then, he looked more weary than upset. "Do you want to know the truth, Eliza? When you came to Flagstaff, and I saw that you were witch-kind, too, I thought you must be a gift from God. I did not dare become interested in another woman who wasn't one of us, not after what happened with

Miss Baker and Miss Terrell. But perhaps another witch...."

"Because things went so well with Nizhoni?" Danica snapped. Yes, what the curse had done to him was terrible, but those innocent women had suffered far worse fates, through no fault of their own, except having the bad luck to marry Jeremiah Wilcox.

At once his dark brows drew together, and his fingers tightened on the knees of his black woolen trousers. "How do you know about that?"

Oh, crap. Come to think of it, no one had said much of anything about Jeremiah's Navajo "wife." Did the good people of Flagstaff think it better to ignore his bad taste in consorting with a Native American woman? Danica didn't know for sure, but she did know she had to do her best to fix this.

"I—people talk, you know," she said lamely. "Perhaps a few did try to warn me."

"Robert Rowe among them?" Jeremiah asked, a certain glitter in his eyes that she didn't like very much.

"What difference does it make? All I can say is that is doesn't seem very...fair...for you to take such risks, when you know what the probable outcome will be."

For a long moment, he didn't reply. The fire crackled away in the background, sounding far too cheery, considering the palpable tension in the room. Then he pushed himself up out of his chair, the movement so sudden that Danica couldn't keep herself from startling.

"Fair?" he said, voice hard. "Is it fair to expect my boy to live without a mother? Certainly he is an innocent, even if my late wife thought I was not."

Anguish thrummed in every syllable. Maybe it wasn't wise, but Danica couldn't keep herself from standing as well, and then went to him so she could place a hand on his arm.

"No, it's not fair," she said quietly. "Perhaps you won't believe me, but I do feel for your son, for your situation. But...." Stopping then, she made herself look up into his face, to register the disappointment there. His pain hurt her more than she'd imagined, seeing it so close. But even if she hadn't been his relative, she knew she couldn't do anything to change the way things were. His story would have to play out, so the future could remain unchanged. She gave his arm the faintest squeeze, then let go. "But I can't be what you need me to be."

Jeremiah gave a nod so faint that she might not have even noticed it if she hadn't been watching him closely. "I understand."

Stepping away, she murmured, "I'll just let myself out."

Before he could say anything else, she moved quickly toward the double doors to the study, then opened the right-hand one and stepped into the foyer. Her cloak and hat still waited for her at the hall tree, and she put them on in some haste, getting the hat crooked. Like that should matter. As she made her way to the front door, the faintest creak from the staircase made her pause and look back.

Jacob Wilcox stood there, watching her with somber dark eyes. God, he hadn't heard that whole exchange, had he?

"Jacob—" she began, but he turned and ran up the stairs, bare feet pattering over the wooden boards.

The world seemed to blur before her eyes. Danica blinked back her tears as best she could. After all, she couldn't fix this. She didn't seem able to fix anything.

Then she opened the door and bolted out into the night, not caring if anyone should see her running like a madwoman away from Jeremiah Wilcox's house.

Let them think what they wanted.

CHAPTER EIGHTEEN

WAS THERE EVER SUCH A LONG, DREADFUL THURSDAY? Danica wasn't sure; she just knew that every minute felt like an hour, and every hour a whole day. Sleep had eluded her for half the night, it seemed, and even when she did manage to fall into a fitful doze, she was haunted by nightmares of being chased, or worse, being trapped in a dark room with no windows and no doors, where she beat on the walls and screamed until her voice failed her, but no one ever came to answer her cries for help.

Even judicious use of her lip and cheek stain only barely kept her looking like death warmed over the next morning. Luckily, Clara was chattering away about the piece of land Elias had just bought, and the house he planned to build on it—the intimation being he would propose in the very near future—and so she didn't seem to notice anything wrong with her housemate. Mrs. Wilson's eyes were far more sharp, and narrowed as they took in Danica's appearance, but she didn't say anything, only set a cup of coffee in front of her before going back to the stove to dish up some eggs and bacon.

The coffee helped a little, at least enough to give Danica the energy to gather up the basket with her lunch and the students' graded compositions, then head out the door. Her destination wasn't the school, however; instead, she walked as calmly as she could to the Hotel San Francisco and went straight to the front desk.

At that hour of the morning, none of the hotel's guests seemed to be up and about yet. Maybe they had all had a gaudy night at the saloon next door. Even the man standing at the desk blinked bleary eyes at her. He looked like he could have used a cup of Mrs. Wilson's coffee.

The evening before, Danica had written Robert a note, then folded it into a very small square and secured it with a blob of wax. Maybe it was crazy, contacting him this way, but she was feeling desperate. Her rejection of Jeremiah the night before might have been enough to keep the Wilcox brothers out of her business…maybe not. She had no idea whether he would even have confided in them. All she did know was that she had to let Robert understand what was going on.

Dear Robert, I fear I might have angered Mr. Jeremiah Wilcox last night, but it couldn't be helped. They know something of what has been going on between the two of us…or at the very least they suspect it…and I'm not sure what we should do next. Please come by the school tomorrow at four. I'll pretend to be staying late and grading papers, as usual.

~Eliza

Should she have signed her name? At this point, the cat seemed to be pretty much out of the bag, so Danica supposed it really didn't matter one way or another.

Especially now, when she was being so bold as to walk into the lobby of the Hotel San Francisco, completely unescorted.

Coolly, hoping it would seem as if what she was doing wasn't completely out of the ordinary, she told the front desk clerk as she handed over the note, "Could you please make sure this gets to Mr. Rowe?"

The man blinked at her, then nodded. "Sure thing, Miss Prewitt."

Of course he would know her name. So much for hoping for anonymity.

"Thank you," she replied, forcing herself to smile. "Much obliged to you."

The man smiled at her in return, but there was something all too knowing in his expression, as if he knew the folded piece of paper must contain something a little more intimate than a mere thank-you. At any rate, she couldn't allow herself to stop and worry about it, since she had to get to the school and open the classroom. By that point it was nearly a quarter to eight.

And then what seemed like an eternity of spelling words and geography and history, although after lunch Danica's energy seemed to desert her almost entirely, and she assigned a composition about Halloween, asking her students to write about their favorite part of the holiday. That got them scratching away—obviously, even kids in 1884 loved Halloween—and it allowed her to more or less collapse at her desk and watch them write.

Finally, though, the day was over, all the compositions left in a neat stack on her desktop. She'd have to grade them, of course, but she could put that task off for a day or so.

If she even stuck around that long. Because what she planned to say to Robert when he came to see her today after school might change everything. She'd tell him the truth, and she'd tell him that Jeremiah Wilcox knew exactly who he was, and so the best thing for the both of them would be to get out of here. Back to the East Coast...back to the future...

right then, Danica didn't care one way or another. She just knew they needed to get away from the Wilcoxes.

A tall shadow filled the doorway, and she smiled. A little early, but obviously Robert had gotten her note.

Then the silhouetted figure stepped into the room, away from the sun that had backlit him, and Danica realized the man wasn't Robert at all.

He was Samuel Wilcox.

She let out a gasp before she could prevent it from escaping her lips. But then she forced herself to give him as steady a gaze as she could manage and said, "Good afternoon, Mr. Wilcox. How can I help you? If it's about that 'D' I gave Clay for his composition on Betsy Ross—"

"This isn't about Clay," he broke in, moving closer to her desk.

No, of course it wasn't. She'd known that even as she spoke. Only a desperate attempt to make his appearance here seem as if it was just part of the regular routine.

Glad that her bulky skirts hid her quivering legs, she stood slowly and made a show of gathering up the stack of compositions and laying them in her basket. "Then what can I help you with, Mr. Wilcox? As you can see, I have a number of papers to grade when I get home."

He smiled then, a thin, unpleasant smile. Funny how she'd always thought of him as the least attractive of the Wilcox brothers, even though they were all physically very similar. It was probably just the disagreeable expressions he often wore which gave that impression. He said, "And here I thought you were planning to stay late and work so you'd have a chance to meet with your lover."

Shock coursed through her, and she took a step backward, nearly tripping over the bulky train of her gown. "I don't know what you're talking about, Mr. Wilcox."

"You don't?" He reached into his waistcoat pocket and produced a small folded square of paper. "This look familiar?"

"Where'd you get that?" she demanded.

"Tom Hopkins at the Hotel San Francisco is a friend of mine. He's been keeping an eye on Mr. Rowe for me, so he let me know the new schoolteacher was leaving notes for him."

Damn. Damn, damn, *damn*. Danica's instincts had been telling her that leaving the note was a bad idea, and yet she'd gone ahead and done it anyway. Desperation had made her stupid.

"I'm afraid that who I leave notes for is none of your business, Mr. Wilcox," she said icily. Could she tough her way out of this? Her gaze flickered over to the clock on the back wall. Not even a quarter 'til four yet.

Please, Robert, come early so you can stop this madman from doing whatever he's planning....

Somehow she knew he wouldn't, though. He wouldn't run the risk of bumping into one of her students, or Mrs. Marshall. If Danica had said it was safe to come at four, then that was when he would come.

"Is that a fact?" Samuel said. "Some might say it is my business. Leaving notes for men in hotels? That bespeaks a loose nature, Miss Prewitt, and I sure as heck don't want someone like that teaching my children."

"Oh, but you're just fine with having someone like that connected to your brother," she shot back.

He didn't blink. "Well, that's an entirely different proposition, isn't it? Because if you're attached to my brother, then you're not associating with the likes of Robert Rowe. And I think that'll be better for all of us."

A retort sprang to Danica's lips, but she wasn't allowed to speak, because in the next second Samuel was lunging for her, arms reaching out to seize her. With a shocking show of strength, he threw her over one shoulder, knocking the air from her lungs.

Not all of it, though. She opened her mouth to scream—would anyone even hear her?—but in the next second the classroom seemed to spin around her like a crazy kaleidoscope, moving faster and faster, blurring, then giving way to darkness.

Slowly, Danica opened her eyes. She lay on a more or less soft surface; above her was a ceiling of peg-and-groove pine that looked oddly familiar. What the…?

Then it came to her. That was the ceiling of her family's cabin, or something which looked exactly like it. Holding back a groan, she pushed herself to a sitting position.

Samuel's hateful voice said, "Careful. It takes a bit to recover from traveling that way."

She looked over at him. He was sitting in a rickety-looking chair of pine with a rush seat. As she glanced past him, she saw that the dimensions of the room were familiar, as well as the huge river-stone hearth. Yes, definitely the Wilcox family cabin, although without any of its twenty-first-century upgrades. The furniture, such as it was, all looked simple and plain, pieces the family wouldn't have bothered to move to their shiny new houses on Park Street.

"That's your talent?" she asked, her voice sounding rusty and tired. "Traveling from place to place in the blink of an eye?" At least she wasn't so out of it that she'd slipped and used the word "teleportation." She was pretty sure the term didn't exist back in 1884.

Samuel looked very pleased with himself. "Yes, and a handy one, too." His gaze sharpened, and he asked, "What's yours?"

"None of your business."

The self-satisfied smile he'd been wearing disappeared abruptly. "You have quite the mouth on you, Miss Prewitt. Well, that'll be my brother's problem."

"Does he know you've kidnapped me like this?"

"No. Sometimes he gets a little squeamish over doing what needs to be done. But once I get rid of a certain obstacle, I'm pretty sure he won't be too angry with me."

Who knew that this great-great-etc.-uncle of hers would turn out to be a full-blown sociopath? Blood feeling as if it was rapidly cooling to ice in her veins, Danica said, "'Obstacle'? What are you talking about?"

"You'll find out soon enough." Samuel went to one of the cabin's front windows and twitched aside the curtain of faded cotton calico that hung there. Judging by the darkening landscape outside, Danica realized she must have been knocked out for longer than she'd thought. It must have been several hours ago that Robert would have arrived at the school-house to speak with her, only to find her gone.

He must be frantic, trying to figure out where she could have disappeared to. He'd be looking all over town....

Oh, God.

"It's a trap, isn't it?" she whispered, hoping against hope that her suspicions were wrong, that Samuel had only brought her here to force her to drop Robert and choose Jeremiah instead. Not that that particular scenario wasn't all kinds of wrong, but....

But the alternative was even worse.

Another of those smiles that made her gut clench. "I guess you are pretty smart, Miss Prewitt. Yes, I'll make sure that interfering fool doesn't trouble any of us again." His right hand went to rest on his hip, and for the first time Danica saw the pistol in its tooled leather holster that hung there.

She didn't even stop to think. One second she was on that threadbare sofa, and in the next she was launching herself at Samuel. In that moment, she didn't care about her own safety. She just had to do whatever it took to keep him from shooting Robert.

But she hadn't counted on how much that teleportation journey had weakened her. It seemed as if her legs would barely support her weight, and Samuel dodged her attack easily, grabbing her by the bicep with an iron grip that kept her from tumbling to the floor.

"Easy, there," he said with a hateful chuckle. "You don't want to hurt yourself."

"Let go of me, you son of a bitch."

He only laughed again. "Like I said, you have got a mouth, Miss Prewitt. Or can I call you Eliza, since we'll be family soon?"

Danica wanted to spit back that she would never be a part of his family, but too late for that. She was already a Wilcox, even if this bastard straight out of hell didn't know it.

"Let go of me," she said through gritted teeth.

He released her arm and she stumbled, thrown off balance. But at least she didn't fall. Straightening, she moved away from him, toward the door.

"Stay right there," he warned her, following a few paces behind. "Not that I don't want Mr. Rowe to see you when he arrives, but we need to do this properly."

"And you really think you're going to get away with this?" she asked, hoping that by appealing to his instincts of self-preservation, he might abandon this insane plan.

"'Course I am." He shifted his weight to one booted foot, hand returning to rest on the butt of his pistol. "Maybe you don't understand the way things work around here, Miss Prewitt. Sure, Mr. Ayer owns the mill, but the Wilcoxes own miles of land all around town. Do you think Sheriff O'Neill does anything without our say-so? If Mr. Rowe goes missing, there won't be any inquiry at all. He'll just... disappear."

To an unmarked grave in a clearing about a half-mile from where she and Samuel now stood. Meaning...what? That you couldn't change the past? Or something even worse?

Growing even colder with horror, Danica wondered if she was the one who'd ended up causing Robert's death. If she'd never come to 1884, then he wouldn't have had any reason to get into an open confrontation with Samuel Wilcox.

This was all her fault. But no, Robert had been shot even before she'd intervened. Unless the timeline had changed the second she intervened...God, this whole time-travel thing was making her crazy.

As she stared at Samuel in horror, she heard the sound of rapidly approaching hoofbeats. He nodded in satisfaction, then came to her and grasped her around the bicep with his free hand.

"Let's go on outside, Miss Prewitt."

How she wished she could resist him. But, as her abortive attack had proved, she didn't have her full strength back. And she had no idea how fast he was with that pistol. His fingers were tapping on the ivory handle, nervous, eager. If she provoked him too much, he might be tempted to shoot her in the leg or something, just to incapacitate her. It wasn't as if he couldn't get her patched up right away again, since his sister Emma was a healer.

"Jeremiah Wilcox!" Robert's voice, strong, carrying.

"Looks like your lover's here, right on schedule. Come along."

He opened the door and marched her out onto the porch. Immediately facing them was Robert, who sat on the back of a bright bay horse. It was blowing heavily, its sides sheened with sweat. He must have ridden it at a punishing pace to get up here as quickly as he could, once he realized where Danica had been taken.

"I'm afraid you have the wrong Wilcox, Mr. Rowe," Samuel said.

Robert's eyes were full of anguish, but he dismounted with easy grace and took a step toward them. "Let her go."

"Now, why would I want to go and do a thing like that?"

A pause as Robert took a quick glance at Danica, as if assuring himself that she was more or less unharmed. "As far as I know, kidnapping is still illegal, even out here in the territories."

"Oh, you a lawman now, Mr. Rowe?" Samuel sneered. "Well, I like to think that possession is nine-tenths of the law. Besides, trespassing is also illegal, and that's what you're doing now. I'll thank you to get off my family's land."

"Gladly. Just hand over Miss Prewitt, and I'll leave."

"Why would I go and do a thing like that after I went to all the trouble of getting her in the first place?" Samuel had ceased his nervous tapping on the butt of his gun; now his hand rested there, relaxed for the moment but ready to strike, like a rattlesnake waiting on a dusty path.

Robert obviously noticed it, too, because he went very still then. Danica couldn't see a gun anywhere on him, but the day was rapidly failing, the only true illumination the yellow rectangle of lamplight from the open cabin door behind them. He could have a pistol hidden under his long black coat. But could he get to it in time?

Then Danica wanted to sigh in relief, because she heard another set of horse's hooves approaching. In the next few seconds, a large black stallion came galloping into the cleared area in front of the cabin, Jeremiah Wilcox astride. He barely waited for the horse to skid to a stop before he dismounted and began to advance on his brother.

"Samuel! What kind of foolishness is this!"

"No foolishness at all, Jeremiah. Just making sure you get what's rightfully yours."

Jeremiah's dark eyes, strained with worry, flickered toward Danica. He gave her the smallest shake of his head, as if to tell her that he had nothing to do with his brother's insane plots.

She believed him. There had been regret and sadness in their parting the night before, but he had known enough to let her go. He would never have sanctioned Samuel's actions.

"She's not mine, Samuel," Jeremiah said then. "She never could be. I know that now. Let her go."

"It's not like you to admit defeat, brother. Once Rowe is out of the way—"

"I said, let her go."

Danica had heard that note of command in Jeremiah's voice before. He'd used it on Samuel back in the churchyard. But back then they'd been surrounded by townspeople, and even the younger Wilcox brother wasn't so crazy as to think he could get away with attacking Robert Rowe in such a public place.

Here, though, out in the middle of nowhere....

During this exchange, Robert had remained standing where he was, eyes flickering as he watched the back-and-forth between the two brothers. Now, though, he stepped forward again, face pale but resolute. "Your brother is right, Samuel. Eliza Prewitt isn't his. She isn't mine, either. She's her own self, not something to be fought over like a war prize. Just let us both go, and we'll leave. We'll never speak of this to anyone else. You have my word."

"Your word?" Samuel sneered. His fingers had begun tapping on the butt of his pistol again, and Danica held herself rigid, worrying that the wrong move might be enough to set him off. "Your word doesn't count for nothing, Mr. Rowe. We took the measure of those like you and your sanctimonious clan back in New England. Far's I'm concerned, you can go straight to hell."

He moved so quickly that Danica didn't even have time to blink. The gun was in his hand, and her ears screamed at the *bang* that followed...and then there was Robert, just like in that vision or visitation or whatever it was, a dark hole appearing in his chest, a hole that immediately began to stain his striped shirt red.

For a second he stood there, eyes staring, while the report from the shot seemed to echo through the woods, ringing on and on, like the tolling of a church bell. Then he slumped to the ground.

Danica screamed, wrenching her arm from Samuel's grasp so she could run down the porch steps to sink to her knees in the dry grass where the man she loved had fallen. No, *no*...this couldn't be happening. She'd come here to stop this from happening.

As she wrapped her arms around Robert, pulling him close, she heard Jeremiah's voice, shaking with fury. "What have you done, Samuel? You stupid fool!"

A low chuckle. "I did what you didn't have the balls to do."

Danica wasn't looking at either of them, had her head bent over Robert. He was breathing still, but in short, harsh gasps. His eyelids fluttered and his mouth moved, but no sound came out. It wasn't hard to figure out why; the bullet had hit him in the chest, piercing a lung. She could hear a horrible wheezing noise with each labored breath.

And the blood. God, the blood. She had to try to stop the bleeding somehow.

Right. All these damned skirts. Might as well put that fabric to some use.

She grabbed the apron overskirt of her cotton gown and tore it away from her waist, then laid it on Robert's chest. Enough pressure to try to slow the blood and keep the air from escaping, but not so much that she would bear down painfully on his punctured lung.

Jeremiah again, not shouting, but every word delivered with such force it might as well have been a physical blow. "You go fetch Emma now. We've got to put this right."

"It'll be right in a few minutes. But not because of Emma's help."

"Samuel, I'm warning you—"

"Warn away. Won't change anything."

A sharp sound, almost like the noise a cork made when it was drawn from a wine bottle. Danica looked up then and saw that Samuel had gone. Used his teleportation talent to get away, now that his work was done. And Danica somehow doubted he'd left to go fetch his sister Emma, the healer.

Cursing under his breath, Jeremiah turned away from the cabin and moved swiftly to be at Danica's side. She was holding the ruin of her skirt against Robert's wound, not because she thought it would help, but because she didn't know what else to do.

Take him home, her mind told her. *The cabin is only fifteen minutes from the hospital. You can save him.*

Of course. She thought of the cabin, but in its current-day guise, with the extra windows added and her Land Rover parked in the driveway. Almost at once, the scene around her began to dissolve…

…Robert along with it. She couldn't feel him, could see him turning transparent.

No. *No.* She couldn't go back to the present day and leave him to die in 1884. With all her will, she forced herself back to the horrible scene she'd just left, with Jeremiah crouched in the dry grass on the other side of her fallen lover, the darkness of encroaching night almost concealing the blood that stained his shirt.

"What…?" Jeremiah began, then shook his hand. "You began to disappear. Where did you go?"

"I was trying to go back where I'd come from. I thought if I could take Robert with me, they could heal him there."

The Wilcox *primus'* face was a study in confusion. "Back to St. Louis? So you have the same gift of travel that Samuel does?"

"No," she replied, hesitating. But then, what did it matter if she revealed her secret now? Still with Robert cradled in her arms, still holding the ruin of her skirt against him since she didn't know what else to do, she went on, "What I said wasn't exactly accurate. I shouldn't have said *where* I'd come from. I should have said *when*."

Jeremiah stared at her. Then he nodded, as if in understanding. "The future?"

"Yes. About a hundred and thirty years from now." Tears flooded down her cheeks now, dropping onto Robert's chest, where they mixed with the blood soaking the cloth she held. "I came here to save him. But I think I only killed him instead."

"You did no such thing. That was all Samuel's doing." The black brows were drawn together, and even in the dim light, Danica could see the way Jeremiah's dark eyes glittered with anger. She wondered what he would do to his brother, once he caught up with him. "So…why can't you return to your time?"

"I can," she said softly. "But I'm not strong enough to bring him with me. And I won't leave him behind."

Jeremiah was silent for a few seconds. "Perhaps I can help."

Did she dare allow herself to hope? But she didn't know what Jeremiah could do. He was a very powerful warlock, but he was not a healer. "How?"

"I'll lend my strength to you. Here." He reached out with one hand, and she lifted her left one from where it had been pressed against Robert's chest, then wrapped her fingers around Jeremiah's.

A shock, almost as if she had touched a live socket, and a strange heat seemed to pulse its way up her arm.

"Do you feel it?" he asked.

"Yes," she whispered.

"Then use it. Use it to take him with you." He paused for the barest moment, and asked, "Who are you, really?"

"Danica," she told him. "Danica Wilcox."

His eyes widened, and some of the strain seemed to leave his face. "So…we will still be here."

"Yes. More of the Wilcox clan than you can even imagine. Strong and happy and prosperous." She tightened her fingers on his, still feeling the heat of his magic flowing into her. "And it *will* get better, Jeremiah. You'll have to be patient, but it will all work out. I promise."

He nodded. "Then go. Save him."

Without truly understanding how she was doing it, she pulled all that magic into her, all that energy. It seemed to spread through every limb, making her tingle with potentiality. Was this what it felt like to be a *prima*? She didn't know, and she didn't have any more time to stop and wonder.

Once again she thought of the cabin in its modern-day form, the driveway, the solar lights evenly spaced along the front walk. Her Land Rover. If only she could move in space as well as time, she'd make sure they materialized right in the SUV so she could bail out of there and head down the hill to the hospital. She'd have to drag him somehow. Or would it be better to run inside and use the satellite phone to call for help?

The world blurred around her, shifting to darkness. Jeremiah was gone, and so was everything else—everything except Robert's now dead weight in her arms. Had Jeremiah miscalculated? Was even the addition of his power not enough to send her and Robert over the gulf of years that separated them from their destination?

But then there was a crunch of dry grass under her knees, and Danica found herself kneeling in front of the cabin. And yes, there was a vehicle parked in the driveway. Not the Land Rover, though…a silver sedan. Someone's Honda?

As her addled brain tried to work its way through that particular mystery, the front door to the cabin flew open, and Danica's cousin Eleanor, the Wilcox clan's healer, ran down the steps. She hastened across the yard and knelt next to Robert, gently pushing Danica's hands away so she could get to work.

"How…?" Danica began. Her mind didn't seem to be processing things correctly. She tried again. "How did you know to be here?"

Eleanor smiled, but she continued to work, tearing away the tie at Robert's throat and swiftly unbuttoning his shirt so she could lay her bare hands on his chest. That was how her power worked—the classic laying-on of hands, so to speak. She pressed her palms against his bloody flesh and then glanced up at Danica.

"Your friend Caitlin. The McAllister seer. She told me I needed to be here."

CHAPTER NINETEEN

ONCE THE BLEEDING WAS STOPPED AND THE PUNCTURED SKIN smoothed over, the two women took Robert by his legs and arms and hauled him into the cabin. Danica worried that such rough handling would disrupt the healing that had already begun, but Eleanor shook her head.

"He'll be fine. But we need to get him into bed. He's still passed out, but soon that will shift over to actual sleep."

All right, she wouldn't argue. After all, Eleanor was the clan healer, and she'd been doing this sort of thing since before Danica was even born. Well, maybe not patching up gunshot wounds. She couldn't help but be grateful, though, that they hadn't been compelled to take Robert to the hospital. That kind of injury would have brought police scrutiny to the clan, and even though the Wilcoxes had a few people on the force, just to make sure these sorts of things got swept under the rug, some anomalies were easier to hide than others.

They took him into one of the spare bedrooms, then laid him down on top of the quilt so Danica could tug off his high boots and set them down on the floor. His clothes were a bloody ruin, however, and she cast a helpless look over at Eleanor.

"I hate to put him in the bed like that—"

"Here," the healer said, and went to the low dresser placed up against the far wall. From the top drawer she brought out a T-shirt and a package of men's briefs.

"Those weren't here before," Danica replied. Again she had the sensation of lagging about two steps behind the rest of the world.

"No," Eleanor admitted. "Angela called me, saying that her cousin Caitlin had called *her*, and that I needed to be at the cabin before six tonight because someone would need medical help, but that I also needed to stop at Kohl's and pick up a few things in these sizes."

Should she laugh or cry? If Caitlin had been there, Danica would have hugged her and then said that was some hell of a second sight, if it told her which sizes their refugee from the past would require. But

Caitlin was hundreds of miles away in Tucson, so Danica settled for smiling and shaking her head.

"Well, that's handy."

"I thought so." The healer gave Danica a searching glance. "It looks like you could stand to get cleaned up, too. I'll take care of putting these on your man."

That would save some embarrassment. Not that Danica wasn't curious to see what Robert looked like…what *all* of him looked like…but sneaking a peek while he was recovering from a gunshot wound didn't sound exactly right. Besides, when she looked down at herself, she saw how her own bedraggled bustle dress was stained with blood, limp and crushed from kneeling on the ground. She didn't think it could be salvaged.

Well, she didn't need it anymore anyway.

She murmured a thank-you to Eleanor and went out of the guest bedroom and down the hall to the master suite. Once there, however, she had to pause and put a hand up against the wall to support her, the shock of the situation finally falling down on her like the proverbial ton of bricks.

Robert was here. She'd done it. She'd saved him.

That is, Danica and Jeremiah together had saved him, with a much-needed assist from Eleanor and Caitlin. Danica knew she could never have brought Robert all the way to her own time without that extra bit of juice from the clan's long-ago *primus*. And what had Jeremiah done afterward, once the shock of her disappearance had worn off and he realized she truly had succeeded in taking Robert back to her own time? Had he gone to confront Samuel over his crime, or had he decided to put the matter aside for the sake of keeping the peace in their clan, since there was no longer any proof that Samuel's actions had resulted in Robert's death?

She had no idea. It probably wasn't the sort of thing that would have been written down in a family diary or anything. Jeremiah had no wife to confide in, and Danica kind of doubted that Samuel would have gone blabbing to his wife Grace that he'd just shot a man in cold blood.

Plenty of time to sort that out later. Danica stripped off her ruined bustle dress, wadded it up, and shoved it in the hamper, then peeled herself out of her corset and chemise, both also stained with blood. How the hell did you clean a corset, anyway? She put it in the hamper, too, since she didn't know what else to do with it.

A shower, but a quick one, working fast to sluice away the blood and dirt and worry and fear. Afterward, Danica thought she felt almost human. She ran a comb through her wet hair, put on clean underthings, and then drew on a pair of yoga pants and a T-shirt. Maybe she should have scrounged the one and only skirt she had with her at the cabin, in order not to shock Robert, but he'd have to come to terms with modern life sooner or later.

Modern life. She'd never had a chance to tell him the truth about herself. He'd wake up in an entirely new century with absolutely no idea of how he'd gotten there.

She went back into the spare bedroom. Robert now wore a T-shirt; the rest of him was concealed under the quilt. It looked as if Eleanor had cleaned the blood off his face and neck, but of course a real shower would have to wait until he was up and about again.

"Feeling better?" the healer asked, and Danica nodded. Tone brisk, as if treating refugees from the past was something she did every day, Eleanor went on, "He should sleep through the night. I healed the wound—he's lucky, because the bullet went right through him—but his body still needs to do some work on its own for him to recover from the trauma. Try to keep him in bed, at least for tomorrow. He can get up and go to the bathroom, that sort of thing, but he should stay inside and rest."

There really wasn't anything Danica could say in response, except, "Thank you, Eleanor."

"That's what I'm here for. You should really be thanking your friend Caitlin, since I wouldn't have known to come if it weren't for her."

And Danica would. Thank God for the satellite phone. At least she wasn't entirely cut off from the world. Enough, though. Enough to give Robert the time he needed to come to terms with what had happened to him. She could only pray that he wouldn't be too angry with her.

"What's the date?" she asked then. Technically, she should have come back the same day she left, but maybe time had passed here while she was gone. Her parents would be frantic....

"September twenty-sixth," Eleanor replied, giving her a curious look. "Saturday."

So it was the same day. Everything that had happened, everything she'd experienced...it had all occurred in the blink of an eye. Did that make it more real, or less? She didn't know. She supposed she'd figure it all out later. Right now, she was just bone-tired.

"That's good," Danica said, and Eleanor came over and gave her a quick hug.

"You need your rest, too. He'll sleep—have no worries about that. So make sure you get some sleep as well."

The healer was probably right. But Danica knew she didn't want to leave Robert's side for too long. What if he did wake up in an unfamiliar place, with no one there to tell him where he was? She couldn't bear that.

"I will," she said, tone noncommittal.

Eleanor lifted her shoulders, as if she knew that arguing the point wouldn't be worth the time. "I'll come by to check on things tomorrow. I'm sure your friend will be fine, but it's better to be sure. Would around eleven be all right?"

"I think so." Lord knows what state of mind Robert would be in when he woke up, but maybe by eleven Danica would have had some time to smooth things out.

"Then I'll let the two of you get some rest." Eleanor went back out to the living room, Danica trailing behind, and retrieved her purse from where she'd left it on the dining room table. After that, she said goodbye and headed out to her car.

Her car. Crap. Danica finally realized why she hadn't spotted her Land Rover when she returned. That's because it was probably still sitting in the parking lot at the Amtrak station.

"Eleanor!"

The healer paused next to the driver-side door, car keys in hand. "What is it, Danica?"

"My SUV—I left it at the Amtrak station. If it stays there too long, it's going to get towed." Danica hesitated then. The last thing she wanted was to leave Robert here while she went with Eleanor to retrieve the vehicle, but....

"Don't worry about that," Eleanor said briskly. "If you can get the key for me, I'll have Travis go with me to fetch it. He can drive it back up here, and I'll bring him home after that."

Travis was Eleanor's oldest son, a couple of years younger than Danica. He'd probably love a chance to get behind the wheel of the Land Rover.

"Perfect," she said. "I actually left the key with it—it's in one of those wheelwell box thingies—"

"We'll find it. You go on inside and get yourself some rest." She smiled, but she also made a shooing gesture before she climbed into the car and started it up.

Despite that, Danica waited until Eleanor had backed out of the driveway and was slowly maneuvering down the dirt lane that led to the main road. Then she shut the cabin door and locked it, even though she knew she was perfectly safe out here.

There wouldn't be any return visits from her ghost. He was sleeping just down the hall.

She padded in her bare feet back to the guest room, noticing for the first time that Eleanor had left a glass of water on the nightstand. The light there hadn't been turned on, though; the only illumination was from the base of the reproduction lamp with the mica shade and amber glass bottom that sat on top of the dresser. It cast a soft, warm glow in the room, not so different from what you might get from a kerosene lamp turned down low. Clearly, Eleanor had been trying to keep Robert's surroundings as familiar as she could. Intuitive, but Danica supposed you could tell from his clothes that he wasn't from anywhere near here.

A chair sat in one corner, and she picked it up and set it down closer to the bed. Even in the dim light she could see the shadows under Robert's eyes, and something around his nose and mouth looked pinched. Well, he'd lost a lot of blood. Eleanor had saved his life, but it still took a good deal of energy to bounce back from an injury like that.

Right then, Danica thought she was going to need a good deal of bouncing back as well. Her arm ached from where Samuel had grasped it, and she could tell she hadn't recovered from his particular mode of teleportation, either. She really should get up and scrounge something to eat. Robert didn't look as if he planned to wake up anytime soon.

She shifted on the chair, and it creaked. Almost at once, Robert's eyelids fluttered, dark lashes beating like worried butterflies against his cheeks. Then his eyes opened, and he turned at once, relaxing slightly when he saw her sitting there.

"You're all right," he whispered.

"I am," she said. "And you are, too. How do you feel?"

His hand went to his chest, to the spot where there had been a bullet hole not even a half-hour earlier. "Wasn't I shot?"

"Yes," she replied, her tone gentle. "My clan's healer fixed you up."

Eyebrows drawing together, he asked, "How is that possible? You're from—" He winced then, as if his chest pained him. Voice dropping to a whisper, he said, "Your clan is a thousand miles away."

"I know." God, they really shouldn't be having this conversation yet. He needed a good night's sleep. After he'd gotten the rest he needed, he'd be in far better shape to hear her revelations. "Robert, please, just sleep. We can talk in the morning. Just know that you're safe now."

"But where—" Breaking off, he seemed to focus on the V-necked T-shirt she wore. "What on earth are you wearing?"

"My dress was covered in blood. I had to change." All right, that wasn't a real answer. But again, she really wanted to avoid getting into all that right now.

He let out a sigh. "Eliza, what aren't you telling me?"

Everything. She reached out and found his hand where it lay on top of the quilt, then covered it with her own. "I swear that we'll talk—*really* talk—in the morning. But the healer told me I had to make sure you got a good night's sleep. So please…can you do that?"

A long pause. Then his hand shifted, and she felt him wrap his fingers around hers. "Very well. I must confess that I am rather tired."

Danica rose from the chair so she could lean over and kiss him on the forehead. "Then sleep, darling. And tomorrow I'll try to explain everything."

He nodded, his eyes slipping shut already. Good. That was what he needed the most. And tomorrow…well, she'd figure it all out then.

Once she'd determined he truly was asleep, Danica crept out to the kitchen and nuked one of her frozen meals, then got out the satphone so she could call Caitlin. By then it was a little after seven o'clock, and Danica hoped she wouldn't be disturbing her friend and her fiancé just as they were sitting down to dinner or something.

But Caitlin picked up right away. "Danica?"

"How'd you know it was me?"

A little laugh. "The same way I knew to send Eleanor over there. Is everything okay?"

"It's fine. *He's* fine. He's sleeping now, thanks to Eleanor and you."

Being Caitlin, she didn't ask who "he" was. "What about you?"

Good question. Danica knew she was bone-weary, and she was worried how she should best break it to Robert that he was more than a hundred years away from everything he knew and loved.

Well, not everything. She could only hope that he would still love her once she told him the truth.

"I'm fine. Tired. And I feel…strange."

"Traveling in time can do that to a person," Caitlin said wryly.

"It was just…I *met* them, Cate. I met people who were just faded images in old, old pictures."

"What were they like?"

"They were…." Danica trailed off there, knowing she couldn't possibly begin to describe her encounters with the members of the Wilcox clan. Lovely, laughing Emma, and solemn little Jacob, and murderous Samuel. And Jeremiah. Danica wondered if she'd ever be able to sort that one out. "Different than I expected."

"That doesn't surprise me. I'd probably be shocked if I met some of my McAllister ancestors in the flesh." Caitlin seemed to hesitate then, as if she was deciding the best way to phrase her next question. "What about him? Do you think he's going to be okay?"

"Isn't your sight giving you any clues about that?" Wishful thinking, probably, but she just had to ask.

"No. I think the important thing was making sure you saved him. After that…I think it's up to you."

Danica wanted to argue with that statement, but she couldn't. The next morning, she'd find out if she was up to the task.

Out of deference to Robert's sensibilities, she made sure to put on her peasant skirt and a long-sleeved T-shirt when she got dressed the next morning. Since she'd showered the night before, she only brushed her hair and pulled it into a long, loose side braid. Hopefully, the ensemble wouldn't shock him too much.

He'd still been sleeping when she peeked into the guest bedroom, so she decided to go to the kitchen and put together some breakfast. Nothing fancy, but toast and scrambled eggs hadn't changed all that much over the years. Maybe the offering of food would soften the blow she was about to deliver.

Just as she was poking around in the kitchen, trying to see if there was a tray somewhere she could use to take his food to him, she heard him say, "Eliza."

Startled, she whirled around. He stood in the entrance to the kitchen, staring at the stainless-steel appliances with an expression of mingled wonder and consternation. Trying to gather her wits, she responded, "Robert, you shouldn't be out of bed."

"I feel much improved this morning." He wore the jeans and a long-sleeved flannel shirt Eleanor had left for him, although his feet were bare, as if he hadn't quite figured out what to do with the tennis shoes. Then he frowned and said, "What is this place?"

"It's—it's my family's cabin." Damn, she really didn't want to have this conversation while standing up in the kitchen. "Why don't you go sit down at the dining room table, and I'll bring you your breakfast. Do you drink coffee?"

"That's what awakened me, I think." He glanced around the kitchen again, eyes narrowed, but to Danica's relief he only said, "Do you have any cream?"

"Just milk."

"That's fine." To her relief, he did head over to the dining room table and sit down.

All right. She poured two mugs full of coffee, then found a little pitcher in one of the cupboards and poured some milk into it. No point in shocking him with a plastic milk container right off the bat. At least the stoneware here at the cabin was that old-fashioned kind with the milky paint spatters on top of dark, dark green. Danica hoped it wouldn't be too shocking, either.

She brought everything out to the table and sat down across from him. He was looking at her, seeming to take in her long-sleeved T-shirt and casual hair. Then he asked, "Where are we? You said your family's cabin, but I just looked out the window. The landscape out there certainly doesn't look like St. Louis. In fact, even though I know it's impossible, I'd say we were still at the Wilcox clan's cabin. The trees look similar, the porch…although I don't know what that thing is sitting off to one side of the house."

That "thing" was probably her Land Rover, brought there last night by Eleanor and her son Travis. They must have come while she was sleeping, because she didn't remember hearing them drop it off. She swallowed, then poured some milk into her coffee and began swirling it nervously. "What if I told you it wasn't impossible, that you still were at the Wilcox cabin?"

He went very still then, ignoring the plate of scrambled eggs in front of him. "What do you mean, Eliza?"

That was the first thing she needed to clear up. "Actually, Robert, my—my name isn't Eliza Prewitt." She pulled in a breath. *Just say it.* "My name is Danica Wilcox."

Those blue eyes seemed to be fastened on her face, boring into her. "You're a Wilcox?"

"Yes. But—but not one of the Wilcoxes as you knew them. I'm Nathan Wilcox's great-to-the-fifth-power granddaughter."

Dead silence. Then, too calmly, Robert reached for the milk and poured a good measure into his coffee cup, followed by a half-spoonful of sugar. He stirred the coffee, kept stirring it.

It was just too awful. Feeling compelled to speak, Danica said quickly, "I tried to tell you. That is, I was going to tell you that time we met in the aspen grove. But then Edmund came along, and everything went crazy after that, and I just didn't have any time."

Still Robert said nothing. He raised the coffee cup to his lips and drained it in one quick swallow, then pushed back his chair and stood. Feeling helpless, Danica rose as well, even as he crossed the front room and let himself out the door onto the porch.

Damn, that didn't go so well. She hurried after him, saw him standing on the bottom step, as if he'd intended to go farther but then stopped when he realized he didn't have any shoes on. Frost glittered on the dry grass, and their breath puffed out into the cold morning air, although the day probably would turn out to be fairly mild.

"It looks the same," he said then, not glancing at her, his attention apparently fixed on the pine forests that surrounded the cabin. "Perhaps not quite as green."

"This part of it is more or less the same. The town—the town has changed a lot."

"I expect it would, in more than a hundred years." This time he did turn toward her. In the morning light, she could see the dark stubble on his jaw, his rumpled hair. In fact, he appeared so much like the way she'd imagined him looking in the morning that she had to suck in a breath and remind herself not to get distracted. "Why?"

She'd known there would be no way to avoid that question. "When I first met you, you were a ghost." His eyes widened at that revelation, and she hurried on, "You were here, haunting this place, because Samuel Wilcox shot you here. And I knew—I knew I had to do something about it. For whatever reason, your spirit reached out to me."

Something about his mouth softened then, as if he was remembering how they'd reached out to one another back in 1884, had believed themselves in love. No, it wasn't believing, but knowing. Her soul had found its echo in his. But did he feel that way as well? "And so you traveled in time to save me? Is that your talent?"

"It didn't exactly start out that way, but...." Quickly, she explained how her gift had originally worked, and how Lawrence had taught her to expand it, to make it so much more. "And so, yes, I went to the Flagstaff of your time, to try to prevent your murder. Only I didn't do such a good job of that."

One eyebrow went up. "I'm here, aren't I?'

True enough. But only because Caitlin's sight had sent help, and Jeremiah had reached beyond his own pain to lend her the strength she needed to bring Robert back across all those years. "But more despite me than because of me. If Jeremiah Wilcox hadn't given me the extra power to bring both you and me back here, you would have died."

"He did that?" The words sounded oddly flat, almost as if they weren't really a question at all.

"Yes. He knew I loved you."

"Did you tell him…who you were?"

"At the end, I did. But I think he would have helped me even if we weren't the same blood."

Robert's mouth twitched. "Are you trying to make me think well of the man?"

"You should," she replied. "He was a good person. I can't say the same for Samuel."

"No, I would think not. I suppose it's a relief to you that your ancestor was Nathan, not Samuel."

Was he teasing her? No, he couldn't be. Not about the man who'd tried to kill him—*had* killed him, in a past that had somehow been erased. "A bit of a relief," she replied, taking care to keep her tone light. "But can we go inside now? It's cold, and our breakfast will be, too, if we don't eat it soon."

Robert came back up the steps but stopped next to her. Danica hardly dared to breathe; he felt somehow more intimidating like this, in his jeans and untucked flannel shirt and morning stubble. He looked like a man she could be with for real, a man she could take to meet her friends and her family, not someone who'd just walked off the set of a western.

But then he was bending to kiss her, mouth warm against hers, tasting of coffee. She reached out to pull him close and felt the strength of his body, the heat of his flesh. God, she wanted him. It was probably too soon for that, however.

"All right," he said. "Let's go in."

CHAPTER TWENTY

ELEANOR DID STOP BY AROUND ELEVEN, AND ALTHOUGH SHE looked less than thrilled to see Robert up and about, she didn't lecture him too much. "Just try to stay around the cabin for now," she said. "No nature hikes."

Robert nodded obediently, and, after she left, confided to Danica, "She reminds me of an aunt back in Boston." The half-smile he'd been wearing disappeared, though, as he seemed to realize he'd never see that aunt again, or any of his family.

His expression felt like a wound through the heart. Would she be enough? Could he learn to start over in a place where everything was strange and alien, and even the woman he thought he loved wasn't who she'd professed to be?

Maybe she should apologize, say something about how sorry she was that she'd had to take him away from his clan. But even as she opened her mouth to speak, he shrugged, as if attempting to shake off the realization that he was now separated from everything he knew by an insurmountable gulf. Instead, he told her, "I think it's time for a history lesson."

First, though, Danica showed Robert how to use the shower in the guest bath. Luckily, one of Cody's friends had left his "guy" shampoo in the shower there, and Danica found a spare bar of soap under the sink. The whole time she was trying very hard not to think about what Robert would look like climbing into that shower. Unfortunately, she wasn't sure how well she succeeded.

If Robert noticed anything strange about her behavior, he didn't show it. He paid close attention to everything she said, then said he'd meet her back out in the living room.

For someone unfamiliar with modern showers, he did okay. Fifteen minutes later, he was back out, changed into some more of the clothes Eleanor had left for him, and actually smiling. Danica lifted an eyebrow at him, and he said, "That was...remarkable. Hot water, as much as you need? I think I like this future of yours."

You ain't seen nothing yet, Danica thought then, but she could feel herself relax slightly. Maybe this would all turn out to be okay.

Time to get down to business, though. She told him everything she could, then fired up the satellite TV to see if there was anything worthwhile on the History Channel. It seemed to be Nazi week once again—no big surprise there—and she switched off the television quickly before Robert could discover the joys of twenty-four-hour cable news. He'd find out about it eventually, she supposed, but Danica wanted to postpone that evil day for as long as possible.

But that interlude led to her having to explain about television, and satellites, and cell phones and computers. His brow furrowed as he seemed to process everything she told him, but he didn't interrupt, and the questions he did ask showed that he was able to grasp the basics of modern-day technology, even if he couldn't begin to understand how it all really worked.

"So," he said, "even though these cellular phones of yours can communicate with one another without wires, they still don't work here at the cabin?"

"Not really," she replied. "It's hard, because of the mountains. Sort of a line-of-sight thing. My phone can't talk to the tower that sends the transmissions because all these hills are in the way."

His brows pulled together as he thought it over. "But the one that uses a satellite—it works because the signal goes up and not across, correct?"

Damn. He was grasping these things far more easily than she'd expected him to. But then, smart was smart, whether now or back in 1884. Danica allowed herself a flicker of hope. He seemed to be doing okay. No, he *would* be okay. He just had to be.

She didn't want to think about the alternative.

And there was so much more, too—the right to vote, and the Civil Rights Movement. Two world wars, and 9/11, and the Internet. By the time the day had worn into evening, Robert finally shook his head and told her, "I think that's where we'd better stop for now. It's—a good deal to absorb."

"Well, considering I just condensed about a century and a half into a couple of hours, I can see why you'd think that way." They'd been sitting on the couch in the family room area, but she rose then and said, "We should probably eat something. I can't really do anything from scratch, but there's a frozen pizza—"

"A what?"

"Pizza. Sort of a big, round, crusty bread with sauce and cheese and toppings. This one is pepperoni. It's a kind of Italian sausage. And there's wine," she added.

His eyes lit up. "Wine. That's something I can understand."

She smiled, relieved that she'd bought those couple of bottles when she loaded up on supplies at the store. "Well, you open it while I get that pizza started."

It definitely wasn't gourmet, but Robert didn't seem to mind. Actually, he'd been snacking on and off all day—bread and butter, crackers and cheese. It was probably his body needing the nutrients to complete the healing process, but Danica knew she'd have to go into town soon to get more supplies. Would Robert be ready to go with her, or would he need a few more days of decompression time? So far he seemed to be handling things remarkably well, but he'd only been exposed to the modern wonders of the cabin's kitchen appliances and satellite TV. What would he think of being surrounded by cars, of going into a huge supermarket with aisles and aisles of products he'd never even heard of?

Well, first things first. They'd eat dinner, and then….

And then what? she asked herself. *It's a little too soon to be jumping into bed.*

She wasn't so sure about that.

They drank the wine and ate the pizza in the living room while a fire crackled in the hearth. It was getting cold enough at night that the cabin could use the supplemental heating, and besides, she hoped the fire would make the atmosphere feel not quite so alien, would be something familiar for Robert. Belatedly she realized that maybe it wasn't the best idea for him to be drinking so soon after Eleanor had healed him, but there wasn't much she could do about that now.

"Danica," Robert said in musing tones.

"What?"

He shook his head. "I'm sorry. I wasn't asking a question. I was just thinking of your name. I've never heard it before. It's beautiful."

For some reason, she flushed, then bent to pick up her wine from the coffee table so he couldn't see her reaction. "Well, styles in names change, I suppose. But 'Robert' is still popular."

"I'm glad to hear that."

A certain warmth in his tone made her glance over at him. He was sitting a proper distance away, with no chance of their legs touching or anything like that, but Danica fancied she could still feel the heat of his body. The tension between them was almost palpable, and she wasn't sure what to do about it.

Actually, she knew exactly what she wanted to do. The question was, would Robert go along, or be hung up on a system of values that no longer had any real meaning in the modern world? Or at least they didn't for her. Her "virtue"—if you wanted to call it that—was long gone.

"Robert," she said, then hesitated, trying to decide on the best way to phrase what she was thinking. "A lot has changed since you—since your time. It's—it's all right for a man and a woman to be together, even if they aren't married."

That remark made him shift toward her, brows pulling together. He set down his wine glass and asked, "Danica, what are you saying?"

Oh, God, this was awful. It had been so much easier to just go out with a guy, mess around on the sofa at his apartment or whatever, and then have things progress naturally to the bedroom. "I'm saying that I want to be together. If you're not ready, I understand, but—"

In that instant, he was reaching for her glass and plucking it from her hand, then pulling her toward him, his lips pressed hard against her mouth, his tongue exploring hers, both of them tasting of wine. Heat seemed to explode up from her belly, bringing with it the welcome ache she'd worried she might never feel again.

"Yes, Robert. Please," she whispered.

That seemed to be enough for him. He scooped her up in his arms and took her away from the living room, back toward the master bedroom, even though he'd never been there before. Once there, he grasped her T-shirt and pulled it up over her head. His hands reached up to cup her breasts, his skin so warm, even through the lace of her bra, his fingers so strong, so sure. She gasped, but she wouldn't let that distract her as she determinedly worked away at the buttons of his shirt.

No trace of a scar where Samuel Wilcox's bullet had pierced his skin. Only smooth, muscled flesh, and a faint dusting of dark hair. She laid her lips against his chest and kissed him, listened to the intake of his breath as she trailed kisses down his front, pausing to undo the buttons on his jeans.

He gasped, "Danica—"

"It's all right, Robert," she whispered. "I want this. I want to be with you like this."

That reply seemed to kill any protests he might make, and he said nothing as she slid down his pants, then grasped the waistband of his underwear and pulled it down as well. He sprang free, hard and ready, and she wrapped her hand around his shaft, moving slowly up and down.

He groaned, then stumbled backward to fall onto the bed. She loved seeing him like that, his lean, muscled body sprawled out across the quilt. In her mind, she'd tried to imagine what he would look like naked, but the reality was so much better than any fantasy her mind could manufacture, from the firmness of his biceps to his narrow waist and strong legs.

Time to join him, though. She slipped off her bra and stepped out of her skirt, then lay down next to him. Immediately he reached for her, his naked body pressed to hers, the heat of him warming her to her very core. Yes, there was his mouth closing on her breast, even as his hand moved over her hip, slipped down inside her underwear, moved into her, stroking gently.

A cry escaped her lips, and she surrendered herself to the sensation, to the way he seemed to know just how to touch her. And this was what she needed—gentleness, someone giving instead of always taking.

Waves of heat washed over her, and she let herself ride those waves, let them carry her to a climax that seemed to explode through every nerve ending, every artery and vein. She clung to him as she rode it out, knowing she needed this release, needed his touch to erase the last memories of Matías Escobar and what he'd done to her.

"Danica." Her name was a whisper of need, and she rolled over to face Robert, to kiss him again, and then once more trail those kisses all the way down to his cock, to take him in her mouth and show him how much she did want this, how much she wanted him.

He gasped, hands softly pushing her hair away from her face so he could see her, watch her. She could feel how hard he was, how on edge, and she stopped after a moment, went to him so she could settle herself on him, feel him fill her deeply, completely.

A moan that seemed to come from somewhere at the very center of his being, and then he began to rock into her, his hands reaching to cup her breasts, to caress her. So wonderful, so amazing, so perfect and intense and incredible that she wasn't sure if she was dreaming.

From the way he was gazing up at her in adoration, it seemed Robert was thinking the same thing. His breaths came more quickly, and she knew he was getting close. Good, because so was she. She held on to his hands as he held her and she rode him, both of them moving as one, in a perfect rhythm that she'd never thought could be possible until that moment.

And then the climax hit him, taking her with it, her own orgasm seeming to be an answer to his, and she collapsed on him, her breaths almost sobs as she tried to understand where this had come from, why it had taken a hundred years for them to create this perfect joining.

His hand moved down her hair to her tangled braid. "I love you, Danica."

"I love you, Robert."

He pulled her to him then, kissing her fiercely, kissing her as if she was the only real thing in his world. Maybe right then she was.

They slept in one another's arms, and though he seemed a little reserved the next morning, Danica chalked that up to coming to grips with the realization that he hadn't "ruined" her by sleeping with her. Certainly he appeared in good spirits as he helped make the coffee, although he said there wasn't much effort involved when all you had to do was push a couple of buttons.

"Well, we've got a cowboy-style pot around here somewhere if you really want to get back to basics," she teased him, and he shook his head and said he'd be all right trying it the modern way.

"After all," he added, "I need to get used to doing things the way everyone does them now."

During breakfast, though, he didn't say much. Danica began to fret, wondering if she had pushed him to intimacy too soon. After all, he'd only been here in the modern world for a day. He could still be somewhat shell-shocked...and she imagined his reactions would only intensify once he was away from the quiet, sheltered idyll this cabin provided.

But then he said, "How did you know for sure?"

"Know what?"

"That I really had died? Samuel—that is, my wound wasn't directly in my heart. Men have survived wounds like that before."

She could lie. But she really didn't want to. She'd done enough lying back in 1884. Making herself meet his eyes, she said, "I found your grave."

He didn't blink. "Where?"

She sighed and set down her coffee mug. "Let me show you."

The hike didn't seem to trouble him at all, which meant that he was, to all intents and purposes, healed. Danica led him up the path to the clearing she had found, and to the sycamore with its little cairn of smooth river stones and the cross cut into its bark.

Only…it wasn't there. Or rather, the tree stood where it always had, but there were no stones, no pale cross on the weathered lower section of the tree's trunk.

"It was right there," she said, pointing.

Robert moved closer and peered at the spot she'd indicated. "I don't see anything."

"That's because it's gone."

He didn't seem too concerned. In fact, he turned toward her and smiled. "That's good, then, isn't it? You might not have prevented Samuel Wilcox from shooting me, but you got me away from that place. There was no one to bury because I came here."

"I—I suppose so." That did make sense. After all, how could Robert's grave be there when he was standing right here, talking to her?

As she gave an abstracted nod, he came over to her and kissed her gently on the cheek. "You did save me, Danica. I've seen those worried glances you've given me when you thought I wasn't looking. You were wondering how I would adapt to this world, this time…weren't you?"

She nodded, not sure if she trusted herself to speak.

He was silent as well, as if considering the best way to phrase what he wanted to say next. For a long moment, he gazed up into the trees, whispering their own secrets into the wind, and the cloud-studded blue sky overhead. "But I know I will adapt, because I know you'll be there with me, helping me along that way. You've given me a second chance. How many men ever get that chance?"

Not many, she thought. Jeremiah Wilcox would, decades after his death. But that was probably cold comfort to a man who would have to spend the rest of his life alone.

She knew she shouldn't be thinking of Jeremiah then. His story was in the past, while hers and Robert's was yet to be written.

Without replying, she went to him and put her arms around his waist. He embraced her then, holding her close, warm and real and so very much alive.

His words came close to her ear, "So let's go, my love. It's time to leave the cabin, don't you think?"

She hesitated. It still felt too soon. After all, what was she supposed to do...have him move in with her at her parents' house? That wouldn't work at all, even after they overcame the shock of truly comprehending where their daughter's new boyfriend had come from.

But she and Robert had this cabin, though, and could use it until they found something better. Not an apartment, but a house, maybe one of the refurbished Victorians near Flagstaff's downtown section, not too far from where Mrs. Wilson's boarding house had once stood. Then Robert could be surrounded by the old and the new at the same time, and maybe the transition wouldn't be quite so jarring for him.

For now, though, if he wanted to see what had become of Flagstaff, of the greater world, then she wouldn't prevent him from doing so. After all, he'd have to come to terms with his new reality sooner or later. She went on her tiptoes and hugged him again, holding on tightly, knowing that soon she'd have to share him with her family, her friends.

"All right, Robert," she said. "Let me show you this brave new world."

AUTHOR'S NOTE

WRITING A STORY SET IN THE PAST OF A REAL PLACE IS
ALWAYS a challenge. Working with the records of a
town like Flagstaff, which really was the Wild West
back in the 1880s, is even more of a challenge. In
Spellbound, I did my best to blend the world of nine-
teenth-century Flagstaff with the world of my witch
clans. Some of the people you read about in the novel—
Mrs. Marshall, Reverend Pierce, Mr. Brannen—did
truly exist, although some license was taken to give
the school two teachers, while the Methodist church
was actually built a year or so later than depicted here.
Other people and locations were invented, although I
tried to make sure I didn't write anything that would
have been hugely out of place during the period.

My thanks to Platt Cline, who wrote *Mountain
Town* and *They Came to the Mountain*, for providing

much-needed research material on Flagstaff's early years. Any errors here, or license taken, are purely my own.

Christine Pope
Sedona, Arizona